VALKYRIE

Books by Conor Cregan

Chrissie
The Poison Stream
With Extreme Prejudice
House of Fire

VALKYRIE

CONOR CREGAN

Hodder & Stoughton

Copyright © 1996 Conor Cregan

First published in Great Britain in 1996
by Hodder and Stoughton
A division of Hodder Headline PLC

10 9 8 7 6 5 4 3 2 1

British Library Cataloguing in Publication Data
CIP data to be inserted

Cregan, Conor, 1962–
Valkyrie
1.English fiction – 20th century
I.Title
823.9'14 [F]

ISBN 0 340 67254 4

Typeset by Hewer Text Composition Services, Edinburgh
Printed and bound in Great Britain by
Mackays of Chatham, Chatham, Kent.

Hodder and Stoughton Ltd
A division of Hodder Headline PLC
338 Euston Road
London NW1 3BH

For Gloria

1943

HE WAS A fake. And Valerie Lynes wondered if he could tell she was faking, too.

When they had finished, he pinned her to the bed. 'It is symbiotic,' he said. 'At this moment, we are both trapped. Me through exhaustion, you through . . . what did Churchill order us to do? Set Europe ablaze.' He stared into her eyes.

She held the stare and stroked his back. His back was smooth, his eyes smoother – blue-green – and she tried to decide whether he was handsome or whether it was something deeper that caught you when you looked at him: his eyes showed no emotion, except maybe a hint that something was missing from this man.

'We know you're a German,' she said then.

The door swung open at the same time.

The first man in held a Webley revolver in both hands. He slammed himself against the open door.

The next man went left of the German, and the third – balding, with bovine eyes – shoved a revolver into his temple. Valerie Lynes pulled the sheet up over her breasts, wrapped it around herself and stepped off the bed.

'These men are Special Branch, and you're under arrest,' she said.

'I could tell your husband about us,' the German said.

'He knows.'

'So Baker Street has decided not to send us back to France together, I take it?'

'Last stop, Paddington,' she said.

The balding policeman pressed his revolver harder into the German's head.

1

'Mits on head, please.' he said.

The German obeyed, very slowly. The policeman at the door, a pale man with a small scar on his cheek, came forward and cuffed him. The third, wearing a fawn mackintosh, stood on the other side of the bed.

'Gentlemen,' the German said, 'please, allow me my dignity.' He looked at his clothes, strewn across the floor. 'I'm still an officer with the Special Operations Executive.'

Valerie Lynes opened a wardrobe and pulled a dressing gown on.

'Go on,' she said. 'Let him dress, Inspector.'

The balding policeman gestured to the pale man with the scar to uncuff the German. He undid one cuff. His colleagues kept their weapons trained on him while he dressed. He was fastening his tie when Valerie Lynes came over to him.

'I insist on dignity,' the German said, 'no matter what the occasion. I suppose there's no point protesting?'

'You meant to kill me in France, didn't you?' Valerie Lynes said.

She ran her hand through his hair. It was the colour of flax just after it is cut, loose, combed from the left and oiled.

He smiled and then touched her face with his fingers.

'Nothing personal,' he said.

'I'm probably going to miss you,' she said. 'Au revoir.'

'Adieu,' he said.

He took her face in his hands and kissed her. Then he looked at the balding Special Branch inspector and smiled. 'You've lowered your weapon.' The man's pupils dilated in shock.

The German's foot came up between the policeman's legs at the same time as his head butted Valerie Lynes on the bridge of the nose. Her neck jerked back and the German forced her jaws apart and wrenched her head in the same movement. Her neck broke as he shoved her into the balding inspector and rolled across the room at the pale policeman with the scar, who had not been able to fire because Valerie Lynes was in the way. The third policeman, in the fawn mackintosh, did fire, but the bullet hit the bed. The German came up beneath the pale man's arms and caught him in the plexus with a single punch. The man buckled and dropped his gun. The German kneed him in the face, opening his scar, and shoved him across the bed just as the man in the fawn mackintosh fired again.

The bullet hit his pale colleague with the scar.

The German grabbed the pale man's revolver and fired two shots

2

into the third policeman's head, knocking the man into the wardrobe behind, then turned back on the balding inspector. The inspector had his gun raised, but the German was faster. He shot the balding inspector in the shoulder and spun him against the wall and then shot him between the eyes.

The pale policeman with the scar was scrambling across the floor towards his dead colleague's weapon by the wardrobe. The German slammed his foot into the man's spine, pulled his head up and pulled his jaws apart.

'Open wide!'

He snapped the man's neck with one movement, then stood back and put a bullet in the back of his head.

Voices from the stairwell grew louder to the beat of running feet. The German picked up the inspector's revolver, and stepped on to the landing. Two men and a woman were out of their rooms. The German kneecapped one of the men and moved down the stairs. On the next floor, he blew away a door lock, and kicked the door in. The room was empty.

He opened a window, climbed out and shimmied down a drainpipe, to the first floor, where he kicked a window in and slipped into a room. A couple were in bed. The German put his finger to his lips, waited for the sounds of all the voices and running feet to pass, then opened the door and walked to the stairs again. He shoved the gun into his pocket, straightened his hair and headed for the lobby.

The shouting upstairs began when he reached the lobby. Two policemen were talking to the desk clerk. One of them was about to call on the German to halt. The German shot the man in the neck and his partner in the chest. He smiled at the desk clerk.

'Just checking out,' he said.

He pulled the front door open and swore. A platoon of soldiers lined the street. And the first volley brought him down.

1

March, 1944

THE BUILDING HAD the look of a mausoleum: a ghostly combination of Victorian neo-classical and Georgian, all buttressed by imitation Doric columns. The whole structure appeared to move in the wind as if it could easily vanish. A good place to meet a dead man.

Ben Kramer hesitated for a moment before going in, but just for a moment.

The room was long. The German sat in the corner, on the *chaise-longue*, reading a newspaper: the Russians had crossed the Bug river in Poland.

'How close was it?' Kramer said.

'I had to put up with a priest.' The German scratched his new copper beard. 'You have no unit identification patches on your uniform, Herr Major.'

He stood up from the *chaise-longue*. He was shorter than Kramer by about two inches, but his shoulders were wider and his physique better. And his hands were manicured.

'Sit down here. Please,' Kramer said.

Kramer sat on one side of the table by the window. The German sat down opposite him. The window was bolted from the outside and it had a steel shutter which could be placed in front of it at night. Otherwise the lead latticework prevented any escape.

Kramer pulled out a folder.

'Erich Haas,' he said then. 'At least that's a name we have from the Swiss. I'll use it if you don't mind. It's more appropriate than the name you were using here.'

'As you please,' the German man said.

'Born . . . I'd say Berlin or thereabouts,' Kramer continued. 'Your accent's a mixture of Brandenburg and Pomerania, but urban rather than rural. Age? I'd say fortyish, but then so am I. Educated . . . here's a university graduation photograph that could be you. Then there's a bit of a gap. Now this is from the French and the photograph is very old but I think you were in the French Foreign Legion in the twenties, and then we have another gap until you turn up in Prague in 1938. The Czech description is a little vague but it is you . . . what I have comes from very different sources.'

Erich Haas's face remained impassive – even the blue-green eyes. He passed a hand through his flaxen hair.

Kramer leaned down to his briefcase and pulled out a second folder. He handed the contents to Haas, photograph by photograph, page by page.

'The Poles say you led the team which captured this bridge in Silesia in '39. But they call you by this name. And here's a blurred photograph I scrounged. Some newsman took it.'

'Very blurred.'

'Yes. You led a team posing as Belgian soldiers through the Ardennes in 1940 . . . helped secure crossing of the Meuse . . . helped secure crossing of the Seine. Do you know Rommel?'

'No comment.'

'I tried to kill him once,' Kramer said.

'Ah! Where you got that?'

Haas pointed at Kramer's leg. Kramer rapped his knuckles on the wood. 'No, that's cancer,' he said. 'When did you begin to kill people for the Abwehr?'

Haas smiled. His eyes were very calm now. 'Look, Herr Major,' he said, 'I've done this kind of thing with your MI5. But you're not MI5, are you? If you think just because I'm at the end I'm going to make some kind of deathbed confession, forget it. I was arrested, tried and sentenced to death. That's life, as they say.'

'You were in Moscow some time in December 1941,' Kramer said. 'You had to shoot your way out. What was the nature of your mission?'

'You seem damn well informed. You tell me.'

'You were sent either to kidnap or kill Josef Stalin. Right? Or perhaps the whole of the STAVKA, the general staff?'

'I'll bet you know the length of my dick.'

Kramer smiled and reached down and pulled out a very thin grey

file with an eagle stamp and *Geheime Reichssache* written underneath:
Top Secret. He handed it to Haas.

Haas opened the file and grinned.

'It's very basic,' Kramer said. 'Straight from Abwehr records.
A simple code and a curriculum vitae, so to speak. Much of it
corresponds with what I've put to you from my other sources. But
the important thing is the letter at the beginning of the code.'

'I should ask where you got this.'

'From people who are busy buying insurance. And even MI5 don't
know about it. You were placed in a Special Operations Executive
circuit in France, from where you were sent here, to SOE headquarters,
in Baker Street. To be sent back to France to organise more circuits,
and staff them with your own people. Then they'd prey on real circuits,
like a . . . a cancer. A killing here, a killing there, suspicion preys on
suspicion and eventually no one knows who's working for whom.
Was that the idea? You're an infiltration and assassination expert,
Erich. What is it they call your kind, The Virus? Apt.'

'And who are you, Herr Major?'

Kramer pulled out another file.

'But you were betrayed,' he said. 'I suspect you know that already.
I know by whom: the Gestapo and the SD in Paris. Avenue Foch
delivered you to us to cover a French collaborator they had infiltrated
into the same SOE circuit as you. We found out about it because we
were trying to infiltrate the very same circuit.'

'Then you must be with the Secret Intelligence Service.'

'Here's the collaborator's statement: he was shot. And that's a
communication between Prinz Albrechtstrasse and Avenue Foch.
You'll recognise the code and the name. If you doubt me, think
about how you were caught. Well?'

'Deep penetration,' Haas said.

'Tell me, how many people should have known your mission? You
boys have no life except your current legend. Your pasts are wiped
clean, nothing so much as a traffic fine. To all intents and purposes
you're dead men waiting to be resurrected.'

'Death has its advantages, I suppose. Although, from where I'm
sitting I can't think of any offhand.'

'There's more, Erich. That little code of yours appears on a
Gestapo Suspects list given to OSS in Berne. Nice that. They betray
you and you're the traitor. Or maybe you were conspiring against
Hitler?'

Now Haas showed some slight emotion.

'You wear the uniform of a British officer and you speak the language of a member of the Secret Intelligence Service, but there is more. Yes?'

Kramer leaned across the table. 'You'll do one of two things now, Erich,' he said. 'You'll consider everything I have to say or you'll go straight back to London and execution. Have you ever heard the words Sherut Yediot, or Shai?'

'They're Jew underground names,' Haas replied. 'From Palestine. Haganah intelligence, that kind of thing. They work with Mossad, getting Jews out of Europe and into Palestine, among other things. Not altogether successful, I suspect.'

'Do you have a view on that? The fate of the Jews of Europe?'

'I don't have views. I don't exist.'

'Nine days ago, German troops occupied Hungary. The Hungarians were getting cold feet. Putting out peace feelers. There are three quarters of a million Jews in Hungary. The SS will kill them all. I want to prevent that.'

'So complain to Himmler. To the Führer.'

'You must have taken an oath to him as a German officer. Still stand?'

'Look at your vast supply of records and tell me. What do you want?'

'I want you to work for me,' Kramer said.

'I won't work for the British. I told MI5 that. Call it professional pride.'

'I'm not asking you to. I'm asking you to work for Shai. I'll pay you a million American dollars, and you'll go free if you succeed.'

There was a long pause. Then Haas leaned towards Kramer.

'I hope I am not betraying my excitement, Herr Major, but you're not a bad interrogator, if you don't mind me saying. One million dollars? I like just hearing the sound of it. And what would I have to do to earn this amount of money?'

'You've killed everything from political commissars to generals, everywhere from the Russian steppes to the cafés of Lisbon. I want you to kill someone for me.'

'For a million dollars?'

'You'll earn it. I want you to kill Adolf Hitler.'

* * *

8

As it happened, the immediate fate of Adolf Hitler exercised the minds of three other men that morning.

No. 21 Queen Anne's Gate, the private residence of the Chief of the British Secret Intelligence Service during the Second World War, is a 1704 period house with the kind of comfort you could still forget existed after four and a half years of conflict. Directly behind SIS headquarters in Broadway Buildings, it was linked by a tunnel to the Chief's office, to enable him to slip in and out unnoticed.

The Chief in question was Colonel Sir Graham Stuart Menzies, a reliable if rather limited figure, appointed to the post in 1939 for reasons as much to do with his social connections as anything else – his family owned a lot of Scotland.

However, sitting across from him that morning, on a piece of furniture that could probably have paid for a Spitfire, was the true heart and soul of the Secret Intelligence Service, its vice-chief, Lieutenant-Colonel Sir Claude Edward Marjoribanks Dansey, KCMG, a man for whom espionage was life itself.

Even at sixty-seven, Claude Dansey was intimidating: charming and ruthless in the same breath. What remained of his hair was a woolly, almost animal, grey, and if he had lost some of the physical power of his younger days, his eyes made up for it. They had a menace, which, added to his moustache and pointed chin, verged on the lethal. And he had the vacuum-sealed lips of the perennial conspirator.

On the other side of Menzies, as if by way of a counterpoint to Dansey, was a cultured American lawyer, Colonel David Bruce, the head of the Office of Strategic Services in London. In his mid-forties, with an Ivy League manner, Bruce looked more like an ambassador than a spy.

'Red Czar on the Seine,' Menzies said, holding up a series of typed blue sheets. 'Bit of a dramatic title, Claude.'

'I wanted to make a point, C. Naturally, we welcome our Soviet ally's success, it's just that too much of a good thing can be distressing. Like getting indigestion after too much cream cake.'

'I do love it when you're being devious and duplicitous, Claude,' Menzies said.

Dansey was the kind of legend that is sometimes bigger than the stories about them. He had begun his spying in Africa in the previous century, slugged Boer sentries with stockings full of sand, fought

Muslim fanatics in Somalia, run a country club in America and his own private intelligence network in Europe.

'But you both agree with the central thrust?' he asked, his eyes darting to each of the men with him.

'This is a hell of a sensitive subject, Claude,' David Bruce said. 'The President's Uncle Joe's number-one fan.'

'I don't know what they slipped him in Teheran, David, but I think the OSS should test him,' Dansey commented.

'We'll bear it in mind, Claude. We're new to this game, trying to find our feet. You Britishers have the whole thing sewn up.'

'You mean we've all the commitments and no money and you've all the money and no commitments, David. Well, here's your chance to increase your input. The facts are, our Russian allies are in Poland and knocking on the door of Romania, our German enemies are stretched to hold them, while we are stuck at Anzio and below Monte Cassino in Italy and have no presence in western Europe. Should our French endeavour this summer fail, then our strategic position will be critical.'

'Manhattan?' Menzies said.

'Ace in the hole, if it works,' Bruce said. 'But it's a year away. You know I'd like to come up with a counter-argument to your analysis, Claude, but I can't. It's flawless – geopolitically. Morally, it stinks.'

'Thank you, David. I appreciate you Americans need your just wars. Will OSS co-operate?'

'Have we a choice?' Bruce asked.

Menzies shook his head. The strain of the next word showed on his face. He was not a man given to instant decisions. 'No,' he said.

'That's what I like about you guys,' Bruce said. 'You always know the right strings to pull. The right moves to make. The right balances to strike. To get what you want. So what we're saying here, in so many words, is we want Germany intact and fighting for the time being? At least, in the east. I can't believe I'm saying this.'

'I do wish you wouldn't put a moral gloss on strategy, David,' Dansey said. 'It doesn't help clear thought. We're talking post-war now, who dominates the continent for the next fifty years. And history has proved that whoever reaches Vienna first is likely to do that. Our Soviet allies may indeed prove to be the freedom-loving democrats our propaganda paints them as being, but we must assume they will revert to type after Germany is beaten.'

'Which is why OSS is keen to cultivate the right contacts in Germany itself,' Bruce said.

'Personally, I'm not at all keen on any of these opposition factions in Germany,' Menzies said. 'And not just because we were taken in by the SS pretending to be one at Venlo in '39.'

'You met Canaris with General Donovan last year in Santander,' Bruce said.

'And it created a big fuss and nothing else. I mean, what's coming out of Germany, David? Army officers worried about their pensions and diplomats with consciences.'

'And Himmler?' Dansey said. 'His people have been making noises in Stockholm.'

'Does he honestly believe we'll deal with him?'

'We may have to. If he moves. Unconditional surrender, while admirable as a battle cry, has painted us into a corner.'

'And what are the possibilities of Himmler making a move?' Bruce asked.

'At the moment, he's trying to be a facilitator,' Dansey said. 'Between them and us. Detached. He's still loyal to his Führer. But . . . he's a cunning one. And if it comes to it he'll reinvent logic to get what he wants. Definitely sees himself as the successor. There is an argument that a clean SS coup, like the long knives affair in '34, would be preferable to a messy civil war. In the medium term. Once we're in a strong position we can rewrite the rules.'

'Don't tell me any more, Claude,' C said. 'I hate having to be economical with the truth at Cabinet briefings.'

'It is in our interests to cultivate certain people's illusions, C,' Dansey said. 'It widens our options in the future.'

'OSS agrees, C,' Bruce said. 'The succession is already under way.'

He looked at Dansey.

'And we must have some control over it,' Dansey said.

'But these German opposition chaps your man, Allen Dulles, has been meeting in Switzerland – his Breakers, David – they're not the people of successful coups,' Menzies said.

'That's precisely the point I'm trying to make,' Dansey said. 'It's an unsuccessful coup we must fear most. One which would precipitate a German collapse before we landed in France. It would really queer the situation for us. I mean, everything they've tried so far has failed, and even a general attempt probably will. Reliable sources say one officer got close to the Führer a couple of weeks back but lost his nerve under the gaze of the bodyguards. If they'd done it a year ago, that would have been fine, but now – well, that's what we're here for.'

Menzies fiddled with Dansey's memo.

'And do you think these opposition types will agree to this: not to make another move against their Führer before the summer? David?'

'They'll listen,' Bruce said. 'They have no choice.'

'And it'll give us a measure of their worth,' Dansey said.

'And their offer of letting us land in Germany if their move proved successful?'

'Like you said, C,' Bruce said, 'their chances of success are very limited.' He looked at Dansey.

'In the end, all we can hope for is a successful landing in France and that they create enough confusion in the Reich for us to exploit,' Dansey said. 'I also doubt their complete independence. The Venlo caveat. I think we should assume that they are not as free as they might think. Which is why we should be flexible.'

'Softly, softly, Claude, please,' Menzies said. 'I have political masters. Don't present me with things I can't decide on.'

'Of course, C. Untraceable intermediaries and vague interchanges. But it's useful. Intelligence is an open book; the trick is to be able to read.'

Bruce laughed. 'You know, sometimes I have to pinch myself and tell myself I'm working with the British Secret Service. You're aware that General Donovan worships you, Claude.'

'Everyone worships Claude,' Menzies said. 'Or fears him.'

'Just how far would the Russians go, do you think?' Bruce asked Dansey. 'If Overlord failed. If Germany collapsed.'

'Look at the title of my memo, David. Stalin talks of Czar Alexander getting to Paris.'

'You think he's serious?'

'He's not a man who jokes a lot.'

Menzies tapped the arm of his chair. 'I find myself in the unenviable position of wishing for German resilience in the east in the next few months. And the continued good health of Adolf Hitler.'

'Then we're agreed. We ask these German opposition people to hold off any move against Hitler until we've landed in France?' Dansey asked.

The other two men thought before nodding their agreement.

Erich Haas nodded when he closed the file in front of him.

'And you can get one million dollars?' he said to Kramer.

'So you're not against the idea?' Kramer said.

'As you point out, I'm a very disappointed man, facing execution, Herr Major. You're offering me a way out. And a million dollars. Suppose I say yes and then I just vanish.'

'We'll find you. Shai will find you and kill you. No matter how long it takes. And if you remain in Germany we'll give your particulars to the Gestapo. I believe that Prinz Albrechtstrasse is a terrible place for those who stay there as guests.'

'Otherwise, I die in London?'

Kramer pulled out a revolver.

'No. After what I've just said I'll kill you now. You were trying to escape. If you agree, we will arrange things.'

'Do you have a cigarette and perhaps a drink?'

Kramer reached into his leather briefcase and pulled out a clear bottle of liquid and two small glasses. He poured into each of the glasses and handed one to Haas. Then he took out a packet of Players cigarettes, lit one, and passed that to Haas. Then he gave him the packet. Haas drank the small glass of clear liquid Kramer had poured for him. And for the first time his eyes warmed.

'Nice?' Kramer asked.

'Nice is too small a word for this. What is it?'

Kramer drank his own glass and winced.

'Poteen. It's Irish and they say you can melt diamond with it. I have developed something of an immunity to it. An Irishman I knew in Spain some years ago always carried a bottle.'

'I'll bet it blew up and killed him.'

'No, he was executed by firing squad.'

Haas held his throat and put his glass down. Kramer poured again.

'A few more of these and you won't need to shoot me – and what's more I won't care,' Haas said. He reached over and poured himself another glass of poteen, drank it and wiped his mouth. 'They'll probably die anyway. Your Hungarian Jews. The SS are very efficient. What they want they usually get. They've been trying to get the Abwehr for years.'

'They have it,' Kramer said. 'Hitler ordered it broken up last month. Your boss, Admiral Canaris, is under house arrest in Thuringia. He was, perhaps, getting too friendly with the opposition. Himmler's picking at the bones of what's left of the Abwehr. Here's an OSS summation from Berne.'

Haas read it and grinned.

'From Allen Dulles,' he said, 'the man who told Lenin to call back when Lenin phoned the Americans in 1917, just before he got on a German train for Russia. Very reliable.'

'Dulles has learned a few things since then.'

'I hope so.'

'Perhaps the SS used you to undermine Canaris. In the end it was unnecessary. Two Abwehr agents in Turkey – the Vehmerens – defected to us, and that did for the admiral.'

'Herr Major, read your files again. I don't exist.' Haas had another drink. 'One million American dollars?' he asked again.

Kramer nodded.

'And help with a new life anywhere you want. One million dollars will buy you anything, anywhere.'

'How would the money be delivered?' Haas asked.

'Switzerland. Stockholm. Buenos Aires. New York. Wherever you want. Half deposited before you carry out the operation and the rest when you are finished.'

'How do I know you won't kill me when I collect?'

'You must trust me as much as I must trust you.'

'When is it to be done?'

'Within a month.'

'Impossible.'

'No.' Ben Kramer stretched his wooden leg. 'He's at his Berghof in Bavaria. This presents a far more manageable target than either his East Prussian headquarters or Berlin. In 1938, a student with a rifle got very close. So it's difficult but not impossible.'

'Sure. But there are possibilities and there are possibilities. I'd have to have the right to call it off if anything goes wrong, if I'm seriously compromised, and know you wouldn't come after me or sell me out to the Gestapo.'

'No, you must go through with it.'

'You drive a hard bargain.'

'The stakes are high . . . and I have to know you're serious, Erich. More trust. If I am not convinced in the next fifteen minutes I will kill you.'

Haas took in a deep breath. He looked at Kramer's files again and took another drink.

'There is an Abwehr account I have access to in Lisbon. That is where you will deposit the money. And I must be allowed to confirm.'

'Agreed.'

'I feel I must point out here that I was caught this time out. Three bullets in me. Your people were kind enough to save my life before sentencing me to death.'

'That's justice. And, as I have confirmed, you were supposed to be caught. Anyway, I don't have the time to shop around. I have looked at everything we have available and nothing comes close to you.'

'So who exactly are you, then, Jew?'

'Will you do it?' Kramer demanded.

Haas drank some more poteen. 'The Russians are across the Bug. Perhaps a man should be looking out for his future. I had ideas. South America. I rather thought I'd like to be a farmer, maybe raising cattle in Argentina or Bolivia. Or mining. Perhaps I'll do both.'

'So we have a deal?'

'What have I to lose?'

'I want to make it clear that if you at any time foul up or look like fouling up, I will not hesitate to kill you.'

'And maybe I will kill you, Herr Major. I could have killed you at least twice during this conversation but I did not. You should be more careful. You will find I am – at those times I choose to give it – a man of my word. And I stand to be a very rich man of my word. So what happens now?'

'Now, we move you. I sign you into my custody. There's a place we can prepare. You must be ready within two weeks.'

'And the British, Mr British intelligence officer?'

Kramer shook his head.

'This is a Haganah operation. You are not the only one who has made a decision to burn bridges.'

Kramer pulled out a buff file and a fountain pen and scribbled something in the top corner and filled in a date. Then he paused and looked at Haas.

'Reconsidering?' Haas asked.

'No, I need a cover code, something to bury you under. You're joining an SIS operation of mine; you need know no details.'

Haas smiled and poured another drink.

'Call me Valkyrie,' he said. 'It's a little private joke. Some people I know of plan on using it to announce the demise of the Führer some day. If they ever get around to it. There's a certain irony in it for the SS and security police, don't you think?'

The central irony of the SS and police empire constructed by Heinrich Himmler under the title, Reich Security Main Office, was the fact that it had no main office.

There was the dour former industrial Arts and Crafts building at Prinz Albrechtstrasse 8, Berlin, which was its postal address, technical headquarters and the official address of the Reichsführer-SS and his personal staff. Most people who had the misfortune to come into contact with the Reich Security Main Office during office hours met their fate in this building because it was also the headquarters of the Gestapo.

But the head of the Reich Security Main Office actually had his office around the corner in the much nicer Prinz Albrecht Palais, at Wilhelmstrasse 102, headquarters of SD Inland, the internal security service of the Nazi Party, while the SS as a whole and Himmler's adjutancy were based in the Prinz Albrecht Hotel, at Prinz Albrechtstrasse 9, a very salubrious *belle époque* building which had been a favourite of the Nazis since before their seizure of power. Overseeing all of this, in true bureaucratic fashion, and to overcome the nebulous nature of the Reich Security Main Office, Heinrich Himmler had offices in all these buildings. And several others.

Standing in his office in the *belle époque* luxury of the Prinz Albrecht Hotel that lunchtime, having just arrived back from Bavaria, the Reichsminister of the Interior and Reichsführer-SS surveyed all the new bomb damage around the area, then picked up a copy of the Bhagavad-Gita, the Hindu holy book, and began reading.

'"... for the protection of the good, for the destruction of evil, for the setting up of the law of righteousness ..."'

Himmler looked up from his book and turned to Gruppenführer Otto Ohlendorf, the head of SD Inland.

In his mid-thirties, functionally handsome, with a slightly receding hairline and a certain romanticism in his eyes that women found

attractive, Ohlendorf's personality had all the vagaries of an intel-
lectual mass murderer. People said it was like a hot-and-cold tap
system without any indication of which was which.

'I was just reminding myself why we fight; why we do what we do;
why we sacrifice ourselves for the nation,' Himmler said.

Ohlendorf gave Himmler the *Deutscher Gruss* salute.

'My lime trees are damaged,' Himmler said then. 'Some day I will
come back and all this will be gone.'

'Never, Herr Reichsführer. Anyway, the Führer was going to rebuild
Berlin, so the terror flyers are only doing his work for him.'

'Very drole, Otto.'

Ohlendorf sat down in front of the desk and Himmler put his
pince-nez on and took up his position.

'You spoke with the Führer?' Ohlendorf asked. 'Concerning the
strategic situation?'

'The Führer thinks SD Inland's morale reports are too pessimistic, Otto.'

'My men report what they hear.'

'The Führer points to the recent production figures and his feeling
for the soul of the German people.'

'The Führer's contact with the German people has been limited
recently. Too many of that mountain crowd he has around him give
him their own fanciful opinions based upon nights spent watching
movies and drinking French wines.'

'Otto, you display a Prussian frankness which I, as a Bavarian,
find borders on the fatalistic.'

'If you doubt my commitment, Herr Reichsführer . . . I speak with
the backing of facts. One cannot deny the facts.'

'But one can interpret them in different ways. Even a *Gralshutter*,
Otto.'

'I'm not sure your reference to me as the guardian of the Holy
Grail of National Socialism is something I am proud of any more,
Herr Reichsführer. Yet there is no one who believes in the doctrine
more than I. We are the master race; no matter what the outcome
of this struggle. Battles may be lost . . .'

'Remember who you talk to, Otto, do not be too frank.'

'The Führer has been betrayed, Herr Reichsführer, by the can-
cerous, self-seeking corruption which attached itself to the state
apparatus and prevented us from prosecuting this war with the
strength necessary. And now they would prevent us from making

17

the necessary strategic decisions if Germany is to survive. You, as Reichsführer-SS, the true guardian of the flame, must take the decisions, no matter how hard, how harsh, how difficult, or what the cost may be, both personal or otherwise.'

'You talk like a prophet, Ohlendorf.'

'I talk like an economist.'

'Is it really true that people are joking that the Führer has written a book called *My Mistake*? I did not tell any of this to the Führer.'

'It is all true. But it cannot be allowed to go on. And you will have to act, Herr Reichsführer.'

'Army Groups Centre and South are in a shambles, you know. Keitel told me you could drive five armies between them and never see a German soldier. I suspect he was exaggerating but the point was made. They are suddenly very close, the Bolsheviks, and everything we have fought against seems to be gathering . . . a storm breaking loose, Goebbels said. But where will it break from and upon what?'

'If we do not remedy the situation, we stand to be in even worse shape this time next year, Herr Reichsführer. Perhaps destroyed.'

'Impossible. We have new weapons. The West will not let us go under, will not allow the Asiatic hordes into Europe.'

'They are in Europe and unless we can come to an accommodation with the Western allies, they will be in Europe for the rest of our lifetimes and Germany as we know and love her will disappear from the map. You discussed this with the Führer? Impressed upon him the gravity of the situation? The need for the steps which have to be taken?'

'There are certain things the Führer will not hear. He says he cannot negotiate, and he will not surrender unconditionally.'

'I suppose one could not expect him to. He is the Führer. Such decisions must then be made elsewhere. To relieve him of the burden.'

'Please, Ohlendorf! This summer's fighting may yet see us victorious. New weapons, fresh divisions. If we defeat the invasion of France, then perhaps the British and the Americans will talk sense. Forget this unconditional surrender nonsense. See the Bolsheviks for the threat they are.'

'And while we're bleeding ourselves dry in France, the Bolsheviks will be over the Vistula and the Carpathians and knocking at the gates of Berlin and Vienna. Time is not our ally. Decisions must be made, Herr Reichsführer.'

'My faith is still with the Führer.'

'Your loyalty is indisputable, Herr Reichsführer. As is ı
But there are questions which must be dealt with. Transcende
questions. Greater than personal loyalty. No one man is greater
than Germany.'

'No, Ohlendorf, no. I will not explore those avenues, I refuse to,
and I warn you, hold your tongue.'

'You would have the socialists and the army traitors in Bendlerstrasse
and Zossen running Germany? Think about it. The same dilettantes
who sold us out in 1918 are at this moment plotting to oust the
Führer and take over this country. I do not think we have the luxury
of ignoring all the realities, Herr Reichsfürer. And what will become
of the SS and all we have worked for in the Party?'

Himmler raised his hand.

'Stop! You play games with my mind; you combine the skill
of an advocate and the detached logic of an economist. Quite
formidable.'

'I have Germany's interests at heart. Should we wait for the enemy
to strike or strike first. Remember 1934.'

'We will strike. We will strike.'

'But where and when?'

Himmler stood up.

'I think you must go now, Herr Gruppenführer. You have work to
do. I have work to do. As the Führer would say, let providence decide.'

Ohlendorf stood up.

'I hope providence realises the urgency of the situation,' he said.

Himmler did not respond.

Later that afternoon, Ohlendorf had to move quickly to catch the
young man ahead of him on the steps of the Gestapo building at
Prinz Albrechtstrasse 8.

'Going back to Berkaerstrasse, Walter?' Ohlendorf asked.

Gruppenführer Walter Schellenberg, the thirty-three-year-old head
of SD Ausland, the foreign intelligence service of the Nazi Party, had
a boyish face that belied his rank. A disarming smile, a buccaneering
spirit and an almost pathological passion for intrigue had all assured
his meteoric rise through the ranks of the SS, since his enlistment ten
years earlier. Another lawyer, he was very different from Ohlendorf in
that he had no faith in anything, except perhaps himself. Schellenberg
was a pure opportunist.

'No. I'm going to Tirpitz Ufer to see Georg Hansen. Not often you get the acting Abwehr chief out of his Zossen lair. I thought Admiral Canaris's old office would be a suitable place to conduct takeover discussions. Hansen can sit at his boss's old desk and I'll be polite and kill the Abwehr with kindness. Want a lift?'

'The Reichsführer's back,' Ohlendorf said, getting into Schellenberg's car. 'He's in the hotel.'

'I know,' Schellenberg said. 'And what did the Führer say?'

'*Ausharren*. Stick it out. It's what the Führer always says. Unfortunately.'

'I'm impressed with his fortitude, even in the light of our current difficulties. Did the Reichsführer impress upon him the gravity of the situation?'

'What do you think?'

Schellenberg opened the glass between him and his driver.

'Drive the long way round,' he said. 'Around the Tiergarten. Let's have a look at our beloved city and see what these people from England have done to it.'

He closed the glass.

'I told the Reichsführer a decision would have to be made,' Ohlendorf said. 'If we're not to fall victim to events.'

'I'll bet he took that well.'

'He's caught on the horns of a dilemma. His loyalty to the Führer and absolute belief in the man and his realisation that the situation demands more sacrifices, great sacrifices. He is a man of integrity, the Reichsführer, great integrity.'

'I really think you mean it, Otto. Well, I've been talking to people in Stockholm and there is possible room for manouevre. But . . .'

'Not if we continue in the direction we are going. We need a more flexible hand at the helm, to use a nautical analogy.'

'You are frighteningly direct at times, Otto. You know you make the Reichsführer uneasy. He's scared of you, thinks you're a fanatic . . . he's really got rather low self-esteem, the Reichsführer. Anyway, there will be change in this Reich, one way or another, there is absolutely no question about that. Our problem, and the Reichsführer's problem, is where we will stand when those changes come about. You've heard about the condition of Army Groups Centre and South in the east?'

'Reports come through all the time,' Ohlendorf said.

'If we had something concrete to offer, we'd be in a better position. I said that to the Reichsführer.'

'He wants to act. But his loyalty to the Führer . . . it is a monumental decision. He must be more than sure.'

'You're an economist, Otto. Surely you can wield that brilliant brain of yours in our favour. He's in awe of you. He thinks I'm Heydrich's old lapdog. I resent him not giving me Heydrich's job, you know.'

'It worries me that Germany may slide the way of 1918.'

'The problem is obvious, Otto, very obvious. And there is only one man who can act. Who must act.'

'But some might construe such ideas as treason, Walter.'

'Only failure is treason. And I will not fail, Otto. The Reichsführer must be persuaded his duty to the state outweighs his personal loyalties.'

'I can only guide.'

'There are ways of guidance.'

The car pulled in on the canal side of the Tirpitz Ufer, just down from No. 72, the old Abwehr building, mostly evacuated now because of the bombing.

'I used to be in awe of that place,' Schellenberg said. 'But now I fear this whole War Ministry block will move on us if we do not take action. As the military situation deteriorates, they will become more focused.'

'We are in a vice.'

Walter Schellenberg smiled.

'We must extract ourselves, for the sake of the Reich. No matter what the cost, no matter what. Take the car, I'll walk back.'

'The Reichsführer wants to rely on providence.'

'Well, I suggest you consider ways of influencing providence, Otto,' Schellenberg said, 'before she turns on us and bites.'

He stepped out of the car and walked across the road.

2

FROM THE OUTSIDE, Broadway Buildings looked like an Art Deco Westminster apartment block, while the brass plates at the door would have had you believe it was a fire extinguisher company and a government communications centre. Inside, it was a rabbit warren commandeered as a filing shed, a labyrinth of corridors, partitions and frosted glass. What might be described as a recess.

From the offices of P6, SIS's German section, Ben Kramer could see the St James's Park tube station across the street and the man in the dark overcoat who had just taken off his hat.

Kramer was about to grab his own coat and follow the man with the hat when a balding head above a youngish face put itself around his door.

'Why don't you ever knock, Teddy?' Kramer said.

Teddy Giles ignored the reprimand. His job specification said he was Claude Dansey's personal assistant, and Giles had learned to accept the little barbs that came with it because the power it gave him was more than a salve for the wounds it incurred.

'VCSS wants to see you, sir,' he said.

'What does Uncle Claude want, specifically?' Kramer asked.

'I'm only the messenger, sir.'

'Is that all, Teddy?'

Giles didn't answer this time.

'I had a meeting planned,' Kramer said.

'I'm sure it won't take long, sir. VCSS was insistent.'

'He always is.'

Kramer knew there was no sense in arguing. Claude Dansey had brought him into the firm in '39 when Kramer had wanted to join the army, and had sent him to Cairo to work with Security Intelligence Middle East and co-ordinate with the Haganah when Kramer had wanted to go to France; then Dansey had sent him to France when Kramer had wanted to stay in Cairo; and finally, when he wanted to go back to France, Dansey had said no. Dansey was the price you paid for the privilege of being in SIS.

Claude Dansey was standing at his window, fiddling with his blackout curtains or looking out at the street, Kramer could not make out which. Dansey pulled the curtains.

'Privacy,' he said. 'Sussex, Ben . . . how are things?' Sussex was a joint SIS–OSS operation to drop teams of observers behind German lines in France prior to D-Day. These teams would watch and report on German troop strengths and movements. Kramer had originally been involved because he specialised in that part of eastern France which had been annexed to Greater Germany and therefore fell under P6's jurisdiction. Now, Dansey wanted to extend the plan to Germany proper, in anticipation of a direct assault across the Rhine following a successful French campaign, and Kramer was assigned to recruit suitable personnel for the job.

'Dripping slowly, sir,' Kramer said. 'Suitable Germans are not easy to find. But we'll get there.'

'We have time. Anyway, that wasn't the real reason I wanted this little chat. I haven't seen you for a few days.'

'I've been busy.'

'Of course.' Dansey paused for a moment. 'How are things in Hungary?' he asked then.

'Awful, I suspect, sir.'

'Yes. We're doing our best, you know. Eden's issuing a warning. How many years did you live there?'

'In Budapest? Eighteen.'

'And then Vienna.'

'And Germany.'

'Yes. Anyway, what I really wanted to toss with you was the new Soviet desk here. The Soviet Union's going to weigh heavily on our minds again soon. I was thinking that you'd be a front runner to head it. Of course, the final decision would be C's, but I'd have an input. What do you think?'

'I'm flattered, sir.'

'Are you interested?'

'One war at a time, sir. I've been offered a job, lecturing in English in Jerusalem.'

'By the same people who are shooting our policemen in Tel Aviv.'

'No. And the Haganah aren't shooting our policemen. The Lehi – the Stern Gang – are. The Haganah are helping us.'

'As we have helped them.'

Kramer winced. 'Indeed,' he said.

'Your leg still hurting?' Dansey asked.

'You could say that.'

'What's the doctor say?'

'He says it's a matter of time.'

'Exactly. You can get over anything in time.'

'I'm not a professional, you know, sir.'

Dansey stood up, suddenly. 'I thought you'd be a bit more enthusiastic, Ben. I think you should remember you are a British citizen and not allow romanticism over a tragic situation to interfere with your work. We're not the ones killing Jews. Remember that.'

'I tell myself that all the time, sir. But it was this country which limited visas to Palestine when the SS were letting Jews out.'

'Regrettable, but we have balances to maintain.'

'With Arabs who follow a man living in Berlin.'

'If we could do more, we would, I told you. We put together that mission for Hungary – with Ennio Sereni. It was just a pity it was too late.'

'A handful of intellectuals and kibbutz girls to try and rescue three-quarters of a million people?'

'We'll help them best by winning the war, Ben. Or perhaps the Russians will do it for us. Think about that. It's a poisonous snake we're faced with. Ben. A very deadly poisonous snake.'

Only when Kramer answered did he get the feeling that they might have been talking about different things.

'Best way to kill a snake is to cut its head off,' he said, regretting it the moment he said it.

Dansey nodded.

'I wish it were that simple, Ben. But it's not. I thought we'd agreed. We killed Heydrich and they just replaced him. And look at the revenge it provoked. The Czechs have never recovered. No one would thank us for wasting our energies on anything like that again, Ben, in spite of P6's optimistic research.'

'Let's agree to disagree,' Kramer said. 'You're right, I'm personally involved.'

'I suppose I shouldn't blame you. As long as it does not interfere with your judgment.'

'No, my judgment is very clear now.'

'So your end of Sussex is going well?' Dansey asked.

'I found a good man yesterday,' Kramer said.

'You know I'd give you leave if I could spare you, Ben. Keep this Soviet thing under wraps, yes? We'll talk again.'

The man in the hat and dark overcoat was standing near Westminster Bridge when Kramer found him. They walked on to Lambeth and a small Georgian house near the river. Maurice Hallan pulled the curtains before taking off his hat and dark overcoat.

'Uncle Claude said it would be easier to kill God,' Kramer said.

'I take it he wasn't talking about himself?' Hallan asked.

'No, he insisted the universe could still carry on without God.' Kramer laughed and then winced.

'You look awful, Ben,' Hallan said.

'I feel worse. I think I'm getting addicted to morphine. What about the money?'

'There,' Maurice Hallan said.

Hallan was one of those seemingly innocuous people whom great causes can drag out of their mediocrity. Physically he had council clerk or bank official written all over him: short, pot-bellied and bald, and his myopia forced him to wear very thick spectacles. Not a courageous man in the conventional sense, he did what he did from a sense of inner conviction.

An archaeologist by profession, he had become involved in helping Jewish refugees almost by accident, when a cousin had asked him to drop off a birthday present in the East End of London in 1936. A Mosleyite march was taking place at the same time. Hallan watched the fascists beat up an old man before urinating on him. The following day he rang a friend who rang a friend.

'Is he all you have, Maurice?' Kramer demanded. 'He's blind, for Pete's sake . . . blind.'

'He's perfect, Ben, perfect. Don't let his handicap put you off. Look at you. Anyway, at this notice, it's all your going to get unless you trawl back over old P6 files and use one of their bods. We have nothing in Trogs that comes near to this.'

Hallan had been recruited into SIS on the recommendation of Ben Kramer, in 1940, and had worked consistently in Research Evaluation and Planning, an area so shrouded in secrecy that its officers were known as Trogs.

'No, no P6, no firm,' Kramer said.

'Just read it, Ben.'

'How come P6 don't have him on file?' Kramer asked.

'That's it. Because he's purely Mossad. What they call a pen. He harbours submarines – Jews who've gone underground.'

The ha Mossad le Alyiah Bet was the full name of the organisation responsible for helping Jews enter Palestine illegally.

Kramer read the document and smiled.

'What would I do without you, Maurice?' he said.

The pen's name was Max Weg and his story was extraordinary even by the standards Kramer was used to.

Born in Russia in 1880 to a German father and a Jewish mother, he had become active in socialist politics while still a student. In 1905, following a bomb outrage in which three civil servants were killed, he was arrested by the Czar's secret police, the Okrana, and beaten so badly under interrogation, he almost died.

Sentenced to death, he escaped and fled to Germany, where he married a teacher.

In 1914, he volunteered for the German Army in order to smash the Czarist regime, taking a new identity in the process.

However, he never saw action on the eastern front and he was not allowed to go to Russia after the revolution.

He came out of the Great War with an Iron Cross, First Class, a Blue Max, a colonel's pension and no sight.

He spent the next year undergoing surgery in different hospitals. Meanwhile, his wife and only child were killed by Spanish flu. Weg emerged from hospital completely alone in the world.

Living on a disability allowance and a small income from a lace business his wife had started, he finally travelled to the new Soviet Union in 1921 and stayed until 1925, when it began to become apparent that the brave new world he had once fought for was not going to come about without terrible suffering and dislocation. While there, he had an affair with a writer who bore him a child. But the affair did not last as long as the pregnancy and the mother did not want to share her child with its father.

When he left the Soviet Union, he went back to Germany and ran his wife's lace business.

In 1929, just before the Wall Street Crash, he sold out his interest in the business and moved to Vienna, from where, in 1930, now fifty and cash-rich, he decided, for no real reason except curiosity, to pay a visit to Jerusalem.

Two things happened at that time which were to shape the rest of his life. He met a young Jewish activist on a kibbutz south of Jerusalem and his former Russian lover was arrested and shot in a Stalinist purge.

So, at fifty, Weg now found himself with a new wife and a five-year-old child he had never seen.

He managed to smuggle the boy out of Russia in 1931, using old revolutionary contacts, and the new family moved to Istanbul where Weg opened an antiquarian bookshop and dabbled in leather trading as a sideline.

At first, it was his wife, Rachel, who worked for the Haganah full time, buying arms and helping undocumented Jews reach Palestine. Istanbul as a choice of family home had been her suggestion. But as the thirties progressed, and the Nazis began to flex their muscles, gradually Weg became more involved.

Then early in 1936, Rachel Weg was arrested in Berlin on currency charges. She was travelling on false papers. Under what the Gestapo always referred to as sharpened interrogation, she betrayed two collaborators, who subsequently died in custody. And Rachel Weg killed herself.

The shock of his second wife's death sent Max Weg into freefall. He would have completely broken down if it hadn't been for a small hard-looking man with a receding hairline and the kind of eyes that splinter souls. The man's name was Shaul Meyerov, one of the legends of pre-independence Israel. And he was laying the foundations of the ha Mossad le Alyiah Bet.

Weg set himself up in a small antiquarian bookshop in Munich's fashionable Schwabing district, near the Hohenzollernplatz, and everyone took him for what he seemed to be, an old blind war hero who had returned to Germany to share the triumphs of National Socialism after years of travelling. The Gestapo called once, to enquire about his son, and Weg's time in Russia. The fate of the boy's mother was enough to convince them that any flirtation Weg had had with his old country's new regime was over. He even filled them in on his experiences there by dictating a fifteen-page report. And his son joined the Hitler Youth.

Nothing existed to tie Weg or his son to the young Jewish woman who had thrown herself from one of the top-floor windows of a nineteenth-century building in Prinz Albrechtstrasse, Berlin.

In spite of, in fact because of, his disability, Weg was able to move around Munich without drawing much more than sympathetic nods. He joined an old comrades' association and could be seen on Party and national days dressed in his old imperial uniform, wearing his decorations, drinking in the beerhalls around the Marianplatz and standing with dignity at the Feldherrnhalle. He was once introduced to Hitler during this period, and Hitler held both the old soldier's hands and made a sentimental remark about his own days in the trenches.

Between 1937 and September 1939, Weg organised one thread of a sophisticated network of illegal Jewish emigration from Nazi-occupied Europe. Because of his work, he could travel; because of his disability, he could travel without interference; and because of his imperial war record, his Nazi Party contacts and his son's membership of the Hitler Youth, his business trips went almost unnoticed by the blockwarts, the Gestapo informers in every building in the Greater Reich.

For a long time he had refused to spy directly against Germany, because it went against his principles and his feelings of residual loyalty towards his adopted country, but then in 1942, more tragedy struck. His son, Ivan, was conscripted and killed at Stalingrad.

Weg considered putting a gun to his head.

Instead, he put a banner in his shop: *Ausharren.* Then he joined the Nazi Party, confident that the racial check Berlin would carry out would only state that he was an ethnic German who had come from Russia to escape persecution before the Great War. The Party gave his name to the Gestapo in Munich, and they sent two agents over to ask him if he would take over as blockwart for his building since the previous incumbent had been killed in an air raid.

Then Mossad put Weg in touch with a courier from Switzerland, and Weg began to spy.

Weg's reports came through a Swiss arms salesman who made frequent visits to Germany, went via the Swiss Secret Service to the American OSS in Berne, who believed all the information was the arms salesman's work, and were then passed on to SIS's German section, P6, through their station in Zurich. Mossad got money and favours from the Swiss and the Swiss got Brownie points from the Allies.

'He doesn't even have to know the nature of the operation,' Maurice Hallan said.

'Definitely,' Kramer said. 'How soon can you contact him?'

'Tomorrow. We just get on to the Swiss. They'll have a man in Munich by lunchtime.'

'All right, tell him we have a special submarine we want docked, no questions asked. I'll fill out the details for you.'

When Max Weg examined the coded message he had received the following day, running his hands back and forth across the special Braille encryption and decoding cards developed specifically for him, he felt a certain excitement begin to creep up his spine.

The Braille cards had the added advantage of being unintelligible to anyone looking at them and he often left them lying around his apartment, and in his bookshop, among other Braille messages of a more innocuous nature.

When he had decoded the message a second time, to make sure, he stood up and made his way across the room to the window of his apartment, pulled the curtain back and opened the window. A breeze and some spots of rain touched his face while he stood there, and he could smell the cement, concrete and embers from the last air raid still hanging in the air.

The air-raid siren took time to enter his head. At first, he heard faster footsteps on the streets. Someone screamed and two doors banged shut. Then there was a hard knocking on his door and the siren had now built itself up to a crescendo.

'Herr Weg, Herr Weg . . .'

Weg made his way slowly to the door and took his time opening it.

'*Fliegeralarm*, Herr Weg . . .'

'I can hear it, I can hear it, Ilse. It's probably a false alarm, or they're going for Augsburg again.'

He reached out and touched her face with his hands. The young woman stood there and let him move his fingers down her nose and around her cheeks. It was a ritual she had once hated but now rather enjoyed, even when the sirens were going and she could hear other residents shouting and scampering down the stairs to the cellars.

'If they go for Augsburg then Munich is close enough to hit by mistake. The Americans have been known to hit the wrong country sometimes.'

'You exaggerate, you know, Ilse, you always exaggerate. But I like that. I like exaggeration. A man with no eyes needs hyperbole now and again. Let me put on my coat. If I am to sit in the cellars with my neighbours, I must have my coat. It is so undignified to be without a coat when you are afraid. And if a bomb hits us, I want to be found in my coat. Last year, I remember hearing two women talk about a man found near the Kurfurstenplatz with only his socks and undergarments on. Very undignified.'

They moved down the staircase, Weg hanging on to Ilse Gern's arm. He had never seen her but he had a picture of her in his mind's eye. She was twenty-seven, he knew that, and she had a strong body weakened now by the continual food shortages and the exhaustion of the bombing and the general fatigue of the war. Her hair was shoulder-length but she liked to tie it up. Her eyes were deep in her head and her cheekbones were sharp and pronounced. One of her ears was slightly bigger than the other and her mouth was hard on top but soft underneath, and there was a constant struggle between the two. And her hands were very soft considering the present crisis.

'The Führer won't be able to find a place for coffee and cakes so easily now,' Weg said. 'All his favourite cafes are full of holes.'

'I don't know when you are being sarcastic or sycophantic, Herr Weg.'

'You should call me Max.'

'I am a product of my upbringing, Herr Weg. Anyway, if I called you Max, I might run the risk of being seduced by you. And what would Mother say then?'

He laughed.

'I wish I was twenty years younger, Ilse.'

'So do I.' She touched his hand. 'You know, Herr Weg, I feel we will lose this war.'

He touched her hand back. 'Ssh,' he said, putting his finger to his lips and moving his head around as if he were looking out for someone. '*Ausharren*, my dear, *ausharren*. I was in the last war. And there are always times when you think it is hopeless. The Führer will see us through, believe me.'

'You sound like Mother.'

'She's a strong woman.'

'And I am not?'

'You are in turmoil still, my dear. How long is Werner dead?'

She led him through a door to a room with nothing in it and then to a small stone staircase.

'One year, five days, three hours . . . God, the smell in here. We'll have to do something about the smell.'

'Did you try for children?'

'Every time we were together. Someone's been pissing down here.'

'So let's stay out of the cellars now,' Weg said. 'I told you, I have an instinct about these things. Comes from my service in the last war. You could tell when a shell was coming your way.'

'I have real coffee,' Ilse Gern said. 'You should report me.'

'I figure the Gestapo has more important business than a young woman with too much real coffee. I'll spare the Wittelsbacher Palais the burden of a report.'

'You are an amusing man, Herr Weg. But I don't know what to make of you. You wear the party badge and you operate as a blockwart, like Mother. But you are not like Mother. Mother does not makes jokes about the Party, about the Gestapo. About anything.'

'I'm an old man. I have lived a good life.'

'And everyone you ever loved is dead?'

He paused and then nodded. 'We share that, Ilse, we share that. It's our secret, isn't it?'

'I sometimes cry at night. Do you?'

'I'm out of tears. I have my work.'

'I sleep with men, a lot of men. I try to find Werner in them, I think. Every time Mother gets a new guest in the pension, I see if he's like Werner and if he is I sleep with him. I do it to forget, too. That's a contradiction, isn't it? I'm confused, Herr Weg. I made love to a soldier last night, in the ruins of a building downtown. To give him pleasure before he dies, I think. But I didn't even know his name.'

Weg put his hand to her face and felt tears. He wiped the tears.

'Where's that coffee?' he said.

They were sitting in her apartment, drinking coffee, when the all clear was sounded a few minutes later.

'See! I was right,' Weg said. 'I was right. They didn't come.'

Ilse Gern laughed but it did not last. Several anti-aircraft guns began to fire.

'Oh, my God!' Ilse Gern said.

'It's okay, it's okay,' Weg said. 'That's stress firing. It'll pass. It

32

always happens, you know that. They're ready and nothing comes but they have to fire anyway.'

He was right; it ended after about five minutes. They sat in silence, drinking Ilse Gern's coffee, listening to the other residents returning to their apartments and discussing the war and the state of the cellars.

'You'll have to do something about the cellars,' Ilse said. 'You're the blockwart here.'

'I'm a blind man, for heaven's sake. What can I do?'

'Now you are being sarcastic.'

He raised his arms. 'Guilty.'

'So the war is not lost?'

'Of course not. And now I have to get back to work. If you want to come up and read some of the new books I have, you are welcome to do so. I'll be at my shop for the rest of the day but I'll be back before the British replace the Americans.'

'Don't joke about that.'

'By the way,' Weg said then, 'speaking of your mother and the pension, I have a colleague coming to Munich around Easter. Could you pencil in a booking? I know you're very busy . . .'

'Anything for you, Herr Weg. You know Mother loves you.'

'You have a cruel streak, Ilse.'

'The Totenvögel was around this morning. Three death telegrams. I heard the screams.'

That night, 30 March, the RAF did come to Germany but not to Munich. They were mauled over Nuremberg.

The following night four German Junkers 88s crossed the English coast and bombed a suburb of London. In a small red-bricked house to the east they heard the sound of the explosions but took little notice. The woman who had gone into the kitchen put her head around the door and leaned into the small breakfast room without looking any of the men there in the eye.

'Anyone kosher here?' she asked. 'Or anything like that? It's sabbath.'

She was small and round at the hips and wearing a coloured apron and wool stockings, and her hair was tied at the back. Her face was young behind and old up front and there was a small amount of powder make-up on the cheeks. The men in the breakfast room looked at each other and then at Ben Kramer. Kramer shook his head.

'No, Irene,' he said.

'In that case I'll do the Spam tie-ups, all right?'

Kramer nodded his head. He could smell the pan heating in the kitchen and the reminders of other meals of potato and carrot and the almost mythical smell bacon and eggs had taken on, which seemed to hang for ever in a kitchen that had fried them. Kramer looked around the room again, at the monotone wallpaper, at the walnut wireless in the corner, the small sub-standard coal fire, empty now, and the metal three-bar electric heater. In one corner there was a small table with a vase of flowers, and various *Woman's Fair* magazines and *Daily Mirror*s lay under it.

'I need a German weapon,' Erich Haas said when Irene Levy had left, 'something no one will immediately notice, something small enough to carry inside a coat, something big enough to make a kill from point blank to two hundred metres. And I need it sighted and silenced.'

'Some kind of stripped-down carbine, Jack?' Kramer said.

The small man beside him, wearing a tank top, braces and thin steel-framed glasses, and picking pieces of bread from a loaf, shook his head.

'No, we're looking at a pistol with an extended barrel,' he said. 'All detachable. Slip the parts into small pockets in a coat.' He began sketching on a sheet of paper with a pencil.

'Mauser?' Haas said. '1932 Mauser, 7.63mm round, selective fire, long barrel, fast exit speed. Police and SS use them all the time.'

Jack Levy shook his head again.

'Forget the speed. Your silencer will kill that. Anyway, you can use a soft nose or a hollow round and over a short distance that'll make the required impact. I was thinking of the Navy Luger. The PO8. Got an eight-inch – twenty-centimeter – barrel, takes nine-millimetre parabellum. I think that's our standard. We can work from that. It's got a wooden stock holster, but we can get rid of that ... even a thirty-two-round magazine, if you want. But you won't need that either ...'

'The police and SS don't carry weapons like that. Mausers, 1932s, 1910s or HSc; Walthers; or Sauers. And the Navy Luger's damn temperamental.'

Jack Levy nodded and stood up and walked over to his fireplace as if he was trying to get the benefit of any heat that might have been left over. They lit a fire early and lived on the residuals after they had used their coal ration.

Levy had been an armourer with the British Army until a Stuka hit the ship he was on in Dunkirk harbour in 1940. Invalided out, he ran a small garage on the Isle of Dogs. In his spare time he moonlighted for the Haganah, buying weapons on the London black market.

'No,' Levy said, 'it's a Navy Luger for a job like this. But we can hide it. I know it's vulnerable to dirt and ice, but we only anticipate one or two actions.'

Haas looked at Kramer. Kramer nodded.

'Jack's the expert here,' he said.

'The money's gone through?' Haas said.

Kramer barely moved his eyes to indicate yes.

'And you'll have a sleeve-gun, too,' Levy said then. 'Silenced tube. Single shot. Very effective over short distances. Quite a little shocker for the uninitiated.'

'You can rifle the barrel?' Haas asked. 'On the Navy Luger? And add some length? At least fifteen centimetres more. Perhaps thirty. And the silencer.'

He demonstrated with his fingers.

'Don't want to unbalance the weapon,' Levy said. 'I'll give you ten inches – about twenty-five centimetres – including the silencer; and we'll add the rifling. How about that?'

'Ammunition?' Haas said.

'The parabellum load should do. Like I said, soft rounds of any kind at a slow muzzle velocity can cause a lot of damage. What do you anticipate as difficulties?'

'Post-strike, I may need to shoot my way out,' Haas said.

'Short or long range?'

'Either.'

'Again, the soft rounds will cause maximum confusion. And the combination of weapons should suffice. Too close a range and you're depending on speed and surprise – soft rounds mean a target stays down. But I'll give you some armour-piercing, just in case. Flexibility is the key here. When do you want all this hardware, Ben?'

'Monday.'

Levy raised his eyebrows.

'I said Monday, Jack. If you can't do it I'll try someone else.'

'Who else, Ben, who else?'

'Maurice Hallan'll be in touch.'

* * *

Maurice Hallan did not laugh or smile at the joke he had just heard. There was a perpetual feeling of being about to lose control somewhere between his stomach and his small intestine. So when he picked up his pint of beer and looked into it, he did not want to drink it.

'I think they water this down,' the man beside him said when his joke had died.

'Just drink it, Larry. Don't look at it and don't think about it.'

The pub was a small low-ceiling, wooden-beamed job with cracks in the walls and tankards hanging from the bar. Hallan found himself watching the silhouettes through the cracked frosted glass in front of him.

'Will you do it, Larry?' Hallan said then.

Larry Amster had been an up-and-coming New York attorney when the Japanese bombed Pearl Harbor. He had expected his asthma and had eyesight to keep him out of the military but the OSS wasn't governed by the normal rules of recruitment and he had a qualification its can-do Chief, Bill Donovan, prized: he was a smart lawyer.

Amster began his intelligence career buying clothes from European refugees in New York, increased his standing rooting out German spy rings in South America, made his name by recruiting his own networks in North Africa, and was eventually posted to London special operations as a reward.

It was no small irony that the OSS operation in London was one of the slowest to find its feet. Being at the centre of things had its disadvantages, not the least of which was the distrust of the American military establishment and the tortuous jealousy of the British Secret Intelligence Service. It had been two years of hard struggle, and only now was OSS starting to move its own agents into occupied Europe. Which was part of the reason for Amster's reluctance in the Piccadilly pub.

'One aircraft, Larry,' Maurice Hallan said after some time without a reply from Amster. 'One pilot.'

Amster's hair was curly and fair and his skin was a kind of unhealthy olive. And he was pimpled and wore steel glasses with thick lenses.

'Why not the Moon Squadron? Why the Black Flight?' he asked.

Of the two clandestine air services used by Allied intelligence and sabotage agencies during the Second World War, the RAF's Moon Squadron, No. 138, flying Lysanders, Halifaxes and Whitleys, was the better known. The OSS's Black Flight was far less publicised, mainly because it went on to be the basis of the CIA's private airline, Air America, in later decades.

The Black Flight got its name from the colour it painted its first three B-24 Liberators, used to ferry OSS agents from North Africa to southern Europe.

In 1943, the Black Flight, now swollen to squadron numbers, shifted its focus to England and began to acquire the appropriate hardware, and the colour schemes began to reflect the various air forces it sought to misrepresent and the cavalier spirit of the OSS. Junkers 52s, Junkers 88s, a Focke-Wolfe Condor bought from an enterprising Galway farmer, three Italian Macchi bombers, complete with one of the crews – even some stolen British and Russian aircraft – all were enlisted into what became known as Donovan's Flying Circus.

'Don't look at me like that, Maurice. I know the way you're looking. Like my mother.'

'You can't see me properly. It's too dark and you've got bat sight.'

'Yeah . . . but I can tell, I can tell. Look, I've always done what's been asked of me but this . . .'

'It's the most important thing I'll ever ask you for.'

'Where the hell's Ben, then?'

'He's got other work. Look, Larry, are you with us or are you just salving your conscience?'

'Hey, come on, you can say that to me?'

Like Hallan, Amster led a double life, though if the OSS had taken the trouble it might have found out that, as a child, he'd spent every summer for ten years shuttling between an exclusive Jewish summer camp in the Catskills and an arid kibbutz in the Galilee.

'How many times have I done stuff without question?' Amster said to Hallan then.

'You counting?' Hallan asked.

Amster cursed quietly to himself.

'One of those blue passes you OSS boys carry with you, Larry, the ones signed by Ike, that'll be enough. Say it's for your end of Sussex.'

'I'm an American, Maurice. I mean, nothing I do for Shai has ever compromised that. I've always been on the level with Grosvenor Street.'

'And you still are. We just need this one favour.'

'So what the hell do you want it for?'

'I'm not going to argue with you, Larry.'

'David Bruce'll have my ass. I mean, this isn't just passing information or helping people get out of Europe, this is theft. I could get disbarred.'

'Yeah, well, you can go to Palestine, practise there. Frankly, I can't abide the bloody place.' Hallan reached into his pocket and pulled out an envelope. 'Details,' he said.

'Jesus. Why do I get the feeling I'm signing a blank cheque for a stranger?' Amster started to wheeze a little then. 'Goddamn weather here, it's always cold and damp. Screws up my chest.'

'Get me the plane, Larry.'

3

THE FOLLOWING MONDAY, the first that April, there was a high smell of oysters rising from the restaurant and bar below Claude Dansey's St James's Street flat. And with the smell came all the salt water and sea breeze images it conjured up in the mind of a rationed stomach. Dansey had tea and toast and a coal fire to beat it back.

Teddy Giles wore a residual hangover with his tweed suit and gentleman's club tie that morning, as he poured the tea before it had drawn and fingered the buttered toast on to the plates.

'It seems a rather large amount of money has turned up in an Abwehr bank account in Lisbon, sir,' he said. 'American dollars. One of those foreign currency things.'

'You're ruining my toast, Teddy,' Dansey said.

Giles looked over at the man sitting on Dansey's right. 'I think Kim should take it from here, sir. It's his find really. I'm just the facilitator.'

Harold 'Kim' Philby, then head of the Iberian sub-section of SIS's counter-intelligence department, Section 5, leaned forward in his chair with a hand in one of his jacket pockets, and composed himself to avoid stammering.

'The money came from the Jewish Star Committee, sir,' he said. 'They're an American relief agency.'

Dansey sipped his tea. Philby wore an aftershave that smelled as if it was designed to cover the alcohol on his breath. 'How much?' Dansey asked.

'Half a million,' Giles said.

For the first time, Dansey's face showed surprise. 'An attempt to buy Jews again?' he asked.

'That's what we thought – at first – and that's what Vee Vee thought, too,' Philby said. 'He told me to watch for developments.'

'What a surprise!' Dansey said.

Vee Vee – Colonel Valentine Vivian – who ran SIS counter-intelligence, had once been Dansey's superior and now was his favourite figure of fun. Monocled and crinkle-haired, he was worse than useless in Dansey's estimation.

'Well, they're fairly desperate right now, the Jews,' Giles said. 'What with Hungary and all that.'

'We can't have them dealing with the enemy,' Dansey said.

'I don't think they are,' Philby said. 'Well, not in that way. The bank account belongs to an Abwehr Tod agent. The Tod programme carries out what the Russians call wet operations. They're . . .'

'Ghosts,' Dansey said.

'Perhaps a melodramatic assessment, but they are talked of in whispers by men in the field.'

'Are you lecturing me, Kim?' Dansey asked. 'I know what the Tod programme is. It's a cadre of assassins and infiltration specialists, who've infiltrated everything from Eben Emael in 1940 to the Kremlin in 1941, and killed generals, fighter pilots and even a Greek colonel's horse. I know what they are.'

'The bank account was opened by this man.' Giles showed Dansey a blurred photograph. 'Captain Kurt Richter.'

'Remind me,' Dansey said.

'One-time submariner, used to work as an agent controller in Hamburg, then moved to Tirpitz Ufer to work directly under Canaris. Ran the Tod programme from its inception.'

'Ran?'

'Richter's dead,' Philby said. 'Committed suicide a few weeks back, after those two Abwehr people in Turkey defected to us. The Vehmerens. It appears Richter wanted Hitler gone. Very popular sentiment in the Abwehr these days. A new man named Hofer runs Tod now. Or what's left of it. Attrition has taken its toll.'

'You're absolutely sure it's the account of a Tod agent?' Dansey asked.

'Absolutely,' Giles said. 'Years of observation and bribery, right, Kim? And a couple of well-equipped defectors.'

Philby pulled out a sheet of paper. 'Look,' he said. 'As you know, once recruited and trained, Tod agents have their entire life history erased, so there's no trace of them. That's why they like orphans.

All they have is a code and a file of their missions. Now, look at the number on this account: eighteen, then the letter T, then four digits . . . Eighteen is the Abwehr code for Portugal, and the four digits after the letter are the agent's personal code.'

'And the letter is his standing,' Dansey said. 'A, a producing agent; F, a courier or scout; R, a travelling agent; H, a sub-agent . . . and T is a Tod agent.' He stood up and breathed deeply. 'So this money, this Jewish money, this half-million American dollars, has been placed in what can be described as the personal bank account of an Abwehr assassin?'

'It would appear so,' Giles said.

'I don't suppose you can tell me who he is?'

'No,' Philby said. 'The code's the only trace with Tod agents. They have no other permanent identity. But we are searching.'

'Well, search hard – both of you. Philby, everyone you can spare and more. My authority. I want to know who he is and I want to know where he is. I feel a strange sensation running down my spine.'

'And what do I tell Vee Vee?' Philby said. 'I feel a certain disloyalty, sir. Going over his head.'

'You let me be the judge of that,' Dansey said. 'You'll find in this game that loyalty is often a matter of perspective. Perhaps you can prove to me you're not just another one of Vee Vee's moronic Indians or Oxbridge homos, Kim. And Teddy, get hold of Ben Kramer.'

An hour later, Dansey was in his office in Broadway Buildings when Teddy Giles knocked.

'Ben Kramer's not around, sir. No one seems to know where he is.'

Dansey closed his eyes. 'Bugger! I feel indigestion coming on. All right, Teddy, keep looking for him. He can't have vanished.'

Several hundred miles away, off the north-west coast of Scotland, a rain storm had passed and the grey lid on the day was opening from the west.

The small island of Beg, in the Outer Hebrides, is surrounded by squat pine trees which have all bent in the direction of the prevailing westerlies, giving the place a look that suggests the top of the head of a giant floating under the water. There is a glacial ravine inland which looks like someone has cleaved the giant's head open, and because of that and the nature of the

41

island some people call it, ironically, given its size, the Bloody Giant.

The surface of the island is rock and bog, good for sheep, bad for growing. The rock is grey and the bogs are black and the island runs with water. Down through the ages people have tried to live there, but usually in vain.

During the Second World War there were two stone cottages on the island surrounded by pines that just about reached the roofs. The trees and cottages were protected by the ravine.

The whole island had once been used as a Special Operations Executive Group A training school, but it had been closed in 1943 for administrative reasons. However, the cottages were still stocked with the arcane implements of SOE's specialist education courses.

A colony of puffins still nests on the west side of the island, where the cliffs fall away about two hundred feet and, overhead, gulls still circle, waiting to pick off stragglers and anything else they might catch.

In 1944, there were richer pickings for the gulls than just the odd puffin. On a clear day you could often see small dots on the horizon, convoys coming in from America, and then the gulls left the puffins alone.

That morning, Erich Haas stood over the body of a basking shark and looked out to sea. Every so often a gull brave enough would land at the shoreline and walk up the pebbles to the rotting shark carcass and begin to tear at the flesh with its beak. Haas watched the next one and let the wind come round and through him. The bird hopped and skipped and jumped towards the dead shark, and the sharp salted air stung Haas's senses into life. Then he whipped the Navy Luger from under his shoulder and fired.

Ben Kramer picked up the dead bird and examined the hole in its head. Then he threw it to one side with the others and breathed in the sea air. Haas had the Navy Luger barrel leaning on his left forearm. He was aiming at the horizon.

'How's it working?' Kramer asked. He pointed at the Navy Luger.

'It's heavier than I remember,' Haas said, 'but I'm starting to hit targets at the right ranges. Another few days to get back into form. I'm just out of practice. Tell me, Herr Major, do you really expect that I will kill the Führer for you?'

Kramer ignored the provocation.

'I think you want to see things that are not there, Herr Major,'

Haas said then. 'I believe you saw service in France. But something happened . . .'

'Come on, let's go back. I want to go over things with you.'

He turned and started walking up to the cliff. Three puffins took off from his right and two gulls above them circled and then came down on the puffins. Four shots rang out. Kramer turned to see the two gulls falling from the sky. Haas smiled and turned the Luger towards Kramer.

Then he swung back and took aim, using his left forearm, and killed the two puffins. More gulls fell on the carcasses of the dead birds, and when the two men were over the crest of the cliff the gulls returned to the dead shark.

'Jack has a .303 levelled at you,' Kramer said.

He nodded at Jack Levy, who sat on top of the cliff with a rifle pointed towards the beach. There were three more guards, but they kept their distance.

'I think I'm starting to understand him,' Haas shouted.

'Who?' Kramer asked.

'The Führer.'

Kramer and Haas did not talk while they ate. When they had finished, Kramer broke some American chocolate and handed Haas a piece.

'You're right, he is a creature of amazing habit,' Haas said. 'Hitler. And very lazy most of the time. If only German taxpayers knew.'

'But only at home,' Kramer said. 'Look, I can't impress on you enough how much this is a man with a sense of assassination, like a hunted animal. Outside his lair, things are rarely scheduled; and if they are, he changes the schedule, or maybe cancels it. He has forty-millimetre armour plating on his Mercedes windows and 18-millimetre plating around the body of the car . . .'

'But he likes to sit propped up and his cars tend to have open or soft tops for viewing and the like . . .'

'. . . and he wears a bullet-proof vest and cap.'

'But only in public.' Haas smiled. 'He takes the cap and the vest off in his lair.'

'You're learning. But he always carries a small pistol.'

'Believe me, Herr Major, I am studying the Führer intensely. He's at his most predictable in his hole. The further out, the less you can rely on his movements. But the hole's where he's best protected. So you gain an advantage and lose an advantage.'

'So let's look at the hole.'

Haas stood up and walked over to the model of the area around Hitler's Berghof.

'The Führer area,' he said. 'Fences electric?'

'No, he likes animals. Neither the outer or inner fence is electric.'

'All right. The Hoheitsgebeit ... the inner area ... the State Security Service guards, the RSD, at these watchposts ... all ex-Kriminalpolizei detectives?'

'Yes. Most people mix them up with the Liebstandarte SS regiment he has around him, but the RSD is his real bodyguard.'

'And only forty?' Haas touched the model of the small Hotel Turken next to the Berghof, where the RSD were based.

'Close protection. Like the American Secret Service. Brains and brawn. And there's another group down in Berchtesgaden. The Liebstandarte SS do the mobile patrols and ceremonial stuff, but the RSD call the shots. And that means this man, Brigadeführer Johann Rattenhuber. Know him?'

Haas shook his head. 'I've heard of him.'

'Fat bastard. Bavarian. They all are. He's been a policeman of one sort or another most of his career. Kept Hitler alive all these years.'

'And the Liebstandarte in the barracks here, behind the Berghof, they're always only at company strength?'

'Most of the regiment's fighting at the front. Guarding Hitler is a treat.'

'And who stays at the Platterhof Hotel?' Haas touched a model of a big building behind the Berghof.

'Nazi dignitaries, that kind of thing,' Kramer said.

'These two watchposts, the one on the road just behind the SS barracks, the other where the ring road around the Hoheitsgebeit swings down to the Salzbergstrasse, are not in direct eye contact. The Platterhof gets in the way and the road dips here.'

'The closer you get the more dangerous it is.'

'Possibilities, Herr Major, possibilities. I was trained to examine all possibilities. I could tell you a story from training about an empty room and a piece of string, but I won't bore you. There are always two guards at the top of the stairs in the Berghof?'

Kramer nodded and studied Haas's face but could tell nothing from it.

'But no more?' Haas asked then. He stepped back from the model. 'Does he always go to bed so late?'

'He doesn't sleep very much.'

'I don't blame him. And the woman, Braun, his mistress, she sleeps with him?'

'Her room's next door.'

'Very bourgeois.' Haas grinned. He touched the model of a mountain behind the Berghof. It had a small building on top. 'Kehlsteinhaus?' he asked.

'It's a teahouse,' Kramer said. 'One thousand metres above the Obersalzberg and thick with snow right now. Inaccessible to all but the most determined. Anyway, Hitler doesn't like it. It has a private road and a four-hundred-metre elevator and it cost millions and he doesn't like it.'

'That's the Führer for you. Is there anything they don't have on this Obersalzberg? I mean hotels, a barracks, a model farm, a piggery, a stud, a school, a cinema . . .'

'It's meant to be a fortress.'

'That's encouraging. I think I feel sorry for myself. You don't look good. Leg hurting?'

'Don't try and make friends, Erich,' Kramer said. 'You're not here to be friends.'

'I always wondered what it would be like to serve a cause. But I have never been so committed.'

'You have that luxury, Erich. Though I suspect you hide things beneath your sarcasm.'

'Only a fundamental dislike of my fellow human beings – present company excepted. But then there are compensations. Money, of which I have never had enough, and women, of which no man can ever have enough. That was the worst thing about facing execution, the thought that I would never again have the chance to seduce a woman.'

'If you're trying to impress me, forget it. If you're trying to make me jealous, I'm way beyond that.'

'These two roads are the only ways off the mountain?' Haas asked. He ran his finger along Salzbergerstrasse, which snaked down the mountain to Berchtesgaden and then touched the village of Oberau, north-east of the Berghof.

'The Oberau road is pretty new,' Kramer said. 'Allows him to drive to Salzburg without using the main road.'

45

'To go to Schloss Klessheim?' Hass asked.

'Owned by the Foreign Ministry. Used for conferences. Horthy signed Hungary over to him there.'

'And what about these tunnels running under the Obersalzberg complex? What's in them?'

'Don't know,' Kramer said. 'News is scarce there. Comes from workers in that camp to the left of the complex. The plans are as accurate as we know. But there are possibilities there. I've marked them for you.'

'Objectively, I would say only a desperate or a crazy man would undertake such an operation. But then I am a bit of both, I suppose. And there are possibilities, as you say. Intriguing and challenging. My ego needs such work. One has to balance so much, don't you think?'

'The closer you get the better your chance of success.'

'The further away, the better my chance of escape.' Haas smiled. 'You know it won't save your Hungarian Jews, Herr Major, no matter what I do. Which begs the question . . .'

'And the answer?' Kramer said.

'Damned if I know, Herr Major.'

Kramer smiled.

'Can you get me an orange?' Haas asked then.

Kramer shook his head. 'In wartime, a million dollars is easier.'

'I'd like an orange. So how are you going to get me there?'

'It's being arranged.'

Holy Thursday was tipping over into Good Friday when Captain Jake Coll sat in the cockpit of a Westland Lysander in a field in northern France. He was drumming his fingers against the instrument panel, repeating the words 'come on' over and over again to himself.

Around him, the sound of the Bristol Mercury 30 nine-cylinder radial engine seemed to echo his anxiety. The agent was late.

Coll looked at his watch: he should go, and now. In the time it takes for a nerve impulse to move, he went through all the reasons why he should go.

The Lysander was the workhorse of Allied special operations during the Second World War. It could, they said, land and take off in a back garden, which was not far off the truth. Coll looked at his watch again.

The bullet hit the windscreen at about the same time Coll saw the

OSS agent; two more bullets hit the Lysander before the agent made another few yards across the field. Then there were more flashes around the field and more rounds than Coll could count hit his machine.

He pulled out the Sten gun lying on the floor of the cockpit, cocked it and fired in the general direction of the incoming rounds and watched the agent stagger, fall and get up. Coll revved the engine and the Lysander's wheels, which had begun to embed themselves in the wet clay, struggled forward.

'Come on!'

Suddenly a searchlight caught him full in the face and a heavy machine-gun opened up. Coll fired his Sten at the light without being able to look at it and while trying to taxi his Lysander into a take-off position.

'Come on!'

The agent was scrambling across the field, firing from a kneeling position with a Browning automatic. Coll could see the silhouettes of other figures moving in the trees at the edge of the field. Another three rounds hit the fuselage of his Lysander, and Jake Coll smelled fuel.

He swore, changed magazines and fired a burst over the head of the OSS agent who was now rolling and scrambling across the field on all fours. And there were German soldiers in the field, too, shouting and kneeling down to fire.

The agent fired off a series of shots. Coll pushed the left rudder pedal and brought the Lysander right up to the agent.

It was a woman, wearing a boiler suit; she was perhaps thirty, maybe younger, and she had short hair. She grabbed for the ladder on the left side of the Lysander, swung round and emptied the rest of her Browning magazine at her pursuers. Coll fired too and the Lysander was hit again, this time with heavier-calibre rounds. It was a strong machine but Coll wondered how much more of this it could take.

'Go, go!'

The woman was not yet inside, and was having great difficulty hauling herself up the ladder, but Coll knew it was now or never. He opened the throttle.

They lumbered over the grass and Coll kept firing with his right hand while flying with his left and looking over his shoulder, watching the Joe, desperately trying to pull herself into the aircraft. Incoming tracer rounds shot by like a display of the Northern Lights and Coll felt the impact of so many rounds he had ceased to count any more, but the Lysander was at take-off speed and he pulled back on the stick and she lumbered into the air.

When Coll looked around again, the woman was slumped in the cockpit, bleeding.

She tapped him on the shoulder.

'Home, James!' she said.

'Just pray there's no night fighters out there. And we're leakin' gas.'

'A charmer. Listen, you spoken for, fly boy?'

She coughed and blood came from her mouth.

'Hang on, hang on a little longer,' Coll said.

'I'm hanging on. How about dinner and some rough loving afterwards?'

'A movie.'

'Yeah, a movie. What's showing? I've been away. Damn, there were a lot of them.'

Coll turned around to her and threw her a flask.

'Whisky,' he said. 'I have a good supplier.'

'I'm bleeding.'

The moon's silver light swept over the aircraft and Coll saw more blood.

'Pretty bad, eh?' the woman said. 'Hey, I know it's against the rules, but what's your name?'

He gave her a name, not his own.

She gave him a name, not her own.

'I like honesty,' she said. 'This kind of work makes you dishonest. You like to get honesty once in a while.'

'So what's a nice girl like you doing in a place like this?'

'Usual story. Boy meets girl, girl falls head over heels with boy, boy turns out to be violent, girl joins convent, boy runs off with girl's mother, mother dies trying to get to the North Pole on foot, girl leaves convent for boy . . . boy gets violent again, girl joins secret service, boy gets killed doing something stupid, girl volunteers for this.'

'Boring.'

'Listen, I'm getting cold. Can you make this thing go a little faster?'

'I gotta move around – night fighters.'

'Screw the night fighters. Get me back in one piece and my body's yours. I hope you don't mind metal.'

'Love it.'

'Kinda weird, aren't you?'

'Just hang on.'

The fuel gauge was struggling to hold the needle in place and Coll could feel the aircraft beginning to slow. The Lysander had quite a wing area, which gave it a lot more lift than the average aircraft, something that contributed to its short take-off and landing capability.

'Don't crash this thing,' she said after a silence. 'I don't want to be killed on my own turf.'

'Hang on, sister, we're about to test the laws of physics to the utmost, but don't worry. I think we crossed the Norfolk coast about three minutes ago. Can't be certain, though, my compass is screwed up.'

'You mean we could be anywhere?'

'I steered by the stars. How about a date in London?'

'Yeah, fine.'

'Listen, we're going to have to put it down before the field. Now there's only one real problem here. The moon's obscured by clouds and I have no altimeter, so we're likely to hit the ground with a thump.'

'Oh, God . . .'

'Here goes.'

Suddenly, the ground was there. He jerked back on the stick, kicked the right rudder to compensate for the wind and strained his eyes to get any kind of a feeling for his height. The aircraft bounced along the ground before coming to a halt at the end of the field.

Coll pulled his flying helmet off and turned to the woman. She was smiling.

'Made it,' he said.

She did not answer.

When Coll reached the small Norfolk airfield that served as a base for the Black Flight, the duty NCO at the small operations hut was stirring a cup of coffee. Master Sergeant Mario Capparelli did not have to be there; his shift had ended an hour earlier.

'Welcome back, sir,' he said. 'I prepared this for you. If you don't mind me saying so, and with all due respect, you look like shit, sir.'

'I feel worse, Mario.'

'Yeah, I heard, sir. Not your fault.'

'Doesn't make it any easier. I mighta got laid.'

'Colonel told me to tell you to get some shuteye; you can fill in your report later. Colonel went up to the house.'

The house was the eighteenth-century Norfolk farmhouse the Black Flight used as a billet and operations headquarters. Only pilots and personnel on duty came to the field, so as not to attract attention. Across the small field, with its single concrete runway, Coll could see the outlines of two Junkers 52s in the hangar. There was enough distance between the station and the local population to prevent prying eyes and enough trees around the perimeter to prevent curiosity tempting eyes to consider prying.

'Oh, I almost forgot,' Capparelli said. 'There's an OSS heavy inside; been here all night, wants to talk to you.'

'I almost had it, Mario, almost . . .'

Jake Coll was still only twenty-nine years old but looked thirty-nine and felt forty-nine. He smoked continuously and drank too much and had constant pains in his stomach as a result. Born in Boston to an Irish father and a Polish mother, he had barnstormed and fought the Russians for the Finns and the Germans for the French before becoming an ace in the Battle of Britain.

He would have led one of the RAF's American Eagle squadrons if he hadn't hit a superior officer when his nerves were the worse for too many flying hours and too much Jack Daniel's.

Pearl Harbor rescued him from an RAF training school in Canada and sent him back to England as a liaison officer with the US Eighth Air Force.

Shot down on a bombing raid over Germany, after many months he made his way back to England complete with an ulcer and a German-Jewish wife. The British promptly interned her as an enemy alien and charged him with consorting with the enemy.

He was awaiting trial when the Black Flight intervened to save the Americans their embarrassment and the British a court martial. And, on mortgaged time, Jake Coll began flying OSS agents into Europe.

Larry Amster was still rubbing his eyes and wondering which parts of his body were not frozen solid when Jake Coll came in.

'Long time no see, Jake.'

'Son of a bitch, Larry . . . where'd you spring from?'

50

'I come hot-foot from Grosvenor Street. I heard about the mission. I'm sorry.'

'Yeah, well . . . it wasn't me. Sounds heelish, I know, but that's the way you get thinkin' these days. Reach into that press and get me the bottle there, will you. I want something for this coffee. So what's OSS head office want with me? I thought you only went to meetings in hotels with six-inch carpets.'

There was a pause. Amster poured the drinks and Coll poured some more for himself.

'How's your wife?' Amster asked then.

Coll shrugged. 'Same. Goddamn Limeys. I'm beginnin' to wonder if she exists any more. I haven't seen her in two months. The Isle of Man, Larry, it's the furthest damn place they could send her. If she wasn't stuck here, I'd go home tomorrow. Let 'em clap me in irons and ship me out.'

'No joy with the brass?'

'Come on, Larry. Our guys want nothin' to do with it and the Limeys have their ways. I go high and I say, this girl's been through hell, she's no Nazi, and they say, the way the Limeys always do, "Yes, Captain Coll, but we must be sure before we process her that she is who she says she is, that she's no danger to the defence of the realm." And all that other bullshit. I reckon she'll be there till after the invasion. That's what I reckon. I'm definitely beginnin' to forget who she is.'

'Too bad, Jake, too bad. What if I could speed things up?'

'Hey, come on, Larry, don't kid me. I just about begged everyone from Roosevelt down for help on this one, but no one wants to offend the Limeys.'

'I have friends who have friends . . .'

Coll stiffened.

'Wait a minute, Larry, why do I get the feelin' I'm bein' sounded out?'

'Because you are. You've flown a JU86R?'

Perhaps the most extraordinary aircraft in the Black Flight's line-up was one of the most specialised aircraft of the Second World War, the Junkers JU86 high-altitude photo reconnaissance aircraft. Flown exclusively by a special unit of the Luftwaffe High Command and capable of altitudes of 45,000 feet and above, the JU86R had a pressurised cockpit and special supercharged diesel engines to enable it to reach the high altitudes. Normally a two-man crew would be in and out and have photographed a target before the defending fighters ever got a chance to see them, let alone try and attack.

The Black Flight had acquired its model after one of the few successful attacks on such aircraft by Allied fighters. The engagement took place at nearly 50,000 feet and the successful pilot had to be treated for frostbite. He lost a hand.

'What do you want photographed?' Coll said.

'I want someone dropped, actually,' Amster said. 'From forty thousand feet.'

'You're kiddin'?' Coll said.

'No. The aircraft's been altered for drops?'

'Sure, but no one's been fool enough to volunteer yet.'

'It is possible, though?' Amster turned a pencil around in his fingers. 'It is possible?'

'Sure, it's possible,' Coll said, running his hand through his red hair, and opening a packet of cigarettes at the same time. He shook his head, lit and drew on his cigarette. 'But I'd hate to be the son of a bitch who has to do it.'

'You'll just fly the mission, Jake, just fly the mission.'

'So, where do you want me to go?' Coll asked then.

'Munich.'

'Far away. Depressurise. Repressurise.' Coll shook his head. 'If that doesn't work I'll have to come low or freeze and if I have to drop down, the Kammhuber Line spiders will eat me up like a blue-ass fly.'

'That's the risk you take,' Amster said. 'You'll only be depressurised for a matter of minutes. And you're flying one of their planes.'

'You have it all figured,' Coll said. 'And for this I get my wife?'

'That's the deal.'

'So what's so special you have to offer me my wife's freedom?'

'The mission will be pencilled in for southern France,' Amster said.

Coll rubbed his upper lip and stared at the other man.

'You're a cool one. What is this?'

'Your wife'll be out in two weeks, Jake. Stateside in three if you want. And with you. There's a posting.'

'Christ, you mean it.'

'You'll go through normal mission procedure, then drop our passenger where we want.'

'We . . .? Who is we?'

Coll reached down and very slowly drew his automatic. He raised it even more slowly.

'I said who is we, Larry? You come here with some half-assed bribery or blackmail, dependin' on how you look at it, and tell me you want someone dropped into Germany but the mission's to be pencilled for France. What's goin' on?'

Amster kept his cool, something he was amazed at.

'A friend, Captain Coll, is asking you to fly a classified mission to help other friends. Now you can accept it or blow my brains out or whatever, but this conversation never happened.'

He stood up and walked to the door. The two men looked at each other. 'It's important,' Amster said then. 'Very important.'

Coll lowered his pistol and shook his head.

'And the time difference?' he asked then. 'There'll be a time difference.'

Amster turned, trying to stop his body shaking. 'Not much. An hour here, an hour there . . . engine trouble, night fighters, high winds, whatever.'

'So who is it? Who's worth all this?' Coll asked. 'You're not a fuckin' Nazi, Larry?'

Amster started to smile and then shook his head, and he had try hard to hold himself together. 'I'm a fucking Jew, Jake, I'm a fucking Jew. Look, you were lucky last night. You might not be so lucky in the future. Take what I'm offering. Your wife's a Jew, isn't she?'

Coll stared hard at him and listened to his breathing worsen.

'Is that what this is?' he said.

'I can't say anything. But you know what's happening to Jews over there.'

'Shit . . . isn't there anyone else?' Coll said.

'You're the only one with enough operational night experience, Jake. And the only one I can lean on. I'm sorry.'

Coll began to laugh. 'At least you're honest. I'm part Jewish myself, you know,' he said. 'My mom was Polish.'

'Welcome aboard, Jake. And this is classified, so not even in your sleep.'

'I never sleep now.'

'I know the feelin'. Let's drink this, enjoy what we can while we can.'

* * *

Gruppenführer Arthur Nebe could not remember the last time he had enjoyed himself. The head of the Kriminalpolizei, Department 5 of the Reich Security Main Office, sat down in the place prepared for him in Heinrich Himmler's office at Prinz Albrechtstrasse 8, in Berlin, intoxicated with that cocktail of hope and fear which seemed to be the staple of the senior ranks in the Third Reich.

A professional policeman, Nebe was a small man with a disproportionately large head and an agonised face. His eyes were duplicitous, his lips verging on the seedy, and the expansive nose almost seemed ready to tip the whole thing over on the bottled shoulders where it rested. Without the SS general's uniform, he might have been mistaken for a low-grade informer instead of the head of a department of the Reich Security Main Office. Not unlike his boss.

Himmler was scribbing notes, and sipping on warm milk. 'How long did the meeting last?' he said without looking up.

'An hour, Herr Reichsführer.'

'Where?'

'A lakeside house. Wannsee. Near the Interpol building.'

'Cheek,' Himmler said. 'Present?'

Nebe pulled a sheet of paper from his pocket and handed it to Himmler.

'Discussed?' Himmler said, reading the names on the sheet of paper.

'The Anglo-Americans have requested that the opposition—'

'The traitors,' Himmler interrupted. 'Subversives.'

'Of course,' Nebe agreed. 'The Anglo-Americans have requested they hold off any move against the Führer until a successful landing is forced in France.'

'Optimism. And their response, these traitors?'

'Agreement. They are anxious to deal. And they're not ready anyway. As you know, they offered to let the British and Americans land here once they had overthrown the Führer, but this was rejected by the Western powers.'

'Whatever you say about the Americans, the British aren't stupid enough to trust such fools,' Himmler said. 'Were you asked anything, Arthur?'

'No more than my opinion. I followed your orders in that matter.'

'And me? What do they say about me?' Himmler asked.

'There is still great division, Herr Reichsführer. Some are willing

54

to countenance an approach, most want you to go the way of the Führer.'

'Well, you must stick up for me, Arthur,' Himmler said, smiling.

'I do my duty, despite all the risks, Herr Reichsführer. I have never neglected my duty to you or to Germany.'

'You still have the faith, as they say, Arthur. You and Ohlendorf are very alike in that way. But then you both commanded Einsatzgruppen in the east. He thinks I should consider making a pre-emptive strike, for the sake of Germany.'

'Ohlendorf is a blunt man,' Nebe said.

'Don't worry, this room is safe, Arthur,' Himmler reassured him.

'Ohlendorf does not realise the nature of your fidelity to the Führer,' Nebe went on.

Himmler nodded and sipped some more milk. 'He is the rock upon which Germany stands; he is my life. If I would do what Ohlendorf asks I would sacrifice myself. For Germany.'

'The Reichsführer is too honourable.'

'Terrible decisions. But if these diplomats and army traitors do move, then I could regret my loyalty. If only ...'

'... the Führer could see strategic sense,' Nebe interjected.

Himmler smiled. 'You've done good work, Arthur.'

'And the Gestapo?'

'I'll keep Müller and his dogs off your back. You have my protection. And I have more terrible decisions to make. Good night, Arthur.'

Nebe stopped at the bottom of the steps outside the Gestapo building, looked up at the upper floors and shivered. The air-raid sirens were sounding. He waved his car on and pointed at his feet.

'Anywhere interesting tonight, Arthur?'

Of all the senior SS and police commanders in Nazi Germany, Gruppenführer Heinrich Müller, the head of the Gestapo, was the one who looked most like a street thug. In fact, like Nebe, he was a professional policeman, having served in the Bavarian political police, specialising in communism, before joining the Nazis. Never a Nazi ideologue, he was a perfect functionary, content, it seemed only to see the state survive.

When he stepped out of the shadow of the doorway, his cropped haircut and vampiric face made Nebe step back.

'You didn't drop in to say hello, Arthur,' Müller said. 'Like a nightcap?'

'No. I've work, Heinrich.'

'I thought you'd done that. Walking? You could get hurt if the British come. But then you could get hurt in all sorts of ways in this war.'

'Is this official, Heinrich?' Nebe asked.

'If this was official, you'd be upstairs and I'd have my sleeves rolled up, Arthur. How's the Reichsführer? Stomach still hurting? Perhaps the strain is just too much for him. Perhaps he needs a rest.'

'You would like his job, Heinrich?'

'I only wish to serve National Socialist Germany; winkle out its enemies. And National Socialist Germany is Adolf Hitler. So anyone countenancing a Germany without the Führer is, *ipso facto*, an enemy. Very simple really.' He looked up at the Berlin skyline and the searchlights. 'I don't think they'll come tonight. You're safe, it would seem, Arthur. But you may not always be safe.'

'I serve the Reichsführer, Heinrich. Loyally.'

'Yes. I serve the Führer, myself.'

4

MAURICE HALLAN SAT back in his chair. 'Moonlight Serenade'
was playing on the gramophone. He sipped his whisky, went over
the operation again, and then cast his eye over the myriad of files
and papers lying on his living-room floor.

Around him, on every table, between the files and papers, were half
a dozen teacups, a similar number of overflowing ashtrays and several
empty cigarette packets. Hallan pulled on his braces and stared at the
blackout curtains, trying to decide whether to open them and watch
the approaching day struggle over the terraced houses. The music
stopped.

'Morning, Maurice. Burning the midnight oil?'

For some reason, Hallan kept looking at Claude Dansey, unable
to speak, almost as if he believed he was dreaming.

'We let ourselves in, Maurice,' Dansey said. 'You know Philby,
here, from Section 5, Iberia, yes? And do I smell tea? Any toast?'

Hallan stood up. Dansey gave a signal and two younger men
appeared from behind Kim Philby and pushed him back into
his seat.

'What say we go somewhere special where your wife won't be
disturbed by a lot of boring conversation, Maurice?' Dansey said
then. 'Get a coat, there's a good fellow. You may, as Captain
Oates so deftly put it during that ridiculous escapade with Scott
in the Antarctic, be some time. We'll have a look around if you
don't mind.'

'I've done nothing wrong, sir,' Hallan protested, while pulling on
his coat.

'You let me be the judge of that,' Dansey said. 'You know, some

57

of my boys want to work on you with various kitchen utensils. You could help yourself by telling me where Ben Kramer is.'

Ben Kramer met a man in Glasgow before making his way to the west coast of Scotland. When he reached the island of Beg that Good Friday morning, the rain had returned and Erich Haas was sorting through a selection of German clothes and uniforms laid out on a wooden table in the cottage. There was a smell of coffee and burnt porridge on the peat smoke that floated around the stone cottage.

'We'll have to have them cleaned,' Haas said to Jack Levy. 'That smell cannot come with me.'

'Jack'll see to it,' Kramer said. 'Everything.'

'Let's see the papers,' Haas said.

Kramer came over to the table with his briefcase. He turned to Jack Levy and the quiet, bearded man carrying a Sten gun beside the door.

'Could you step outside, Jack,' he said. 'This is an eyes-only thing. You understand?'

Levy's face became strained but he nodded to the other man, a relative who had done time in the Commandos, and the two of them stepped out into the rain and lit cigarettes.

'I'll have to be scrubbed, too,' Haas said.

Kramer emptied the contents of his briefcase on to the table. Identity cards and papers fell out on to a black waistcoat with a satin lining. He picked up a small grey linen-covered German soldier's paybook.

'*Soldbuch*,' he said. 'You'll be able to deal with the alterations to your hair?'

'No problem.' Haas touched the promotions section of the *soldbuch*. 'I was promoted from the ranks?' he asked.

'Yes. Your age . . . If you began as an officer in that unit, you'd be a general by now.'

'I'd be dead. Do you know the attrition rate for field officers in the German armed forces?'

Kramer picked up a series of thin brownish-yellow documents.

'*Urlaubscheins* – travel permits, tickets of leave – good for the whole of the Swiss border area. And these are for various journeys around Bavaria and Austria. And these are empty. You can fill them in yourself with a little kit we have.'

Kramer rooted through more documents.

'I don't know what good this will be but it's a letter of authorisation signed by Reichsführer Himmler. It's so good the great man himself wouldn't recognise it as a forgery. Use it sparingly.'

'I'm impressed,' Haas said. 'The Abwehr have a castle in Thuringia where this kind of thing is done.'

'It's where they have Canaris at the moment, I'm told, under a kind of benevolent house arrest.'

'To make the old bastard feel at home.'

'Okay,' Kramer said then. '*Arbeitskarte*. A work permit for foreigners. They definitely don't have your fingerprints on file?'

'Abwehr Two destroyed everything to do with me when I signed for the Tod programme. I don't exist in any official sense.'

'I found you. This goes with the *arbeitskarte*. It's a provisional passport for aliens resident in the Reich. But don't use this and the work permit unless you absolutely have to. I didn't pick you to act as a Belgian. Your chief asset is you're German.'

'I'm beginning to wonder if I am any more.'

Kramer picked up three small brown books.

'Your German civilian *ausweis* in the legend you asked for, two more back-up *ausweis*, marriage certificates, ration cards, etc. And here's a few photographs of girls and children.'

Kramer walked around the room in a circle and rested by the fireplace, where a turf fire was burning. He warmed his hands, then put them in his pocket. He pulled out a silver disc with a German eagle on one side and a legend and number on the other.

'Gestapo silver warrant disc,' he said.

Haas's pupils visibly dilated. He came over to Kramer and took the disc out of his hand and examined it.

'It's genuine?' he asked.

Kramer nodded.

'Where the hell did you get it?'

'That's not your concern. It'll get you through road blocks and annoying checkpoints. It will not get you into the Führer area on Obersalzberg. And if anyone takes the time to check the number with Prinz Albrechtstrasse, they'll find it belongs to a man who's attached to the German legation in Madrid. Only use it where absolutely necessary.'

'I'm impressed, Herr Major.'

'I repeat, it will not get you into the Führer area on the Obersalzberg. For that, you need a *sonderausweis*, signed by the head of security, Rattenhuber, and Hitler's chief adjutant, Julius Schaub, stamped with an RSD monthly stamp. And even then there's a ninety per cent chance they'll nab you.'

Haas began to smile.

'But you have one for me anyway,' he said.

Kramer pulled out a Red card with a place for a photograph and a gold bar across it; at the bottom were three RSD monthly stamps.

'It's good for this month, Erich. The inner area. But walk in displaying that and you won't walk out displaying it.'

'The challenge of it all. Have you ever slept with another man's woman, Herr Major? It is the most satisfying of conquests. I only sleep with such women.'

'I'm not impressed, Erich.'

'Your wife is having an affair.'

'We're divorced.'

'She has slept with someone you know, who takes delight at seeing your face when you know they have been together. It's the extra centimetre you Yids don't have that women like.'

Kramer hit Haas in the face and the German staggered and held himself up against the table. Kramer's face was red, his eyes dark. He steadied himself against the fireplace. Haas wiped his lip.

'First blood, Herr Major,' he said. 'I was hoping you'd say that if I spoke like that again you'd kill me. I'm trying to figure you out, Herr Major. You are a driven man, yes?'

The door opened and Jack Levy and his young companion stepped inside the cottage.

'All right, Ben?' Levy asked.

'All right, Jack. Go and get something to eat. Tell Sam and Ken they're on duty. You look wretched.'

Levy nodded and pursed his lips. When the two guards had gone, Kramer went over to his briefcase. 'You ever dropped from forty thousand feet, Erich?' he asked.

Haas smiled and shook his head. 'You're joking?'

'Junkers JU86R. You freefall to three hundred, pull your cord and . . .'

'You have an evil streak to you, Herr Major. No wonder you didn't threaten to kill me. You figure I'm already dead.'

'You're dead until you do this job, Erich. And if he's not dead by the end of the month, everything we have on you goes to the Gestapo and the Shai will dedicate itself to tracking you down.'

'Eye for eye, Herr Major. Tooth for tooth, life for life.'

'He dies or you die, Erich.'

The tiled walls of the basement buckled into the depressed flagstone floor, while a large wood-burning stove with a teapot on top stood cold in a corner. There were wooden shelves around the walls and the furniture was thick and had been repainted a few times. There was a picture of the King and Queen on one wall and a squanderbug poster on another; and two ration books lay open on a wooden bench beside a collection of brown paper bags, all folded. Maurice Hallan shivered.

'Valkyrie, Maurice,' Dansey said. Then he exhaled. 'Now we've torn your office to pieces, we're tearing your house to pieces and you are going to chokey. This is the number of a Lisbon bank account.' He handed Hallan a slip of paper. 'It is also the personal code of an Abwehr killer. A very wealthy Abwehr killer. I should congratulate you, Maurice, on a job well done. You're planning to kill Adolf Hitler, aren't you? It can only be him. No one else is worth a million dollars. Feel free to correct me.'

Hallan kept looking at the slip of paper and shaking his head.

'Do you know how many man-hours we've spent tracking that code number?' Dansey asked.

'I can't tell you anything,' Hallan said.

'Sweet Jesus, Maurice, some of my boys would like to play gravity games with you,' Dansey exclaimed.' Do you know what I mean? Indulge in a bit of reconstruction. But it's so imprecise. Not me at all. I prefer to reason with a man. Your wife will end up in chokey, Maurice, if we find she so much as knew the colour of Ben Kramer's eyes, I promise you that. Five, ten years for treason. Maybe longer. It depends on the jury and what evidence they're presented with.'

Hallan's head was moving in small jerks. 'Three-quarters of a million Jews,' he said.

'One dollar and thirty-three cents a head,' Dansey retorted.

'We have to do it. I mean, what's the problem? Surely, we all want him dead. Surely.'

'Listen, you stupid little prick, do you understand anything about the real world? I'm talking about the strategic whole, Maurice, the macro-situation. Not the selfish interest of one small group of people. Have you stopped to think for one moment what would happen if this succeeds? Germany collapsing. Us still stuck in Southampton. Ivan the Terrible wading across the Rhine, planning to holiday at Calais.

We've put a monumental effort into this struggle and we're not going to have some over-eager schoolboys, playing assassins, fucking it all up for us. So where is Kramer?'

'I can't tell you what I don't know.'

'Look, you and your gang of Zionist fanatics have put the security of this realm in the gravest peril; and I will have answers.'

'I am a patriot, sir,' Hallan said.

Claude Dansey closed his eyes and sighed.

'I'm not against the idea in principle,' he said. 'I told Ben Kramer that. Yes, we discussed it. My God, everyone's discussed killing Hitler at one time or another. The Americans were even contemplating poisoning him. But none of us were really going to waste the time trying. And certainly not now. Not until we're in a position to exploit it. If it didn't anger me so much I might be tempted to say I admired your loyalty, Maurice. But your loyalty to this realm is paramount. Look, we understand your motives. Come on, we've worked well with you people for years now: Palmach, 51 Commando, we're on the same side. Your people in Jerusalem and Tel Aviv, they're helping us run the Stern Gang and other lunatics to earth. This has been a long war, Maurice, and no one has suffered more than the Hebrew people. But we're approaching the most crucial phase and we can't afford to have anything foul it up. So where the hell is Kramer?'

'I don't know, sir.'

Dansey stood up. He turned to a bigger man standing in the shadows of the basement.

'Right, get it out of him any way you can; and sweat his wife, too.' He turned back to Hallan. 'You know our firm doesn't officially exist, Maurice, so anything we do doesn't happen. I hope your missus is as dedicated as you are.'

He walked towards the door.

'Moon Squadron!' Hallan shouted. 'We're sending him out by Moon Squadron tonight, pencilled in as a Sussex drop . . .'

Hallan kept shaking his head. He began to cry.

'You know I'm not proud of this, Maurice,' Dansey said, 'but I have considerations.'

In Munich, that Good Friday, the Stations of the Cross had ended in the Church of Our Lady off Neuhauserstrasse, and Max Weg made his way through the crowd and past a group of Hitler Youth making a gate collection in the Frauenplatz. One of the Hitler Youth offered to help him negotiate some steps near a fountain. Weg reached into his pocket and gave the boy a coin and a pat on the head. Then a voice cried his name.

Weg recognised the voice and automatically turned his head in the direction of Lowengrubestrasse, to his right.

A dark-haired man in his mid-forties, with black eyes and a sad if romantic face, came over and put his hand out. Weg put his stick down between his legs and held out both his own hands and allowed the man to take the grip before closing it.

'Herr Kriminalkommissar,' Weg said. 'At the stations?'

'Good God, no. I'm an atheist,' the police inspector said. 'Anyway, my job is my stations.'

'For the architecture, then?'

'If the terror flyers have their way there won't even be that left to us. Have you seen the Michaelskirche or the Peterskirche?'

'I was down at the Peterskirche the other day. Someone wanted to know if I had a book which would help with the restoration. The Führer has ordered that all such buildings be rebuilt. But what's the point if they keep coming over and wrecking them. So how's the crime rate?'

'Worse than ever.'

'You'd think it would be low, with the war and the community spirit.'

'Max, I think you're a cynic underneath all that naïvety.'

'Willy, I'm a German.'

Wilhelm Koch had been working in his office at the headquarters of the Munich Kriminalpolizei on Ettstrasse 2 since ten o'clock the previous night, trying to make sense of four bodies fished out of the River Isar, and if Max Weg had been able to see his eyes he would have noticed that Koch had reached a stage of exhaustion that was affecting his health.

'So you're working hard,' Weg said. 'Even on Good Friday.'

'Harder than ever on a day like today.'

'Yes. I called over last Sunday, and you were out. Working on the sabbath.'

'I'm not sure I shouldn't arrest you for using a word like that. I'm sure it breaks the Jewish sections of the criminal code.'

Weg pulled his lapel and showed his Nazi Party badge. 'I have connections,' he said.

'I hear you had real coffee on Briennerstrasse last week, Max.' Briennerstrasse contained the Nazi headquarters in Munich, the

Brown House, as well as the headquarters of the local Gestapo, the Wittelsbacher Palais.

'If they had coffee,' Weg said, 'I should have given you some.'

Koch nodded and looked around at the crowds of tired people coming from Mass, heads bowed and eyes frozen. They had a skeletal look and moved mechanically.

'I thought perhaps we could have a game of chess, Max. I wanted to sleep but I'm not able to. I tried in there.' He pointed to the offices of the Kriminalpolizei, which occupied the whole block from Ettstrasse around Lowengrubestrasse to the Frauenplatz, a big green building with a functional solidity about it. Except now there were shrapnel holes in the walls and strips torn from the roof and windows boarded up and taped and the perpetual smell of smashed drainage and lime. 'I know it's Good Friday and all but I need to exercise my mind.'

'Let's go to the shop,' Weg said. 'I've things to sort out there. I have done my religious duties.'

'How does the Party react to such piety?'

'The Party is . . . ambivalent. There were many members there today; times like ours make men seek help where they can find it. Anyway, the Reichsführer insists his men believe in God.'

'Enough, enough, you'll convert me to at least one of your faiths. How are things up there in Schwabing?'

'There's a crack in my window but it wasn't a bomb; some little tearaway threw a stone at it.'

'You should have phoned the police.'

'They never come.'

Apart from military service during the First World War, Wilhelm Koch had been a policeman all his working life. In 1923, he had been part of the team that had arrested the leaders of the failed Nazi beer hall putsch in Munich, among them a young radical politician named Adolf Hitler. By 1933, when Hitler took power, Koch was already an inspector, but he never got another promotion.

'So what are your problems, Willy?' Max Weg said when they were sitting at a leather-covered desk in his bookshop, preparing to play chess. Weg had two pieces concealed in his hands. Koch touched one of the hands and Weg swung the board around.

'What is this I'm drinking?' Koch asked, puckering his mouth.

'I got it from a Party guy down at the Brown House last mouth. It's herbal tea; he says it comes straight from the Führer's stocks.'

'The Führer drinks this? That explains a lot. You got any schnapps?'

'I was waiting for you to ask,' Weg said. 'So what has you working so hard, Willy?' He stood up and went over to a bookshelf, took away a book and pulled out a bottle of schnapps. 'The only really valuable thing I have here,' he said. He pulled two small glasses out of a drawer and poured the schnapps. 'To the future.'

'You definitely are a cynic, Max,' Koch said. And then he moved a chess piece and told Weg his move.

They played for another fifteen minutes, during which time, Koch took one of Weg's pawns and Weg took one of Koch's knights. And Weg poured more schnapps.

'You do sound very tired, Willy,' Weg said a number of times.

'Black market gangs. Pulled bodies out of the river yesterday, Max. Cut to pieces. It's gangsterism. I've seen things, but this kind of stuff, it's gangsterism. Even for butter now. You know what butter's worth on the black market? And those Gestapo assholes at the Wittelsbacher Palais, they're useless when it comes to real police work.'

'I think you are very tired, Willy,' Weg said. 'Perhaps you should call it a day and go home to your wife and your son and rest.'

'My wife? I think not. Would you report me because I bad-mouth the Gestapo?'

'Not me, Willy, but others might hear and the way things are in our Reich, things could be misunderstood.'

'You shouldn't pour schnapps into me if you want me to be discreet. The Gestapo attracted all the guys who wanted to move quickly. They're fine when they're dealing with corrupt officials and criminals with low IQs, but for the real stuff, the stuff that needs trained detection and evidence, they're amateurs. And so I'm left to pick up the pieces.'

'Retire.'

'To what? Heinz got his call-up papers, Max.'

Weg pulled his head up. The eyes made Koch feel uncomfortable.

'Oh God, I'm sorry,' he said.

'Barely seventeen. And he's jumping to get in. Jesus, he won't stand a chance.'

'How's Maria taking it?'

'Like any mother, she's blaming me.'

'So you don't want to go home?'

'I don't have a home. Things are breaking down, you know. Things . . .'

'We are all being asked to make sacrifices, Willy.'

'Yeah, well, you'll forgive me if I'm not as idealistic as I once was about all that kind of thing; I see the grubbier side of the Reich, the corruption, the profiteering, the hoarding, the gangsterism, the favouritism. Other things. Maybe you could have a word, you know, have Heinz posted somewhere he won't get into too much trouble.'

'I don't carry that much weight, but give me the details and I'll see what I can do when he's trained. We'll have to wait till then.'

'I wouldn't ask only I'm afraid Maria will have a nervous breakdown. I once tried to get into the RSD, you know, to guard the Führer. Did I ever tell you that?'

'When was that?'

'Oh, years ago. It was exciting then. I thought because Rattenhuber knew me – we were in the army and the Landespolezei in Bayreuth –, I'd have a chance. But everything stopped for me then. I've been treading water ever since, trying not to drown.'

'Destined to pass history but never enter it.'

'The odd thing about that is I was sympathetic in '23 and the Führer was very polite to all of us.'

'You were doing your duty. He understands.'

'Yeah. I don't think it was the putsch that kept me out of the RSD. Rattenhuber and I were good friends, you know. He was a captain. I was what I still am. Now, he just gives me the courtesies. I suppose he has his position to think of. You won the Blue Max, didn't you?'

The small bell at the shop door rang and Koch turned his head. Ilse Gern stood inside and nodded at him.

'Excuse me, Herr Kriminalkommissar, I didn't realise . . .'

'Oh, we're just paying chess, Ilse,' Weg said. 'Old men with nothing better to do.'

'You speak for yourself, Max. How are you, Ilse?'

'I am well, Herr Kriminalkommissar,' she said. 'Considering.'

'Please, my name is Wilhelm. And I'm off duty. Would you care to join us for a cup of herbal tea or a schnapps?'

'No, thank you. I just wanted to drop these over, Herr Weg. Mother baked them and felt you might like some.'

She opened a wrapper and revealed two small cakes.

'I can smell them from here,' Weg said. 'Tell your mother she is very kind.'

'And you will come to dinner on Sunday?'

'Yes. Though I have that book-binder I told you about arriving some time in the next couple of days. So I may have to cancel. I must keep my colleagues happy.'

Koch shook his head. 'I always wonder where you find customers in times like this, Max,' he said.

'*Objets d'art*, Wilhelm. Never go out of fashion. Think of Göring. Thank your mother for the cakes, Ilse.'

She came over and put the package on the table and looked at the chessboard. Koch smiled and then winced. For a moment he smelled her scent and everything he had felt or was feeling dissipated and he hung on that smell.

'You fancy her,' Max Weg said when Ilse was gone.

Koch was going to argue.

'And it shows, doesn't it?'

'Well, at least you have something nice to consider. I have her bloody mother trying to get into my trousers. She thinks I can do favours, get her things.'

Koch tapped the table.

'Now what makes her think that?'

Weg moved one of his bishops into a position where Koch could take it.

'You did that on purpose,' Koch said. 'Why?'

'Sacrifice for the greater good,' Weg replied. 'Tell me more about how things are in our dear city.'

In a corner of the wooden maturity of the Café Heck, near the Odeonsplatz in Munich, that day, two men in SS general officer field uniforms sat in front of two cups of real coffee. Neither drank.

Around them, at various tables, bodyguards sat and drank the coffee supplied by the Munich Gestapo, while Gruppenführer Heinrich Müller and Brigadeführer Johann Rattenhuber, the commander of Hitler's bodyguard, the RSD, talked.

'He reports directly to the Reichsführer after each meeting. Nebe.'

Müller stirred his coffee. His face was statuesque, almost frozen. Rattenhuber, a very fat man, with a certain jovialness in the folds of his skin which disguised his real personality, touched the Iron Cross, first class, on the left breast of his tunic.

'With due respect, Heinrich, what would you like me to do?' he asked.

Müller smiled. 'You know, I miss working in this city sometimes,' he said. 'I was a good cop. Like you, Hans.'

'You still are, Herr Gruppenführer. And you will appreciate the need for evidence before a move is made. The Reichsführer is perfectly entitled to ensure the security of the Führer and the state in whatever way he deems necessary. If we had a transcript of one of these meetings Nebe attends . . . but even then, if Nebe is working for the Reichsführer, then that is all there is to it. Have you pressed the Reichsführer?'

'He tells me it is not my business.'

'The privilege of rank.'

'Have you spoken with the Führer? We must be allowed to act, Hans.'

'Herr Gruppenführer, I must ask you to be careful in your implications. Heinrich, there are some suspicions I may not hear, not without firm evidence. In the end, it all boils down to trust. And the Führer trusts the Reichsführer, implicitly.'

'I trust no one.'

'Not even me?'

'You just look after the Führer, Hans. These are difficult days.'

Teddy Giles knocked and entered Claude Dansey's office without being asked. Something Dansey noted.

'News from the Moon Squadron, sir. Everything going out tonight is accounted for. Seems Hallan was lying.'

'Bloody little shit. Any news of Kramer?'

Giles shook his head.

'He can't have vanished.'

'Perhaps Haas is already gone,' Kim Philby said. He was standing in shadow. Giles had barely noticed him.

'No,' Dansey said. 'Kramer'd be in his office, looking smug. Anyway, Hallan wouldn't have lied if that was the case.'

'Perhaps they don't plan to send him by plane,' Philby suggested.

'I checked shipping. Nothing there either,' Teddy Giles said.

'You're learning, Teddy.' Dansey smiled. 'No, they have to get this man to Munich quickly and easily. They'll drop him. One man, you can risk a drop.'

'Then perhaps we're looking too close to home,' Kim Philby said.

'The Americans,' Teddy Giles added.

The three men stood looking at one another.

'Get on to Grosvenor Street,' Dansey said to Giles. 'See what their Black Flight has leaving in the next few days.'

'They're not likely to be immediately co-operative,' Philby said.

'If it's necessary, I'll talk to David Bruce myself. But try not to tell them what they don't need to know. And Teddy, get me a list of all the bodies working on the American side of Sussex – you know, backgrounds, all that kind of thing.'

Dansey was looking out of the window. It had begun to rain.

At a window in East Anglia, between King's Lynn and Norwich, Eric Haas sat oiling the Navy Luger, watching the rain fall. The window was broken in two places and some of the rainwater was seeping in and running down the window to the sill and gathering there before dripping on to the carpet. Haas watched the water trickle to the edge of the sill and tried to figure out when it would fall to the floor. The walnut radio across the room vibrated to the humour of ITMA, and the faint smell of carrots tickled Haas's nose and made him think of somewhere else.

'I don't understand the jokes,' he said to Ben Kramer. 'It's very provincial.'

'That's why it's so popular.'

'I prefer Bob Hope.'

'Actually, I'm more Wodehouse,' Kramer said.

'He's a traitor.'

'I can laugh at a traitor. All the best writers are traitors or spies or both. You Germans have no sense of humour.'

'We elected Adolf Hitler,' Haas said. 'I took this job.'

'You sound as if you don't know yourself, Erich.'

'There are always things we don't know, Herr Major. You don't know if I will do this and I don't know if you won't try and kill me afterwards.'

'You know what will happen if you betray us, Erich,' Kramer said.

'That works both ways, Herr Major.'

'I wish you only success, Erich.'

'Tell me, did many people die because of you?' Haas asked. 'When you were working in France.'

'Just one.'

'I have killed many people, but no one has ever died because of me.'

69

'I needed a woman.'

'I have learned to deny myself. I get pleasure from it now.'

'Her name was Valerie Lynes,' Kramer said. 'She was helping to catch a German infiltrator. Shadowed him all the way to London. Played the role right to the end.'

'When did he seduce her?' Haas said. 'Your wife's lover?'

'Right after she wrote and told me how much she loved me.'

'That is the way of such things.'

Teddy Giles came running up the corridor with the confident humility of an accountant caught fiddling his clients' tax returns by a curious inspector: he had something to trade.

'Tonight,' he said. 'The Yanks are sending a man to France. By JU-86R. That's a high-altitude aircraft which has been specially adapted. The flight's been signed out by a chap named Amster who's working on their end of Sussex.'

'Don't tell me, Amster's a Jew,' Dansey said.

'Bingo! And he's been seen with Ben Kramer and Maurice Hallan.'

'Two men answering Kramer and Haas's description were spotted at Peterborough,' Dansey continued. 'Where's that Black Flight field exactly?'

They slipped into Dansey's office and Giles went over to a map on the wall and pointed to an area between Norwich and King's Lynn. 'Here, near this village, Tetham.'

'And what have you told Grosvenor Street?'

'Nothing yet. Just said I was checking for Sussex. I thought you'd want to break the news to Colonel Bruce.'

'Ever the diplomat, Teddy.' Dansey was already up and grabbing his coat. 'You know, sometimes I have faith in you. When we stop this nonsense, I might even promote you.'

The moon hung left of the wind-sock, through a line of thin trees with new leaves rustling in the spring breezes drifting in from the Wash. And Ben Kramer could see the vaguest outline of the JU-86R on the runway.

Jake Coll was at the window of the Nissen hut, tapping the blackout screen, looking at maps of Germany when Kramer came in. He looked at his watch as he stepped inside.

'You know they call us the vampires on account of we only come out at night,' Coll said. 'Black Flight. Look at the colour of my skin. White.'

'Close the door, please,' Haas said to Kramer. 'You are in breach of blackout regulations.'

Kramer shut the door.

Haas sat in the corner of the hut, reading magazines and drinking water. Beside him, sitting at what passed for an operations desk, Mario Capparelli sank his fourth coffee. Haas closed his eyes and tried to concentrate on anything but the smell of the coffee he could not have.

'Could we stop drinking coffee,' he said to Kramer. 'It's beginning to annoy me.'

'The raid should be heading out round about now,' Kramer said. 'Time to go through final checks.' He gestured to Larry Amster.

'Yeah, sure,' Amster said, looking pale. 'The sooner this is over, the better. I hate waiting.'

Amster nodded at Coll, who zipped up the one-piece flying suit he had on. Haas did the same.

'You're sweating, Larry,' Kramer whispered.

'I'm a lawyer, for God's sake, Ben.'

Kramer went over to Haas.

'Tell me again that bit about freefalling from forty thousand feet in the dark, counting the way down to three hundred feet before pulling the rip cord.'

Kramer tried to smile.

The black telephone on the sergeant's desk rang just as Amster was dimming the lights in the hut before opening the door. Capparelli, who was one of those administrative NCOs who manage to keep a dozen things going at once, listened without emotion, nodded, put the phone down, and wrote something in a notebook.

'Weather?' Coll asked.

'Yes, sir,' Capparelli said. He tore out the page and gave it to Coll. Amster went to open the door.

'Don't open the door, Mr Amster.'

Haas saw the Browning first. Capparelli was still behind his desk.

'And turn all lights on, please, Jake.'

'What is this?' Kramer said.

'Capparelli?' Coll queried.

'What the hell's going on, Sergeant?' Amster asked.

'Appears your flight's been cancelled,' Capparelli said. 'Stand down, sir. And you're under arrest, Major. Mr Amster, too. I have orders to hold both of you and that man.' Capparelli was standing up and holding the Browning in both hands.

'It seems you have overstepped your authority, Herr Major,' Haas said.

'Look, I don't know what this is about but we have a deadline for this man and it must be kept, Sergeant,' Kramer said.

'I'm afraid I can't allow that, sir. Weapons on the floor, gentlemen, very slowly.'

'I'm authorising it, Sergeant,' Amster said.

'I'm sorry, Mr Amster. Do as I say.'

'Damn it, Sergeant, obey your orders,' Amster said. He pulled out his blue OSS card. 'You see this? I can have you transferred to combat. Right now, Sergeant.'

Capparelli shook his head.

'That's as maybe, Mr Amster, sir, but I want you and the other gentlemen over against the wall . . . all of you, please. You too, Jake.'

Coll found that his hands were shaking.

Claude Dansey watched the hedgerows through the darkness as the cars sped north-west towards Tetham. He took out a service revolver and checked it.

'If it comes to it, kill them all,' he said.

In the Nissen hut Capparelli kicked the automatic pistols across the floor.

'I'm gonna have your ass for this, Mario,' Jake Coll said.

'You can do that, Jake, just as soon as the MPs get here.'

'Mice and men, Herr Major,' Haas said, smiling. 'I feel I must tell you that whatever our personal business arrangements, I have no intention of staying here like this.'

Capparelli turned the Browning on him. 'I have no idea who you are, sir, but if you open your mouth one more time, I'll blow your brains out.'

'And that is the difference between you and me, Sergeant,' Haas said. 'You give me a warning.'

'No, Erich!' Kramer shouted.

Haas was already moving. And when Kramer and Coll moved, Haas flicked out the steel tube concealed in his sleeve.

He fired one silenced shot. It caught Capparelli in the right shoulder, below the blade. He staggered and dipped and then swung his pistol at Kramer.

'Ben!'

Amster went to push Kramer out of the way. Capparelli fired.

'Oh, Jesus . . .'

Amster staggered against the wall of the hut and fell on to his knees, holding his stomach. 'I think he's killed me, Ben,' he said.

Kramer looked over at Capparelli, who was lying across his desk, holding his shoulder, cursing.

'Shit!' Haas said to him. 'I meant to get you through the head. Hey, not a bad weapon, this sleeve gun. Needs practice.'

Coll bent over Amster and tore open his clothes to see the wound.

'I'm cold, Jake,' Amster said.

'Hang on, Larry.' Kramer looked at Coll and then at Haas. 'Get him out of here, Coll, get him out of here.'

Haas picked up the Browning from the floor. 'I think we had better move,' he said, pointing it at Coll.

'Jesus Christ, Major,' Coll said to Kramer. 'What the fuck . . .?'

'There's no need for the gun, Erich,' Kramer said. 'Is there, Captain?'

'Go, Jake, go, please,' Amster said. 'I'm begging you.'

'Do your job, Coll, just do your job,' Kramer urged.

Coll hesitated some more. He stared at Capparelli and shook his head.

'Your wife's out, Jake,' Amster said. 'I kept my word. Jesus, I can't feel a thing.'

'If you don't mind, Captain . . .' Haas smiled. 'I assure you, what we're doing here is from the highest motives. Right, Herr Major?'

'I can't see,' Amster whispered.

'I'd rather not have to force you,' Haas said to Coll. 'But I will if it's necessary.'

Coll reached over and took Larry Amster's hand.

'Best motives, Jake,' Amster said. 'Best motives.'

Coll nodded and turned to Haas. 'All right, let's go,' he said.

Haas smiled. 'I won't stay for pleasantries, Herr Major,' he said to Kramer.

'And I won't say good luck.'

Haas continued smiling. 'It would only invite bad . . .'

Coll walked out into the darkness. And Larry Amster died.

The JU86R had just cleared the runway when Dansey's column reached the airfield. Some of the men fired their handguns. The aircraft climbed into the night and Dansey swore to himself.

Coll reached maximum ceiling over the sea.

'Don't worry about it, you're not committing treason,' Haas said to him. 'I am. I've discovered treason has better working conditions.'

'I've been tryin' to decide whether to push the column forward,' Coll said. 'But I've been alive too long for dumb heroics, I think. You're not carryin' the plans for the invasion of France?'

'Would that I were. No, I am carrying something far more deadly, a little revenge. So, don't think about doing something stupid like pretending to be at the target when we're not. I read maps, I know navigation. I can even fly when needed, Captain. And I can understand one of these machines. It's a British invention and I have been briefed.'

Jake Coll switched on the H2S transmitter when they crossed the European coast. It showed a picture of the terrain below, gathered from radar echoes.

'What made you co-operate?' Haas asked somewhere over the Rhine valley.

'I made a deal.'

'We are similar people.'

'Then I wish you luck,' Coll said. 'I'm gonna need it.'

They did not talk again until Coll said, 'About fifteen minutes.'

Haas did not respond. He was going through a routine, tightening his straps so there would be no marks to give him away when he landed.

Ten minutes later, Coll nudged him.

'I'll depressurise in three minutes.'

Haas pulled down his goggles and turned on his oxygen and then tapped Coll on the shoulder. Coll watched the H2S and then his own maps and pulled in close to Augsburg before turning west again. He depressurised the cockpit.

Outside, the noise of the supercharged diesels began to increase and Haas could feel the pain in his ears.

Coll tapped him on the shoulder, took one more look at the H2S and then turned back to him.

But Haas was gone.

5

GLANCING AROUND THE Edwardian elegance of Claude Dansey's St James's Street flat later that morning, while his host poured the tea and he cut the buttered toast, David Bruce could not help pondering the nature of men like Dansey, who could get hold of such quantities of things like butter when the weekly ration per person was two ounces.

'I feel like the worst kind of heel, Claude,' Bruce said. 'I liked Larry Amster. And this going behind the President's back, it sets a precedent, you know. I'm afraid OSS is dipping its toes in the mire.'

'Necessary, David. And what the President doesn't know isn't going to hurt him. You're protecting him. Like I am the Prime Minister.'

'And C?'

'There are certain things he doesn't want to know about. And C is a man who likes to mull over decisions. Time is of the essence here. You understand?'

'I'm beginning to, Claude. You'd rather I didn't tell Bill Donovan?'

'Not unless it's necessary. He'd have to tell the President; and that would put the President in an invidious position.'

'So we just tell the Germans there's an assassin gunning for their Führer? At this Munich address?' Bruce pointed to the address of Max Weg's bookshop on the sheet of paper in front of him.

'No option,' Dansey said.

'We can't go direct to the Gestapo,' Bruce continued. 'Surely. They probably wouldn't believe us.'

'That's why you're here, David,' Dansey said.

'I appreciate your candour, Claude. If you'd been a little more candid earlier we might have nipped this thing in the bud.'

'Spilt milk, David. And no time for sensitivities. Allen Dulles is going to have to arrange a meeting with someone from the German opposition. We can feed it into the system that way. Those Breakers of his can start to earn their spurs, as we say.'

'They'll think we're crazy,' Bruce said.

'They'll do as they're told. Or we won't ever bite. Allen will insist on that. Tell them we'll serve them up to Himmler if they don't co-operate.'

'Jesus, Claude, do you sleep well?'

'Very well. Our Zurich station will help where Allen needs it. And Allen needs to keep this to himself. No records.'

'Allen Dulles would spin cartwheels for you, Claude. I'm not sure he'd do something like that for me. He's in awe of you. We all are. You're the kind of guy I read about when I was a kid.'

'A last hurrah, David. The baton is being handed over as we speak. A decade from now, when I'm dead and you're an ambassador, we British will work for you Americans. So let us enjoy our last late summer of freedom.'

'I don't know if you're serious sometimes, Claude.'

'Neither do I, David.'

'And direct action?' Bruce asked then.

'Yes. For insurance.'

'Almost a death sentence for those involved. He doesn't have a chance, does he? This German guy, I mean.'

'We're not doing this for fun, David. Tod agents are something of an awesome legend in intelligence circles. They say they can walk through walls. Read what I've given you, David. And I'll need to see what you have on file that we might use at short notice.'

'The files are yours. What a decision – eh?'

Dansey tapped the table. 'Come on, David. If you're going to take over the leadership of this business then these are the decisions you will have to make.'

'You put it so nicely, Claude. Jake Coll hasn't returned.'

'Your problem, David.'

'And yours? This Kramer, where is he now?'

'In one of our detention centres. He's not going to talk, though. Damn shame your man, Amster, was killed. Maurice Hallan might talk. We're going to use MI5 Ham Common methods there. Nothing physical, but lots of psychological stuff. The problem here is time.

Though I think we have enough to act on. We were lucky Hallan had it all laid out on the floor when we picked him up.'

'Hell of an insurance policy you're writing, Claude.'

'Look what we're trying to underwrite, David.'

Otto Ohlendorf stood under the shade of a chestnut tree in the Tiergarten, near an anti-aircraft position, and looked up at the Siegessaule in the middle of the Charlottenburger Chaussee. Then Walter Schellenberg signalled to him to enter the tunnel under the road.

When they reached the top of the monument, Ohlendorf had to pause to catch his breath. He saw the rings, on the last two fingers of the left hand first, and then the cuff stripe of the Reichsführer-SS, and then the pained, bespectacled, fowl-like face of Heinrich Himmler.

'Perhaps you need another tour of front-line duty, Otto,' Himmler said. 'It's only two hundred and eighty steps. I thought we should get above it all, so to speak. Away from the atmosphere of destruction.'

He walked around to the south side of the platform and pointed to the south side of the Tiergarten, where the Allied bombing had caused immense destruction.

'The work of terrorists,' he said. 'Inhuman. Tell him, Walter.'

Himmler stared up the Charlottenburger Chaussee to the Brandenburg Gate and the Unter den Linden beyond.

'One of SD Ausland's agents in the Forschungsamt came across this intercept yesterday,' Schellenberg said.

The Forschungsamt was Germany's signals interception organisation. Technically, it was the fiefdom of Hermann Göring, but all Nazi intelligence agencies had agents there, feeding them the best information.

'It's a transcript of a radio message from the NKVD station at the Soviet Embassy in London to their Stockholm station. *Mokrei dela* is Russian for what they term a wet job – where killing is involved.'

'And Sohnchen?' Ohlendorf asked.

'Someone they have high up in SIS. You see he refers to the Hotel, that's SIS, and the number two, that's Claude Dansey, the vice-chief of SIS; it was his network we broke up when we captured Payne-Best at Venlo in '39.'

'You always manage to steer things around to Venlo, Walter. Your crowning achievement.'

'Just read it, Herr Gruppenführer,' Himmler said without looking around.

'And Israel?'

'Jews,' Himmler said.

'But this is the important bit,' Schellenberg said. 'You see this – Czar . . .'

'Yes,' Ohlendorf said. 'I'm not too well up on cryptic messages but it would appear someone wants to kill this Czar. Yes?'

'Well done, Otto,' Himmler said. He was pulling out a small cigar. He lit it cupped in his hands. 'Czar is the NKVD codeword for the Führer, Herr Grupenführer Ohlendorf,' he said then. 'It's supposed to be an insult.'

'It was sloppily sent,' Schellenberg said. 'As if they were in a hurry. But it would appear that some kind of assassin has been sent here to kill the Führer.'

'A Jew?'

'Or sent by Jews . . .'

'You see, Ohlendorf, your work in the east, our work now, it has a terrible purpose. These people would attack our very heart,' Himmler said.

'Is it genuine?' Ohlendorf asked. He handed the piece of paper to Schellenberg.

'Very much so,' Schellenberg replied. 'This was a random intercept. In a code no one knows we even have access to, let alone are listening to. It's about as real as these things get, Otto.'

Himmler continued to smoke while the other two men stayed quiet. Then he turned to them. 'So, what do you think, Otto?' he asked.

'I think we have met providence, as the Führer would say, Herr Reichsführer.' There was a long pause, so that each of them could be sure the others understood what was being said.

'I love springtime in the Tiergarten,' Himmler said then. And he left them without saying anything more.

'Do you ever get frightened, Walter?' Ohlendorf asked when the Reichsführer was getting into a car below them.

'All the time, Otto. It's what keeps me going.'

'The Reichsführer doesn't look well.'

'The Reichsführer has such heavy responsibilities. He suffers physically.'

'Do you suffer, Walter?'

'Why did you join the SS, Otto?'

'I am a National Socialist.'

'Well, I joined because I needed a job. And there was only one way to get work – the Party. And in the Party, the best route to the top was the SS. I didn't want to be a foot slogger so I touted my brains and got into the SD. I'm not going to let it go without a fight.'

'I definitely don't like you, Walter. You'll be selling your memoirs when I'm climbing the scaffold.'

'I'll put in a good word for you, Otto.'

Max Weg could smell people before he heard them, and often he could hear them before they entered his shop. He could smell separate odours and hear sounds that tiptoed through the background noise of Munich, even during an air raid; and he knew the smell and the sound of an air raid.

He knew the sound of incendiary, high-explosive and deep-penetration bombs; and he knew they usually fell in sticks of eight. And when it was over there was always a silence, then a deep pungent odour of burning, the sharp smell of lime and the sound of single voices.

When people asked him how a blind man could sell books, he said it was a matter of knowledge and trust. He could tell each of his books by touch and smell and the dealers he dealt with he trusted; his sense of trust was something people felt and it gave him an edge where there should have been none. That Easter Sunday afternoon, while church bells were still ringing, he was arranging three new books on a shelf behind his desk when the entry bell over the door of his shop rang.

'We're close.' He continued running his fingers around the gold embossment of the nineteenth-century on leather volume birds.

'I wonder if you could help me,' a voice said. Weg was already making judgments based on scent, tone, step and breathing.

'If I can . . .'

'I think you can. Though I walk through the valley of the shadow of death I will fear no evil.'

'For thou art with me; thy rod and thy staff they comfort me.'

'Heil Hitler, Herr Weg.'

'Herr Rotach . . . welcome.'

Erich Haas put his suitcase down, smiled and reached out and took Weg's hand.

'I'm sorry I'm late. I got held up by the Americans.'

81

'You will take a coffee with me?' Weg asked. He still had not let go of Haas's hand. 'It is the best coffee. Illegal. We can discuss your request. Lock the door, would you.'

He led Haas to the back of the shop, opened a door hidden behind a bookshelf and revealed a small flight of stairs.

'Very dramatic, don't you think?' he said. 'I have a passion for cheap spy thrillers. There's another one over there leading to the basement. You have a trace of a French perfume that one doesn't easily come across here in Munich. I think you should perhaps borrow some cologne I have.'

'Thank you.'

'And your hand has slight traces of a leather I have not smelled since they picked an American flyer out of the ruins of a church three streets that way. A woman I know took his jacket. You should have a bath.'

'What happened to the flyer?'

'I think they hanged him before the police could get to him. Though the police were not in a hurry. It is getting like that around here. Could you push that, please.'

He pointed to a bare wall as they reached the top of the stairs.

'Will anyone come?'

Weg smiled and went into the small room.

'No. Not today. I'm not open. Anyway, I know my customers by name. You think ordinary people have much time for antiquarian books now? They look for food and stay clear of bombs. They are tired and they sleep when they have spare time. Everyone is tired.'

'You speak fondly of them.'

'They are my friends.'

'And enemies.'

'That is the way of life, as they say.'

The room at the top was furnished in an off-white colour that reminded Haas of a cheap funeral parlour in middle America; the curtains were torn and the chairs were all broken in one way or another. The wallpaper was coming loose from the top and there were lines of forgettable novels round the skirting board, all leaning in one direction. The novels had not been read in some time because there was a thin undisturbed layer of dust on them. In the middle of the room was a small desk and a chess set laid out for a game, and three bottles of moderately old wine. Someone had drunk from one of the wine bottles: a crystal glass, with a sediment of red wine caked to it, stood over the stone fireplace to the right of the desk, between a bad oil painting of a beautiful girl and some ugly souvenir beer mugs. The fireplace was empty except for a couple of sticks. Haas had noticed that most of the trees around the area had been felled.

'No one gives you wood,' he said.

'They do,' Weg said, 'but I sell it on. I have good clothes. If it's a choice between wasting small amounts of wood on a fire which would not heat an ant or having tradeable goods, I opt for the latter all the time. You have to be a businessman here in this Third Reich. Please sit down over there.'

He gestured to one of the chairs by the fireplace.

'Heat rises,' he continued. 'The others, in this building, they all have fires and their heat rises and keeps this place warm. Now, you'll want that cup of coffee.'

'Don't bother,' Haas said. 'I'd rather work.'

'Oh, we'll work. But today is Easter Sunday and a day for coffee. Now I want to run my hand over you, if you don't mind. Please don't think I am some kind of pervert. It is something I find necessary. You can close your eyes when I touch your genitalia, if you like. I don't mind.'

Haas watched the older man kneel down beside the chair and then run his hands around his body, very slowly, pausing at different places for a while, moving quickly at others.

An hour later, they were drinking coffee and Weg was cutting a slice of sausage for a piece of bread. 'You have any problems during the air-raid alert this morning?' he asked.

'Not like yesterday. I followed the crowd into a shelter near the Hauptbahnhof. No one was too inquisitive down there. Just afraid.'

'Tired and afraid. Your moustache is recent. You have shaved off a beard in the last few days. And your shoes are too clean and that suit has traces of British Army metal polish. Someone who handled that was using the stuff. Now my nose is very sensitive but it could make a difference at a crucial time.'

Haas sniffed his suit and could not smell anything. Then he began to scuff his shoes.

'Anything else?'

'Yes. You're too clean. No one here washes that much. Don't wash for a couple of days and rub your hands on the walls of bombed buildings. You like the coffee?'

'Fine.'

'It's more than fine. I have a contact who brings it in from Turkey. I sell what I don't use.'

'Does that not attract attention?'

'Didn't they tell you? I'm a Nazi. Fully paid-up member of the Party. I'm a local blockwart. I get invited to the Wittelsbacher Palais for coffee and cakes and the Brown House for Party days. Occasionally, I inform on people just to keep my hand in. Don't worry, the kind of scum I inform on don't deserve any sympathy. So what can I do for you, Herr Rotach?'

'What did they tell you?'

'You're not a Jew, are you?'

'Is that relevant?'

'You're not circumcised. It doesn't matter. I just meant that you've never worked for us before. We don't tell each other what we're doing. I get a request; I follow it through.'

Haas stood up and went over to the curtains and looked through the small chink. 'Don't pull those – blackout regulations. Being blind I would not know. I'd have to inform on myself. And that would not be good for either of us.'

'I need a place to stay,' Haas said then. 'Separate from you.'

'Yes. That is arranged.'

'I need a secondary base in which to keep certain items and to fall back on if the need arises. And I may need you to carry out certain tasks for me. They didn't tell me you were blind.'

'Do you foresee difficulties?'

'It depends. I am working to a tight deadline.'

'You have me interested. I feel the hairs on the back of my neck standing up. I assume you have equipment you would rather not carry round in case of spot checks by Gestapo or other agents of the state. That you can store here. It is about as safe as anywhere in this city – which is not saying a lot if you consider the damage the British and Americans have done in recent months. The British have been very quiet in this area since Nuremberg, and the Americans are only coming as far as Augsburg. I suspect everything is being concentrated on France in preparation for the invasion.'

'Tell me what people talk about, what their concerns are, bits of gossip. Fill me in on the general situation.'

'Adolf Wagner . . . heard of him?'

'The old Bavarian gauleiter . . .'

'He's dying of drink in Bad Reichenhall. And Speer is sick over at Schloss Klessheim. Nervous breakdown, they say. But that is Gestapo rumour, not ordinary citizen stuff. And Frau Göring seems to be going the way of her fat husband. They're all sick, it seems. Maybe even the Führer. No one sees him these days. Some people even say he's dead. He isn't. He has ordered various civic buildings rebuilt. Good of him, don't you think?'

Haas came over to the desk, sat down, moved a chess piece and called the move. Weg replied.

'I read palms, Herr Rotach,' he said. 'I have read yours.'

Haas moved another chess piece and called the move. 'Tell me what I ask, no more,' he said. 'I have decisions I must make.'

Claude Dansey tapped his fingers on the arms of the chintz-covered chair. He pulled his upper lip down and and allowed his lower lip to touch his moustache, then he directed his pointed chin at Teddy Giles.

'How the bloody hell did that happen?' he asked.

'He must have had it hidden, sir,' Giles replied. 'He was good at hiding things, Hallan.'

'What the bloody hell did you do to him?'

'Nothing. No rough stuff, sir. He was crying a lot last night, the guards said.'

He looked over at Kim Philby.

'Bugger!' Dansey shouted. 'I told you to go easy on him. Not kill him.'

'He killed himself, sir,' Kim Philby said, glancing at the floor to maintain control of his speech. 'And Vee Vee's asking questions, sir. I do have a sub-section to run.'

'You work for me, Philby. Remember that. Don't go and cock things up by proving to me that I was right all along about you Oxbridge types – that you're not up to the job. Let's face it, young Kim, you have a lot to prove, your pater being sympathetic to undesirable Arabs and having been detained at His Majesty's pleasure under 18B for a time. You were decorated by the Spanish Caudillo, weren't you? How the hell did you get into the firm? You're not a German agent, are you?'

Giles broke what might have been tension by smiling at Philby's misfortune, and Dansey quickly swung round to him.

'I don't know what you think is so funny, Teddy: I've a good mind to have you sent to darkest Africa. I don't take it kindly when you drive my suspects to suicide, you know.'

Dansey stood up and walked over to the marble fireplace. He picked up a porcelain figurine and turned it over in his hands.

'Haul in every Zionist in this city. I want all of them in for questioning.'

'There could be a problem there,' Giles said. 'I mean jurisdiction-wise. The Colonial Office are anxious not to antagonise now that Ben-Gurion and company have swung in behind us in Palestine. We need their help with the Stern Gang.'

'Do what I say. Despite this damn mess, these people know what side their bread's buttered on. Get them all in and sweat them, Teddy.'

'But, sir, there's definitely a problem here. I mean, what they were doing, it's hard to present it to people as being treasonous.'

'Well, it bloody well is, Teddy, believe me.'

'No court would convict. Kim?' Giles said, looking for support from his friend.

'Treason is a peculiar beast,' Philby said. 'It has many coats for many seasons.'

Dansey placed the porcelain figurine back on the marble mantel-piece. 'Oh, for heaven's sake,' he said. 'When you two scholars are finished your sophistry, I'd like your minds concentrated on the job in hand. God, the man might be in place to move at any moment.'

'No, he'll need time,' Giles said, 'for a job like that.'

'And now you're an expert in assassination, Teddy?' Dansey retorted. 'I really hope you don't react badly to tropical insect bites.' He thought for a moment while Giles tried not to look uneasy. Then he slapped his hands together. 'All right, Philby, you can go now,' he said. 'And for heaven's sake, go easy on Ben Kramer.'

He followed Philby to the door and stepped into the corridor with him.

Teddy Giles was pulling files from a briefcase and placing them on a glass coffee table when Dansey sat down again. 'Teddy,' he said. 'What do you think of Philby?'

'Oh, Kim's the best, sir. The best.'

Dansey muttered to himself. 'I expect you're probably right. I just wonder whether we're talking about the same thing.'

Giles was not listening. One of his files had fallen to the floor. He was picking up the typed pages. 'Sorry, sir?' he said.

'It doesn't matter. Just a pain in my gut. Probably more of the ravages of old age. I used to be a strong man, Teddy. So what have you got for me?'

'Well, at short notice and with everyone looking for qualified people at the moment, it's hard to come by any talent. Most of the German-speakers we have are either communists or Jews, or both, or ethnic German types – quite a few Swiss and the like – who'd sell their own grandmothers for the right price.'

'I have a great affinity for the Swiss,' Dansey said.

Giles grinned.

'Well, I went through the Pioneer Corps first but had to drop everyone there because we're looking for people who have some kind of training in this work. There isn't time to train them. So, the obvious areas for trawling were our German section, SOE's German Section and No. 10 Inter-Allied Commando's No. 3, Miscellaneous, Troop. X Troop. With all its various Germans and ethnic Germans and so forth. Actually, Maurice Hallan and Ben Kramer had most of the files one way or another. Now SOE's German section is full of communists and assorted Reds of all kinds. I mean, that place seems like a branch office of the communist international at times.'

'That's something I'm not unaware of,' Dansey said.

'They've been liaising with the NKVD, dropping German communists in for them. Not terrifically successful but it keeps us in contact with our Soviet allies and the firm has been taking advantage of the situation to try and recruit potential for the coming post-war era. And therein lies our problem with them. The ones we might rely on we don't want to expose and the ones we might expose we can't rely on. No. 10 Commando's X Troop has a few people who have done this kind of work for us, but most are ethnic Germans who speak with various accents and are ignorant of the area in question. Most of the genuine Germans in No. 10 Commando are Jews or left-wingers with records as long as your arm who haven't been in Germany since 1933. So you see our problems?'

'There is a point to this lecture, Teddy?'

'Well, yes, sir, I was coming to it.'

'I am running against a deadline.'

Giles picked up a few files. 'These,' he said. 'I have gone through everything we have and they're the only ones who come near to requirement. Deficiencies taken into account. The hazardous nature of the operation means that we can afford to be less than careful.'

He took out a single file. 'And she's particularly interesting if you tie it in with this.'

In Germany at that moment, a balding thirty-four-year-old diplomat broke pieces of ersatz bread in his hand very slowly while he looked out of the window at a deserted lake shoreline south of Berlin. When he had eaten the bread he rubbed the base of his neck and sighed because he had a headache he could not shift; he had been ill on and off for a few months and working too hard, and he had just returned from an unplanned overnight trip to Switzerland.

Together with the other two men in the drawing room of the lakeside villa that evening, Adam Von Trott Zu Soltz was at the centre of a growing conspiracy to overthrow the Nazi regime in Germany. By the spring of 1944, a number of disparate conspiracies had coalesced into a definite structure based around the War Ministry buildings in Bendlerstrasse, Berlin. Von Trott had emerged as their foreign policy adviser.

'This is the British.'

'It is all of them, Claus,' Von Trott said. 'Dulles was the main speaker. The British man hardly said a word. Just nodded the way their Foreign Office people always do when they know they have you.'

Colonel Claus Von Stauffenberg scratched his right arm at the stump where his hand used to be, and stood up. Two years older than Von Trott, and terribly wounded in North Africa, Von Stauffenberg was the engine of the Bendlerstrasse conspiracy. In October 1943 he had been posted as chief of staff of the General Army Office in Berlin. While Von Trott had been an anti-Nazi from the first, Von Stauffenberg more typically represented his class in that he had, at first, welcomed the order brought by the new regime and only very slowly came to the realisation that the nature of Nazism made it impossible to tolerate in any shape or form. This late conversion accounted for his zeal.

'My God, we only just agreed to hold action until a landing had been forced in France. We agreed to that even though it meant wishing for German defeat on the battlefield. They asked for that as a proof of our bona fides and we agreed; but this, this is insane. Insane.'

'Not from their point of view, Claus; it's what we've been peddling to them for months now – the Russian threat. At least we know now they believe it. Think, Claus, they're offering us what we want.'

Von Stauffenberg rearranged the patch covering his left eye socket before putting his hand on Von Trott's shoulder. Then he turned from the window suddenly. 'Martin?'

Major Martin Hofer had been head of the Tod programme at Abwehr Two since his predecessor, Kurt Richter, had taken his own life in preference to Gestapo interrogation.

The son of a career diplomat who committed suicide and a Swedish mother who died of hepatitis while running guns to Mexican rebels, Hofer was born in Switzerland and raised in Germany by his grandparents. He flew fighters while under age in the First World War and won the Blue Max, prospected for diamonds in South Africa in the twenties, flirted with the Nazis in the early thirties, and joined the Abwehr soon after Hitler came to power.

He was involved in the occupations of Austria, Czechoslovakia, Poland and France, and advised the Franco Government in Spain during the Civil War before his private epiphany in Russia in 1942.

Wounded in an air accident, he was being transported by train, drifting in and out of consciousness, when he witnessed the clearing of a Jewish village by an SS *einsatztruppe*. At first he thought he had been dreaming, but the images of the long line of children shot in the back of the head by smiling SS soldiers kept returning. He joined the Abwehr end of the conspiracy against Hitler on his return to duty.

'Claude Dansey,' Hofer said. 'This has Claude Dansey written all over it.'

'He is your man?' Von Stauffenberg asked. 'This . . . this Valkyrie?'

'If it's him, yes. The code number corresponds. Richter seems to have given them a library of Tod material.'

'And he uses our codeword. It's a bad joke,' Von Stauffenberg said.

'The British and Americans will deal with us, something we've been begging for, if we do this for them' Von Trott said. 'And what chance has this assassin anyway?'

'He got this close to killing Stalin in 1941,' Hofer said. 'The Führer called it off. Didn't want to tempt providence.'

'My God,' Stauffenberg said. 'Then he could do it?'

'Yes,' Hofer said. 'But Adam's right. It has to be stopped. For Germany's sake. Believe me, Claus, my heart says yes, let it happen, but my head says go for the deal with the Anglo-Americans. This is difficult, Claus, very difficult.'

Von Stauffenberg shook his head and sat down.

'Do you think they'll stick to their offer to deal with us, Adam?' Hofer asked.

'I don't know, Martin, I don't know. But it's better than what we've been facing. Makes us respectable.'

Hofer exhaled slowly, the way condemned men do when they are trying to cope with the sentence.

'Just like that?' Von Stauffenberg said. 'They just call up and offer us conditions we have been begging them to accept. What if it's some kind of disinformation trick?'

'No, they were very clear, Claus. Almost courteous, definitely anxious, I'd say. I've never seen them so mannerly around me, and so nervous.'

Hofer slapped his hands. 'A delicate situation,' he said.

'Delicate? This is positively gossamer,' Von Stauffenberg said. 'And what if we do not get a chance when the British and Americans have landed in France? My God, I feel like a traitor. Breitenbuch ... he should have done it, no matter what. He was right there in the Berghof, but he lost his damn nerve. And now we're tied to our word and a heap of promises. This could be the only real chance we ever have, this Jew-hired assassin. Long shot and all as it is ... The Führer isn't a man to lend himself to assassination, is he?'

'So what do we do?' Hofer asked.

Von Stauffenberg shook his head.

'What can we do, Martin?' Von Trott said. 'We need to deal. It's no good toppling the Führer if the Western Allies treat us the same way as they treat him. We're trying to save Germany, gentlemen.'

'It's a change having them relying on us,' Von Stauffenberg said.

'Dulles sounded like he had discovered the Third Secret of Fatima,' Von Trott said.

'Always a bit slow, the Americans ... we've known the Third Secret of Fatima since 1918,' Hofer said. 'You want me to tell you?'

'No!' Von Trott said. 'You'll have to go to Schellenberg, Martin. It's got to come from Abwehr sources to be believable. Abwehr Two Tod is perfect. And perhaps it will win the Abwehr some space before it is packaged and taken over by Schellenberg's gang. Claus?'

Von Stauffenberg just kept nodding.

In Munich that evening, Erich Haas passed a heavily bombed building on the corner of a small street between the Englischer Garten and

Leopoldstrasse. He wore a brown coat and a felt hat and carried a small leather suitcase. A group of women were searching the rubble of the bombed-out building and there was a banner, with '*Es Liebe Deutschland*' written on it, draped from the remains of the building. A lone *ordnungspolizei* private stood at the opposite corner of the street. He wore the ribbon of an Iron Cross, second class, across the buttonhole of his uniform, a silver wound badge, which indicated he had been wounded more than once and less than five times, and a Winter War ribbon.

The orpo rubbed some dust from his blue uniform and looked at Haas. Haas nodded. The orpo nodded back.

The pension was down a lane beside a small shoe shop. The shoe shop had closed. There was a furniture workshop beside it but it was burnt out. Some boys were scavenging inside. One boy held half a dozen cigarette ends in one hand. They were made from cork and wood shavings and pieces of rotten vegetable matter and plant roots, and they tasted like poison.

The woman who answered the pension door was sixtyish and somewhat thinner than she might be. She carried a copy of *Volkischer Beobachter*, the Nazi Party newspaper, under her arm, and she had a pair of cracked spectacles hanging from her neck by an old piece of twine. Haas bowed.

'Frau Gern? Frau Gerda Gern?'

The woman nodded.

'I believe you have rooms,' Haas said.

She nodded again and kept looking him up and down.

'Yes. For how long?' she asked.

'Perhaps a week, no more than two, I think.'

She looked over his shoulder. 'I can't give you breakfast. And I only have a double room free. And no refunds for having to go to the shelters.'

'Fine, fine, I'll take the double.'

'You're a traveller?'

'Of sorts. Karl Rotach. I am a book-binder. Herr Weg, Herr Max Weg, you know him? He recommended you.'

'Yes, I know Herr Weg. And you are his friend? Yes . . . yes!'

'Acquaintance. I met him the last time I was in Munich. I do work for him and others. It was before all this. Quite a mess. But not as bad as Berlin. You should see Berlin.'

'It is bad enough.'

He pulled out an *ausweis* and showed it to her. The woman pulled on her glasses and looked at the document.

'You'd better come in. The British might come tonight. You must have been out during the alert this morning.'

'I took shelter.'

'Well, we have a shelter in the basement and there's a shelter down the street. I don't like it. I have mattresses down in the basement but I charge for them. Night isn't so bad now. The British have not been around these parts for a couple of weeks. We hit them heavily when they came to Nuremberg.' She touched her paper. There was an article by Josef Goebbels in it. 'Perhaps the Reichsminister is right and they are being turned.'

Haas nodded.

'You are in Munich to repair books?' she asked when he was inside. 'I would not have thought there was much need for books these days.'

She looked at him. Like Max Weg, she was a blockwart, one of the thousands of Gestapo informers who kept the secret police abreast of what went on behind the closed doors of the Greater German Reich's hotels and apartment blocks.

'I have to earn a living. I have various clients – private, universities, technical colleges and schools,' he said. 'I travel once or twice a year. I have an interest in antiquarian books, too. That's how I know Max. We still do business.'

'He's a strange one. I think he has private money. Have you?'

'No. There are times when I wish I did.'

'Don't we all. These are difficult times.'

She led him up two flights of dusty wooden stairs and in through a door that had taken a large fragment through the centre and was patched up with newspaper. Inside, there was a foyer of sorts, a semi-circular counter with a bell on it and some pre-war tourist brochures, covered in fine dust. There was an acrid smell. The woman went behind the counter. 'I must see all your documents.'

'Of course.'

'You are aware of all the restrictions?'

'Yes. I travel all over the Reich.'

'Fill in this, please, it's for the police. There is a station two streets that way. The officer in charge is a friend of mine. He may call. But he relies on me.'

'Indeed.'

'You will fill out this form, too, please. For me. I will keep this until you are ready to leave. Now, where's that key?'

Haas filled out the personal details form in a block script and handed it back to Gerda Gern.

'Why are you not at the front?' she asked.

Haas held her gaze. 'I was at the front. Some of me is still at the front. Which is why I am no longer at the front. My discharge papers are inside the *urlaubschein*.'

She coughed. 'Food coupons?' she asked.

'I have enough,' he said. 'I will eat at restaurants where they are not needed. And Herr Weg has invited me to share his rations.'

'Yes, well, I think you will not do too much business here, Herr Rotach. People have other concerns. Books . . .'

'I see nothing but resilience here. I think you don't give the people of Munich enough credit, madam. Here's my card, in case you wish to request something of me. My mother company's Swiss, I'm afraid. That's a Zurich address. But we have good contacts around Europe. I've heard we've even done books for the Reichsmarschall.'

Frau Gern reddened slightly. 'I do not have time to read anything except the newspapers, Herr Rotach,' she said. She rang the bell on the desk. 'This is my daughter, Ilse. Ilse, show the gentleman to room number three, please.'

Ilse Gern was wearing glasses and a scarf around her neck. Her sandy hair, off-blue eyes and sad, vulnerable mouth drew Haas to her before he could stop himself.

'*Gruss Gott*,' she said.

Haas was still looking at her, letting his eyes dally on the way, watching her tongue touch her upper lip which had dried suddenly. She stepped forward and took Haas's bag and then turned. Haas looked at the mother, smiled and followed the daughter.

'Oh, Herr Rotach, if you wish to eat free of coupons . . .'

Haas stopped and turned to Gerda Gern.

'Yes, well there's a restaurant down the street with soup and potatoes. The bread is like the coffee and the cigarettes ersatz. I think we have been eating paper bread since 1942.' She grinned. 'My humour has been described as inappropriate. You can get other things to eat, of course . . .'

Haas came almost to attention. 'Black market trading is a serious offence, Frau Gern. I am here to deal in books, not to face a criminal trial.'

Her face became impassive and when she had regained herself she frowned. 'Enjoy your stay,' she said.

A man in Waffen-SS uniform, with the cuffband of the Germania Division, came out of one of the rooms along the corridor and nodded to Haas. He looked Ilse Gern over and smiled at her. Haas made a note of the man's size.

'Ah, Herr Untersturmführer!' Frau Gern said to the SS officer. 'Good evening!' He did not reply.

Ilse Gern put Haas's leather case on the single bed in the room. The room was not much bigger than the bed; there was a table and chair stuffed into one corner and a walnut wardrobe in another.

'The water doesn't always work, so if you need some please take the basin down to me or my mother.' She pointed to the enamel basin under the small wash-basin.

'And if the electricity goes, there are candles in the drawer beside the bed. Please do not use them for anything else, they are hard to get now. We close the shutters at night for the blackout. It is best not be out after dark. There are gangs in Munich now. They are orphans or refugees from up north and they live in the ruins and elsewhere. The police find it hard to catch them. If there is anything else?'

Haas shook his head. 'I see you wear a wedding ring,' he said.

'My husband is dead.'

'I'm sorry, it was stupid of me. I was just trying to be polite. Make conversation.'

'Men do it with me all the time. They think because I am here I am available. And men who stay in hotels want women who are available.'

'I'm not like that.'

'Why aren't you in the army? You must be of age.'

'As I told your mother, I was invalided out. Some of my stomach is misplaced. The Russians.'

'My husband died there.'

'I've said I'm sorry.'

'He was always shaking. You don't shake. For a man with severe wounds.'

'I will try.'

'Now I am the one who should say sorry.'

'I wouldn't be so hard on your husband. If he was in Russia then he will still be shaking wherever he is.'

'We have not had it so bad here in Munich. Their long-range fighters come here, but we have not had a really heavy raid since last autumn. It is the refugees who are becoming the problem. Many people come to Munich to get away from the bombing up north. Even the Führer, they say. He is up at Berchtesgaden now. They say he has a mistress and he will not come down until the bombing has stopped.'

'I don't think your mother would approve of what you are saying.'

'I don't care. My mother works for the Gestapo because she can get food out of it. And when someone else comes along she will probably work for them. That's my mother. My husband was a believer. In Hitler. He was in the Luftwaffe but he fought on the ground – a gunner. I miss him. You will find it easier to get things here than in Berlin. Many things still come in from Switzerland.'

'If I want to take a bath?' Haas said.

'The bathroom is down the hall on this side. Please only use the amount of water marked on the side of the bath. We are trying to conserve.'

Ilse Gern went to leave the room but held herself at the door and watched Haas take off his coat and scarf and place them over the bed. He then lifted a suitcase on to the bed, opened it it and took out a bar of soap. He looked over at her.

'You want some?' he asked. 'I can spare it. I get it from a cousin. Between you and me.'

He took out a knife and unfolded it and cut some soap from the bar and handed it to her.

'No, thank you,' she said. 'Were you really in the army, Herr Rotach? Or do you have a friend or a relative who keeps you in a safe job? You and my mother should get on well. Very well.'

And she left.

Haas locked the door.

6

CLAUDE DANSEY HAD just thrown a pencil across his office on the fourth floor of Broadway Buildings when the phone rang. He listened, put the phone down, got up from his desk, picked up the pencil, scribbled a note, put on his long black coat and left.

He crossed the road, entered the St James's Park underground station and caught a westbound train to Victoria.

At Victoria, he almost fell over a family that had been sleeping in the tube tunnels. The smell of over-stewed tea and human body odours danced tangos with his senses and Dansey found himself cursing as he climbed the steps out of the station. When he reached the top, he stopped, looked around and then crossed to Vauxhall Bridge Road and headed into Pimlico.

The hotel was leaning to one side and the paint on the walls was flaking. The walls were pockmarked with shell splinter holes. Most of the windows had paper stuck across them in lines to prevent shattering. Dansey walked in past the man at the desk, nodded and headed upstairs. Three flights later, he crossed a small landing and knocked on a brown door.

Teddy Giles opened the door just enough to allow Dansey through. The room was bare except for three lounge chairs, a small coffee table and a single bed in the corner. Dansey took his coat off without looking at the woman in the corner.

She was in her early thirties, about five six and blonde. Her face was hard and unattractive, her dull grey eyes being slightly too far apart and her cheeks uneven. Her body was linear and squat at the middle and she wore a brown uniform without any insignia as if it did not belong to her.

Dansey gestured to her.

The woman sat down. Dansey let his eyes run down her legs because they were the best thing she had and it might make a difference. Then he looked at the rest of her again and decided the legs did not make up for what was lacking elsewhere.

'Ruth Wachs . . . born 1916 in Ulm . . . Jewish. Father beaten up by stormtroopers, 1933, family moved to Vienna. You fought with the communists there in 1934? And with the Reds in Spain in 1936?'

'I fought fascism. I fight fascism,' Ruth Wachs said.

'You were married to a poet – an American in Spain – and stayed behind to nurse him even at the risk of your own life. Foolish.'

'He was my husband. And I escaped.'

She had. And made her way to Paris. When France was overrun, she joined a resistance group as a courier. In 1942, she began operating as an organiser for the Special Operations Executive, until an ambush led to her circuit being almost completely wiped out.

'You went back after the ambush,' Dansey went on.

'I was needed,' she said.

In January 1943 she was part of a team dropped into France to blow up a radar installation; the mission was successful but in the fighting retreat only Wachs made it back alive.

Later that year she was part of a mission in Italy charged with destroying a bridge. She ended up being stretchered out by boat with a bullet in her back.

She had been recuperating ever since.

'You have never been back inside the Greater German Reich?' Dansey asked.

'I have never been sent,' Wachs replied.

'It has been a long time, then?'

'It's not a place you forget.'

'But you are a Jew.'

'And you are perceptive.'

'Don't be facetious.'

'The last time one of you people talked to me like this I was shot in the back. It is a sobering experience.'

'Which you do not wish to repeat?'

'To be quite honest, no. But then I'm here. And there's a war on. And I want to win it. We lost in Vienna and Spain, I'm tired of losing.'

'Tell me, do you know Munich well?'

'I grew up nearby. It's all in my records.'

'Answer my questions,' Dansey said. 'I have a job. But I'm not sure if you're the right person for the job.'

'You have a thing about women?'

'Not *per se*.'

'I know your argument,' Wachs said. 'Yes, a good-looking woman attracts attention. But I am not a good-looking woman. You never once looked into my eyes during this conversation. And I work on it. I never attract attention. Not even so much as a wolf whistle. I speak seven languages, I can shoot things you can't see and I would have been a doctor if Hitler had not taken a keen interest in my education.'

'You have killed many people?'

'Enough.'

'You have any problems there?'

'Not now. It's an acquired taste.'

'You're a communist. I don't like communists. In some ways they're worse than bloody fascists. They have a creed that is positively religious in its beneficence but brutal in its imposition. It attracts soft-headed writers and intellectuals who are desperate for theories of everything and economics lunatics who want palliatives which will bring about Utopia.'

'I'm not a communist any more. And I hate the Nazis far more than I ever loved communism. I do not believe in creeds. I want to win this war. I've been fighting a long time.'

Dansey put down the papers and thought for a few seconds. 'I have someone I want killed,' he said.

'In Germany?'

'It is critical that it is done, even at the cost of your own life. I tell you this because I need someone who will go on to the bitter end.'

'And I am that person?' Wachs asked.

'Your record says you might be. Anyway, I have very little time and even less choice. He's in Munich. I want him located and killed very quickly.'

'Located and killed? You sound unsure.'

'It is a developing situation.'

'So, why does he have to die?'

Dansey looked over at Teddy Giles, who dipped his head as if he wanted no part of this. 'Because he will make an attempt on the life of Adolf Hitler. And we do not want that.'

'You're joking?' Wachs said.

'I don't joke about such things.'

'Well, forget it.'

'I thought you might be difficult.' he said. 'Please, look at this.'

He picked up another file and handed it to her. 'Simon Wachs,' he said, 'is your brother, yes?'

She began to read the typed papers and nodded at the same time.

'Seems he's got himself mixed up with those Stern Gang radicals in Palestine, Ruth. That policeman shot the other day in Tel Aviv, your brother was caught with the smoking gun in his possession. It's enough to hang him.'

She stopped reading. 'You bastard,' she said without looking at him.

'Save it for the policeman's widow. I am merely forced to do things, Miss Wachs, where there are greater considerations. If you co-operate, brother Simon can be charged with manslaughter; if not, he swings. It's that simple. And I will have you interned in solitary for the duration of the war. If necessary, I will have you killed. So we understand one another. You're technically an enemy national and I am always wary of enemy nationals, especially Germans, no matter what their political hue.'

Wachs read some more and then stared at Dansey for a while.

'It's not something I wanted to do,' Dansey went on. 'Your brother deserves to hang. But I have responsibilities. So, take it or leave it, now.'

Wachs forced a pathetic grin. 'That is, as they say, an offer a girl can hardly refuse,' she said, putting her brother's file down. She picked up a packet of Players cigarettes and lit one. 'Why don't you just tell the Germans, let them do the dirty work?'

'Because I want you to do it. With no fuss.'

'And I'm expendable?'

'If you like.'

'So tell me about it,' she said.

And he did.

When Dansey had finished, Teddy Giles gave Wachs a dossier on Erich Haas. Dansey rang down for some tea.

'Why is he going to kill Hitler?' Wachs asked then.

'Not your concern,' Dansey said.

'Why do you want him stopped?'

Dansey smiled. 'I bet you do this for amusement,' he said. 'You know he's their biggest strategic liability. Hitler. Think about it. Without him, they might be doing far better and we would not be having this conversation.'

'Your logic has a certain inescapability, but I suspect it's a veil. If this was April First, I'd say you were playing a practical joke.'

'I assure you, this is no joke,' Dansey said.

'I met him, you know . . .'

'Valkyrie?' Giles said with some disbelief.

'No, Hitler. Years ago. Before he came to power. I was a small girl and we were out for a walk in the country and I got separated. There was a group of men in *lederhosen*, talking. They found me and took me down the mountain to an inn. One of them was Adolf Hitler. He held my hand and gave me sweets and bought me a cold lemonade and talked to me. He did not know we were Jewish. None of my family looks Jewish. And when my mother and father came along he told them to watch me in future or I would be difficult. I did not know who he was then. I saw him later on a newsreel and I knew then. He was a nice man in 1925, I thought.'

'I have a selection of people for you to look at,' Dansey said. 'I want your selection in an hour. But they are not to know the reason for the operation.'

'So I am to save Adolf Hitler's life? Even at the expense of my own? You have to admit, there's a deliciousness in that. I sometimes wonder if the world is really a fair place.'

'Indeed,' Dansey said.

And he thought of something and grinned.

Otto Ohlendorf was tempted to grin. Instead he scratched his chin, as if Martin Hofer had just given him a bad weather forecast. Hofer studied the general's face and came to the conclusion that it held at least two, if not more, separate personalities.

Hofer had gone to Walter Schellenberg's office in Berkaerstrasse that morning, only to be confronted with Ohlendorf too. Hofer was convinced their offices were connected by tunnel. And somewhere in the back of his mind was the feeling he had made a mistake.

'We do get information concerning attempts on the Führer's life almost hourly now, Hofer,' Ohlendorf said. 'In fact, I have a statistic here which puts it up there with sightings of Rudolf Hess and escaped prisoners-of-war in our league table of informants' titbits.'

'With due respect, Herr Gruppenführer, Abwehr Two, Tod, can hardly be equated with society informants, however important the latter are to SD Inland's operations.'

'Respect and point duly noted. And you have not informed Brigadeführer Rattenhuber at Führer headquarters, or Gruppenführer Müller in Prinz Albrechtstrasse 8? Why not?'

'I thought it best, given the Abwehr's soon-to-be-close links with SD Ausland, to approach Gruppenführer Schellenberg first. Abwehr Two, Tod's work is very sensitive and the less people who know the origin of the information the less likely a compromise.'

Schellenberg grinned his boyish grin and tapped the table. 'So how did you come by this assassin tale?' he asked Hofer.

'It is no tale, sir. It is genuine. Abwehr One is not the only organisation with access to information. Abwehr Two, Tod, has its own contacts. Even more sensitive in many ways because of the nature of our work. You are aware of how we work . . . deep penetration, infiltration . . .'

'Are you saying you have a man in England with access to information like this?'

'Merely answering that would compromise existing Tod operations, sir.'

Schellenberg nodded and sighed.

'It's all very fantastic, Hofer,' Ohlendorf said. 'The British hiring one of your men to kill the Führer.

'I have made a sketch from memory,' Hofer said. 'And I have given you the address in Munich. It should be a simple case of watching the address and arresting whoever turns up.'

Hofer nodded at the sketch and the address of Max Weg's bookshop in Munich.

'Quite an artist. You should sit and chat with the Führer some day,' Ohlendorf said.

Schellenberg nodded. Then he picked up the sketch Hofer had made and looked at it. 'It would be helpful to know the full extent of your information and your sources, Hofer, without in any way compromising your agents in the field, God forbid. I appreciate their situation. You do realise the problems this creates for the Abwehr? If it is the case that this is a recorded defector, then your already difficult predicament may indeed become more precarious.

And since I am to inherit this I would appreciate it if we could limit the Abwehr's exposure to any further scandal. Who else knows about this in Abwehr Two?'

Hofer thought for a moment. 'No one. It's a direct source to case officer trade. And I did not think it appropriate to inform Oberst Baron Von Freytag-Loringhoven at this point, because technically my section has full autonomy inside Abwehr Two. Gentlemen, ordinarily I would have gone straight to the Gestapo and the RSD with such information, but given the delicacy of the situation vis-à-vis the Abwehr and the Reich Security Main Office, I felt it better to come to Gruppenführer Schellenberg. To ensure prompt action.'

'Very thoughtful,' Ohlendorf said. 'It all sounds a bit like that affair with the British last year before they invaded Sicily. The man in the water with the wrong information. Remember that, Walter? And it was the Abwehr who gave it the seal of approval. You boys have lost your touch, Hofer. You need a bit of SS ingenuity.'

'The Führer's not exactly unprotected, Hofer,' Schellenberg said.

'Begging your pardon, I don't think you quite understand how serious this is. This man will try to kill the Führer. I have no doubt of that.'

'We appreciate your concerns, Herr Major,' Schellenberg said. 'But if the British can plant a body with secret papers on it and make us believe they are going to invade the Balkans rather than Sicily, then perhaps they can do the same with this assassin business and have us chasing a ghost all over Germany. We have already spent valuable man-hours chasing scores of terrorist prisoners-of-war all over this Reich, man-hours which detract from our war effort. Think of that.'

'But, with respect, Herr Gruppenführer . . .'

'That's the second time you've said that, Hofer,' Ohlendorf said. 'You know, when a Wehrmacht officer uses the term "with respect", I'm inclined to laugh. You knew the Vehmerens who defected in Istanbul, didn't you? I mean, they were social companions of yours and those diplomats you call your friends. You know, Gruppenführer Müller would like to take ten or fifteen of those dandies and work on them with various gardening tools. But, alas, the Reichsführer is too fond of due process to allow that. Right, Walter?'

Hofer felt he was sweating. What did they know?

'You should realise in the Abwehr that the Reichsführer and the SD are on your side,' Schellenberg said. 'The little admiral would not be in his present position if he had borne that in mind. You see, the Reichsführer sees the whole picture – the mark of a statesman, don't you think?'

'I have never questioned the Reichsführer's competence. He has my full support and the support of the Abwehr,' Hofer said.

'Well, since the Abwehr is in the process of being wound up, I don't think the Reichsführer is particularly excited at that revelation, and as for your own loyalty, Hofer, you can best show that by obeying orders.'

Hofer was sure he was sweating now, but he felt he had to press the issue to help his case. 'If the Herr Gruppenführer believes . . .'

'Oh, spare me the indignation, Hofer,' Ohlendorf said. 'I know what goes on, everywhere in this Reich. I know what people are thinking before they think it. Do you understand me? Now it appears to me that what you are bringing to me is a fragment picked up from someone's waste. And I think to myself, perhaps the Abwehr just wants to embarrass the SD in front of the Führer. Possible, you will agree, given the tension between SD Ausland and the Abwehr. You see, embarrass the SD and it rubs off on the Reich Security Main Office and the SS and the Reichsführer.'

'Not at all, sir. I believe my information to be genuine. At least warranting serious investigation and surveillance.'

'And that will happen,' Schellenberg said.

'This killer,' Ohlendorf said then. 'I assume, as his case officer, you are probably the only person who can positively identify him.'

'Probably,' Hofer replied.

'Then we will need you,' Schellenberg said. 'Assuming our enquiries come up with something. However, we would appreciate discretion, Hofer. Tell no one else for the moment, not even your wife. How is your wife?'

Hofer felt very cold. He did not answer as it was not a question.

'Good,' Ohlendorf said. 'All right, dismissed. We'll be in touch.'

'But, Herr Gruppenführer, the time factor . . .'

'Dismissed.'

Ruth Wachs sat on the floor of a hotel bedroom in Paddington, examining a series of German handguns, and appropriate silencers. Walthers, Mausers, Lugers, they lay stripped on a green tarpaulin. Her gas mask container hung over the chair behind her with her jacket. She reached over and picked up a Walther P38 and began to handle it. Her skirt rose up and the man beside her stopped what he was saying and glanced down at her legs.

'I don't sleep with gentiles,' Wachs said.

'My great-grandfather was Jewish.'

'Do you have a foreskin?'

Paul Kaestner heard the laughter from the other man in the room; he frowned.

'I prefer my men without a hat, so to speak. It gives me more power.'

She stared into his eyes and he had to turn away.

Kaestner was thirty years old, a Sudeten German from Czechoslovakia who had trained to be a concert pianist in Berlin until the Nazis broke his fingers. He had fought with the Polish Army in France in 1940, been interned as an enemy alien when he came to Britain, then joined No. 10 Inter-Allied Commando.

In 1943, he was dropped into southern Austria to identify German Army units moving towards Italy; he survived for four months living alone in the mountains and was eventually picked up by submarine.

That winter, he was parachuted into Czechoslovakia to gather information on a factory making parts for the German rocket programme; the mission was betrayed in Prague and Kaestner only avoided capture and death by hiding in a small cubby-hole for five weeks, something he still refused to discuss.

He was a quiet man, with a face that verged on the ashen when he was angry. But he did not want to argue with Ruth Wachs now.

'We are running against the clock here,' Teddy Giles said. 'I'm under instruction to have you out of here this evening. So concentrate on your legends and your weapons.'

'I get seasick,' the third member of the team said. He smiled.

Mathius Schumann had once been a professional boxer and his face bore certain of the traces of his former calling. A member of the Hitler Youth, until he killed a fellow member in a knife fight, he had fled to America via Shanghai, where he fought the Japanese, and worked as a low-grade enforcer for one of the five Mafia families in New York. Then, in 1940, he murdered again and was forced to flee to Canada; arrested there, he was offered a choice – deportation and the electric chair or a job with British intelligence.

He had survived several raids behind German lines in North Africa and Italy, including the ill-fated attempt to blow Rommel's fuel supplies in Tobruk in 1942, and Ben Kramer and Maurice Hallan had even considered him as a potential assassin. They had rejected him for many of the reasons Dansey and Giles had offered him to Wachs.

'If we drop the three of you in by parachute, we stand a good chance of losing one of you,' Giles said. 'If we lose one of you it compromises the rest of you. The sea is the best way. If you stick to the timetables we've given you you'll be in Munich by the day after tomorrow. Your papers are good.'

'Tell me, Teddy,' Ruth Wachs said, 'have you ever been to Germany?'

Giles felt a certain inadequacy; his operational experience was limited to trying to blow up a dam in Romania in 1940. He pulled rank. 'I'd rather not have this conversation,' he said. 'Your legends and your weapons.'

'If I'm sick when we land in Brittany, the Nazis will know,' Schumann said. 'The Gestapo look out for such things.'

'Well, then don't be sick,' Ruth Wachs said.

'Or we'll have to kill you,' Paul Kaestner added.

He picked up a Mauser HSc, screwed a silencer onto it and loaded a magazine. 'I don't know why you picked me. I'm not a killer,' he said to Wachs. 'I'm not like him.'

Schumann stared at Kaestner. 'Hey, I'm not jumping about working with you. You look soft to me. I bet you're a commie like her.'

'Shut up, both of you,' Wachs said. 'I chose you because I need you.' She picked up a photograph of Erich Haas taken by MI5. 'Keep memorising this, every detail. We want to get the right man.'

'Who is he, anyway?' Schumann asked.

'None of your concern,' Giles said. 'Need to know and all that. You have your orders, you have his destination, you have your Joan-Eleanor transmitters.'

He picked up one of the small hand-held transmitters lying around the room. The Joan-Eleanor was the first real hand-held transmitter–receiver radio system available to Allied agents behind enemy lines. Developed by the OSS, it usually required a friendly aircraft flying overhead with a large transmitter, to which the agents on the ground could send and receive messages without the bother of carrying around the old bulky suitcase radios. SIS had adapted the Joan-Eleanor system to enable agents to contact one another within a small radius by simple Morse signals. The agent receiving the message did so by touching a small metal plate on the transmitter and received a series of tiny electric pulses through the fingers. There was no sound involved.

'Do I get conjugal rights?' Schumann said to Ruth Wachs. 'I mean we're married on the way in, and I like to live my legends to the full.'

Wachs picked up a silenced 1932 Mauser and fired it between Schumann's legs. It all happened so quickly that Giles dropped the cup he was holding and cursed.

'Now, you know how I like my men,' Wachs said. 'Clear?'

Schumann nodded and smiled.

'You want to take a Sten?' Teddy Giles asked then. He was ticking off a checklist.

'Teddy, leave the technicalities to us,' Wachs said. 'You just take care of logistics. No Stens. We're going to Munich. Stens stick out. Anyway, we need small reliable firepower. This address, Teddy, do you know what it is?'

'Boffins are tearing through street directories and the like, going over everything we have from the Munich area, but we may not have the time.'

'So we have an address and a mugshot which probably doesn't look like him and a city stuffed with people,' Schumann said. 'Simple.'

Giles watched them sort through weapons and decide who would carry what. When they had finished he took out a small tobacco tin and opened it.

'L-pills,' he said. 'Painless.'

Schumann began to say something but stopped himself.

'You have had people tell you this?' Kaestner asked. He picked one of the lethal pills out. He smiled. 'Look, I'm not interested in being caught. I've no more fingers for them to break.'

'All right, all right, enough fun . . . legends and weapons,' Wachs said. 'Let's see if we can upset their plans.'

Searchlights still combed the Bavarian sky and the odd anti-aircraft gun loosed off a shell in fear. The clouds had come in low and it was spitting rain. Haas smiled when Ilse Gern opened the pension door.

There was a gramophone playing in the background, a love song.

'I decided to bring him home myself,' Max Weg said. 'We were playing chess.'

'He beat me,' Haas said, pretending to be slightly drunk.

She nodded to him and he lifted his hat.

'Please . . .' she said, gesturing to them to come in.

Haas watched her walk ahead of him up the stairs. He was aware she knew he was watching and he felt a degree of pleasure in that.

Wilhelm Koch sat in a soft chair in a small room behind the check-in desk, reading a magazine. There was a colour photograph of a German soldier following a tank somewhere in Russia. It was summertime and the man's sleeves were rolled up.

'Wilhelm, Max is here,' Ilse Gern said.

The police inspector pulled himself out of his chair and threw on his jacket. And though he was smiling he looked a little bit uncomfortable. 'Max!' he said to cover his embarrassment. 'What has you here this time of night? You're not running a black market?'

Weg was even more surprised to see Koch there, but his face showed nothing. 'Alas, no, Willy. I am escorting a colleague from out of town. A fine chess player. Right, Karl?'

Haas laughed. 'Karl Rotach,' he said, putting his hand into Koch's. Koch shook it and looked at Ilse as if they were harbouring a terrible secret.

'Herr Rotach deals in books, too.'

'Another bloody scholar,' Koch said.

'Willy is a cop,' Max Weg said. 'So don't tell him about my illegal activities or we'll have a very cold night in one of his cells.'

'How many times do I have to tell you, Max, that's Gestapo stuff. The Kriminalpolizei don't work like that. Well, not unless ordered. Anyway, we're professionals. You ask your friends at the Brown House who they ring when their houses are robbed or their cars are stolen or their kids run off. They don't call the Wittelsbacher Palais, I'll tell you that. You in town for long, Herr Rotach?'

'A week or so, perhaps.'

'From . . .?'

Haas thought for a second. 'Berlin,' he said.

Koch shook his head. 'I believe things are very bad there. Yes?'

Haas thought again and looked around.

'It's okay, Karl, Willy's not going to report you for anything. Anyway, that's my job and I just might report him for drinking my not quite strictly legal stocks of Scotch and Bourbon. Karl was invalided out after Kursk. Now if you could spare me a hot drink, I'll make my way back home, Ilse. I've delivered your guest and my work is complete for tonight.'

'I have some wine. I could heat that.'

'Excellent. Karl? Willy?'

Koch looked at Ilse Gern and she nodded to him.

'A nightcap,' Haas said. 'Good thinking, Max. You haven't lost your touch. As long as we're not interrupting you two?'

'Oh, no, no,' Ilse Gern said.

'I was going anyway,' Koch said.

'Oh, well, then forget the drink, Ilse,' Weg said. 'If Willy is going he can escort me home. Police escort. The best.'

'Yeah, yeah, sure,' Koch said, aware that he sounded even more confused and out of control.

'We can have that drink some other time, Ilse,' Weg said. 'And I'll see you tomorrow, Karl.'

Koch was grabbing his coat and hat, and was about to follow Weg to the stairs when he turned to Haas. 'Herr Rotach, you play chess?'

'Moderately,' Haas said.

'Perhaps we could have a game.'

'Yes, if I have the time.'

Koch studied him again; Haas smiled.

In his room, Haas assembled his different papers and checked them and then replaced them in the false bottom of his suitcase. Then he took off his jacket and pulled the sleeve gun from a pocket in his right sleeve and placed it under his pillow. Finally, he took his suitcase and went over to the walnut wardrobe and placed it inside.

He had just lain down on the bed and was thinking about a nightmare he used to have as a child when the gentle knock on the door came.

'Yes,' he said.

'Herr Rotach, it's Ilse.'

Haas pulled himself up and walked over to the door and turned the key. He opened the door three seconds after turning the key.

'Oh, I'm sorry,' Ilse said. 'I didn't know you were asleep.'

'I wasn't.'

'I was boiling some milk – we have a relative, he's a farmer and he gives us more milk than we need – and I made too much. Would you like some?'

Her eyes were wide open the way Haas remembered young girls' eyes from years ago when he was at teenage dances. He looked her up and down and told himself to refuse the drink. 'Yes, that'd be nice,' he said.

Two minutes later she came back with a cup of hot milk. Haas sat on the bed and beckoned her into his room. She looked into the corridor and then half closed the door behind her.

Haas pulled his shirt over his vest and one of his braces over his shoulder and drank the hot milk and for a minute they stood watching each other, smiling, drinking milk.

'The inspector and I,' she said then, 'we are friends.'

'It's none of my business.'

'No, but in case you thought . . .'

'It's none of my business. He's a nice man.'

'Yes. I went to Berlin in '39 for a week with my husband. He didn't like it. Have you ever been to Rome?'

'Yes, I've been to Rome.'

'I don't like Rome. I liked Berlin.'

'Where's your mother?'

'We have an apartment . . . above Herr Weg's. But she is probably in the shelter – in the cellars. She likes to sleep there.'

'And the night porter?'

'He's on fire watch. Two or three days a week, I stay here.'

Haas looked at her for a while and told himself to say he was tired. 'It's good milk,' he said.

'When I was younger I wanted to go to many places but when I got to them I didn't like some of them. Have you a wife?'

Haas shook his head and Ilse then retreated from her question.

'Oh, I'm sorry. I'm so nosey. I like to know about people. It's what I like about this place. The world comes to you. I talk too much. You don't look like a book-binder.'

'What does a book-binder look like?'

'I don't know but I'm pretty good at these things. I have seen hundreds, maybe thousands of tradesmen, and you don't look like any of them. You look more like a soldier to me. If perhaps a little old.'

'Thank you. But that's over.'

'And now I'm a little tight. I have a bottle – I put it into the milk. You want some?'

He told himself to get rid of her. 'Sure,' he said, 'I'd like that.'

She slipped back down the corridor and came back with a bottle of white wine.

'What I was going to heat for Herr Weg,' she said. 'It helps me sleep. When there's a raid on, in Augsburg or somewhere like that, and the sirens are going in the night and our guns are firing, it's hard to sleep. The guns fire at nothing, all damn night. Did you hear it this evening?'

'I was playing chess.'

Ilse looked around the room as if she were thinking of something to say.

'Would you like to stay and talk?' he asked.

'Oh, no, I must stay at the desk.'

'I thought . . .'

'I'm sorry. I am tight. Maybe I can stay here for a while. Do you get frightened by the raids in Berlin?'

'You get used to it. I travel a lot. My job.'

She looked as if she were straining to keep the conversation going. 'Is it very bad there?' she asked.

'Some areas. Below the Tiergarten, near the Zoo, there's a lot of damage. It's patchy. Some places always get hit, some never get hit.'

'Sometimes I get excited by it. By a raid. I want to go out into the street and scream. Sometimes.'

'I understand. You carry an excitement in your eyes.'

She pulled her eyes away from him and stared into her milk for a while. The warmth running through her body held her there. And the alcohol was releasing more. 'So why do you not have to fight any more?' she asked suddenly in a changed tone. 'My husband was killed fighting. And you're here in our hotel, drinking our milk with our wine . . .'

'I'm sorry,' he said.

'Yes, I'll bet you are. I'll bet you damn well are.' She looked down at the floor again. 'I'm sorry, I'm sorry,' she said. 'I get tight and I say things I don't mean.'

'Sure you do. *In vino veritas.*'

'What's that?'

'It means you should go. Listen, I'll have to get some sleep. I have a lot of work to do. The book trade is depressed.'

He handed her his cup. She did not take it at first. Then she did. 'I'm sorry,' she said again. 'I don't want to be like that. I can't help it. I promise it won't happen again. I promise.'

He stood up and reached over and took her arms. 'It's okay. You're probably right,' he said. 'Has Herr Koch served at the front?'

'In the last war. He doesn't talk about it. We're not lovers. I let him touch me. It feels good . . .'

Haas reached up and touched her face and let his hand run down to her breast.

'You had a good day?' she asked.

He took his hand away. 'I must sleep.'

'They say the Führer has ordered the rebuilding of the Theatre. Do you like the theatre?' she asked.

'No,' he said.

It was a calculated negative. Ilse Gern felt slighted and showed it. Haas was aware his face was in danger of showing no emotion, something almost as bad as showing the wrong emotion in a situation like this. He faked a smile. 'I do not have time for it. I like to watch films when I can.'

'Oh, yes,' Ilse said. 'I like films. But it is so difficult.'

'Everything is difficult . . .'

There was a sound in the corridor and two voices. And Ilse Gern left the room.

7

MARTIN HOFER OPENED his eyes again and looked at his watch; it was two in the morning. He rubbed his eyes and stared at the two men in leather coats, standing at his apartment door.

'Herr Major Hofer,' the younger one said, 'SD – Inland. Would you please get dressed. You must accompany us.'

'Where?'

'Get dressed, Herr Major,' the older man said. He was very square and his eyes looked like frosted glass. He showed identification and then pushed his way in. The younger man with him shoved his hand into his trenchcoat pocket and pulled out a small Mauser pistol. 'Inside, Herr Major.'

'Look, what's happening? What's the charge?'

'Let's begin with activities contrary to the security and well-being of the state. Put your trousers on.'

The older SD man went into Hofer's bedroom and took his uniform and threw it at him. 'Put it on, please.'

Hofer began to dress and the younger SD man went to the window and looked out.

'Are you taking me to Wilhelmstrasse?' Hofer asked. He waited a few seconds. 'To Ohlendorf? To Prinz Albrechtstrasse?'

The older man smiled and lit a cigarette. He sat on the arm of a chair and smoked while Hofer fumbled with his clothes.

'Field Marshal Keitel will not be pleased,' Hofer said then. 'I am a Wehrmacht officer. Not under SS jurisdiction.'

'Shut up and put your damn uniform on properly. As you say, you're a German officer, Herr Major. Try and look like one.'

Hofer was beginning to shiver with fear. He had heard of this so

113

many times, people he had known, or known of, being taken away, vanishing.

'*Nacht und Nebel*?' he said then. 'Is this *Nacht und Nebel*?'

In 1941, Hitler had issued his decree whereby people perceived to be endangering German security, who were not to be executed immediately, could be made to vanish without trace into the night and fog.

'You ask too many questions for a traitor, Herr Major,' the older SD man said.

'I am a Wehrmacht officer. If I am to be charged it must be by military court. If I am to be arrested it must be by military police.'

'Of course, of course,' the older SD man said then. 'You hear that, Werner? You're the lawyer. Tell him.'

Werner thought for a while before he spoke. 'Well, it's like this, Herr Major. The Abwehr is being absorbed into SD Ausland; SD Ausland is a department of the Reich Security Main Office; the Reich Security Main Office is the concern of the Reichsführer SS, therefore you are the concern of the SS. Which is why we are here, Herr Major. Bring your coat. It's chilly. There's a fog outside.'

'I wish to make a telephone call to Zossen; I wish to contact Oberst Von Freytag-Loringhoven or Oberst Georg Hansen.'

'Disturb such distinguished Abwehr officers at this time of the morning? I think not, Herr Major. Perhaps later, when they're available. Had their beauty sleep, so to speak.'

Hofer tried to regain control of the situation. 'You would do well to consider what you are doing, Herr . . .?'

'I am Untersturmführer Werner Tor; and my colleague is Hauptsturmführer Alois Mann. No relation to the writer, thank God.'

'Well, Herr Untersturmführer, Herr Hauptsturmführer,' Hofer said, 'do you know who I am?'

The older SD agent pulled out a sheet of paper and read out a potted biography of Hofer. 'You have a pretty wife, Herr Major,' he said then. 'Probably covered in coal dust now, if she's in Silesia like it says here.'

'You bastard.'

'Accident of birth, Herr Major,' Mann said. 'You and your kind, however, seem to achieve the status under your own steam. Congratulations.'

Hofer thought about making a move for a pistol he kept in a

drawer to his left, but Werner Tor had his Mauser trained on him all the time. Mann shoved Hofer's head down when they were putting him into the back of the black car on the cobbled street below. He pulled out a pistol and the younger man put his away and got into the driver's seat.

'This is a mistake,' Hofer said. 'Something is very wrong here.'

'Funny, everyone says that. I wish people like you had better imaginations. But then perhaps an imagination is not what you need to be a traitor. Particularly when one considers the terrible price demanded by the Führer. Terrible, Werner?'

'Terrible, Alois.'

'Listen,' Hofer said, 'I have discovered a plot against the Führer. There's an assassin . . .'

'There's always an assassin,' Tor said, 'so shut up, please. You think we like these early morning duties? We have wives, too, Herr Major, and right now I'd like to be with mine. No offence intended. Come on, let's get this over with.'

Hofer tried to stop himself shaking.

Claude Dansey had fallen asleep. He woke suddenly in a puddle of lazy yellow light from a green desk lamp and took a sip of stagnant water from a beaded glass. Then he continued sifting through a series of dog-eared reports from an empire where the sun seemed to take pleasure in setting early now, occasionally glancing at his blackout curtain, shuffling in the draught of an ever so slightly open window. Outside, the ungrateful weather spat small drops of spite at the window pane.

His body felt giddy and his leg trembled. For a man who was almost seventy, Dansey could put in a tremendous amount of work in a day, but the back end was mortgaged to this excess several times over and the bank of human life was drawing close to calling in its loan.

He sifted through the reports like a high-speed camera; now and again he would mark something with a cryptic note.

The knock on the door announced Teddy Giles almost at the same time as the balding head put its sheen into Dansey's office.

'Yes, Teddy?' Dansey said, intending to intimidate.

'Just to say they're over, sir,' Giles said, holding his own. 'Landed about half an hour ago.'

'Keep me informed. Any news from Germany?'

'Nothing more since Swiss station made contact.' He scratched his nose. 'It's a funny old world we live in, sir.'

'Curious, Teddy. Just curious. Look, I can't make it to Maurice Hallan's funeral tomorrow. Will you go along.'

'Are we giving him honours?'

'No. Just to see who turns up. Five will have it covered anyway, but we should have a presence. You ever feel powerless, Teddy?'

'Always, sir.'

'It's not a feeling I'm comfortable with. I've spent all my life watching power work. I like the feel of it, I like the moves it makes. You remember that.'

'All the time, sir. We're beginning to get disturbing rumours from Budapest, sir.'

'I know, I've read it all. But two months from now hundreds of thousands of our troops will be wading ashore in France, Teddy, wet, sodden, under fire . . . I want that to be worthwhile. You see the point?'

'Russian advance seems to be slowing down.'

'Can't take the chance, Teddy. Philby got anything from Ben Kramer yet?'

'I don't think so, sir. But if anyone can, Kim can.'

'You're a real fan.'

'He's the best, sir. Kim.'

'C fancies him for the new Soviet desk.'

'Good choice.'

'I rather fancied Ben Kramer. Have you heard of the Manhattan Project, Teddy?'

'No, sir.'

'Well, I can tell you this, Teddy, if we don't settle Europe out with some degree of satisfaction, we're going to see destruction on such a scale . . .'

He shook his head and rubbed the hairs of his moustache and then took his glasses off.

'Anyway, I'll be dead . . .' he said then.

Martin Hofer's apartment was between Gneisnaustrasse and the Landwehr Kanal, in the Kreuzberg district of south central Berlin, and the SD car first turned on to Blucherstrasse and then right on to Belle Alliancestrasse at the Blucherplatz before crossing the canal and heading towards Friedrichstrasse.

Hofer could hear his heart beating now and feel his body shivering.

But the car did not swing left into Zimmer and Prinz Albrecht strasses; instead it continued on up Friedrichstrasse and turned right at the Weddingplatz fork for the road leading to Oranienburg. Mann smiled at Hofer.

'Where am I being taken?' Hofer asked for the fifth time. He never would have believed he could be so disappointed at not being taken to Prinz Albrechtstrasse. As they left the northern suburbs of Berlin and swung off the main road, he asked the question again.

'People get lost in fog,' Werner Tor said from the front seat. 'I am a lawyer, as you know. I know about evidence. You would do well to study the law. For instance, if there is no body in a murder, it is extremely difficult to prove a crime has taken place. You see, crime is such a relative thing. Some Jew scientist's idea. I'm not terrific on Jew ideas, they're always dirty. You religious, Herr Major?'

He drove for three-quarters of an hour, then pulled the car in off a road and up a dirt track into a forest. The temperature was down and Hofer figured they were near a lake.

'We have a long way to go,' Tor said. 'I think you should take a leak, Herr Major. So you don't piss all over us.'

The car stopped.

Hofer's mouth was dry when he stepped out of the car. The wind from the nearby lake caught him and unbalanced him. He watched Mann get out of the other side, keeping his Mauser trained on him over the top of the car.

'I think we'll take our leak over there, Herr Major,' Mann said. 'Back in a few minutes, Werner. Keep the engine running.'

He gestured with the pistol and then reached into his pocket and pulled out a Walther P38.

'Recognise this?' he said to Hofer. 'Yours, I believe.'

They walked into the trees, Hofer staring straight ahead, Alois Mann pushing the barrel of the P38 into his skull.

'Now, down on your knees. I believe you know the drill.'

'Do you know what department I run in the Abwehr?' Hofer asked.

'Does it matter? Oh, and I want you to know, this is personal, Herr Major. You're a traitor and, if you ask me, you're getting off easy.'

'I run the Tod programme. Killers.'

'I'm impressed. Now shut up.'

'You should be more than impressed. You made a big mistake, coming here alone, Herr Hauptsturmführer. I train killers who can take your life by looking at you.'

'Just shut up . . .'

Mann had cocked the P38 when he realised he had made a fundamental misjudgment. He had time to curse his superiors but nothing else.

Hofer brought a sharp stick up under his ribs and his left arm across the barrel of the P38; the pistol went off.

Mann was staggering, trying to get the P38 to bear on Hofer when the Abwehr man kicked the pistol from his hand and then slammed his boot into the dying SD man's chest. Finally, Hofer came up behind him and grabbed him around the neck, holding his left arm with his right hand. He twisted the neck violently and jerked Mann up. Mann twitched on the ground for a while.

A few minutes later, Werner Tor watched the man in the leather coat approach the car. He turned and grinned and began to say something. The bullet went through his right eye.

Ben Kramer was feeling weak, finding it harder to resist interrogation now. He sometimes wondered if he had given anything away without realising it. And then he thought of Erich Haas and it gave him strength. To some extent he had handed on his life to Haas.

The cell door opened very slowly.

'I have to ask you . . . so-me . . . more questions, Ben.'

'Go away, Philby.'

'It doesn't do to stay quiet with this service, you know that, Ben. We can be persuasive. It's not my particular bent but I believe we can do certain things, usually with drugs, and the effects are disturbing.'

'Don't threaten me, Philby. I'm a dead man anyway.'

'I can assure you, Ben . . .'

Kramer smiled and then started to laugh.

'You don't understand,' he said. 'I'm dying of cancer. A few months at most. Be a blessing, I suspect. Now let me sleep.'

Philby nodded. 'Maurice Hallan's dead,' he said. 'Committed suicide. You know you shouldn't have done it, Ben. Bad form really.'

'Like father, like son, eh, Kim?'

Philby turned and walked out. Kramer felt a weakness come over him and he had to close his eyes and wince to control himself. He concentrated on Erich Haas.

Since he had arrived in Munich, Erich Haas had been looking for tails, but that Tuesday only the Föhn followed him. The Föhn is a strange atmospheric occurrence peculiar to Munich and its environs which causes headaches and feelings of depression. And while he struggled with it, he never really knew why he decided to go ahead with the operation. Just once, while he was waiting for a bus, he whispered something to himself about why he was doing the job, but when he thought about it afterwards he was not sure he had. And he was still going through with it.

He left the Pension Gern while the night porter was still at his desk. The night porter was a surly balding man with a large lower lip and bloodshot eyes that gave the impression that he saw things other people did not.

When he left the pension, Haas walked very slowly towards Max Weg's shop. Now and again he stopped and checked and walked on. And when he reached the shop he stood across the street for a few minutes.

'I have selected these for you to carry,' Max Weg said. 'And for God's sake bring them back, they're valuable.'

He handed Haas three large books on mathematics printed between the seventeenth and eighteenth centuries. Haas placed the books into a small suitcase, also supplied by Weg, and snapped it shut.

'Here are the names you asked for; each of them is looking for a book-binder. They are all personal friends.'

'You'll be here tonight?' Haas asked.

'All night. If there's a raid, stay in a shelter, don't come here. The wardens clear us out and I will be required to urge people to their shelters. You are carrying a weapon?'

'No.'

'Good. Good luck. Be careful today. The Fohn makes people irritable.'

Haas was going to say something but he did not.

He took a tram to the centre of town and got off where the bombing had broken the tramlines and walked to the Hauptbahnhof.

The Hauptbahnhof was slightly punctured from the Allied bombing and smelling of high-explosive residue, coal dust and human body odours. Haas passed three soldiers asleep against a wall just inside the station concourse. A train was pulling in and more soldiers were leaning out of the windows, shouting at people on the platforms. Haas looked around and then went over to a restaurant marked '*Markenfreies Essen*', which meant it sold coupon-free meals.

The restaurant was nothing more than a canteen with a few broken tables around it. It was full of people in thick coats and every uniform of the German armed forces, but few of them were talking. There was one meal on offer, a thick stew. Haas stood behind two policemen, who were talking about a girl they both fancied. He listened to them and glanced across at a sign asking everyone with more than half an hour to wait to go into the underground waiting rooms. Another train came in and more soldiers got off.

He finished his stew quickly, bought a paper at a news stand and then ordered an ersatz coffee and drank it while reading the paper. When he was finished, he gave the paper to a soldier beside him, went over to the ticket desk and bought a second-class ticket to Kufstein, a small town just over the old Austrian border, west of Berchtesgaden. He checked his watch and bought another paper and then made his way to a platform on the right-hand side of the station.

The Innsbruck train left at nine, packed with soldiers, refugees and foreign workers. It travelled slowly through the flatlands south of Munich, and, after it met the Inn river at Rosenheim, began to climb into the glacial valleys of the Bavarian Alps. Three-quarters of an hour out, it was pounding along the line of the Inn river, in a long valley, flanked by alpine crags covered in pines, and the railway crisscrossed the river and the main road to Innsbruck while the blue sky gave way to flat clouds and rain and the Fohn gave up its pursuit of Haas for a time.

Haas sat by a window, across from a thin woman dressed in brown, who kept smiling at him. He smiled back but did not talk to her. He read his paper and then closed his eyes and then, almost two hours out, he saw a castle with pointed red roofs on the towers on a rocky crag above a small town where the River Inn had turned brown.

The police were checking papers at the station in Kufstein; but the rain had forced them indoors and they were just glancing at people's *ausweis* and travel permits. Two Luftwaffe officers and their girlfriends got into an argument with one of the orpos and one of the Luftwaffe officers kept shoving his Knight's Cross at the policemen. Haas managed to slip by, virtually unnoticed, during this argument.

Then the rain got heavier.

Haas crossed the Inn river by the Innsbrucke and turned right down cobbled streets towards the fortress. For a few minutes, he looked at the fortress, perched above the river, then he walked to the edge of town, stopped again and looked around him at the jagged limestone cliffs. Then he began walking towards Wörgl, the next town along the valley.

The river, to his right, was swollen with the spring rains and Haas listened to the sound of the water flowing while he walked. A Mercedes truck passed him and the driver nodded and Haas gave a small wave.

An hour and a half later, he was in Wörgl. He bought a ticket for Salzburg and took the late morning local train.

At St Johann in Tirol, a pretty resort town high up in the northern reaches of the Kitzbuhler Alpen, he got off the train, walked round the town once and down a road for about two kilometres – the Wilder Kaiser and the Kitzbuhler Horn either side of the town were his reference points – and then came back. No one paid any attention to him and except for a few *Gruss Gotts,* he went unnoticed.

He got on the next train for Salzburg and stared out of the left-side window as the train dipped south away from and then swung northeast towards Berchtesgadener Land, that area of southern Bavaria, centred on Berchtesgaden, which thrusts into Austria. In Hallein, which is about five kilometres from Berchtesgaden, he crossed the Salzach river and walked towards the old German–Austrian frontier before doubling back and taking another train a few more kilometres to Salzburg.

It was mid-afternoon. He found another coupon-free restaurant, had more stew and then went to a bar in the old town and had a beer. The rain had returned.

Once again, he crossed the Salzach river on foot and walked across Salzburg for about an hour until he reached the outskirts, near the autobahn to Munich. It was flat and desolate and the Schloss Klessheim in the distance, surrounded by a high wall, would have had a certain draw to it, if it weren't for the SS checkpoints surrounding it, the swastikas adorning it and the wide sweep of open ground around it. Haas made an instant decision and turned round before he was noticed.

He passed through a Gestapo checkpoint at the train station at about 4.30 in the afternoon.

* * *

Max Weg heard Wilhelm Koch's footsteps and then smelled him
before the inspector spoke. He was walking towards his shop that
afternoon, and found himself angry, but not at Koch.

'Worried, Willy?' he said, listening for a tone in the policeman's
breathing.

'Can I talk to you, Max?'

'Always. Time for a game of chess?'

'No, not really. It's about that fellow, Rotach.'

Weg felt his heart miss a beat. He hoped his face wasn't showing
any sign of what was going on inside him.

'What about him, Willy?'

'Well, how . . . how well do you know him?'

'Through business. That's all. He was in the Army.'

'Yes, I know, but how well . . .?'

'What do you mean?'

Koch looked around and then tapped his feet. Weg was waiting
to hear that Koch had sent an order for a records trace to Berlin.
He could feel his own pulse in his ear, as if the artery were going
to explode.

'Do you think he's interested in Ilse?' Koch asked then.

Weg started to laugh and the release made him laugh more. He
slapped Koch on the back. 'Oh, no, no. As far as I know he has
someone in Berlin. A secretary, I think. And he's been married, I
believe.'

Koch was smiling now. Nodding his head and smiling. 'Good,
good, that's good.' he said. 'It's just . . .'

'Oh, it's always just . . .'

'Yes, isn't it? Listen, I'll try and get away for a game this evening
if I can.'

'If I'm not at the shop, I'll be at my apartment.'

'And he's not interested, you think?'

'No. He'll be gone in a matter of days. Another town . . .'

'Good. I was going a bit crazy. Going to ask for any records we
have on him. Crazy, eh?'

'You like her, don't you?'

'Yes. She makes me feel clean. It was just the way she looked at
him last night.'

'Don't worry about Karl. He'd have said something if he was interested. Anyway, he's a book-binder, and you know how unromantic
we are in our trade.'

'What would I do without you, Max?'
'Win at chess, I suppose.'
They both laughed.

Adolf Hitler was just about to pick up another cream cake and bite
into it when the rodentine features on the face of his chief adjutant,
Gruppenführer Julius Schaub, broke the slivers of sunlight that had
managed to slip into the Berghof salon through the camouflage netting
and the window screens.

'Reichsführer Himmler would like to talk with you, Chief, urgently.
Rattenhuber's with him.'

'I'm having cakes,' Hitler said. The confection in his hand began
to seep cream and one drop ran slowly over his hand and dripped
to the floor.

'It's very urgent, they say.'

'All right, all right.' Hitler shot a glance at the young woman in
the green dress across from him. 'You'll have to go, Tschapperl,' he
said. 'Later . . .' She obeyed without question. 'And get Bormann,
will you, Julius,' Hitler said then.

Heinrich Himmler entered only when Schaub indicated he should.
He stood to attention and gave the *Deutscher Gruss*. He had never
been a member of the mountain set and his position in the hierarchy
was dependent far more on his abilities as a functionary than on any
personal relationship he had with Hitler.

Rattenhuber, on the other hand, had been guarding Hitler for a
decade and was very much a part of the set-up on the mountain,
often performing minor favours, as well as his bodyguard duties.
He simply clicked his heels in front of Hitler and stood behind his
boss, Himmler.

Hitler shook hands with Himmler, more as a means of settling the
Reichsführer in than because of any real affection.

'My Führer, I have somewhat disturbing news,' Himmler said.

Hitler gestured to him to sit down. Rattenhuber simply put his
hands behind his back and stood, pointing his belly at his Führer.

'How unusual,' Hitler said to Himmler. 'People only ever come to
me with disappointment these days.'

'My Führer, there is at this moment a grave threat to your security,'
Himmler said.

Hitler looked at Himmler as if the Reichsführer had just told him
the sun was out or the time of day it was.

'There is always a grave threat to my security, Heinrich. That's why I have Hans and his RSD lads and the boys of the Liebstandarte and God knows how many thousands of other SS men. That was why I formed the SS. You came here to tell me this?'

'This would appear to be more specific and immediate,' Rattenhuber interrupted.

Himmler appreciated his help. 'Two SD agents were discovered murdered in woods north of Berlin this morning. Brutally murdered,' he said. 'They were investigating a circle of traitors with Abwehr links and had just made their most significant arrest.'

Hitler stood up, walked over to the window and thumped the cream-coloured screen. 'Traitors in the Abwehr, Heinrich. Tell me something I don't know. I'm beginning to believe the whole bloody organisation has been working against me. That fucking little Greek. Don't tell me he's involved here, Heinrich.'

'No. We have no evidence of any involvement by Admiral Canaris. I have a report from Reich Security Main Office, if you would care to read it. We are sure the conspiracy runs deep, though.'

'Hans?' Hitler said to Rattenhuber, rubbing Himmler's nose in it somewhat.

'Naturally, my men are investigating it, my Führer,' Rattenhuber responded. 'Dienstelle 1, here at Führer headquarters, and Dienstelle 9 down in Berchtesgaden, are being put on full alert. And we're liaising with Gestapo A4 in Prinz Albrechtstrasse. We know who we're looking for. It's only a matter of time.'

'His name's Hofer, my Führer,' Himmler said. 'Major Martin Hofer. He is currently the head of the Abwehr Tod programme. Which is the reason for our concern.'

'Tod . . . Tod . . . Yes . . . what is that exactly? I seem to remember it from somewhere.'

'Assassins,' Rattenhuber said. 'Trained by Abwehr Two to, well, kill key enemy personnel.'

'You called them off Stalin in '41, my Führer,' Himmler said. 'Remember?'

Hitler tried to think but he could not remember. He waved his hand. 'I have never believed in assassination as a means of warfare. It tempts providence. So find him and pick him up and get whoever else is in this with him. What about that Junker fellow who runs Abwehr Two, Von Freytag-Loringhoven? I mean, he's a classic example of the Zossen spirit. All of them up there are bloody traitors. Active or passive, they are bloody traitors. I'll eat Keitel alive for this, Heinrich.'

'The Field Marshal, knows nothing of this.'

'He's Wehrmacht, they're all the same.'

'Not all, my Führer. But we do need to weed out the old guard.'

'Like trying to separate grains of sand. Do you think he'll try and kill me, Hans, this Hofer?'

'He's alone, with few options left,.' Rattenhuber nodded as if he were thinking beyond his words. 'But now we're warned, we should pick him up easily. Best to be prepared.'

'How many times have they tried to kill me, Hans? They must know by now only I can kill me. I control my life. And my destiny.'

'And the destiny of Germany, my Führer,' Himmler said. He touched his Party badge to emphasise the point.

'Yes, thank you, Heinrich, very commendable. I want you to go to Zossen, gentlemen, and haul in anyone who even asked directions from this Hofer.'

'I have your full support for the measures which must be taken?' Himmler asked. 'Your orders to the Wehrmacht high command that those we see fit to charge will be dismissed from the service so the full gravity of the law can be turned upon them? It's a stinking festering hole, the Abwehr.'

'I don't see why you want to take the damn thing over, Heinrich. We should have just made them an infantry unit and shipped them all east. Four days later they'd all be out of our hair and we could concentrate on winning this war. I can't fight internal subversion and a war, gentleman. I want rigorous methods used against this . . . this Hofer. Take him alive, gentlemen. Alive. Then let Müller's boys go to work on him . . . the arrogance of the man. The arrogance. Doesn't an oath mean anything to German officers any more?'

'Not those scum.'

Martin Bormann burst into the salon, unannounced, buttoning his tunic.

'No need to ask where you've been,' Hitler said.

Rattenhuber grinned. Himmler remained impassive.

'I was . . . I was . . . interviewing a prospective employee, my Führer.'

Hitler snorted. 'I know what you were doing, Herr Reichsleiter, I know what you were doing. I only hope I don't lose valuable time handing out more maternity leave. Between you and the

Liebstandarte, sometimes I think I'm running a bloody brothel here, Herr Reichsleiter. Anyway, it appears there's an Abwehr officer who does not have my best interests at heart on the loose in the Reich, Martin. Hans will brief you on what's been discussed. I'll leave it all in your hands, of course, Heinrich. But I'm not going to let this interfere with my running of the war.'

'He will be caught and dealt with, my Führer,' Himmler said.

'I'm glad to hear it, Heinrich. Tell me, how's Gauleiter Wagner, Martin?'

'Not good,' Bormann said. 'A matter of days. Perhaps less.'

'If he goes, I'll have to go to the funeral.'

'I would advise staying put until this matter is settled,' Rattenhuber said. 'For security. Hofer is dangerous – he's killed twice.'

'Impossible!' Bormann said. 'The Führer has engagements. Mussolini is coming.'

'Yes, Martin . . . thank you for reminding us. So you had better find this traitor, Heinrich. I refuse to cower. I've survived more of these bastards than I care to remember.'

'Precisely, my Führer,' Himmler said. 'It would be an insult to your dignity to let such a man interfere with one second of your schedule. Hofer will be found. And Rattenhuber will protect you.'

Hitler nodded his approval at the Reichsführer-SS. Rattenhuber felt as if someone had dumped a heap of farm waste on him. But he was diplomatic enough to hold his displeasure.

'Now I'm going upstairs, if that is all,' Hitler said then. 'And I don't want to be disturbed for at least an hour. Get me those air-raid reports for yesterday, Martin, and the latest situation report in Carpathia.'

The three men with him came to attention.

Outside in the afternoon air, Johann Rattenhuber found Heinrich Himmler lighting a small cigar.

'Herr Reichsführer,' Rattenhuber said, 'what were SD Inland doing arresting a traitor? Surely that's a Gestapo matter. The SD being brains rather than brawn . . . which appears to have been these two dead men's downfall.'

'There were intelligence co-factors; advanced knowledge and suchlike. SD Inland territory.'

'Should have taken along some Gestapo people, though.'

'Hindsight is twenty-twenty; foresight a little more blurred.'

'I'll keep that in mind, Herr Reichsführer,' Rattenhuber said.
'And help me find Hofer.'
'Of course.'

A little over two kilometres below the mountain, Erich Haas stood on
the bridge in front of Berchtesgaden railway station and considered
how remarkably vulnerable Adolf Hitler was.

Despite the checkpoints and the fences and the scores of bodyguards,
when you considered the height, vastness and inhospitable nature of the
back of the Obersalzberg mountain, suddenly the death of the Führer
of the Greater German Reich was more of a positive prospect.

He stopped his considerations when he saw one of the uniformed
detectives at the RSD checkpoint outside the station watching him.

'Purpose of your visit?' the RSD detective said. Haas pulled off
his glasses and rubbed the condensation from them, put them back
on and handed his *ausweis* over to the detective.

'Book-binder,' Haas said. 'I was visiting a private customer in town.
Herr Helmut Keller, Schiessstrasse 12. Know him?'

The detective shook his head. 'Like I know everyone. Open the
suitcase, please, Herr . . . Rotach.'

Haas smiled. He feigned nervousness. 'Mathematics,' he said. 'Herr
Keller is a mathematics scholar. Retired here from Hamburg. I am
repairing the leather.'

He opened the small suitcase and the detective examined the
books inside.

'They're antiques. Be careful, please,' Haas said.

The detective looked him over again: the glasses, the blue-green
eyes, the greying moustache, the grey streaks in his hair, still visible
under the rim of the felt hat. 'All right. Go,' he said.

Haas raised his hat to show more of the grey dye he had streaked
into his hair, and scratched his slightly stubbled chin, shaved that
morning to achieve the effect of appearing academic that evening.
A long streak of soup on his tie added to the effect, as did the smell
of beer from his breath. The detective watched him enter the station,
and Haas watched the detective through the glass in the door, then a
young girl came down the steps, and the detective lost interest and
began checking the people coming in.

8

MARTIN HOFER DOWNED the soup in one. He was unshaven and dressed in civilian clothes and looked the worse for having slept rough for two nights.

'You want some more?' Adam Von Trott asked.

'I think it'll probably kill me, Adam,' Hofer said, grinning and shivering. 'I haven't felt this bad since the last war. And then I was at ten thousand feet being chased by four Sopwith Camels. God, I'm too old for this.'

Von Trott poured some more soup into Hofer's cup and handed it to Claus Von Stauffenberg, sitting next to the Abwehr major. Von Stauffenberg took time to pass the cup on to Hofer. 'Remind me never to get a job as a waiter,' he said. 'I'm getting the hang of it, it's just that one eye makes your sense of distance impossible to determine. Right, Herr Gruppenführer?'

In the corner of the room, Gruppenführer Arthur Nebe, wearing tweeds, was more nervous than usual. 'I cannot protect you, Hofer,' he said.

'I'm not asking you to, Herr Gruppenführer. All I'm asking – all we're asking – is that you order your men in Munich to raid that address and arrest the relevant individuals. A police matter.'

'So simple?' Nebe had picked up a small book and was flicking through the pages.

'It's Stefan Georg,' Von Stauffenberg said. 'A favourite poet of mine.'

'Too damn romantic for me,' Nebe said. 'I must say, quite a spread you have here. I almost feel out of my depth. A bit like you, Hofer. You must go to Switzerland. For all our sakes.'

'And our predicament, Herr Gruppenführer?' Von Trott said. 'Martin's the only one, bar yourself, who's in a position to act here. If you don't act, then Martin must.'

'I will not expose myself like that,' Nebe said.

'And if the Reichsführer is making his move?' Von Stauffenberg asked. 'Perhaps you will be dispensable, Herr Gruppenführer, which will leave you very exposed. Have you considered that?'

'You should show more respect, Graf Von Stauffenberg,' Nebe said. 'Hofer, here, is a wanted traitor now; with two murders to answer for. No evidence to the contrary. Have you considered that? I've seen the file.'

'They were going to kill me, Herr Gruppenführer,' Hofer said.

'Yes. Well, you cannot be allowed to fall into Gruppenführer Müller's hands, that's primary here. For all our sakes.'

'I should think that what's primary here,' Von Trott said, 'is stopping this assassin, surely. If he is allowed to succeed, then that clears the way for your precious Reichsführer, Herr Gruppenführer. *Treue* Heinrich, as the Führer so laughingly calls him. You know he's stabbed every boss he's ever had in the back. Remember Ernst Rohm? Himmler was his truest subordinate. Then . . .' He drew his hand across his neck.

'Adam's right, Herr Gruppenführer,' Von Stauffenberg said. 'If Himmler or his dogs use this to pre-empt us then all our efforts, not to mention our lives, are worthless. We won't have to worry about who will deal with us because it'll be a people's court and a rather slow death.'

Nebe visibly shivered.

'I will protect myself,' Nebe said. 'Have you considered the possibility that this assassin story might be a British trick? They have done such things before and would not hesitate to do so again. To create chaos, to sew doubt.'

'Raid the Munich address, Herr Gruppenführer,' Hofer said.

'On what charges? On whose order? On what information? To find whom? I have no desire to disappear into the fog, Hofer.'

'He'll throw you to Müller some day,' Hofer said. 'The Reichsführer. And Müller will take great pleasure playing football with your head. You are with us now, Herr Gruppenführer, there is no going back.'

'And if I did as you suggest?' Nebe said. 'I am surely not going to go to the Führer and say the Reichsführer and two department chiefs of the Reich Security Main Office are liars intent on seeing his demise. I do value my own life, gentlemen. I do intend to come through all of this.'

'Given your record?' Von Trott asked.

'Adam!' Von Stauffenberg snapped.

'You should speak with more respect, Von Trott. I did my duty as a soldier in the east. My duty.'

'We know what your duty was, Herr Gruppenführer Nebe. Germany will be paying the price of your duty into eternity.'

Nebe stood up. His small stature made the gesture seem ridiculous, given the nature of the three men he was trying to impress.

'Gentlemen, this meeting is terminated. I advise you to make your way to Switzerland, Hofer, where the facilities for a healthy life are more readily available than on the upper floors of Prinz Albrechtstrasse 8. If I or mine should come across you in the course of our duties then I will be forced to follow my orders in respect of murderers and traitors. And I will not allow you to fall into Gruppenführer Müller's hands, with or without orders from the Reichsführer.'

He was opening the door when Von Stauffenberg spoke.

'Arthur, the die is cast. You should remember who your friends are. More importantly, you should remember who your enemies are. Otherwise, we will all end up at the sharp end of one of Gruppenführer Müller's more vigorous interrogations in Prinz Albrechtstrasse 8.'

'I cannot help you,' Nebe said. 'I cannot go against the Reichsführer on this. I will not.'

'He will surely go against you, Arthur, some day.'

Nebe shook his head and left.

'What do you think?' Von Trott said to Stauffenberg when the Kripo chief's car had crunched along the gravelled avenue leading to the castle.

'I think he will not do anything. If Himmler suspects he knows about this then Himmler will move against him. Otherwise Müller might indeed get him and Himmler does not want that at this moment. Müller would have the Reichsführer's job, if he could. And all our heads.'

'Can you do this, Martin?' Von Trott asked Hofer. 'Find Valkyrie and kill him?'

'I'd rather go to Switzerland.'

'But it must be done and you're the only one who has the wherewithal,' Von Stauffenberg said. He showed his crippled hand.

131

'Thank you for putting it so bluntly, Claus. I feel like I'm in a vice and every minute someone turns the screw.'

'Only every minute?' Von Trott smiled. 'It's every second with me. Claus?'

'I'm due back in Berlin.' Von Stauffenberg nodded at Hofer. 'You do realise you're on your own now, Martin. We can't help any more.'

'Yes. The vice is a little tighter. The time shorter.'

Erich Haas looked around him one more time, then threw the cigarette away and ducked into a line of trees and waited.

He was two kilometres outside Wörgl, on the road to Kufstein, at a spot he had made a note of two days earlier during his first reconnaissance of the area.

He waited five minutes and watched the road and the fields and then made his way along the line of trees, heading east, up a steep incline and into a pine and oak wood.

When he had gone about a kilometre, he stopped again, pulled out a map and a compass and took several bearings. He jotted the bearings down in a small notebook, checked the map and the compass readings again, and then began to move quickly through the trees and up a steeper incline.

He climbed up the limestone crags, out of the valley and on to the snowy rock of the surrounding massif. Then he stopped and took another compass bearing and moved across the northern reaches of the Kitzbuhler Alpen for ten kilometres. It snowed twice and Haas kept himself warm with a small flask of schnapps Weg had given him.

When he had reached a certain point marked on his map, he stopped, took another compass bearing and went to the foot of a small brown crag flanked by tall pines.

Then he opened the small suitcase, took out an entrenching tool and began to dig. When he had dug down four feet, he gathered small stones and heaped them into the bottom of the hole until they covered the floor to a depth of five centimetres; then he took a waterproofed canvas sack out of the suitcase, checked the contents – a suit of clothes, some identification papers and a small parcel of rations, mostly chocolate and hard American biscuits – replaced them and placed the sack in the hole.

He covered the sack with more stones and then with twigs and filled the hole in. Then he found a large brown speckled rock and placed it over the hole and spread leaves and broken twigs around the site. Then he took a piece of bread and a lump of cheese from his pocket, sat down and ate. It had stopped snowing and was raining now. He rested for an hour before heading back the way he had come, checking the compass bearings he had taken.

When he reached Kufstein, he went into the railway station toilet, cleaned his shoes, his suitcase and changed his shirt, then came out and bought a ticket for Innsbruck.

In Innsbruck, he went to a bar in the old town and had a beer. The Inn river was green at Innsbruck and the rain had returned. There was no checkpoint at the station when he bought a ticket on the last train for Munich. The train was full and he had to stand for the whole journey.

Max Weg was playing chess with himself and losing. He opened a medieval book on courtly love and let his hands spread over the vellum; the doorbell brought him back from where he had strayed.

'Herr Weg, Herr Weg . . . have you heard the news?'

'I have heard no news today, Frau Gern. I have been working too hard. Taking advantage of the lack of air-raid warnings.'

Gerda Gern approached Weg very timidly, then reached out and took his hand. 'I was sure you would know,' she said.

'Know what, Frau Gern?'

'You being influential in the Party and all. What should we do?'

'Well, if you'd just tell me what has happened, I might be able to proffer some advice on what to do about it.'

Gerda Gern nodded and composed herself. 'Gauleiter Wagner . . . he's dead. I just heard. In Bad Reichenhall.'

Weg did not say a word. He very slowly pulled his hand away from hers and sat down in the chair beside the table he was working at. 'You're sure?'

'Yes. Straight from the Brown House. I want to know what to do. Should I send condolences to the Brown House? Should I send flowers? Should I send them to the Führer? The Führer will be upset. It's so difficult to know what to do, to know what is for the best.'

'Take a chair, take a chair,' Weg said. 'Let me think.'

'Of course,' she said, 'of course. You met him, didn't you?'

'Once or twice. Socially.'

'You want to be alone.'

'No. No. I was expecting it; we all were. But sometimes even things we know are coming are hard to take.'

'I could not agree more. But it is important to do the right thing. I was wondering if . . .'

'. . . if I might have a word with someone in the Brown House and find out what's expected?'

'You read my mind, Herr Weg, you read my mind.'

'It is a faculty of being blind, Frau Gern.'

She blushed and he sensed it. He reached out and took her hands and held them. 'I think I'll close the shop, as a mark of respect,' he said.

'Should I close the Pension Gern?'

'No, no, Frau Gern, no. You are vital to the war effort.'

She beamed and squeezed his hands. 'Oh, thank you, thank you. I was concerned. I didn't know what I should do there. You're a fine man, Herr Weg, a fine man. And I'll tell you what, I'll bake you a couple of cakes, all right? Small, mind, I don't have too much in the way of ingredients these days. With almond. The way you like it.'

'You don't have to, Frau Gern.'

'I insist. We Party people should stick together. And call me Gerda, please.'

Weg smiled.

When the last train from Innsbruck that evening arrived in Munich Hauptbahnhof, the air-raid sirens were going. Erich Haas followed the rest of the passengers into the shelters. The sirens stopped wailing fifteen minutes later when no aircraft came and the all clear was given five minutes after that.

Weg's shop was shut when Haas got there; a simple notice said it would not reopen until Gauleiter Adolf Wagner had been laid to rest. There was a small wreath under the black-rimmed notice and the words '*Es Liebe Deutschland*' across the wreath. Haas waited for dark before going to Weg's apartment, watching Weg's window from a secluded doorway, for fifteen minutes, before approaching the building.

'You were in the mountains,' Max Weg said. He was checking the mathematics books he had given Haas to carry with him as cover, feeling them for blemishes, smelling their leather. 'You have eaten cheese and you put your hand into something an animal dropped.'

Haas moved a chess piece on Weg's board but did not tell

the old man the move. They did not speak for two or more minutes.

'Hitler will come to this funeral,' Haas said then. 'Yes?'

'Almost certainly. Wagner's an old fighter. A former gauleiter.'

There was another long pause.

'I want you to find out everything you can about the arrangements for Wagner's funeral,' Haas said. 'Everything, Max.'

There was a third, very long pause. Then Weg's mouth opened slowly. 'My God, I know what you're here for,' he said then. 'Is it possible?'

'Nothing's impossible, Max. Improbable, yes; difficult, always. Opportunities, Max, one must take one's opportunities.'

'But if it's not impossible, it's surely folly for you.'

'Is it folly for man to follow his nature? You just do as I ask, Max. It's for a good cause.'

Max Weg approached the table and moved a chess piece. 'I heard your move,' he said. 'Check.'

'But not mate,' Haas said, and he moved another piece.

'For the first time in years I am frightened,' Weg said.

'Wish me luck.'

'I want to ask so many questions but I will not.'

'Just do what I ask, Max.'

'Check,' Weg said, and moved another piece. 'I need a drink.'

One floor above them, Wilhelm Koch sipped from a glass of clear liquid which tasted of liquorice and smelled of peppermint. The warm glow he had been feeling all evening, watching Ilse Gern, had developed beyond mild lechery into an unbearable desire. He had that ache which men have when they are aroused to a point where they no longer really care about the person in front of them, only the conquest.

'Did you know him? Gauleiter Wagner?' Ilse Gern asked him. She was cleaning grease from a plate with cold water and an old rag.

'I arrested him once or twice before the *Machtergreifung*. He always remembered it. They have long memories.'

'Did you really arrest the Führer?'

'I was there.'

'And it has affected your career?'

He shook his head even though she had her back to him. 'I'm the only one who has affected my career. I think I should have joined the SS. Or left Germany.'

'Why didn't you?'

'Which? I didn't leave Germany because I had nowhere to go and I didn't join the SS because I think I'm a snob. They were street thugs, I was a detective. Now maybe I'm at their level. It's too late now. I'm settled, they're settled. Are you wearing perfume?'

'A little. You like it?'

He stood up and shuffled over to her in the way that men who are not seducers by nature do, when they know it can only end in humiliation and yet they have to try. 'You're very beautiful.'

He went to touch her neck but she flicked her hair and it knocked his hand to her back and he caught her bra under her dress. He pulled his hand away. She smiled at his discomfort. 'Perhaps you should go now, Wilhelm. Your wife will be wondering.'

'She's a witch.'

'She's your witch.'

He put his hand on her shoulder, gently at first, then, because he could not control himself, he shoved it under her dress to her breast. She pulled away and pushed his hand off.

'I'm sorry,' he said. 'I think you're so beautiful.'

'You've told me. You should go, Wilhelm.'

He moved towards her. 'I want you.'

She sidestepped him. He caught her and pulled her to him and kissed her. She half responded, then pulled back and kicked his shin. The physical pain did not hurt as much as the emotional.

'I'm sorry, I'm sorry,' he said. 'Please, forgive me, please. I wouldn't hurt you.'

'It's all right, Wilhelm, it's all right. It's just tonight I'm not in the mood. The Föhn, perhaps. I think it's still around. And my time is here . . .'

He did not understand at first, then it dawned on him. 'Oh, I'm sorry, I'm sorry. I didn't realise.'

'I don't broadcast it.'

'I thought you and that book-binder . . . it's been on my mind. I can't get rid of it.'

'You're married, Wilhelm. There can be nothing between us while you're married.'

'But you do care? If things were different?'

'Of course I care. We're friends, aren't we? We'll always be friends.'

'I just thought . . . you and him . . . you're not . . .?'

'You have no right to ask me things like that, Wilhelm, no right. Anyway, the answer's no. But you've no right.'

'I can't help it, I can't help it. I think about you all day, everyday.'

'You mustn't. I know things are bad at home but you must control yourself, Wilhelm. You're a police officer.'

'Yes. I have arrested homosexuals and Jews; exchanged memos with the Wittelsbacher Palais, with terms like night and fog and special treatment in them. All in a normal day's work. Because that's all I can do now. I am a servant of the state. And I need the state like a servant needs a master. I need the structure. I need the orders. I need the security. All of it. Would you take me for a murderer, Ilse?'

'I don't know what you mean, Wilhelm.'

He shook his head and reached for his coat. His lechery had transformed itself into humiliation, as it always did.

'I'll see you again,' Ilse Gern said. 'I'll see you again. We'll talk.'

He hung on to those words as if they were salvation itself, and hated himself for doing it.

Ilse Gern touched her breast where Koch had scratched it and thought of another man.

When she knocked on Haas's door in the Pension Gern the following morning, there was no answer.

'He's gone out, dear. I don't trust him. He doesn't shave properly.'

Ilse Gern did not look at her mother. 'He's a friend of Max Weg's,' she said. 'A business friend.'

'And Herr Weg is blind.'

'Perhaps Herr Weg needs a wife,' Ilse said.

'Do you think so? I don't think our friend Rotach is interested in a wife. You're making a fool of yourself.'

'I enjoy it.'

'That's what I fear.'

Ilse turned finally and walked towards her mother. 'Actually, I have a message from Herr Weg for Herr Rotach; to meet him for a drink, later. Perhaps Herr Weg wants to recruit Herr Rotach for the Party.'

'They'll take anyone these days. Herr Weg should know better. He does need a wife.'

'I don't want to argue, Mother.'

'I've baked two small cakes. I think I'll take them around to Herr Weg. He's in his apartment?'

'In mourning for Gauleiter Wagner.'

'As it should be. You mind the desk, dear.'

'When did Herr Rotach leave?'

'I don't remember.'

That same Thursday morning woke Ruth Wachs from behind a forest. And as she watched the landscape fly by north-west of Munich, manicured fields and wooden outhouses and single small figures scurrying between barns in the chill of dawn, the sun's rays slipped by them and through the trees and hedgerows, and small herds of cattle stirred, while birds landed on their backs for the first meals of the day.

Wachs touched Mathius Schumann's foot.

'I was having a nice dream,' he said, looking at the others sleeping in the carriage. 'We were making love, *liebchen*.'

Wachs watched a wiry infantry NCO stir and waited until both his eyes were open before answering. 'It's the only place we ever do it any more, darling,' she said, and she made her face go red. It was easy because she was angry. They were a day late.

They had been dropped on the coast of Brittany by a sixty-five-foot Breton tunnyman, part of what amounted to a private SIS navy berthed in the mouth of the Helford river near Falmouth.

Brittany was the fiefdom of the Free French, and it was supposed to be deliberately kept quiet and free of sabotage activity to facilitate the landing of agents and a regular escape and evasion service which ferried downed Allied pilots and the like back to England from its coastline.

However, someone had forgotten to explain this to a small communist cell around Rennes; they blew up the railway line a kilometre outside the town and Wachs and her two colleagues missed their subsequent connection in Paris. And the knock-on effect of connections missed meant they lost the Wednesday.

The early morning Munich-bound train was slowing now and more bodies were moving and stretching and lighting what passed for cigarettes. Those without cigarettes watched those with

with an intensity usually reserved by hunting animals for their prey.

The compartment door slid open and an orpo sergeant and a plain-clothes Gestapo agent in a tweed suit with a watch and chain stood before the six passengers in the compartment.

'Papers ...'

One by one, the people in the compartment handed over their *ausweis*, foreign workers' permits, passports, and various travel permits. It was a mechanical process, a repeat of what had taken place at regular intervals throughout the journey, the orpo sergeant asking questions, the Gestapo agent just looking and listening.

'Married?' the sergeant asked Ruth Wachs. He looked at Schumann's *ausweis*, pawing the brown cover.

'Barely,' Schumann said.

'I asked your wife,' the sergeant said.

Wachs nodded.

'You are going to Munich?'

'Vienna. It says so in my permit. In Munich for a few days only. We have family who have moved there.'

'Address?' the Gestapo man said suddenly.

Wachs looked more confused than she was.

'The address of your family in Munich.'

'Dusseldorferstrasse 44B, near the Kolnerplatz,' Schumann interrupted. 'You know it?'

The Gestapo man was going to make an issue of the interruption but he had been awake all night doing this and wasn't in the mood. 'I'm not from Munich,' he said, sensing a definite hostility in the compartment.

'It's in Schwabing,' Schumann said. 'Nice area.'

'And what do you do for the Foreign Ministry, Herr ... Raum?' the Gestapo man asked.

'I work for a department which liaises between the Foreign Minister and the Foreign Minister's representative at Führer headquarters, Dr Walter Hewel. Do you know Dr Hewel? Nice man. Terrible dress sense, the Führer says. But then, I'm not on duty at present, I'm on leave, otherwise I would be irritated. Call Führer headquarters if you like when we get to Munich. But not before eleven. The Führer doesn't appreciate it.'

The orpo sergeant looked at his colleague and the Gestapo man held his gaze on Schumann for a couple of seconds, then started to scratch his chin. 'Have a good trip,' he said. He left the sergeant to give back all the papers and got out of the compartment as quickly as possible. And all the time Schumann stared at him.

On the platform in Munich Hauptbahnhof, Ruth Wachs leaned towards Schumann's ear as he was lifting up a suitcase. 'You ever even think of doing something like that again, I'll kill you myself,' she whispered.

'I got us through, didn't I? And I don't see any sign of our friend. So he goes to Dusseldorferstrasse. So what? We change identities now, anyway. I know what I'm doing. I know shit like him. Waiting for a pension, both of them. You see the stains on his shirt? He's divorced or something. And jealous of marrieds. Come on, we're late.'

On another platform, Erich Haas had just bought a paper; he boarded the Salzburg train just before it pulled out of Munich Hauptbahnhof.

In Salzburg, he bought a coupon-free meal and a beer and then a ticket to St Johann in Tirol.

It was a slow ride and took longer than it should have because of the changes. Haas wore a tweed jacket and knee-length *lederhosen*, high socks and hiking boots – and the obligatory Tirolean hat with a feather. And his knapsack did not look out of place with the others on the train. Even though recreational mountain walking was frowned upon in wartime – and skiing banned – people used their leave and spare time to get away from the privations when they could. Some men carried legally held shotguns in the hope of bagging some bird meat for the dwindling tables. The writ of the Reich Security Main Office ran least in these mountain areas of Bavaria and the Austrian Tirol.

But then, it was least needed there; Adolf Hitler had not chosen the area strictly for its scenic beauty or its inhospitable topography and winter climate.

It was a crisp Tirolean day, the kind Haas remembered from what he liked to call the years before; he could afford a smile at a pretty girl and a raise of the hat to a woman in black who had obviously lost someone. He stopped to read the names of the recent dead at the beautiful church of St Johann, even knelt in a pew and muttered something that appeared to be a prayer.

Outside the town, he walked along the road to Lofer and Bad Reichenhall for about ten kilometres; then, when he was sure he was alone, he cut into the mountains for the second time.

Wachs and Schumann had split up at the railway station; Wachs had gone to meet Kaestner in the Englischer Garten where they had become the married couple. They had booked a double room in a pension on Augustenstrasse north of the Hauptbahnhof.

It was early afternoon when they met Schumann in a beerhall near the Isar river.

Schumann was sitting at a wooden table, reading a newspaper, dressed in a long dark coat and a grey scarf, with a felt hat down on the bench beside him. The beerhall was smoky and damp and there was a hole in the roof at one end where a fragmentation bomb had come through. The fragments were still in the stone walls.

'I've found the address,' Schumann said. 'It's a bookshop. Just off the Hohenzollernplatz. There's just one slight problem . . . it's closed. Some bigshot called Wagner's dead and our boy ain't opening till he's buried.'

'Adolf Wagner,' Wachs said. 'He used to be Gauleiter of Bavaria. Didn't you read the briefing?'

'Yeah, yeah, sure. I tried to look inside but the windows are glued together with paper. I asked a woman across the road about the place. It's owned by a man named Weg. I got that.'

'I don't suppose you got a home address?' Wachs asked.

'She didn't know. Anyway, she was asking more questions than I was.'

'Damn,' Wachs said. 'This is not good.'

'We have the name,' Kaestner said.

'Yeah, all we have to do is put an ad in the newspapers, Paul,' Schumann said. 'Or better still, ask the cops.'

'Don't be a smartarse all the time, Mathius,' Wachs said. 'When is this funeral?'

Schumann shrugged.

'We have to find out,' Wachs said. 'I'll do that.'

She was already making calculations and trying not to give this away to the other two.

'So what do we do now?' Kaestner asked.

'We'll take it in rotation to watch the bookshop,' Wachs said. 'Starting now.'

Kaestner sat back and stared into space. 'Why? I can't see why we don't just try and track down this Weg.'

'Because we'll draw notice,' Wachs said. 'Anywhere we can sit without being noticed, Mathius?'

'Difficult,' Schumann replied. 'Some of the area's wrecked from bombing. We can sit in a café on the platz. Maybe one at a time. And there're a few benches around.'

'What's the point?' Kaestner asked. 'If our man isn't coming?'

'The shop's closed, Paul, that's all,' Wachs said. 'We cope with what presents itself. And I give the orders.'

'It's looking a bit open-ended,' Schumann said. 'And that's going to attract attention soon. No matter how careful we are.'

'You got a better idea?' Wachs asked. 'If it comes to it, gentlemen, we are expendable.'

'I could break in,' Schumann said. 'I know how. Leave no trace.'

'No,' Wachs said. 'Not unless we have to. We don't want to risk scaring them off. Especially the target.'

'So how long do we stay?' Kaestner asked.

'As long as it takes,' Wachs said. 'There is a deadline.'

'Want to tell us about it?' Schumann asked.

'No.'

'The longer we stay, the more exposed we are,' Kaestner said.

'Exciting,' Schumann added.

'Jesus, we're assuming the target will come anywhere near this shop, or look anything like his photo,' Kaestner said. 'Who is he, anyway?'

'It's not your concern,' Wachs replied. 'Look, there's a good chance one or both of them will come near the shop in the next two days. So we watch it as planned. We can't try and trace every Weg in the city, Paul. And I don't want to make a move unless we're forced to. So, we wait and hold our nerve.'

Kaestner nodded and sighed.

'For what . . .?'

Two SS NCOs walked past them and Wachs stopped herself speaking. Schumann noticed the obvious hiatus and grabbed her and hugged her. 'Must be great to have your wife here . . .' he said to Kaestner. 'My God, you miss a woman.' He kissed her cheek.

Wachs leaned towards Kaestner. 'Kiss me,' she said to him. She kissed him. 'Keep talking,' she whispered to Schumann. 'Keep talking. Ask us what we're going to do, stuff like that.'

Kaestner felt embarrassed. He pulled away from her kiss and then tasted a sweetness that held him and he joined the kiss.

Schumann grinned and winked at him.

'We should get moving,' Kaestner said. 'We're losing time.'

Three hours later, in his apartment, Max Weg smiled at Gerda Gern and broke a small cake in half. 'You're really too good to me, Frau Gern,' he said.

'Please, call me Gerda . . . Max. I'll call again?'

He smiled again. 'Please do. Goodbye.'

She closed the door very slowly. Weg ate some cake.

'So what's the news on Wagner?'

Erich Haas stepped from the bedroom and stood against the wall, combing his hair. He could smell a mixture of perfume and cheap almonds.

'Monday,' Weg said. 'They will bury the esteemed gauleiter on Monday. Big ceremony from the Feldherrnhalle to the Konigsplatz. He will be interred with the heroes. Goebbels will give the oration. Anyone who's anyone will be there. I'm invited.'

'Security?'

'An ant will have to show a pass to get to its hill.'

'Hitler definitely coming up from Obersalzberg?'

'Of course. The Führer would not miss an occasion like this. You know, I have been trying to figure you . . .'

'Well, don't.'

9

THE FOLLOWING EVENING, Mathius Schumann tapped the sole of his foot on the white gravel of the Englischer Garten while the last brittle rays of sunlight broke up on the tips of trees and the spikes of spires. Darkness had already invaded the east of the city and the cool of dusk was relieving the Föhn when the day finally acquiesced and the pressure began to lift. In front of Schumann, the green rush of the Eisbach whispered excited secrets while around him a breeze began to stir the trees.

Sitting beside him, Ruth Wachs looked left and right and behind her, and then stood up from the bench. About ten metres to the right, and hidden by the trees, Paul Kaestner watched the Eisbach flow by and checked for interruptions.

'I mean, what did you expect? We'd catch them having coffee and cakes?' Schumann asked. 'You gotta let me break in.'

Wachs shook her head. 'And if you find nothing, and we end up scaring our man off?'

'Well, I hope you have a better idea, because another day of hanging around that shop with no joy and we're gonna have the Gestapo down on us like flies around shit. And that'll scare our man off. Why do I get the feeling I'm a lab rat?'

'Teddy Giles and that old bastard he works for . . .' Kaestner said. 'Jesus, we could be working for the Gestapo and not even know it the way those two think.'

'We have our orders, Paul,' Wachs said. 'That's all.'

'Well, I hope this fellow's worth it,' Kaestner said.

'There was a guy watching me this afternoon, Ruth,' Schumann said. 'You gotta let me break in or I'll be made.'

'Were you in America for long?' Wachs asked him.

'Jesus, didn't you hear me? We have to make a move or back off. And I ain't backing off.'

'Keep your damn voice down,' Wachs said.

'Mathius is right, Ruth. We have to face the probability that neither of them will turn up before the funeral,' Kaestner said. 'So standing around that shop does nothing but expose us. Maybe we should just wait till the funeral's over.'

Wachs thought for a while and considered telling them what she knew. Then she pursed her lips and nodded. 'All right, all right,' she said. 'We'll continue to watch the shop and we'll try and trace Weg. Maybe he lives nearby.'

'Oh, yeah, excuse me, sir, but we're trying to find a Herr Weg so we can kill a friend of his,' Schumann said.

'Don't aggravate me, Mathius,' Wachs said. 'We have a job and we will do what is necessary to complete it. As I deem it necessary.'

'Well, then, let me break in,' Schumann said.

Wachs ignored him and went over to Kaestner, who shook his head. 'I'm not a killer, you know,' he said. 'I'm a musician. I'm not sure I could kill anyone. I never have.'

'You leave that to me,' Schumann said.

Wachs sighed. 'You and I are going to have to ask the questions, Paul,' she said then. She turned back to Schumann. 'And if we don't have anything by tonight, Mathius breaks in.'

'Okay,' Schumann said. He slapped her on the back.

Wachs was about to turn to Kaestner when he elbowed her in the arm. A flashlight was moving in the trees and two voices were talking in clipped sentences.

'Shit!' Schumann said.

He threw himself into the undergrowth beside the river. Kaestner was reaching out to grab Wachs and pull her with him when a flashlight beam cut off his escape.

'Kiss me,' Wachs said. She shoved him against a tree and kissed him. 'Pull my skirt up,' she whispered through the kiss. She began pulling at his trousers. Kaestner hesitated.

'Do it,' Wachs said. And she began to make small noises.

At first the two orpos just stood watching the scene in the pool of light, smiling at one another. Then one of them nudged the other. 'Excuse me,' he said then.

Very slowly, Ruth Wachs turned her head; Kaestner followed,

breathing quickly. Below them, in the undergrowth by the river, Schumann was holding his silenced Mauser.

Wachs squinted as the first policeman shone the torch in her face. She pulled her skirt down and feigned embarrassment and Kaestner turned his body from the light and began to do up his flies.

'No screwing in public parks,' the second policeman said, laughing. 'By order of the Führer. Lowers public morals. She'd better be pregnant, mate, or we'll have to fine you.'

Ruth Wachs was wiping her mouth. 'We . . . we're married. We were carried away,' she said.

'Sure, sure,' the policeman with the torch said.

'Papers,' the other policeman said.

Wachs fumbled with her handbag and pulled her coat around her body. 'I don't . . . usually we find . . .' she said.

The policeman with the torch examined her *ausweis* and then took Kaestner's. 'Well, if you take my advice, mate, you'll find a more civilised place to make it with your missus than a clump of trees.'

'But I like it like that,' Wachs said. 'It excites me.' She looked for his rank and saw he was a sergeant. 'Herr Meister.'

The sergeant felt his throat become dry.

'Come on, Walter,' his companion said. 'Take their names and let's go. You two get out of here. There are gangs who use these woods at night, black marketeers, others, and they won't hesitate to slit your throats for a mark or what you're giving for free – love. And if the British come tonight, this is not a good place to be either. Haven't you noticed the craters? There's an unexploded bomb less than half a kilometre away.'

He noted the names and handed back the *ausweis*. 'Okay, where are you staying?'

'We're going tomorrow,' Kaestner said. 'We're on leave. Going to Vienna.'

'Doesn't matter. Procedure says I have to check all this.'

'It's a pension . . . I'm not familiar with Munich.'

'Well, how the hell did you expect to get back, then? There's a blackout. Look, what were you doing here?'

The rustle in the undergrowth distracted all of them. Both policemen suddenly pulled their pistols.

'Hey, you, get out of there,' the sergeant said. 'Out now or I fire.'

Schumann came out with his hands in the air.

'Who the hell are you?'

147

'I'm with them.'

'What is this? What the hell are you doing?'

'I like to watch,' Schumann said. He grinned.

'Well, you're in a lot of trouble, boy. You're all in a lot of trouble.'

Schumann moved between Kaestner and Wachs. 'No, you are, friend,' he said, still smiling.

He pulled his silenced Mauser out from the small of his back and shot the sergeant in the head. The other orpo was raising his pistol when Wachs kicked him between the legs. He went to cry out when Wachs shoved her hand into his neck and choked off the cry. Then Schumann shot him in the face.

For a few seconds the three of them said nothing, and all there was was the wind.

'Oh, shit, shit . . .' Kaestner said then. 'What the hell did you do that for?'

'Stupid bastards,' Schumann said. 'Should have minded their own business. Quick, strip them. Jewellery, everything. Give me a knife, someone.'

Wachs had already started to strip the body of the dead sergeant. She reached into her sleeve and pulled out a small penknife. 'Will this do?'

'Come on, Paul, strip him. Don't look if you don't like this. I'm going to mutilate them. Put a round in each of that fellow's eyes.'

Kaestner nodded and raised the Mauser.

When he had finished, Schumann toppled the first body into the Eisbach and the current whipped it away. 'It'll be morning before they're found,' he said. 'Then they'll have to make sure they're the two cops. We're buying time here.'

'The uniforms,' Wachs said.

'You two go now. Make sure there's no blood on you. I'll bury the uniforms. See you tomorrow. Go on . . .'

Wachs nodded and she and Kaestner checked themselves in the light of the police torch, scrubbed off some blood stains and then disappeared into the darkness of the Englischer Garten. Schumann drove the penknife into the soil at his feet and began to dig with his fingers. Somewhere in the distance the air-raid sirens were beginning to wail.

Erich Haas lay in bed listening to the sirens, too. The first guns had begun to open up to the west of the city. but he could hear no planes and no bombs. He closed his eyes and went over things in his mind again. He had spent most of the day in a beerhall with Weg and some of his Nazi acquaintances. Then they had walked around central Munich, surveying all of Hitler's favourite haunts – the Café Heck, the Osteria restaurant, the Carlton Tearooms on Briennerstrasse, Hitler's nine-room apartment on the Prinzregentenplatz, the Feldherrnhalle, the area around the Konigsplatz where Wagner would be buried – and Haas had reached another decision.

He did not hear the first knock on the door. The second made him reach out for a pistol he had secreted. Then there was noise in the corridor and voices. He cocked the pistol.

'Herr Rotach . . .'

'Yes . . .'

'It's Ilse, Ilse Gern, we must go to the cellars. There's an air-raid warning. Would you please get dressed and come out.'

'I don't hear any bombing.'

'It is a warning. Perhaps it is only Augsburg or down at Wiener Neustadt. They make aircraft there, you know. You must come.'

Haas got up and dressed himself, slowly. He was still thinking about the job and why he was going through with it. You could still walk, he told himself once or twice, but he knew there was no chance of that. He had made his decision way back, in an instant, maybe before he even realised it.

When he opened the door he expected to see Ilse Gern standing there. Instead he found the corridor empty except for the back of one old man running for the stairs in his dressing gown. Haas walked to the desk and listened to the silence.

'You should be in the cellars.' He swung round. Frau Gerda Gern stood with her arms folded. 'Please,' she said, 'to the cellars, if you would. I must check the rooms.'

He watched her go down the corridor, knocking on people's doors, opening them when there was no answer. When she got to his room she went to open the door.

'I'm here, Frau Gern,' he said. He held up his key.

She did not even respond.

Haas smiled and turned and went down the stairs.

Ilse Gern stood at the cellar door in her dressing gown, smoking a cigarette. The cigarette was made from leaves and wood shavings and the smell was a sickly sweetness which made Haas wince slightly.

'I hate them,' she said. 'But we have nothing else, do we? Is Mother coming?'

'She's checking the rooms.'

Ilse shook her head. 'She embarrasses me. I am sorry. She is not a bad woman, she just takes it all very seriously. Being a blockwart. You should see her on Party fund-raising days or when the Führer's birthday comes along. It's the Führer's birthday on Thursday. We'll have a banner hanging from one of our windows, saying something very patriotic. Mother's afraid her gift will not please the Führer.'

They were an hour in the cellar before the all clear was sounded. It had reached a stage in the city when it was better to go through the motions of a raid than to do nothing. It was as if the calm they were enduring, with only the odd flight of De Havilland Mosquitoes or stray American raiders during the day, were a rehearsal for something they knew must come.

The patrons of the Pension Gern gradually drifted up the old wooden staircase to their rooms. Two or three opted to stay where they were, in case the big one did arrive. Frau Gern went around the cellar like a military commander, checking on the condition of her subordinates, and Haas could see that this was what drove her in her life, this feeling of being needed. He watched her and then watched her daughter. Ilse stayed quiet during the period of the alert, looking at the ceiling more than the others, her face tense and her eyes white, and Haas made a note of it.

He waited for Frau Gern and Ilse to go up before leaving the cellar himself. He exchanged some pleasantries with an old couple who ran a shop in the same building and shared a glass of schnapps with an air-raid warden who had chosen to take shelter there. Ilse Gern looked back twice when she was leaving the cellar, at Erich Haas the second time.

Haas then followed the two women up the stairs.

Someone had put 'Lili Marlene' on a gramophone player and the music filtered through the thick walls of the nineteenth-century building like a whisper.

Ilse was standing by his room, holding a candle, when he reached the desk again. He stared at her and she turned her head slowly to him as if she had been caught doing something illicit and half wanted approval for it. He looked for her mother, but Frau Gern was not there now. Ilse might just have turned, made an excuse and gone past him, but she did not. She just stood there.

He watched her chest move under her dressing gown and the way her hair fell on her shoulders and how she held her face behind her hair so that she could hide some of it from him. Then he saw the

candle flicker and she moved her hand and the light from the candle
lit up her face in a curious yellow. There was darkness of various
intensities the further away from the light you got. He was not even
sure she had seen him.

'Can I help?' he asked.

'Are you the last?' she said.

They both looked up and down the corridor. 'I believe I am,' he
replied. He reached into his pocket, took out his key and opened the
door of his room. 'You're shivering,' he said then. 'Are you cold or
frightened?'

'I'd better go.'

'Good night, then,' he said. But she did not go. Her hand shook
more. 'I enjoy the raids,' she said.

He reached out and touched her hand and steadied it. 'You are
cold,' he said.

'Mother's asleep. She always goes to sleep quickly when there's
been a raid alert. She can't stay up after midnight any more. She
pretends she can but I know she can't. That's why she does all that
concerned blockwart business. She has to have something to keep
her awake. I could stay awake all night after a raid alert.'

Haas touched her face with his finger. 'Come in . . . please.'

She stepped into the room and Haas closed the door. Then he
killed the candle flame with his fingers. Ilse placed the candle in the
small bowl on the table beside the door. Very slowly Haas leaned
his body close to hers and gently kissed her on the lips.

'You excite me,' she said. 'I can sense excitement. Most of the men
in this city reek of mundanity. They're civil servants or Party workers
or reserved occupations. All the excitement has died on the Russian
front. My husband was exciting. I don't think you're a book-binder,
but I don't care.' She took his hands and put them to her face. 'Try
not to make too much noise. I don't want Mother to hear. I can do
it without saying a word now.'

When he brought her the first time she bit into his shoulder and
cried small tears without a sound; the second time she came faster
and he let go just before she was finished; later, they both came
together, very slowly, almost painfully.

Some time just before the darkness left, Haas woke and touched
Ilse Gern on the stomach and she rolled over on to him. 'I have to
go,' she said, kissing his body. 'Mother will be getting up.'

She sat up and reached down for her clothes on the floor and tried to pull her nightdress over her while Haas kissed her neck. 'Please, Mother will be getting up soon. I must be back in my room.' She turned and touched his lips.

'Will you come tonight?' he asked

'Of course,' she said, giggling. 'And I am the three brass monkeys rolled into one. Hear no evil, see no evil, speak no evil.'

'I am a book-binder,' Haas said.

'I don't care what you are, Herr Rotach.'

'My name is Karl.'

'Herr Rotach,' she said.

She stood at the door and picked her candle from the wash-bowl and put it in her pocket. 'You and Max be careful,' she said then. 'I know he has Party connections, but black marketeers get no mercy from the Gestapo. Tomorrow I have time off and we can use my apartment if you want. I'll cook you something.'

'Perhaps in the evening.'

She nodded and smiled. 'We can make noise there,' she said. 'The walls are good.'

'And your policeman?'

'Wilhelm! He is a sad man, you know. He wants me because he wants a woman to replace his wife. She hates him. I may indeed marry him some day when I need to . . . but now . . . I don't need to. He is a sad man.'

When she had gone, Haas sighed, lay back and looked at the ceiling.

When he woke, Wilhelm Koch had a head cold and a headache; the head cold was physical, the headache metaphorical. Both were irritating. One caused him to lose his temper; he drank schnapps for the other.

'This is not my day, Theo,' he said to the detective sergeant standing in front of him. 'What's the time? My damn watch isn't working.'

'Seven fifteen, sir.'

'Did you go home last night, Kriminalmeister?' Koch asked.

Theo Brandt smiled on one side of his face. 'I am newly married, sir. Heidi . . . well, she likes me home. Even for a few hours. And there was no raid last night.' He pulled two photographs from a buff file and placed them in front of Koch.

'Jesus Christ!' Koch said.

'They were pulled out of the river an hour ago; we think they're two orpos who didn't come back from patrol last night. Quite a job done on them.'

'Black marketeers?'

'All the hallmarks. I've contacted the Gestapo.'

'That's all I need now. Some Wittelsbacher Palais kid telling me my job.'

'Movers and shakers, sir.'

'And when you're in the SS, Theo, will you move over there?'

'Speaking of all that, we may need their co-operation today, sir,' Brandt said,

'Oh, shit, I almost forgot. Preparations for Wagner's funeral.'

'Higher SS and Police Führer Von Eberstein wants roadblocks everywhere. And Kriminaldirektor Schmidt is wetting himself over these two killings. Screaming for people on every street.'

'When can we get an autopsy?' Koch asked then.

'Not before eleven. It's Saturday. Pathology does not work to wartime schedules.'

'Haul in everyone we know,' Koch said, looking at photographs again. 'Jesus Christ, there're some real animals in our Reich, Theo, know that?'

Brandt did not answer.

When he had gone, Koch went to the window and watched the broken city creep into life.

The first roadblock had just established itself on Dachauerstrasse when the Mercedes truck swung into the Leonrodplatz in north-west Munich, close to an S-bahn stop.

Martin Hofer got out of the cab without looking at the three uniformed *ordnungspolizei* in front of him. The three orpos were discussing the rumours which had already begun to circulate about the state of the two dead men fished out of the river earlier. Hofer could not believe his bad luck.

'Papers!'

The voice followed Hofer for a moment before he realised the demand was directed at him. He had not slept properly since Wednesday, having hopped on a train before being forced to sleep in a box-car on a railway siding and then steal a bicycle.

Twice, he thought about giving up and heading for Switzerland. He made it to the Abwehr Two safe house in Regensburg on Thursday night, taking the clothes, money, weapons and false papers that were there.

The next morning the Gestapo burst in. Hofer only just made it out of the back door and over several garden walls. All he could think of was Arthur Nebe shaking his head in Stauffenberg's castle. He cursed the Kripo chief and then the whole SS state, and after that he had no more energy for curses and he gave up any idea of going to Switzerland.

'Me?' he said to the orpo, knowing that he had just committed the cardinal error of seeming to be smart with the police. And, true to form, the two orpos shouted at him to halt and come back to them. One of them was pulling a carbine off his shoulder and shouting down the street for a Sicherheitspolizei agent – Hofer could not tell whether he was Gestapo or Kriminalpolizei – who was in the process of getting into his car.

'French?' the orpo asked Hofer.

He nodded. 'Yes. I don't speak such good German. I'm looking for work. There's my *Nichtdeutscher Dienstausweis*; here's my *urlaubschein* and my alien's passport and my *arbeitskarte*.'

'Jesus, we do all the fighting and you boys get all the work,' the policeman said.

'So much for the purification of the race,' his colleague added. He had lowered his weapon.

'Soon there'll be more bloody foreigners than Germans.'

'And we'll all be dead on the fucking Russian front.'

'I was asked to help,' Hofer said. 'So I came. To help.'

He thought he was through when the Sicherheitspolizei agent came along and insisted on checking his papers all over again. He was a Kriminalpolizei detective. Barely awake, rubbing a stubbled chin, sniffing.

'Open your bag, please,' he said while reading the alien's passport. Hofer hesitated. 'Your bag, please,' the Kripo detective said again.

The orpos with the carbines covered Hofer; the other pulled the small bag off his shoulder.

'My papers are in order,' Hofer said.

The orpo began to search the bag. 'Two policemen were brutally murdered last night. We're checking the fleas and lice today, to see if their papers are in order. Jesus, you haven't got any, have you? You French are all filthy.'

Hofer had backed off. There were fifty thousand Reichmarks in the bag, concealed in a pair of trousers; if they found the Reichmarks they'd detain him, if they detained him, they'd find the Walther tucked into the small of his back, and if they found that . . .

He swung his leg into the kneecap of the orpo with the carbine, slammed his fist into the Kripo detective, and made a bolt for it, down Dachauerstrasse, across the road. The orpo with the carbine fired but the round went high and by the time he had slammed another round into the breech and taken aim, Hofer had scrambled over a wall and into the garden of a mansion with a flagpole. A small aircraft was taking off from the airfield to his left, and all he could hear was shouting when he hit the ground. He was sweating and damning his luck and praying for more luck and wondering why the hell he hadn't gone to Switzerland.

Paul Kaestner stood at the hotel window overlooking Augustenstrasse, watching factory workers in heavy coats making their way to work with a slow, almost painful gait.

'I feel sorry for them,' he said.

Ruth Wachs stirred in the chair across the room and opened her eyes.

'Who?' she asked.

'Them, outside.'

'Don't,' she said when she had rubbed her eyes.

'You should have let me take that,' he said, pointing at the chair.

'I don't think so. You would have looked worse than you did and I might have asked you into bed with me. Did I embarrass you last night?'

'I was too frightened. My God, what we did to those two . . .'

'I could state the obvious.'

'Poor bastards.'

'Save your pity. We did all right last night. Quite the passionate lover. Pretending, anyway.'

He turned from the window and shoved his hands in his pockets. 'Now, I think you're playing power games with me. I won't allow that. I must shave.'

'Paul,' she said when he was shaving, 'I want to know I can rely on you.'

He paused before replying. There were sirens outside on the street. Moving vehicles. 'So do I,' he said. 'So do I.'

* * *

Hofer slipped out of a side gate on Augustenstrasse, tried to slow his breathing. He could hear the sirens around him; he wondered who the hell had been so stupid as to kill two policemen. Then the face of SD Hauptsturmführer Alois Tor came into his mind.

He had dumped the papers he had been using, pulled out some new ones, and switched jackets from a clothes-line.

He put his hands in his pockets and crossed the street. A truck was coming down Augustenstrasse at speed. It halted at the junction with Schellingstrasse and soldiers and orpos poured out on to the street, shouting at pedestrians, asking for papers. Two soldiers confronted Hofer.

He presented new papers – German – and the soldiers looked at him and then let him through.

When Hofer reached the end of Augustenstrasse, he walked over to a tram stop near Karlstrasse; the tram stopped and Hofer took his place in the queue, which was slow because there were fewer trams now. He felt his pulse lower and his breathing even out and he thanked God and some other deities for giving him some luck. He stepped on to the tram.

'Frenchman!'

Hofer did not turn until the Mauser pistol was touching his back.

'Your hands up or your body out flat.'

Hofer turned his head slowly, as if he were going to attempt to bluff his way out again. He thought about reaching for the Walther in the small of his back. The Kripo detective from the Dachauerstrasse road block smiled, touched his jaw, where Hofer had punched him, and swung his pistol and knocked him to the ground.

Erich Haas left the Pension Gern just in time to see the residue of Martin Hofer's arrest being cleared from the streets. He passed two checkpoints without difficulty.

He took the Salzburg train, changed at Freilassing for Berchtesgaden, but got out at Bad Reichenhall and took a bus. The security in Berchtesgaden was more apparent than it had been but there was a relaxed feeling among the soldiers and detectives. Haas went to a small house near the town hall in Berchtesgaden. A little silver-haired man with a roughly hewn face and smooth hands answered the door. He blinked in the midday sunlight and raised his hand; a church bell rang.

'Herr Keller? Herr Helmut Keller?' Haas asked. He put out his hand and took Keller's. 'Karl Rotach . . . Herr Max Weg of Munich gave me you name and since I was in the area . . .'

'Ah, yes, yes, the book-binder. Yes, please, come in. *Gruss Gott.*'

'Yes, *Gruss Gott.* I am from Berlin. I would have come sooner but I have had other engagements and the terror flyers are making life very difficult in the cities these days. Not to mention problems with travel. Soon, I will not be able to travel any more. This trip was only through the good grace of some Party colleagues in Berlin.'

'You're in the Party?'

Hass pulled his overcoat lapel to one side and revealed a gold Nazi Party badge.

'An old fighter . . .'

'Yes. Not too many of us left, Herr Keller.'

Haas stepped inside the small house and glanced left and right to see who had seen him.

'Herr Weg said you would charge a reasonable price, Herr Rotach. Will you do the work here or in Berlin?'

'Oh, Herr Weg allows me to use his facilities in Munich; it would not be feasible to take books back to Berlin. And I would have to charge prices no one could afford.'

'Of course. May I offer you a drink?'

'Please. I'd like to see the books, Herr Keller. You've known Herr Weg a long time?'

'We're old comrades, so to speak.'

'You'll be going to Gauleiter Wagner's funeral, then?'

'No, not me. I'll watch the Führer go. Too old to go to Munich these days.'

'I suppose so.'

He led Haas up four flights of very narrow stairs to a small room at the top of the house. It was all treated pine and the smell of resin was sweet and almost sickly, except for the sharp tang of leather.

'All mine,' Keller said. 'My children.'

He touched an old book. Haas was looking out of the window at Berkwerkstrasse and Salzburgerstrasse below and the first checkpoint on the road up to the Berghof. And he was making a calculation in his head.

'Can you do the job?' Keller asked.

'I think so,' Haas replied.

*   *   *

The meeting broke up into cliques at six o'clock; and the cliques were still talking at seven. Wilhelm Koch tried three times to get away from his *kriminaldirektor*, a rather stiff man with one eyebrow, but three times his superior had called him back to discuss some minor detail of the orpo murder investigation or some other enquiry. Koch's headache was back, but this time it was real. On his fourth attempt, when he had explained every detail of every case on his desk, he managed to break free and reach the door.

'I do hope you can guarantee these criminals will be in custody before the Führer comes.'

If he had not recognised the voice, Koch would not have turned around. 'Herr Brigadeführer.'

Johann Rattenhuber waited for Koch to come to something like attention before proffering his hand. 'If I didn't know it I'd say you were trying to avoid me, Koch,' he said. 'It's been a long time, Wilhelm.'

'Several years, sir.'

'I have been travelling. Führer headquarters.'

Koch nodded and moved on to the balls of his toes.

'So you're on top of this, then?' Rattenhuber asked.

'Doing our best under the difficult circumstances in which we all work.'

'That wasn't what I asked.'

'No, sir. To be honest, I don't expect to find anyone for this. To be honest, we could pin it on some old criminal with a record, and that would satisfy the Higher SS and Police Führer, and others. But that would be an honest assessment.'

Rattenhuber smiled. 'You always were honest. To a fault, I suspect, Wilhelm. But I appreciate it.'

'We've hauled in everyone we could think of and the Gestapo have hauled in everyone they could think of. And then there's a score or more of people who were just hauled in today because their papers weren't right or their faces were dirty.'

'Now you're betraying your other weakness, Koch. Not an admirable quality.'

'There just aren't the men for homicide detection any more, sir. Too many other interests have to be served. Anyway, numbers aren't enough. Experience is what counts and that's been frittered away.'

'Don't be too honest, Wilhelm.'

'At least I can claim overtime for working weekends.'

Rattenhuber put out his hand again.

'You weren't refused entry to the RSD because of your performance, Wilhelm,' he said. 'There were more sensitive reasons, you know. I'm sorry about it. I could have used you. If you weren't so opinionated sometimes.'

'I'm better off here, I think, sir. It's what I like doing. Keeps me out of mischief.'

'I'm glad to hear it. Look, we must arrange a social gettogether sometime.'

'It'll probably take a week to interview all these people, sir.'

'You have tomorrow.'

Saturday had just become Sunday when Max Weg staggered into his apartment building near the Leopoldpark, the worse for a whole day's drinking with Nazi Party members. He had to stop and find the bannisters three times before attempting to climb the stairs, and just when he reached his own floor, the air-raid sirens went off.

'Allow me to save you from the staircase, Herr Weg.'

'Ilse . . . I'm perfectly able to make my way down to the cellars. Well, I would be if I was not the slightest little bit drunk. But in honour of Gauleiter Wagner.'

'You do mock, Herr Weg. I am not mother, so there is no gain for you.'

'You see right through me, Ilse.'

'Was Herr Rotach with you today?'

'For one drink. Then he left. He has business. I am closed. Losing business for the honour of the dead Gauleiter Wagner.'

'Yes. Mother says Frau Steiner – the lacemaker – had a couple asking where you lived. Keen customers.'

'Who were they?'

'I don't know; but Mother wanted to tell you. She's at the pension tonight. I'm going on duty in an hour. Frau Steiner couldn't tell them where you lived anyway, she didn't know. Mother was angry at her. Foolishly. "You've probably cost Herr Weg business," she said. And all that kind of thing. I'm sure they'll be back if they're that keen.'

'I'm sure they will. But your mother's right. It could be too late.'

Claude Dansey barely looked up at Teddy Giles. 'Nothing?'

'Nothing.'

Dansey tapped his fingers. 'All right.'

'You should get some sleep, sir.'

Dansey took his glasses off and leaned back in his chair. 'I've got a special job for you, Teddy. Call it a test. If you pass, and this German business works out in our favour, maybe we'll see about getting you something better paid. Away from Africa. You're ambitious, aren't you, Teddy?'

'What's the job, sir?'

That afternoon, Erich Haas put the finishing touches to what he had been planning. He buried his third gunny sack south-west of Hallein and east of Berchtesgaden, across the Salzach river from the village of Golling. It was a warm day and he carried his knapsack on one shoulder. After walking in the hills, he took a local train back to Hallein, and then began to walk towards the village of Oberau, about two kilometres from the Berchtesgaden.

This was the most dangerous move of his preparations, as he was utterly exposed if Hitler's security should decide to put on a show of strength or if one of the local population should become suspicious. He was banking on a straight walk-past by a Sunday hiker going unnoticed, as anyone who seems to know where they are going does not provoke suspicion. He also hoped that the time of day and the day itself would have civilians and military alike concentrating on other matters.

It was a risk he had to take, and for that he enjoyed it. Like going into Max Weg's shop the week before. He'd half expected to run right into the Gestapo, even after watching the bookshop for a day, but that had not happened. And now he was almost ready and luck and skill and nerve had brought him to this. It was a good feeling.

'Are you lost?'

He was standing on a bridge in Oberau, looking at a house on a hill ahead of him and making a mental note.

'You can't go that way. That's the Führer's house.'

The little girl came from the direction of the small church with the onion dome and she wore a blue coat and an apricot frock.

'No,' Haas said, 'I'm not lost. I'm just taking in the view before the sun goes down.'

'You're not from here.'

'Berlin. Where do you live?'

'Up there; Daddy's dead.'

'I'm sorry.'

'So am I. What's your name?'

Haas kept moving his eyes to see who was watching; no one seemed to be. A little drizzle had begun to fall and it was flecking the packed snow in the field next to him.

'Karl . . . my name is Karl.'

'I'm Doris, Doris Schieff. I'm called Doris because my mother likes English names. She lived in England. We should not be fighting the English. Did you fight the English?'

'Once.'

Haas reached into his pocket and pulled out a boiled sweet.

'Mummy told me never to accept things from strangers. Daddy did, too, but Daddy's dead. The English killed him. Mummy's upset.'

Haas put the sweet back in his pocket. He touched the little girl's head. 'You should go inside. You'll get wet.'

'Where are you going?'

'Salzburg.'

'I don't like Salzburg.'

'Me neither.'

Haas moved his eyes and took in every feature he could and logged them all. 'I've got to go now,' he said.

'I won't tell if you give me that sweet,' Doris Schieff said.

'Tell what?'

She shrugged. 'Whatever it is you are hiding. I bet it's in that.'

She pointed at his knapsack. Haas froze for a moment and considered an option. Then he reached into his pocket and pulled the sweet out again. 'Deal,' he said. 'Friends?'

'Mummy told me never to make friends with strangers.'

Haas began to laugh. 'She's right,' he said.

Doris Schieff turned and ran back towards the church and Haas walked on down to the main Salzburg to Berchtesgaden road for a bus he knew would be there.

Mathius Schumann broke a splinter of wood between his fingers and began to clean one of his fingernails. 'Now what do we do?' he asked.

Ruth Wachs examined the Braille cards in front of her, then chewed the skin around her own fingernail. 'You covered yourself?' she asked. 'Footprints, all that?'

Schumann sipped his schnapps and raised his eyebrows. 'I just wish someone had mentioned that our shopkeeper's blind. Small detail London might have added. At least, we've narrowed his dwelling down to a square kilometre around the Leopoldpark. Only marginally impossible now. I'll bet you got some peculiar looks, yeah? I can't wait to turn up at the Hohenzollernplatz again. I think I'll wear a sign: Anyone know Max Weg?'

'Shut up,' Wachs snapped.

'Another nice mess you've gotten us into,' Schumann said then. And he flicked his tie and scratched his head.

Wachs slammed her hand down on his. 'Just grow up,' she said.

'You know, you're beginning to annoy me, sister.'

'The feeling's mutual.'

'So what do we do?' Kaestner asked.

'Tomorrow,' Wachs said. 'Tomorrow. No matter what. It has to be.'

'What do you mean?' Kaestner asked.

'I mean we do whatever is necessary at whatever cost to ourselves, Paul. I mean that he'll move tomorrow. He has to.'

'Wagner's funeral,' Schumann said then. 'Hitler'll be here.' He smiled and shook his head. 'Shit!'

At first, Kaestner returned a confused look, then his mouth opened more than it should, then he began shaking his head in small jerks. 'Oh, no . . . no,' he said. 'You're joking?'

'I wish I was, Paul,' Wachs responded. 'I wish I was.'

'But why?'

'London doesn't want it.'

'You have to give it to them,' Schumann said, 'they saw us coming.'

'No,' Kaestner continued. 'No way. Mathius?'

'Orders are orders, as they say here. If it's a choice between a rock and a hard place . . .'

Wachs reached over and grabbed Kaestner's wrist. 'We'll get him,' she said. 'We'll get him tomorrow.'

'You're both crazy.'

'Only slightly,' Schuman said. 'It's a peculiar world.'

Kaestner closed his eyes and listened to his heart beat.

10

ERICH HAAS LAID the parts of the Navy Luger out on the bed, assembled it, adjusted the telescopic sight and took aim at an old tourism photograph of the mountains south of Munich. He focused the weapon on the nearest of two men standing on a hillside, wearing *lederhosen*. Then he stripped the weapon, placed the parts in the pockets of his coat, hung the coat on the back of the door and washed himself. It was Monday 17 April 1944.

'You are leaving us, Herr Rotach?' Frau Gern asked at the desk in the foyer.

'I hope to finish my work today, Frau Gern.'

A Wehrmacht officer and a young girl came out of a room at the end of the corridor and hesitated. The girl kissed the soldier and he grinned. Then they passed Frau Gern and Erich Haas without saying anything.

'Newlyweds,' Frau Gern said then. 'Foolish. But still, we need the children.'

'If I could have my bill?' Haas asked.

'Of course. You will not be attending Gauleiter Wagner's funeral with Herr Weg, then?'

'I suspect he'll have others to go with.'

'Yes. The Führer is sure to be there. Have you ever seen the Führer?'

'From a distance.'

She totted up the bill with a pencil and wrote it out on a small slip of rough paper. Haas reached into his pocket and pulled out the money, which he counted out, very slowly, on the desk. 'I'll pay my respects,' he said. 'I promise.'

'I am not sorry you are going,' Gerda Gern said.

Haas did not move. Frau Gern looked up but continued writing. She took the money from the desk and recounted it.

'Is Ilse at home today?' Haas asked then.

'Or meeting Kriminalkommisar Koch. He's very fond of her. And she's very fond of him. I think she wants him to propose. And he will. When this business with his wife is sorted out. He has been hurt by his wife, you know. That makes a person slow, deliberate, suspicious. But that's fine.'

'Then I wish them the very best,' Haas said. 'Say goodbye to Ilse for me.'

'Are you married, Herr Rotach?'

'No, Frau Gern. The right girl wouldn't have me and the ones that would I didn't want.'

'We can't always get what we want.'

'But we can try. We used to say that in Russia, when things were bad.'

Haas entered Weg's shop through the back, via a lane.

'I thought you had asked me to be here so you could kill me,' Weg said. 'I came early. Are you going to kill me?'

'I had considered it, but it's not necessary,' Haas said.

'I bet you're not as hard as you sound.'

'You don't know the half of it. Get rid of all this stuff when you can.' He put his suitcase in the corner of the room.

'I may need it,' Weg said. 'I suspect attention may focus on me, one way or another.'

Haas looked at the chess board. 'Your move, Max,' he said.

Weg sat at the table and moved a chess piece. 'Checkmate, I think,' he said.

Haas looked at the board. 'Yes,' he said after a while.

Then Max Weg heard the sound of footsteps on the stairs and the shop bell.

Paul Kaestner was sitting on a bench at a tram stop in the Hohenzollernplatz, reading a newspaper and listening to a small radio in a nearby café broadcast the Wagner funeral – Hitler had arrived at the Feldherrnhalle – when Erich Haas came out the front door of Weg's bookshop.

At first, Kaestner could not believe it was Haas. Twice, he looked at the photograph he carried.

By the time he had come to terms with it being Haas, the assassin had crossed Hohenzollernstrasse and disappeared into a side street.

Kaestner dropped the newspaper on the ground, checked the weapon in his pocket and followed. But when he turned the corner into the side street, Haas was gone again. Kaestner leaned back against the wall and slammed his hand against the stone washing and shoved his silenced Mauser pistol back inside his coat pocket. He tapped out a pre-arranged Morse signal on his Joan-Eleanor transmitter.

A minute later, Ruth Wachs was walking towards him. 'Where?' she asked.

Kaestner nodded, then described Haas.

'Go right, then turn down towards Augustenstrasse,' Wachs said. 'We'll flank him.'

She passed on without stopping, crossed the cobbled street and turned towards Kurfurstenstrasse to her left. Kaestner turned right and headed back in the direction of the Hohenzollernplatz before turning south again.

Haas was at the church at the Josephsplatz when Ruth Wachs saw him. She had time to consider pulling her Mauser and trying a shot. Then he disappeared into the building. She huddled into a corner and tapped out a morse signal.

She entered the church perhaps two to three minutes after Haas, pushed through the communion lines and walked up and down the side aisles to and from the altar. Nothing. She walked back towards a man with his hands in his pockets, a plainclothes security policeman, probably Gestapo. He looked at his watch, sighed, caught the priest's eye and tapped his watch. The priest nodded once.

Ruth Wachs scanned the congregation again, and then mouthed an obscenity. Haas was gone.

Outside the church, five ordnungspolizei wandered up and down the lines of people leaving, telling them to hurry up, and checking papers now and again. On one of the church walls someone had scrawled: 'Enjoy the war, the peace will be much worse.' The authorities had tried to scrub it off but had only succeeded in dulling the paint.

People began to mutter and a couple of them took their frustrations out on the policemen, who just shrugged their shoulders. No one seemed to be afraid of the orpos, not the way Wachs remembered before. She stopped at the end of the street.

Kaestner was standing across the road. Wachs looked around before crossing over.

'He must have gone straight in and out,' Wachs said. 'I should have known he'd do a procedural run. Shit! Where the hell's Schumann?'

Over in Ettstrasse 2, Wilhelm Koch's headache was gone but his head cold was getting worse. He looked at Martin Hofer's mugshot one more time. 'How long have we had him?' he asked his sergeant.

'Since Saturday,' Theo Brandt said.

'A.m. or p.m?'

'The bad one.'

'How the hell have we had him that long and not recognised him? What took us so long to identify him?'

'We must have pulled in fifty to a hundred suspects on Saturday, sir, for this orpo murder business. He was just another. And we are pressed. Gauleiter Wagner's funeral ...'

'You know that man's more trouble dead than he was when he was just a pickled politician.'

'I think you're trying to upset me, sir.'

'No, Theo. I'm your superior, it's impossible for me to upset you. I was half hoping he killed the two orpos,' Koch said.

'Gauleiter Wagner?'

Koch grinned.

The small bearded face of Theo Brandt nodded at the heap of files. 'Hofer was carrying a Walther ... they were both shot with the same silenced Mauser,' he said.

Koch read the autopsy report. 'It's not going to gain you and me promotion, Theo. Well, you maybe ...'

'Surely he's really Gestapo business, sir, isn't he? Conspiracy to endanger the life of the Führer ... activities contrary to the well-being and security of the Reich, etc., etc.'

'Yes, but he is first and foremost a murder suspect. And anyway, Kriminaldirektor Schmidt says we're to handle it. Orders from Berlin. Nebe, personally.'

'Who's Schmidt not trying to impress?' Brandt asked.

'I just follow orders, Theo.'

'And he stands beside the great and the good at the funeral.'

'Where he thinks he can announce Hofer's arrest to the Führer or the Reichsführer or whoever,' Koch said. 'I bet Higher SS and

Police Führer Von Eberstein's in on this. Nice bit of arse-licking to the Reichsführer. And for us, it's just more work for little reward, Theo.'

'Enemies of the state bring more notice than any number of gang murders. Even of orpos.'

Koch blew his nose and stopped himself sniffing by smoking again. 'I need this like a bloody hole in the head, Theo.'

'Praised be that which hardens, as the Reichsführer would say.'

'Cheeky bastard. Get me some more schnapps.'

'And the prisoner – Hofer?'

'Wheel him in. Let's see if we can get a statement and have the Führer forgive me my past indiscretions.'

'May I ring my wife, sir? I was expected home yesterday.'

'By all means, Theo. Tell her you'll be home in 1954, and then give her my apologies. Then ring my wife and tell her I won't ever be home.'

Hofer was smaller than Koch had imagined, and his growth of stubble and tired eyes gave him the appearance of an animal about to be used for vivisection. He lowered himself into the chair provided and kept looking around him, as if he were expecting a bullet.

'I read here you are no longer a serving officer, Herr Major, but I'll use your rank anyway. Smoke?'

Hofer shook his head.

'Good,' Koch said. 'I only have so many. Now I just want to get things clear for my own report. Then I'm sure others will want a word. But that is your problem, Herr Major, not mine. If you will insist on trying to kill the Führer, you must expect the consequences. Now, please tell me the sequence of events surrounding the deaths of the two SD men, Mann and ... er, Tor.'

'Are you trying to make fun of me, Herr Kriminalkommissar?' Hofer asked.

'Please, Herr Major, I have a head cold, and I have a major murder investigation in this city and a massive ceremonial problem draining resources. You'll appreciate that my patience is limited. My time even more so. I just want a statement. For our files. Then you'll be charged, put through the proper procedure and so forth. We're not thugs here, despite what you may think. Now, please

... tell me what happened, where you went, what you did, who you talked to, all that kind of thing. Up to the moment you were caught.'

Hofer was convinced that Himmler, Ohlendorf or Schellenberg was watching or listening, or both. Perhaps even Arthur Nebe. He watched Koch's face for any sign. 'I'd like something to eat,' he said then. 'I haven't eaten for over a day.'

'Oh . . . well, yes, I'll see what we have. There are shortages. You've no coupons, I suppose?' Koch smiled, picked up a black telephone receiver, pressed a switch on an intercom and called for some food. 'I'm afraid there's only *suppengrün* available,' he said when he had put the phone down. 'There's some bread, though. Not great but edible. The SD men?'

'They were going to kill me,' Hofer said. 'They were going to kill me because . . .' Then he shook his head. 'It doesn't matter. I'm dead anyway.'

'I assure you, in my custody you are safe.'

'My God, Herr Kriminalkommissar, where are you living? I was a victim of *Nacht und Nebel*. You do understand *Nacht und Nebel*?'

'A regrettable procedure. But you were plotting to kill the Führer. It says so here.'

'I don't know if you're a knave or a fool or both, Herr Kriminalkommissar.'

'When were you planning to do it? Gauleiter Wagner's funeral? Down at the Feldherrnhalle or the Konigsplatz? And who else is involved? This is only for my own curiosity. I am a homicide investigator. Other people investigate plots. I investigate murders.'

'Whatever you have been told is untrue. Though I do not expect you to believe me. Is this room secure?'

'You won't escape.'

'Not what I meant. I meant do SD Inland or the Gestapo have a wire in here?'

'My God, I think you could claim some kind of mental illness as a mitigation. This is a *kripoleitstelle*, not some SS brothel. You could annoy me, Herr Major.'

'Lock the door, will you.'

'Jesus! You're the first prisoner I've ever had who asked for that, Herr Major. That is insanity. But then again, reading about how you killed one of these SD men, I feel I must warn you that I am armed and there are two detectives in the next room. It is a substantial drop to the ground outside and there are *ordnungspolizei* guards out there. By the way, you didn't kill two orpos in the Englischer Garten the other night?'

'I think you're missing the point here, Koch.'

'Which is?'

'I was arrested because I had information of a genuine assassin here in Munich, here today, who will kill the Führer. Hired by the British. Have you ever heard of the Abwehr Tod programme?'

Koch shook his head.

'Assassins, run by Abwehr Two. Completely anonymous, utterly untraceable. I run – ran – the section. This assassin is one of my men. Turned. He vanished in England earlier this year.'

'Go on. I like a good story.'

'I informed Walter Schellenberg and Otto Ohlendorf, and that night I was picked up by our two deceased friends. They took me to a wood to kill me. I had no choice. I am trying to protect the Führer.'

'From what I hear of the Abwehr these days, that's quite a novel position, Herr Major. It's a good story, I'll give you that, but I warn you, the Gestapo are humourless sods.'

'I didn't expect you to believe me.'

'Would you in my position?'

'No, probably not.'

'However, I will inform the Reich Security Main Office of what has transpired. Perhaps the Gestapo will want to pursue it. Müller hates Schellenberg and Ohlendorf, I hear. Likes to embarrass them. It's not really my area, political assassination. I deal in the lower grades of homicide.'

'I suspect you'll be dead in twenty-four to forty-eight hours, Herr Kriminalkommissar. Don't worry, I'll be dead before you.'

'Please don't try and kill me or yourself. It upsets the men and it means more paperwork for me.'

'This is a waste of time and you're a bloody fool, Koch,' Hofer said. 'Why don't you do us both a favour and shoot me while I'm trying to escape.'

There was a knock on the door and a young woman entered carrying a tray with soup and bread.

'Ah, the food,' Koch said. 'Just in time to prevent me from losing my temper. You know you're an arrogant bastard, Hofer. Exactly what I'd expect from a traitor. And now, if you'll excuse me, I have work to do. *Bon appetit*. Don't go anywhere. I'll be back.'

Mathius Schumann was standing at the junction of Karlstrasse and Luisenstrasse, cursing his two colleagues, tapping mercilessly on his Joan-Eleanor, watching the snaking lines of people taking up positions near the Konigsplatz for the Wagner funeral.

He had been wandering around the area of the Leopoldpark, with the vain notion that he might just pick up the trail of Max Weg, when Kaestner's message came through on the Joan-Eleanor. Schumann launched himself south, without really thinking, in an attempt to try and cut Haas off from the funeral area, but was forced west by the security around the Konigsplatz and Briennerstrasse. Now there was no sign of Haas and he could get no response from Wachs and Kaestner.

The gravelly solemnity of Adolf Hitler's voice echoed from a loudspeaker.

Schumann was about to head up Karlstrasse, towards the Wagner funeral, when he glanced south towards the Bahnhofplatz.

The man was standing about a hundred metres ahead of him, looking back towards the Konigsplatz, his collar turned up, wearing glasses and a moustache. He was slightly stooped and looking older, but it was him.

Then Erich Haas turned and stepped out on to the street behind a tram.

Schumann tapped furiously on his Joan-Eleanor once more, checked the silenced Mauser in his pocket and shoved his way through a group of people discussing the funeral.

An SS officer warned that when the cortège left the Feldherrnhalle for the procession down Briennerstrasse, everyone should keep quiet. No one paid any attention.

Schumann saw Haas again at the Bahnhofplatz. Then Haas disappeared into a crowd of workers and Schumann stopped and scanned the heads.

'Berchtesgaden,' he muttered to himself.

Inside the Hauptbahnhof, Erich Haas went to a ticket counter and bought a second-class ticket to Berchtesgaden. They would expect an attempt on Hitler at the funeral, perhaps, not from the third floor of a town house in Berchtesgaden.

The station was humming with the business of wartime travel, while a loudspeaker broadcast the proceedings from Gauleiter Wagner's funeral. Haas heard Hitler's voice and stopped for a few seconds. On one platform, two orpos were arguing with a group of drunken soldiers, threatening to get the military police. The soldiers were really in no mood to have three cops tell them what to do.

Finally, three Gestapo agents came out of the station police office and tried to calm the situation down. A sergeant went to hit one of them but he lost his balance and fell on to the tracks. When his comrades finally dragged him up on to platform again, bruised and almost unconscious, it seemed to defuse the whole row and the Gestapo and orpos were content to have it so.

One of the orpos brought the sergeant a glass of water and the policemen and the soldiers discussed Russia for a while until the policemen seemed to become uncomfortable and pulled away from the conversation.

Mathius Schumann entered the station as Erich Haas was walking up the platform towards his train. Schumann caught up with him just as the assassin had reached it. Schumann started to draw his gun. Solemn funeral music beat out the glacial pace of events now as he forced his way towards Haas. And then the music was gone.

The air-raid sirens had begun.

For a moment, the huge swell in the station stopped; for several seconds it began to deflate; then the sirens stopped. A false alarm. In the silence that followed, as whoever was in charge of the public address system tried to reconnect the Wagner funeral broadcast, the panic began and the crowd reflated.

Schumann's eyes caught Haas's as Haas was about to board the train. Then Haas saw Schumann's silenced Mauser.

Schumann went to fire, but the swell of people making for the shelters, urged on by policemen and rail guards, knocked him off balance.

Haas swung his right hand up in one movement and flicked his wrist. A small metal tube appeared out of the end of his sleeve. Schumann struggled to bring his Mauser to bear again. But Haas fired first. At the same moment, the crowd shifted direction.

Haas's silenced sleeve-gun round went through a fifty-eight-year-old train guard. The man toppled over in the middle of the scrum and the scrum moved again and took Schumann with it. Haas jumped into the carriage against the current.

Schumann pushed through the dozen or so people who were beginning to realise that the train guard was dying under them. The man was groaning and a small trail of blood ran to the edge of the platform, through some white grooved lines, and dripped on to the track. A man cursed and a woman called for a doctor.

Schumann tried to get at the carriage Haas had jumped into but was forced back by five men who were trying get out. He was pushed across the platform and against the wall. He began searching the train windows, trying desperately to get off the wall. The loudspeakers in the station were now pleading with the crowd to stop panicking, the emergency was over.

Inside the train, Erich Haas had ducked into a toilet. Outside in the corridors people were shouting at each other, some still trying to get out, others telling them the alert was over, to get back in. The sounds of fear and frayed tempers had mixed so that you could not tell the one from the other. One woman wanted to bring a second suitcase with her and it was caught and blocking other people's exits. A man behind was yelling at her, and two men who were refusing to leave the train, were arguing that it was a false alarm, the sirens had stopped. But no one was in a mood for listening.

Haas drew some water from a tap in the toilet and rubbed his face.

Every thought and every permutation of thoughts went through his head in the seconds he worked. He pulled out the sleeve-gun and reloaded it and slipped it back in place. Then he took a deep breath, opened the door slightly, looked out and stepped back into the corridor.

Some people had opened the doors on the track side and had jumped down between the trains. Haas looked out, then up and down the carriage, and then jumped after them.

Mathius Schumann reached the train at the same moment. But when he went to follow Haas, he was pushed back by two men with four suitcases trying to get out. Schumann hit one of them and forced his way past. But Haas had vanished again.

Haas pushed his way along the gravel and then slipped under the coupling of two carriages and pulled himself up on the concrete platform and headed for the concourse. He ran right into the three policemen, who had been arguing with the soldiers before, and who were now directing people into an underground waiting room that served as an air-raid shelter, still unaware that the alert was over.

Haas tried to explain that the emergency was over, but the policemen made him go down and soon he was following the crowd into the shelter.

Schumann reached the concourse through the gap between the trains as the policemen realised their mistake. He moved up and down, wiping his mouth, breathing heavily, muttering to himself, cursing, tapping his Joan-Eleanor.

Behind him, someone was shouting for the police. A train guard had been shot, people muttered to each other; and the story changed to two train guards and then two guards and a cop and then there were too many stories.

For fifteen minutes, Erich Haas was stuck in the underground waiting room. When he got out, there was a group of policemen gathered around the dead train guard. Several people who had been nearby when the event had occurred were giving highly charged versions of what they thought had happened. And more policemen were flooding the station.

Haas went with the flow, dipped his head and followed the throng out of the Bayerstrasse exit of the Hauptbahnhof. When he was out, he swung round on his heels and then headed for a tram stop at the Bahnhofplatz.

With the sunlight, events seemed to condense to manageable proportions. The city outside was moving at the pace of the all clear. The radios said the Wagner funeral procession was heading down Briennerstrasse to the Konigsplatz. Erich Haas composed himself, made a decision and then crossed the road to the next parked tram.

Paul Kaestner reached the edge of the Bahnhofplatz as Haas was crossing the platz. Behind him, Ruth Wachs was beginning to pick up speed. And in front of the Hauptbahnhof, Mathius Schumann had stopped.

The tram driver rang the bell.

Kaestner saw Haas as the assassin was getting on the tram. He had a clear shot and went to draw his Mauser, but then hesitated. And, as he did so, Haas disappeared into the tram, and it moved off. Kaestner let his gun slip back into his pocket.

Wachs grabbed him by the sleeve.

'He's on the tram. I missed him.'

Wachs swore. 'Back that way,' she said, pointing to the Konigsplatz. 'And up Karlstrasse.' Kaestner nodded and moved off, still nodding.

Schumann came running across the Bahnhofplatz to Wachs. 'He was going to Berchtesgaden. He was going to do it there.'

'He's on the tram,' Wachs said, gesturing with her head. 'Take the left side of the street.' She crossed the platz and accelerated into a slow trot.

Adolf Wagner's funeral procession had reached the Brown House, the Nazi Party headquarters, at the Konigsplatz end of Briennerstrasse. The solemn music was weaving its way through the streets from radios and its natural echo was a faint background noise in the distance.

Wachs and Schumann caught up with the tram at the Karlsplatz. It disgorged and absorbed equal amounts of people. Wachs paced up and down the footpath, looking for Haas. Schumann searched the tram from across the street, shaking his head. Then the tram bell rang again. Wachs signalled to Schumann and jumped on board.

The tram turned right towards the Sendlinger Tor, Schumann shadowing it from about thirty metres. On board, Ruth Wachs pushed her way along the spine of the tram, squeezing her body through the herd of commuters and the curtain of stale breath. Twice, she thought a man in front of her was Erich Haas. When the tram came to a halt again, she tapped out another signal on her Joan-Eleanor. Haas was gone. Again.

Paul Kaestner was standing at the barrier between Karlstrasse and the Konigsplatz, facing five SS guards and three ranks of spectators, when the pinprick pulses of his Joan-Eleanor tickled his fingers. Ahead of him, the sea of people made sudden waves in the solemnity around the Propylaen, while the strained, almost pained voice of Josef Goebbels began a eulogy for Adolf Wagner.

For a few moments, Kaestner hesitated again, watching the crowd, and beyond them the legions of Nazi dignitaries paying tribute to the old drunken gauleiter in the neo-classical splendour of the Konigsplatz necropolis. Then Kaestner swallowed what was choking him, pulled back from the crowd and slipped back up Karlstrasse, towards the Feldherrnhalle. Mathius Schumann had spotted Haas again, moving east.

Erich Haas came to a halt at the Marienplatz in the centre of Munich. The bomb damage in the platz and the spectators and mourners, coming and going to Wagner's funeral, had forced people into lines, winding their way through heaps of rubble. Policemen and soldiers patrolling the area were doing random searches, while several loudspeakers blasted the ceremony from various windows and open doors. One of the Nazi banners near the Neues Rathaus fell, snagged on a wall and then ripped itself apart.

Haas checked his back once more, then shoved his hands in his pockets and headed north towards the Feldherrnhalle and the Odeonsplatz. Twice he stopped, once to straighten his hat in a shop window, the second time to do up his shoelace.

Behind him, Mathius Schumann stayed out of sight, worked his Joan-Eleanor and drew his Mauser pistol.

On Sendlingerstrasse, about three-quarters of a kilometre behind Schumann, Ruth Wachs was now running.

And Paul Kaestner had reached the Maximilianplatz, about five hundred metres from the Feldherrnhalle. But he'd stopped again.

Erich Haas touched the Navy Luger inside his coat and watched the crowds streaming from the Feldherrnhalle, down Briennerstrasse, towards the sound of the excited voice that darted around the streets from the loudspeakers and radios. He stood for a minute, looking towards the Konigsplatz, surveyed the buildings around the platz and came to the same conclusion he had reached before. Then he headed for a bus on the other side of the Odeonsplatz.

Mathius Schumann came at him from the Theatinerkirche side of the Feldherrnhalle.

This time, Schumann had his pistol levelled at Haas before Haas saw him. But he fired while on the run, aiming with both hands. A woman yelled at her children and two men dived to the ground. The silenced round flew right of Haas and embedded itself in a middle-aged woman who was pulling herself on to the bus ahead of him. And because of the slow speed of the round, the woman took a while to realise she had been shot. A small trickle of blood came from her mouth and she fell back into a man's arms and then on to the street.

Haas ducked into the bus, swung his arm across his body and fired the sleeve-gun. Schumann staggered a bit, shouted for people to get out of the way, and then fell, got up and fell again.

And the bus moved off.

A small crowd of people who had missed the bus was gathered round the dead woman, trying to figure out what had happened to her. The man into whose arms she had fallen felt blood on his fingers and raised them.

'My God,' he said, 'she's been shot.'

Schumann was up again, running after the bus. He fired another round but it hit the bodywork of the bus and splintered on impact without anyone even noticing it because of the noise of the vehicle.

Four orpos in the Odeonsplatz drew their carbines. A squad of SS soldiers shouted a warning to each other and pulled their rifles off their shoulders.

Kaestner, who had reached Briennerstrasse near the Carlton Tearooms, was going to shout a warning to Schumann.

But two of the policemen called for Schumann to halt. Another had his weapon up at his shoulder in a firing position.

Schumann, who was weakening fast now from his bullet wound, swung and fired at the orpo with his rifle pointed, and caught him dead centre in the head. The man fell by the kerb.

The other three orpos loosed off a round each before Schumann could train his Mauser on any of them. Two of the orpo rounds hit Schumann, who spun and fired another round from his own weapon. It struck a child in the face. Then the real screaming started in the Odeonsplatz.

Schumann picked himself up again, and was hit by three rounds from the SS squad. He staggered, fired twice again, and then fell to his knees and watched the bus moving up Ludwigstrasse. The last thing he did was point his arm in that direction.

Paul Kaestner shoved his Mauser pistol back into his pocket. Fifty metres to his right, at the Feldherrnhalle, slapping the side of her coat, Ruth Wachs was shaking her head. And in the middle of the platz, Mathius Schumann was dead.

Martin Hofer had finished his soup when Wilhelm Koch came back into the office. 'You don't think I'm going to Prinz Albrechtstrasse willingly?' he said. 'Shit, Koch, are you drunk or really stupid? What are your orders?'

'I have no orders as yet, Herr Major, except to hold and interrogate you on the SD murders. Gauleiter Wagner's funeral has slowed procedures, and it doesn't do to insult me, it won't help your position. This assassin of yours. You have proof? I am a detective. Usually I like proof.'

Hofer followed him around the room with his eyes, trying to decide. 'It's a bit late now, don't you think?'

'The Führer's still alive, as far as I know. But then I'd expect that since you're here.'

Hofer reached into his pocket and fumbled about. 'Have you got a pen or a pencil?' he asked Koch.

'You're not going to stick it in my eye? I've heard about you spies.'

'I'm going to write down an address. That's where you'll find the assassin. Or someone who knows where he is.'

'Description, too, Herr Major,' Koch said sarcastically. 'Like to know who we're looking for. For the files.'

'I can do better. I'll sketch him for you. I used to study art.'

'Funny, that. So did the Führer. Something in common. So, can I take it you admit you killed the two SD men?'

'Yes. Why not? I killed them because they were going to kill me.'

'You'd make a statement to that effect?'

'Yes. And I would like to speak to Gruppenführer Arthur Nebe.'

'So would I. But I don't seem to move in your circles.'

Koch pressed his intercom and called for a secretary and some large sheets of paper. Paper was kept locked away now because of its scarcity.

'You have a good technique, Herr Kriminalkommissar.'

'It's better if you talk to me voluntarily than the Gestapo involuntarily.'

'Yes, if you say so. I stole their car, those two SD clowns, made my way to several Abwehr safe houses, used the equipment there. I almost made it.'

'I cannot feel compassion for you.'

'You don't believe me, do you?'

'It doesn't matter. I'll have a statement, an admission to the murders, the rest is up to higher authorities. Out of my hands.'

'Is it that easy for you?'

'My duty is to keep law and order, no more, Herr Major. I keep out of politics. It's bad for my health, I've found.'

There was another knock on the door.

'Paper! I hope you're a good artist, Herr Major.'

'There is an assassin here, Herr Kriminalkommissar. He's here and he will kill the Führer, given the chance.'

'You are very melodramatic, Herr Major. I expect that's the spy in you. I'm a policeman, far more plodding.'

Hofer took a pen and dipped it in ink and began to write the address of Max Weg's bookshop. His hand shook and twice he had to dip the pen in the inkwell again. Koch stood at a distance, as if it were all so absurd he did not want to be seen to show interest.

At that moment, Theo Brandt burst into the room, grabbed Koch's coat from the stand by the door and tried to check his own personal weapon at the same time. 'Multiple shooting in the Odeonsplatz. Train guard dead in the Hauptbahnhof. The orpo captain who rang in was near-hysterical. Shouting about the Führer being in town. I think he feels he'll be sent east.'

Koch dropped his hand from his mouth and some of the ash from his cigarette fell to the floor. 'Jesus Christ, this city's turning into Chicago,' he said. 'I'm sorry, Herr Major, I'll have to postpone this.'

He called in two detectives and told them to escort Hofer to the cells.

'Assassins and gangsters, they'll be the death of the Reich,' Brandt said, helping Koch into his coat.

'That could be interpreted as treason, Theo.'

'Speaking of which,' Brandt said, 'RSD Dienstelle 1 have been on the phone. There's a *sturmbannführer* says Rattenhuber is kicking up a stink about what's happened.'

'That fellow, Hofer, says there's an assassin out to kill the Führer. *British-hired.*'

'If only life was that simple. Perhaps that's what makes traitors. Imagination.'

'Tell your wife she might not see you again till the next century, Theo.'

'How much do assassins make?'

*   *   *

Arthur Nebe unfolded a Weimar Republic banknote and laid it on the coffee table in front of him. Adam Von Trott Zu Soltz tried to count the zeros.

'You couldn't even buy a loaf of bread with it,' Nebe said. 'But then you gentlemen move in circles which probably did not even notice the great inflation. Swiss bank accounts, access to hard currency' – he turned and looked out of the window – 'private estates. The kind of freemasonry a name with a Von gives you access to. You know, he hates you people most of all. The Führer. I think I agree with him.'

'It would not be the first time,' Von Trott said.

'You could be a bore, Von Trott.'

Claus Von Stauffenberg leaned over the coffee table and picked up the banknote. 'If Müller should get Hofer, your Reichsführer's protection will have all the value of this banknote,' he said.

'I'd like to know how you discovered we had him – Hofer,' Nebe said.

'Your boys in Munich put in a request for a copy of Hofer's army file,' Von Stauffenberg replied. 'That request made its way through to the General Army Office and was forwarded to me. One of the privileges of the General Army Office is its ability to place sympathetic officers in positions of influence within the Wehrmacht structure. You might explain why I had to hear about it this way, Herr Gruppenführer?'

'It is imperative he does not fall into Müller's hands. All else is superfluous,' Nebe said.

'Has Himmler asked you to kill him?' Von Trott asked.

Nebe felt hemmed in on the couch. He stood up. His small frame walked across to a period chair, where he sat down and crossed his legs. 'He will be transferred to SD Inland at the earliest possible moment. Then it is out of my hands.'

'And you are safe,' Von Stauffenberg said.

'We are all safe, Herr Oberst.'

'And if this assassin succeeds?' Von Trott asked. 'How safe will we be then? The Reichsführer will seek scapegoats. It would solidify his position with the faithful. Perhaps even placate Müller's lust. And if Müller takes any one of us alive, how long do you think it would be before your name began to pass lips? You will release Hofer. Today. Then you will order a surveillance of that address in Munich and arrest any and everyone who appears there.'

'Who the hell do you think you are?' Nebe said.

'Your salvation, Herr Gruppenführer,' Von Stauffenberg said.

'You're mad, both of you. If I did what you said, how long do you think it would be before I wound up on the end of a rope or face down in a ditch? The Reichsführer is not a forgiving man. No, I will obey orders, and hand a prisoner over to another branch of the Reich Security Main Office.'

'And they'll kill him. And our assassin will kill the Führer.'

'I don't know that.'

Von Stauffenberg grabbed the Weimar banknote and crushed it. 'If you will not comply with our request, Herr Gruppenführer, we will be forced to inform Gruppenführer Müller of Hofer's arrest. I'm sure he'll be interested.'

'Don't threaten me,' Nebe said. 'You'd be slitting your own throats.'

'And yours,' Von Trott pointed out.' The priority now is to find this assassin. If it's necessary, Claus and I will try and find him. But Müller would be more effective.'

Nebe shook his head. 'My God, you are naïve people,' he said. 'Do you have any idea what it would be like in Müller's custody? And is that not what the Reichsführer wants? All of you out of the way. You will do nothing, gentlemen, for your own sakes. Hofer will be dealt with under due process. He will endanger no one. And this assassin – this British assassin – he will vanish, I suspect, once the Americans and the British have attempted to land in France.'

'And the Führer?' Von Stauffenberg asked.

'Is safe.'

'You're very confident, Arthur,' Von Trott said.

'I told Hofer to go to Switzerland.'

Outside, on the damp gravel an hour later, Von Stauffenberg turned to Von Trott. The latter was pale. 'We are faced with a stark choice,' Von Stauffenberg said. 'Valkyrie must be stopped.'

'With what consequences for ourselves?' Von Trott said.

'Unlike Gruppenführer Nebe, Adam,' Von Stauffenberg said, 'we have sworn our lives away. We are dead men, like Hofer's assassin.'

Erich Haas watched Ilse Gern struggle with a large bag in the doorway of her apartment. When she was inside, he switched on the light. She jumped. 'Oh, God!'

'No, just me. I thought I'd surprise you. You told me where the key was.'

She looked at him with her mouth open, as if everything she had ever wished had been granted to her in that instant. 'I thought . . . I thought . . . you'd checked out.'

'I was going, yes, but I came here instead. I had to see you again. I should have told you. Sorry.'

'It's all right, it's all right . . .'

She came over to him and they embraced and kissed.

'There was trouble, did you hear? I thought . . .'

'. . . I was involved?'

'They say it was black marketeers, a shooting at the Odeonsplatz.'

'I was watching Wagner's funeral. I'm not a black marketeer, Ilse, I promise you. Do you believe me?'

He kissed her hand. She nodded. He kissed her eyes and then ran his finger across her lips.

'I didn't think I'd see you again.'

'I must care.'

'I care. You're my choice. We don't get many choices in this life, do we? Most of mine seem to be made for me without consultation. But this I choose. Next I'll be asking you questions about yourself.'

'I can only stay one night.'

'Please don't . . .'

'I wanted to go.'

'Please, don't tell the truth.'

'I'm hungry.' He reached into her bag.

'Turnip,' he said. 'Very rare these days. Now who's black marketeering?'

'I have my contacts. But the Gestapo caught a man across town and he was executed last week. That's why I was afraid for you.' She picked up the turnip. 'This is quite a delicacy. Shall I boil it?'

'For me?'

'It's good to make love on a full stomach.'

'Cut it in half.'

He kissed her. They held the kiss and Haas moved his hand around her body and made her sigh. She reached down and touched him between the legs. 'You're harder than the turnip,' she said.

'Is that a compliment?'

She saw his coat hanging up. She walked over to it and pulled his hat off the coat-stand.

'Making yourself at home. I'm spoken for. A *kriminalkommissar*, I may remind you.'

'Well, call him, if you want him.'

'I just might. What will people say? She takes strange men to her apartment.'

'I'm tired, Ilse, it's been a long day. Cook the turnip or don't.'

'I'm sorry, Karl, I'm sorry. Please . . .' She came over to him and put her arms around him. 'I'll cook it. I will. I have bread, too. Please don't look like that. Oh, God, I'm sounding like a little *hausfrau*, aren't I? I'm sorry. I'm glad you're here.'

'Cook the turnip and hope the British don't come tonight.' He smiled and ran his arms around her. 'I get lonely too, Ilse. You don't mind me saying that?'

'No. It's very sensitive. Did you see the Führer?'

'No. I missed him. Too big a crowd. I saw Goebbels. He made a fine speech.'

'Perhaps another time. The Führer.'

'Perhaps.'

'You're not married, are you? It wouldn't make a difference but I'd like to know.'

'No, not married, Ilse.'

And Haas let himself think about the man he had killed, and again he wondered.

Ruth Wachs got up and walked across the hotel room to the wall. 'Is there anything in that room that could lead them to us?' she asked.

'Nothing. Absolutely nothing. But his Joan-Eleanor's going to raise a few eyebrows, and sooner or later they'll find the papers are fake. Thank God he's dead. Stupid bastard.'

'The desk clerk here saw me with Schumann.' Wachs said.

'For how long?' Kaestner asked.

'Long enough. What the hell were you doing back there? You had him.'

'Don't bitch at me.'

'You didn't move, Paul. You didn't move.'

'There wasn't time.'

Wachs put her hands in her hair and ran them through the sweating strands. 'My God . . . Simon,' she said. Then she shook her head.

'Simon? Who's Simon?'

'Never mind. Never you damn mind. We had him. We had him and he got away.'

'We've got to get out of here, Ruth.'

Wachs slapped the wall. 'Running, Paul?' she said.

'No, I'm not. But maybe I'm not as keen on dying as you seem to be. It's not a prerequisite for success. Look, we stopped him.'

'He can try again.'

'It's time to get out.'

'The time to get out is when he's dead. That's the time to get out. And he's not dead.'

'But he knows we're here. I mean, what's the bloody point?'

Wachs shook her head. 'Enough soul-searching.' she said. 'He hasn't gone back to the bookshop, that's for certain.'

'No,' Kaestner said. 'And he won't go anywhere he was before for fear of it being blown.'

'So, he's hiding somewhere.'

'With Weg?'

'We'll have to get hold of him,' Wachs said.

'You want to go back?'

'The shop's the only line we have. The only starting point.'

'Ah, shit, I don't know, Ruth, I don't know. I don't know if I can do this any more. I'm no killer. We're too exposed. I don't think I can do it. I just don't think I can do it.'

'We have to kill him. No matter what the cost. We have to kill him.'

'Why?'

She went to the bed, sat down and ran her hand across the coverlet. 'I need you with me, Paul,' she said. 'Don't let me down.'

She leaned over and kissed him.

11

A DRIPPING PIPE tapped a warning note on the depressed floorboards of an upper floor in the Spanish café off Soho Square. Kim Philby sat in the corner, eating gazpacho and breaking bread, occasionally glancing out of the restaurant, through a latticed window, at the building across the street and the shadows the sun threw on the walls. The man sitting opposite him very timidly touched his lips with his spoon.

'They do the best gazpacho in London,' Philby said. 'And damn hard to get in wartime.'

He put his feet up on the small cross-spar between the legs of the wooden table and placed a piece of bread in his mouth. The diminutive man with the high forehead across the table looked confused, possibly by the contents of the meal, more probably by Kim Philby's stutter. 'Enough home economics, *Sohnchen*. Now . . . Centre is very keen that this Valkyrie business should help the career of a lead instrument of ours inside the Reich. Centre feels the Hotel's reading of the situation is perhaps verging on the pessimistic, but not implausible. However, there is a balance that has to be maintained. And, despite what Claude Dansey thinks, Centre is anxious for Anglo-American participation in the shape of a second front. At least to save us from bleeding ourselves dry. We may indeed reach Paris but with three men and a hay-cart. Hardly in the best interests of socialism. Or our mutual serious institution.'

'So we wish it stopped, too?' Philby said. 'The assassination.'

'Patience, *Sohnchen*. Now, if the Führer of the Greater German Reich were to meet his demise in the next weeks, what would be the outcome? Possibly, there would be a neat changeover, perhaps

185

Himmler or Göring, and the German war effort would continue as normal. Not likely, though. Possibly there would be a military coup, a deal with the West and a Germany unconquered. A third option is a civil war in the Reich, between the Nazis and the Conservatives, SS against Wehrmacht, which would perhaps leave the front open to dramatic exploitation – your Colonel Dansey's analysis. Centre is of the opinion that the danger to the Reich would cause an alliance of convenience to be formed and, ergo, as they say in the best English public schools, we have a deal with the West again. Our imperative is to avoid a deal with the West at all costs. The alliance must not be broken. And Germany must be conquered. Otherwise, we will be back to 1941 all over again and socialism will have made no advances. If the plan of campaign continues the way it is moving now, the Red Army will be in Berlin within two years, perhaps less.'

'However, Centre is very interested in weakening the conservative opposition in Germany. The fate of our instruments in the so-called Red Orchestra has worked for us in one way but left the balance of opposition forces uneven. And it is part of our war strategy to eliminate the conservative Junker element, particularly in the army. And perhaps the best way to do this is to force their hand, make them move when they are unready.'

'And what if they succeed?' Philby said.

'Centre feels that, given our advantages, it's worth the risk. Anyway, we have our managers, so to speak. This lead instrument I mentioned, whose career we wish to further. The thing is for our people to emerge more powerful. A question of balancing interests. And weighing the risks.'

'Uncle Claude and the OSS are making very friendly noises to the German opposition; promises have been made.'

'Yes, Hitler is fast becoming an irrelevancy. And Himmler and his pets, Schellenberg and Ohlendorf have been making overtures through Stockholm for over a year now. The Reichsführer seems to think the West will deal with him, eventually. To prevent us getting our greedy hands on Germany and other places. Will they?'

'Not with him. Not with any Nazis. This has become a personal crusade with Roosevelt and Churchill. It's why they're frowned on all contacts so far. It's still unconditional surrender.'

'If one didn't need their zeal one might be tempted to say Roosevelt and Churchill were myopic. But it does give us some room.'

'You know something I don't?'

'Always *Sohnchen*. Always.'

'Eat up, I want to get out of here,' Philby said. 'Never know who might . . . drop in.'

'My boys are watching. I'm a Venezuelan businessman helping the Allied cause. I am five feet three, weigh too little, have a pale complexion, broken veins in my face, stomach trouble, wear glasses and am balding. Hardly your average Chekist, yes?'

'You'd slit my throat if someone nodded.'

'Please, you'll aggravate my ulcer. Now, this Soviet Desk job, you are definitely in the running?'

'Rumours. Now that Ben Kramer's been eliminated.'

'And your current performance will have an effect?'

'I'm not sure Uncle Claude fully trusts me.'

'Earn his trust. Earn it, Comrade. Use this situation.'

They walked through the city to the river. There was a couple kissing where the late afternoon sun's rays were broken by chestnut trees. Philby felt the sun on his back. Even in April it was pleasant.

'Whatever happens in this matter, Comrade,' the Venezuelan said, 'it won't make much of a difference. But we must exploit it as it runs. You'll keep Island station informed so on-going decisions can be made. We're not strong enough to hold all of Europe – yet.'

They shook hands and the Venezuelan walked across Blackfriars Bridge while Philby stared into the river and drifted back in time with it.

Erich Haas had developed his skills as a lover beyond merely satisfying his own urgent need, beyond any emotion. When he ejaculated inside Ilse Gern that morning, it was the third time she had come. He released his seed in a sudden deliberate frenzy, just as she was on the edge of losing control, and the shock of his movements made her cry out and the violence and duration of the act brought her close to a kind of pleasure that was almost pain. And before he had finished, she had lost all control of herself.

When it was over, Haas held her like a predator holds its prey; then he rolled off her.

Ilse stretched over to him. 'Please, please . . .' But he pulled away from her and got out of bed.

'I've got to go now,' he said. 'Business.'

'I thought you were going to kill me,' she said. 'I thought I was going to die.'

'Never,' he said. 'Never. I'll be back. I promise. There's a contract; there's a lot of money in it. It's in danger of not going through. I have to see if I can salvage it.'

'Yes, tell me that. I like it. You lie well.'

'Where would you like to go?' Haas asked her.

'Well, since we're fantasising, how about the South Seas?'

He knelt on the bed and took her head and kissed her. 'The South Seas it is, then. No fantasy.'

'My husband wanted to go there. He was always fantasising.'

'Don't tell me, it was the last thing he said on his last leave?'

'He didn't have a last leave. He just went and he didn't come back.'

'Probably best.'

'I'm getting comfortable with it,' she said. 'You have a good body, Karl Rotach, for a book-binder who's been invalided out of the army. Your wounds are small.'

She stroked his body by a small scar and watched him come hard and smiled. For a minute or two he teased her with it.

'I'd have expected something bigger,' she said.

His prick lengthened. She giggled. 'I meant the scars. This one looks like a knife wound.'

She licked his prick. 'If you think I'm going to swallow you again, you can forget it,' she said then. 'I'm full. Only down here now.'

'I have to go.'

'Probably best. I think you will kill me the next time. If you are a black marketeer, will you get me some stockings?'

'I'm a book-binder, Ilse, like any other book-binder only more so.'

'You don't talk like a book-binder, Karl, you talk like a soldier.'

'I have been that.'

'Mother doesn't trust you.'

'She's right.'

'She's trying to seduce Herr Weg. She thinks it'll help my uncle win building contracts and get us some more money.'

'She could be right there, too.'

'I think she spends more money on the Party than we've ever made; I hate her for that.'

'She does her best.'

'Oh, yes, and the Führer's going to notice another painting among all the ones he usually gets on his birthday. You should see it, it's grotesque.'

'I should like to.'

'Well, you can't, it's already gone to Schloss Klessheim, as a surprise. Some surprise.'

Haas was silent for too long and he gave something away; he was not sure if Ilse picked it up. 'Is she going to give it to him personally at Klessheim?' he asked.

'She'd love that. But since his birthday's on Thursday and she hasn't received an invitation . . . well, every 20 April she gets excited, thinking she'll be invited, and every year she's disappointed. Maybe that's what she's trying to get from Herr Weg. It's all a secret, you know, I shouldn't have even told you.'

'No. Careless talk costs lives. I need to wash.'

'I'd offer to help only I can't walk at the moment.'

'Would you press my shirt and trousers?'

'We're not married, Karl.'

'I'm pretending, Ilse.'

In their hotel room on Augustenstrasse, Ruth Wachs looked in the mirror and saw Kaestner watching her from the bed. 'You can take your eyes off me now,' she said. 'Pleasure time is over.'

'You might pretend that you care,' he chided.

'I might. But I can't afford the luxury. My head's clear, that's enough. Thanks. You weren't bad.'

'You make a man feel so wanted.'

'You think a little sweaty sex behind the lines counts for anything?'

'That's not what it sounded like.'

'Don't flatter yourself. You should hear me when I want to kill a man.'

'Are you trying to impress me?'

'I'm telling you that what we did was nothing more than professional. I'd pay you only I can't afford the money.'

'Have you killed many – men?'

'Not as many as I've had as lovers.'

'So where do I rate?'

'Predictable. I was thinking about where he'll have moved. Where's safe.'

'We've lost him.'

'No.'

'Do you ever question yourself?' Kaestner asked then.

'Look, we slept together. That's it, Paul. It's nothing special. Now we have a job to do.'

'You're . . .'

'I hope you're not going to say beautiful. I know I am not beautiful. I'd be dead if I was beautiful. I'm not beautiful.'

'I was going to say you're a bitch.'

Kaestner picked her shirt off the bed and threw it to her. She adjusted her bra and then turned to him and started to button her shirt. He watched her walk around the room picking the rest of her clothes off the floor.

'You know what you remind me of?' she asked.

'What?'

'A boy I used to know. He always wanted something more. Not because he wanted it but because he wanted to say when we did things and what we did. I loved him and was quite happy to do what he wanted when he wanted it, but I realised that it wasn't what I thought was happening.'

She sat on the bed and pulled on her stockings and clipped them to her suspenders. 'I remember we were making love – it was the third or fourth time that afternoon, so we were really moving – and I was so excited and saying I loved him and all that kind of thing, and he was also excited – but when I looked into his eyes I saw something I did not expect . . .'

'Tenderness?'

'No. We weren't thinking the same thing.'

She pulled on her skirt then stood up and straightened it and went over to the chair and took her jacket and brushed the strands of carpet from the back of it.

'You have a burn mark at the back of your leg,' he said.

'You've a bruise on your shoulder.'

Kaestner got out of bed and began to dress. Wachs sat down and checked her handbag. 'Come on, let's go and find that bookshop owner, that's our first move.'

'Your logic is inescapable. And terrifying.'

'And wear a different coat and don't wear a hat. Wear a scarf.'

'I think you're trying to impress me now,' Kaestner said.

'Perhaps I am.'

*   *   *

Claude Dansey was reading *Mein Kampf* when Teddy Giles entered his office. Giles paused before approaching Dansey's desk. Dansey's tight lips tightened some more, as if they were crushing something between his jaws and trying to keep it quiet at the same time.

'If this is bad news, Teddy, you're going to central Africa.'

Giles paused and looked at the sheet of paper he was carrying, before handing it to Dansey. 'From Germany, sir,' he said. 'Schumann's dead.'

'The other two?'

'Still alive, as far as we know.'

'What the bloody hell are the Germans playing at? Get on to Switzerland and tell them to make contact with those German resistance friends. I knew they were useless sods.'

'Hitler's still alive, sir.'

'And the Russians have brushed away German armies like autumn leaves. We should have crushed those bastards in 1918. But no one had the gumption for it. Everyone sent troops and paid lip service but no one was willing to make the effort. Ever hear of a man named Reilly? Sidney Reilly?'

'Of course, sir. The ace of spies.'

'Rubbish. I'm the ace of spies. But Sidney and his crew were this close to overthrowing the Bolsheviks. We'll have to find a better way of keeping order in Europe when this is over.'

'Do you think they'll get to Berlin before us? The Russians?'

'Yes, probably. But that isn't the point here. Merely getting there isn't the point. It's who's there with you and how strong they are. If the Germans do stop us on the beaches, it'll be the devil to pay. Out of our hands. I hope you're not planning on visiting the Continent in the next fifty years.'

'You're too pessimistic, sir.'

'And you're definitely lining yourself up for Africa. How's that special job I gave you coming along, then?'

'Tell the truth, I feel a little disloyal there, sir.'

'Loyalty in one direction, disloyalty in another. The trick is choosing the right direction, Teddy.'

'It'll be on your desk next week.'

'Who knows, you might just end up with a senior position here, instead of Africa.'

Wilhelm Koch pushed through the strings of detectives, clerks and typists twisting along the corridor of the Ettstrasse Kriminalpolizei office, trying to cope with the residuals of the head cold he still had; his throat choked on the mucus dripping from his nose and he kept trying to clear it without making a sound.

One or two people, mainly women, squirmed when he tried and Koch just walked on past without looking any of them in the eye, thinking they could add that to his middle age and body odour and nicotined breath and all the other things the typists and junior detectives talked about when they were trying to impress each other.

Someone had once referred to it as the freemasonry of youth, and Koch could not figure out when membership was terminated, but it seemed to have more to do with rank than age. He stopped feeling sorry for himself when he reached his office again.

'Theo . . .?'

The sergeant did not smile in his usual slightly sycophantic, slightly mocking fashion; he just shoved a few sheets of paper into Koch's hands. 'He killed the two orpos,' he said without explanation.

Koch read the typed sheets.

'Our mystery man in the Odeonsplatz. His weapon fired the slugs. And see here, he's false, everything about him is false.'

'Fingerprints?'

'Nothing on that from Berlin yet.'

'And that transmitter?' Koch asked.

'I thought we might ask the Gestapo there,' Brandt said.

Koch frowned. 'It's our patch – murder.'

'He was shot with a silenced tube weapon,' Brandt said. 'Our mystery man. The type Allied agents use.'

'Abwehr supplies?' Koch asked.

'Gestapo rounded up all the Abwehr villains in Munich when they broke up that currency racket last year.'

'Speaking of Abwehr villains, where's that Hofer fellow?' Koch asked.

'He's being sent to Berlin today,' Brandt said. 'Here's the order. Reich Security Main Office are sending a special detachment. From SD Inland.'

'SD Inland? Bypassing Wittelsbacher Palais altogether. The Gestapo'll be pissed off.'

'Direct orders of Gruppenführer Nebe, from the Reichsführer himself, according to Kriminaldirektor Schmidt.'

'Look, ring the Gestapo and tell them what we've found out about the transmitter and the weapons. See if they've had anything similar. If SD Inland are getting Hofer we'd better do a bit of sucking and get some credit from the Wittelsbacher Palais, then maybe we can use them in these orpo murders without having them walking all over us. They're going to be so sore about us handing Hofer over to SD Inland.'

'Not as sore as Hofer.'

Brandt left the office, and Koch called for tea and bread and then leaned his head on his desk.

He was chewing a piece of bread when Brandt returned. 'We've got him,' he said before he was in the room. 'Our dead man in the Odeonsplatz. Pension owner on Bayerstrasse rang in. Says he heard about the shooting and one of his guests didn't come back last night.'

'Get someone over there, Theo.'

Brandt nodded and Koch felt something stab at the breastplate of despair covering his heart. He tossed it aside. 'What's that?' he asked, nodding at the buff file Brandt was carrying.

'Oh, I almost forgot. It's Hofer's statement. The one he was writing for us. I was going to get it typed and send it to Berlin with him.'

'Anything interesting?'

'Haven't had time to look at it yet. It's handwritten and we're very busy, sir.'

'Give it here. I want to see him before he goes anyway. In case someone asks a question.'

Brandt smiled and gave the file to Koch. 'You are good at protecting yourself, sir,' he said.

'If I don't, who will?' Koch asked.

He put Hofer's file to one side, and watched his sergeant leave again before picking up his bread and sipping his tea.

Erich Haas slipped out of the door of Ilse Gern's apartment and eased the latch shut before going across to the staircase. The stairs were dusty white marble and Haas had to place his feet carefully so as not to make a noise while he listened for activity in the other dwellings. The smell of watery soup and reheated meat tripped down the staircase beside him, sometimes pausing to take on another odour and then move on again. Haas stopped at Max Weg's apartment.

'I thought you were dead; I've been expecting the Gestapo since yesterday,' Weg said when Haas was inside.

'He was trying to kill me. He killed the woman. He killed the kid. I shot the train guard, by accident.' He went over to the window and looked out.

'Not Gestapo, then?' Weg asked.

'Couldn't be. Like you said, they'd have picked you up by now. I've been upstairs with Ilse. She's asleep. I left a note.'

'There's no one following me. I swear it,' Weg said. 'I know footsteps.'

'Yeah, I believe you, Max, I believe you. I've been watching the street from upstairs. And I've been taking a leaf from your book: listening. He must have been British.'

'What . . .?'

'This is a Haganah job, Max. As I understand it, the British don't approve of their actions. I expected something like this but when it didn't materialise. I thought they just couldn't find me. It seems I have managed to bring two sides in a world war together for a few days. My contribution to world peace. Nice, isn't it?'

'Frau Steiner,' Weg said then.

'Who's Frau Steiner?'

'A woman who makes lace; works in a shop near mine. A couple were asking where I lived on Saturday. Said they were curious customers.' He thought for a while longer. 'Frau Steiner didn't know where I lived.'

'Shit, Max, why didn't you say something?'

'I can't believe the British would stop us.'

'Max, are you familiar with Niccolo Machiavelli's *The Prince*?'

'Of course.'

'Then believe me, our dead friend was probably British. Or hired by the British. I've been at this too long, you know. And there are probably more.'

'They must know the shop. If there are more.'

'More than likely. But they don't know here, otherwise they'd have come here. You haven't been out this morning?'

'You were waiting to see if they would come,' Weg said. 'Up there.' He nodded towards Ilse Gern's apartment.

'Don't philosophise,' Haas said. 'I'm trying to survey the ground with my limited information.'

'But why haven't the British told the Germans if they want this stopped?'

'Now you're beyond philosophy to facts. And facts are what I am short of. Time to change my appearance again, Max. I want that brown dye I left with you, and the suitcase.'

'You're still going ahead with this?'

'I haven't been ordered off. And there're three-quarters of a million lives depending on me. Noble, yes? Not that I am losing sleep over that. I am losing some sleep over the one million American dollars awaiting me. Somehow, the harder it becomes the more attracted I am to it.'

'I think you're a little insane, Karl. Or whatever your name is.'

'I don't exist, Max.'

'They'll kill you. Whatever chance you had before, you have none now.'

'Nothing succeeds like success.'

'Everything you gave me's still at the shop.'

'Well, you'll have to go and get it, Max.'

Weg licked his lips. 'And if they're waiting for me?' he asked.

'In and out the back way. I'll be watching from here. Make sure to stop outside when you get back here, so I can see who's around you.'

'Checkmate for me, yes?' Weg said.

Haas slapped him on the shoulder. 'There's a lot of money waiting, Max. Maybe I'll share it with you.'

'I can hardly wait.'

'It's my call, Max.'

'And I must obey.'

'Go get the stuff, Max. And Max, I want you to talk to Ilse when I'm gone, tell her I cared, all that kind of thing.'

'Very noble.'

'I don't want her hurt.'

'I couldn't tell anything from your palms, you know,' Weg said.

Haas watched him stop on the footpath and exchange a greeting with two people on the other side of the street and then disappear in the direction of his shop. Then Haas pulled two bottles of black dye and an *ausweis* from his coat and went to work on his hair.

When he had dyed his hair jet black, he took a cutthroat razor and began to shave the sides military style. Then he took his moustache off.

It took twenty minutes to transform himself into the photograph in the *soldbuch*.

Wilhelm Koch was studying the various autopsies and ballistic reports while eating when he finally opened the file with Martin Hofer's statement. The file contained several handwritten pages and a pencil sketch; there was an address at the top of the first page, in block capitals and underlined. When Koch saw the address his mouth stopped chewing, and when he looked at the sketch his mouth went so dry he had to down the rest of his tea in one.

'Theo!'

'It's an SIS flat-bed operation,' Hofer said.

'What the hell's that?' Koch asked. He was undoing Hofer's cuffs over the seat of the car.

'Straight tasking. Limited back-up. No more than one person, probably.'

'Max . . . Max Weg. My God, I can't believe it.'

'You know this Weg?'

'He owns that bookshop in Schwabing, the address you wrote down. I've sent men there.'

'He's trained to act alone, Valkyrie, and survive on his own. He will not, if he uses his Abwehr training, rely on anyone who is not strictly necessary for the job in question. We trained these people very well for the Tod Programme, Herr Kriminalkommissar. They carry out their assignments to the letter; it's their way. If we don't get to him first, he will get to the Führer.'

'You had better be right or we'll both be in Prinz Albrechtstrasse tonight.'

'I'm not sure we can avoid that.'

'Rotach checked out yesterday morning, Herr Kriminalkommissar,' Frau Gerda Gern said, shutting her guest book. 'Perhaps Herr Weg will know where he's gone. They are friends.'

'Where's Ilse?' Koch asked.

'Oh, she's at home. The apartment. Yesterday was her day off. She should have been in by now, actually. She's so . . .' Frau Gern's face went pale in an instant and Koch turned.

'God. Ilse . . .'

12

THE APRIL SUN tiptoed along one side of Hohenzollernstrasse in Munich, holding itself at a discreet distance behind Max Weg as he turned into the shade of a narrow pencil-line street. There was a slight breeze shuffling down the narrow street and several trees, newly sprouting leaves, bowed gently as Weg passed. Behind the sun's rays, a couple stopped at the junction of Hohenzollernstrasse and the narrow pencil-line street and then walked on, arm in arm.

Ruth Wachs and Paul Kaestner watched Weg tap his way along a shaded stonewashed wall. When they were past the junction, Wachs pulled her arm away from Kaestner's and continued on down Hohenzollernstrasse before cutting right into a cobbled lane. One of the buildings in the lane had been hit by a bomb. Kaestner followed directly behind Weg.

Wachs paralleled Max Weg as he tapped his way down two streets. An old woman in a square hat blocked her view of him for a few seconds, but she caught him again on Friedrichstrasse. This time, Paul Kaestner moved across to parallel Weg, shadowing the blind man from about a hundred metres.

When he reached his own street. Max Weg slowed, put the suitcase he was carrying down and felt inside his pocket for his keys. The building he stood before was plain grey solid stone, periodically pocked with bomb and shell splinters, the odd window cracked and held together with gummed paper. It had a turret at one corner, before an alleyway that led to the back of the building and some small allotments.

Ruth Wachs watched Weg from the shadowed doorway of a bombed-out building in a side street. She pulled her Mauser out and let her hand drop to her side so that you could not see the weapon in the shadow of the doorway at that time of the morning.

Weg fumbled with his keys.

Paul Kaestner folded his newspaper, and reached deep into his coat pocket. His mouth was dry and the early morning wind dried it some more, dried it so that he was sucking at the air for moisture. He entered Weg's street on the opposite side, kept walking for fifty metres and then crossed towards the blind man.

Wachs saw Kaestner and moved. She heard the cars before she saw them.

The four black Citroens came from opposite ends of the street and halted on either side of Weg, who just about to pick up his case, and in front of Kaestner as he crossed the street.

Two Kripo detectives leapt out of one car, grabbed Max Weg and pinned him to the wall. Two more detectives got out of the other car and took up covering positions on either side of Weg's apartment building. Kaestner stopped.

'You live here?' one Kripo detective asked him.

Kaestner was looking at Weg. 'No, I . . .'

'Then move on.'

Kaestner looked around him. Weg was asking the men what they wanted. One of them picked up his suitcase. Theo Brandt took Weg's keys and opened the main door to the building.

Kaestner shoved his hands in his pockets and moved on.

Weg was still asking the detectives what they wanted with him, asserting that it must be some mistake, giving the names of leading Nazis he knew, when Wilhem Koch stepped out of the lead police car, feeling a small trickle of sweat running down the side of his face and his knees begin to shake. 'Good morning, Max,' he said.

'Willy, if you wanted a game you only needed ask me. No need to bring all this.'

A truck had pulled into the street from the Hohenzollernstrasse end, disgorging a dozen or so *orpos*, carbines at the ready.

'Where is he, Max?' Koch said.

Weg smiled. 'The appropriate thing to say would be I don't know what you're talking about, wouldn't it?'

'You're in a lot of trouble, Max.'

'You don't know the half of it, Willy.'

'Why?'

'More exciting than chess.'

Theo Brandt came out of the building, rubbing his forehead, followed by two more detectives. 'I think you'd better come up, sir,' he said.

Ilse Gern was laid out on the bed with a sheet drawn over her. The blood from her wound was seeping through the coarse fibres of the sheet and her right index finger was pointed out from a fist, as if she were trying to show Koch something.

'*Der Gast ist König* . . .' Brandt said. The guest is king.

Koch stared at Ilse Gern and allowed himself a moment of personal grief. Then he swung round on one heel. 'Find out how long she's been dead.'

When Max Weg had run his hands over the body he stood up and stepped back and bowed his head for a moment. 'Praised be that which hardens,' he said, 'Isn't that what your boss, the Reichsführer, says?'

'Theo, can you leave us, please,' Koch said.

Brandt hesitated.

'I said, leave us, Theo. Get Forensic down here and go slide your hands over this man's apartment downstairs. If there's a fly in it without the right papers, I want to know why. Search the whole building. Tear it apart. Then the block, then the street.'

Brandt left the bedroom and Koch locked the door after him. Weg was sitting on the bed beside Ilse Gern, touching her dead body again.

'I want to kill you,' Koch said. 'I want to put my hands around your neck and squeeze the life out of you, you bastard. Who is he?'

'I don't know, Willy. And that's the truth.'

'Is he here to kill the Führer?'

'I won't say anything further without a lawyer,' Weg said. He barely smiled.

Koch stood up and swung at Weg and knocked him across the room. 'Look at her, you bastard! When the Gestapo get hold of you, Max, when Wittelsbacher Palais get hold of you, you'll need a surgeon. Look at her!'

'I can't, can I? Too long a sacrifice makes a stone of the heart, as the poet says.'

'They'll send you to Prinz Albrechtstrasse, Max. And then, if you're still alive . . . I hope they fucking tear you apart.'

Weg was picking himself up. 'Listen to yourself, Willy, listen. You should have joined the SS when you had the chance. Policeman . . .'

Koch swung his fist and caught Weg square in the jaw. The blind man fell back across the bed and rolled on to the floor.

'For God's sake, Max, why?' Koch pleaded.

'I'm sorry he killed her; for her sake.' Weg was rubbing his bleeding lips.

'This is treason, Max.'

Weg shrugged. 'I hope so. Tell me, Willy, do you know what happens to Jews in the jurisdiction of the Third Reich?'

'You're a Jew?'

'I know I don't have a big nose and I don't own a bank and I don't eat chicken soup – you can't get chickens these days anyway – but, yes, I'm a Jew. If you want to help me, then draw your gun and shoot me. Shoot me before the Gestapo get me. Say I was trying to escape. Please!'

Koch shook his head. 'I can't . . . I won't.'

'I didn't kill her.'

'Does it matter? You bastard. I loved her.' He swung and hit Weg again.

'I would prefer it if you killed me, otherwise the Gestapo will take me and torture me. And I'm not sure I can withstand much of that. You would be doing me a favour. And satisfying your desire for revenge. Believe me, I have no particular wish to die. But I have less wish to go to the Gestapo.'

Koch swung and hit him again. 'Bastard!'

One kilometre east of them, across Leopoldstrasse, Erich Haas glanced down at the dead body of a man who had accepted his Gestapo silver warrant disc at face value; the man was a reserve fireman and a friend of Max Weg in the Nazi Party. Haas drank a cup of herbal tea.

Across the room, on a bed, an SS uniform he had hidden at Max Weg's apartment was laid out.

In Berlin, Arthur Nebe sat across the desk from Heinrich Himmler, desperately trying to read the impassive fowl-like face in front of him. Himmler had his *pince-nez* on and was reading files, not looking at Nebe.

'It would appear we have ourselves a situation, Arthur,' Himmler said. 'I had hoped we could manage this satisfactorily. But events have overtaken that wish. And Muller is very anxious to interrogate Hofer. Whoever informed him did not have our best interests at heart. I think, given the circumstances, handing Hofer over to anyone would create more problems than it would solve. I think we need another solution.'

'A final solution. Herr Reichsführer,' Nebe said.

'Exactly. This fellow, Koch, he's obedient?'

'If a little outspoken. Somewhat naïve. He was instrumental in the investigation of Fraulein Geli Raubal's death in 1931; annoyed the Führer somewhat.'

'Yes, yes, I remember him now. The Führer was very fond of her. In my opinion he has never really recovered from her suicide.'

'Well, it was his gun, wasn't it?' Nebe said.

'As I remember it, your friend Koch implied more than that. I hope his previous arrogance has been blunted.'

'He'll do what he's told. He has done so before – terrorist escapers, Jews, that kind of thing. Not one to be entrusted with special action but a suitable auxiliary. Kriminalkommissar Koch is a man married to the system he serves. And he's a good detective. It appears he even has a murder confession from Hofer.'

'Admirable. But make sure everything comes to you. Everything. Hofer is a skilled intelligence officer and he could manipulate the naïve.'

'Even Gruppenführer Müller.'

'Müller knows you've met Hofer, Arthur,' Himmler said then.

'I've met many people. I rely on your protection, Herr Reichsführer.'

'Müller will try to get at me through you.'

'Fire him.'

'I have no cause. Anyway, what is the old saying? Keep your friends close and your enemies closer, Arthur.'

'And which am I, Herr Reichsführer?'

'I'd like to know who told Müller your men had Hofer, Arthur.'

'So would I, Herr Reichsführer. What do you recommend?'

Paul Kaestner kept rubbing his hands. Sweat gathered at his eyebrows and the corners of his mouth. And the mouth struggled with the words.

'It's crawling with police . . . crawling. The whole bloody city.'

'Calm down, for God's sake,' Ruth Wachs whispered. She put her hands on Kaestner's and kissed them. 'Just calm down.'

'I thought they had me,' Kaestner said. 'Shit, I'm not up to this. I'm not up to this.'

'You are up to it, you have to be.'

'Look, the police are on to him; we've been hung out to dry. London told them.'

'We saw an arrest; that was all. The cops picked up the old blind man; maybe he's a black marketeer, maybe he insulted Hitler; they don't need much of a reason to arrest in this country, Paul.'

'Look, I'm out. It was a simple case of find a shop and kill a man; now it's find a needle in a haystack and avoid the hay. We stopped him, that should have been it.'

'We were sent here to kill him, and we will kill him.'

'And where are we going to find him?'

Wachs looked around the beerhall. It was filling up. And a cloud of steam followed some of the groups as they sat at the tables, drinking a watered-down version of what they were used to. There was a coupon-free kitchen serving *suppengrün* and ersatz coffee but only a few factory workers were standing at it.

'All right, all right, so the Nazis are looking for him, too,' Wachs said. 'I never thought I'd wish them luck.'

'So let's go, let's get out. Let them get him.' Kaestner picked up his newspaper and went to get up from his seat.

Wachs grabbed his hand and pulled him back to the table. 'You move and I'll kill you myself,' she said.

He looked into her eyes. 'My God, you would.'

'Try me. Now think, just think. If the Gestapo are on to him, he has to act. And quickly. And that means Berchtesgaden.'

'No. No. You can kill me now, but I'm not doing that. It's suicide. And I'm not committing suicide. Not for that.'

She touched his hand and then put her finger to his face. 'We're a good couple,' she said then.

'Stop it.'

She nodded to herself. 'It's his birthday the day after tomorrow. Hitler.'

'Shit! Christ! If I get out of this I'm going to kill Teddy Giles and that old man he works for.'

*   *   *

Teddy Giles watched the anti-aircraft crew go through their paces and then threw a large breadcrumb at a squirrel. The squirrel looked at the bread for a while, stepped back, looked round, then lifted the bread and ran back to its tree.

'Waste of good rations,' Kim Philby said. 'You were raised too well, Teddy.'

'It's called making friends, Kim.'

'What can you possibly hope to receive from a squirrel?'

'Perhaps I'll be reincarnated as a nut.'

'Very optimistic.'

The sky over Hyde Park had darkened and spots of rain appeared on the pathway in front of them. The anti-aircraft crew left their 3.7-inch gun for the shelter of a truck.

'I hope the Germans never attack here when it's raining,' Giles said. He threw another piece of bread at a pigeon.

'You're sure he's dead?' Philby asked. 'Schumann.'

'Zurich was adamant.'

'And the other two, this Wachs woman and the Czech, Kaestner?'

'Who knows? The thing Uncle Claude and I can't understand is what the bloody hell the Germans are doing. I mean, it had to have been him – Valkyrie – who shot Schumann. It had to. Unless our team ran slap bang into the Gestapo. There was always the chance of that. But they're expendable. I do hope you know what a risk I'm taking for you, Kim. If Uncle Claude knew we were discussing this, I'd get kicked all the way to Africa.'

'Friendship, Teddy. Like with the squirrel. And I'm sure I'll be looking for people of your calibre if I get the Soviet desk.'

'I bloody hope so. That's the future.'

'So, we can take it this assassin is still at large?' Philby asked.

'We're somewhat in the dark. But, yes.'

'And our people – if they're alive – are in pursuit?'

'And the Germans do not appear to have acted.'

'Tricky. And this address they found on Maurice Hallan?'

'Some sort of bookshop, according to Research.'

'And Uncle Claude, does he have an option, if it all fails?'

'Jesus, Kim, don't even talk like that. He doesn't tell me. He doesn't tell me anything, really.'

'I will, Teddy, I will.'

'You are a charming bastard, Kim. Do you know what I'm supposed to be doing now? I'm supposed to be doing a deep background check on you. For Uncle Claude's eyes only. A kind of test. I bet he has ten other people doing the same thing on ten other people, and so on. He hasn't asked you to check me out, has he? You Section 5 johnnies are very good at that.'

'No,' Philby said. 'Dug up anything?'

'On you?' Giles shook his head and smiled. 'I hope you're not having an affair or anything, Kim. Be embarrassing.'

'Would I?' Philby said. 'If you want me to help, I will.' He took out his pipe and lit it despite the best efforts of the rain.

'Come on,' Giles said, 'the rain's getting heavier.' He stood up.

Philby looked up at him. 'Are you following me?' he asked.

'Of course, old man. Even have a few pictures. Nothing I can blackmail you with, though. Yet.'

'I work hard at that.'

'That's my problem. I'm sure Uncle Claude will want at least one weakness.'

'Well, let me see what you've got and I'll see if I can't help you there. Nothing to damn me, just something to make Uncle Claude think I'm human.'

'Making friends.'

'Precisely.'

Wilhelm Koch put the phone down with a certain discomfort.

'It seems I am to meet Gruppenführer Arthur Nebe, finally,' he said to Hofer. 'And your transfer to SD Inland is off. So you need not worry about the prospect of them bumping you off any more. Or other such fantasies.'

'And Valkyrie . . . Rotach?'

'When we get the posters out, then we'll have a face for people to search for, Herr Major. There's no point chasing something when you don't know what to look for. I've ordered a personality check from Berlin.'

'I bet that'll come quickly,' Hofer said. 'Anyway, it'll do nothing but prove me right and show you there's no point chasing something that's already gone.'

'I've ordered everything by way of transport sealed off in this city. But it takes time, Herr Major. This is a big city. And there are other pressures. Now we must wait.'

'For what, Herr Kriminalkommissar?'

'Because I have orders to do so. And things to consider. Right now all I have is a murderer on the run, and your word – the word of a wanted traitor and self-confessed murderer himself – that this man is a British assassin on his way to kill the Führer.'

'You have Weg. Your friend.'

'And he's saying nothing. Anyway, he lied before. And you lie for a living, of course. So you'll excuse me if I am a little cautious. For all I know Max Weg could be one of your men. I'm walking somewhat blind here.'

'There is more happening here than you can possibly imagine,' Hofer said.

'Now, that I'm inclined to believe.'

'Well, believe this, too. You had better find Rotach, Herr Koch, or there will be more trouble in your life than you can cope with.'

'You're trying to frighten me.'

'You should have been frightened a long time ago, Herr Kriminalkommissar.'

Five minutes later, in the Haidhausen area of Munich, Erich Haas stepped off a tram. He wore the uniform of a major in the Waffen-SS and the personal papers of an Ulrich Beck, a thirty-five-year-old officer with the Das Reich Panzer Division. Several younger women watched him cross the broken street to the Ostbahnhof and noted the Ritterkreuz at his throat with oak clusters and the gold wound badge which signified he had been wounded more than five times. Haas smiled at one blonde girl and she blushed. The two orpos at the entrance to the Ostbahnhof barely looked at his red Party membership book, grey *soldbuch* and *urlaubschein* before letting him through. He deliberately looked one of the policemen in the face because the man had a Winter War ribbon; Haas let his leather coat slip back to reveal his own decoration and the policeman came to attention.

'Good leave, Herr Sturmbannführer,' he said.

'Thank you, Wachtmeister.'

The corporal showed off his own silver wound badge by expanding his chest.

It was two o'clock on 18 April, and he could hear police sirens. In front of him, the train to Innsbruck was pulling into the station.

The clatter of typewriters drummed Wilhelm Koch through the carriages of another train that afternoon – Heinrich, the private train of Heinrich Himmler, and if his location unsettled him, the noise seemed to be warning him.

'The Reichsführer was good enough to lend me his train,' Arthur Nebe said. 'He's a good ally, the Reichsführer.'

He was standing on a Persian rug in front of a leather-topped table. A copy of the Bhagavad-gita lay open on the desk.

Nebe wiped his hands on the legs of his trousers. 'This woman you found dead. She was your mistress?'

'No.'

'You know Hofer worked for Abwehr Two – sabotage and subversion? He is a man who deals in illusion.'

'It had occurred to me. But I have met Rotach. The man Hofer calls Valkyrie.'

'No one saw him kill the girl, no one saw him enter or leave the apartment, no one saw him enter or leave the block. In fact, he might be in Berlin for all we know, perfectly ignorant of what's happened. Ilse Gern was not exactly mean with her favours, Koch. Forgive me, but the truth is often painful.'

'Hofer sketched him independently, sir. Rotach. And I have Max Weg.'

'Whom you are holding on charges the Gestapo would be ashamed of. There is no evidence he is a Jew. Or anything of that nature. He is, however, a well-connected Munich Party activist. People are complaining, you know. And he's blind, for God's sake.'

'I do my duty where I see it, sir. I believe there to be a strong chance there is an assassin in the Munich area, a man who will kill the Führer.'

Nebe looked at some papers. 'Yes, some kind of ghost resurrected by the British from an Abwehr Two defector. Strange Hofer should pick you of all people to deliver his information to. This Reich has many enemies, Koch.'

'But Rotach exists.'

'And we will find him. But there is a vast chasm between a common murderer, if that is what this book-binder is, and a political assassin. No matter what you may wish to believe.'

'And if my request for a trace of his origins in Berlin proves him to be other than he said?'

'It still does not prove he is an assassin,' Nebe said. 'We're policemen, Koch, we work on evidence. And the only evidence we have of an assassin points to Martin Hofer. The file is thick enough to stop a bullet. However, you appear to believe your own theories over your own superiors.'

'If I had not met Rotach . . . If Hofer had not sketched him . . . If Max . . .'

'Your personal feelings are clouding your judgment, Wilhelm. That's exactly what Hofer wants.'

'I am a good detective,' Koch protested.

'Exemplary. But somewhat over-zealous at times. Cost you entry to the RSD, you know? The Führer didn't take kindly to being accused of murder.'

'I did not accuse him.'

'Well, it doesn't matter now,' Nebe said.

And for a minute or two he scratched his head and wiped small beads of sweat from his face. Then he walked over to the window and pulled up a blind. 'Look, I want you to let Hofer go,' he said then, stumbling slightly over the words, 'and to desist in your investigations into anything connected with this matter.'

Koch's heart almost leapt out of his mouth. 'But, Herr Gruppen-führer, he is a self-confessed murderer. He killed two of Gruppenführer Ohlendorf's men. Surely if—'

'You think I would willingly countenance the release of such a man if it were not in the best interests of the state?' Nebe said. 'As I said, treason has many allies, Koch. Finding out who is always the problem. That is why Hofer must be let free and nothing he says believed.'

'And what do I tell him?'

'I ordered his release.' For a moment, Nebe's eyes closed.

Koch was beginning to feel almost faint.

'And if you are asked, you must say he escaped,' Nebe said then. 'He's done it before. He's a resourceful man. You will be protected, Koch. Acting in the interests of Reich Security. Trust me.'

Koch thought for a while and scrutinised Nebe's face, with its smiling poison. Then he stood up and came to attention. 'As you order, sir.'

Nebe faked another smile. 'Good,' he said. 'Just do your duty, Koch. Come on, I'll walk you to your car. It's in the best interests of the state, you know. The best interests.'

Koch's mind was elsewhere.

When Heinrich Himmler sat down at his desk on the same train, he lit a cigar. 'What do you think?' he said to Walter Schellenberg.

'As soon as he acts. I think you can order his arrest for treason, Herr Reichsführer.'

'And providence continues its course,' Otto Ohlendorf said.

'Of course. Providence,' Himmler said.

Erich Haas stood at the window of the Innsbruck-bound train and watched the green of the Inn river rush past beneath and heard the sound of the carriages trundling over the metal bridge before the train began to slow down.

There was a dynamic, as powerful as the flow of the river, which he could not have gone against it even if he had wanted to. And he did not want to.

'Cigarette, Herr Sturmbannführer . . .'

Haas looked at the great girder of a figure to his right. The paratrooper wore a camouflaged *fliegerbluse* with an Iron Cross first class pinned below the left breast and a gold wound badge.

Haas went to shake his head and then realised that the paratroop sergeant was asking him for a cigarette, not offering one. 'You're a cocky one, Oberscharführer,' he said.

'When you jump out of serviceable aircraft for a living, it helps to be cocky. Anyway, we're a penal unit, so frankly we don't have any manners, sir. Russia?' He tapped Haas's Das Reich cuffband.

'On leave, Oberscharführer.'

'Well, I'm off to Yugoslavia. We all are.' He nodded towards a group of paratroops further up the carriage. 'That thing holding us up is on the way to a cushy number in Italy.' He nodded in the direction of the train ahead of them. 'We could be a while. So how about that smoke, sir?'

Haas pulled out a packet of pre-war French cigarettes and gave them to the sergeant.

'France has its compensations, Herr Sturmbannführer,' the sergeant said.

'I'll tell you when the invasion comes, Oberscharführer. I think I'd prefer to be fighting terrorists rather than sitting on a beach.'

'You've obviously never been to Yugoslavia.'

'What was your offence?' Haas asked.

'I shot an officer: a *sturmbannführer*.'

The sergeant lit one of the French cigarettes and the train lurched and then slowed and skidded to a halt. He opened the window in front of him and called a military policeman over. The military policeman was going to swear until he saw Haas. 'Their engine,' he said, nodding to the ammunition train ahead. 'Carrying too much load. Maybe you boys will all have to walk.'

'I've walked before, Feldwebel,' Haas said.

'I thought this lot would save me walking,' the paratroop sergeant commented.

'You damn paras think the sun shines from your own arses. Give me a cigarette?'

The sergeant looked at Haas, who nodded. '*Heil Hitler,*' he said, handing over the cigarette.

'If you're trying to aggravate me, Oberscharführer, then you'll have to do better than that,' Haas said.

The sergeant smiled. 'A weakness of mine. Where did you win your Ritterkreuz?'

'Russia. You?' Haas pointed at the Iron Cross.

The sergeant touched his Winter War ribbon. 'Near Moscow, I think. It was snowing. I used to be an officer, you know.'

'Stalingrad?'

'Sure. There's been worse since. Prokhorovka, yeah?'

Prokhorovka was a small village near Kursk in the Soviet Union where the German Citadel offensive had ground to a halt the previous July. The Das Reich division were part of the SS spearhead during the attack and suffered huge loses.

'We could compare battles all day,' Haas said.

'Yeah, I suppose. It's just the Das Reich are such arrogant shits, don't you think?'

He stubbed his cigarette on the window pane. Then he flicked the butt at the military policeman, who was turning white. 'Hey, you're out of order, Oberscharführer,' he said. He touched his neck shield to emphasise the point.

Haas looked at the sergeant and pushed his hands into his pockets. He let the sleeve-gun slip down. 'The Feldwebel is right, Oberscharführer. You're out of order. Now, I'll let it pass and put it down to fatigue . . .'

The paratroop sergeant came a step closer and Haas could smell alcohol on his breath. He touched Haas's coat. 'A couple of my lads were in the Das Reich. Want to come and say hello?'

'I don't think so,' Haas said. 'And take your hand off my coat.'

'Just being friendly, sir. SS scum to SS élite.' He turned his head

and leaned out towards the military police corporal. 'When is that
bloody train going to move, Feldwebel?'

'You all right, sir?' the corporal asked Haas.

'I'm fine. The Oberscharführer here is going to offer me a drink
of that . . . what is it, Sergeant?'

'*Sljivovica*. Plum brandy. They make it in radiators in Yugoslavia.
Sends you mad if you drink enough of it.'

'My kind of drink.'

The paratroop sergeant smiled and brought his face close to Haas's.
'I'm particular . . .'

'Shut up, Oberscharführer,' the military police corporal said.

'You'd have to be particular. The nearest zoo's in Innsbruck, I
think,' Haas commented to the sergeant.

Some of the sergeant's comrades at the other end of the carriage
sensed that something was going on and were beginning to make
their way up, through the various people, calling to the sergeant to
come away. He just swore at them.

Haas flicked the sergeant's hand away; the paratrooper drew his
pistol and shoved it in Haas's face.

'What the hell are you doing, Oberscharführer? I'll have you
court-martialled.'

'Like I give a fuck, Herr Sturmbannführer. Give me a reason why
I shouldn't waste you here and now?' He turned his eyes to see who
was watching.

'Don't upset me, Oberscharführer,' Haas said.

'It was a shit like you put me in this mess,' the sergeant said. 'I
hate guys like you. Shining examples of SS manhood. All mouth and
heil, mein Führer. Jesus Christ!'

The military police corporal was pulling his machine-pistol into a
firing position. 'Drop it!' he shouted.

'Stay out of it, Feldwebel,' the sergeant said. He turned his head.
'Everyone stay out of . . .'

Haas brought his knee into the paratrooper's groin and his forehead
into the man's nose; he swung the sergeant's arm around behind his
back and slammed his heel in behind the paratrooper's knee. The
pistol fell to the floor when the arm was dislocated, the sergeant
went down on his knees and Haas rabbit-punched him and sent him
sprawling down the aisle of the railway carriage.

'Now,' Haas said, holding the man's pistol to his head. 'Give me
a good reason why I should not blow your brains out. Gorilla.'

'You'll end up an *oberscharführer* in Yugoslavia,' one of the paratroopers said. He stood back from Haas with his hands out. Three or four civilians in the carriage were looking out from compartments. Others ignored the incident. The military policeman was in the train now and pushing his way towards them.

'It's all right, it's all right,' Haas said then. 'Just an accident, yes?'

The sergeant nodded. 'I think my fucking arm's broken,' he said. 'Sweet Jesus . . .'

'No, just out of place.'

Haas leaned down and grabbed the offending arm and slammed his foot into the paratrooper's back and jerked the arm back into place. The paratrooper roared and more people leaned out of compartments. Haas held his hands up.

'Incident over,' he said. 'It's fine now, Feldwebel. These trains are slippery. So who has this Yugoslavian plum brandy?'

The military police corporal nodded and began to retreat. The rest of the paratroopers gathered around their sergeant. One of them handed a bottle to Haas.

'So, what's your name, gorilla?' Haas asked the paratroop sergeant. 'Since we could be here for a while. I ought to know the name of a man I'm going to have court-martialled.'

The sergeant smiled. 'Thann, Michael Thann. You?'

Haas put out his hand.

Martin Hofer dropped the pencil; Koch picked it up and sat down. He watched a small spider crawl up the undulating wall of the cell; the sound of dripping water beat time in his head.

'They're going to kill you, too,' Hofer said.

'I am aware of the possibilities of my situation, Herr Major. Particularly since my immediate superiors seem to be unavailable for comment. However, I have my orders.'

Theo Brandt knocked on the open cell door and entered, carrying a map and two files. 'The *fraulein* was probably killed with the same weapon our friend in the Odeonsplatz and the train guard were shot with,' he said. 'Preliminary autopsy says the round went straight . . .'

'Yes, yes, Theo, I don't need the exact details,' Koch said. 'They're sure of this?'

'As can be . . . I'm sorry, Wilhelm.'

Koch folded his arms, sighed and stared at the spider again. 'All right, Theo, I'll see you in my office. I don't suppose that personality check on Rotach has come back from Berlin?'

'No, sir. Several of the phone lines are out. Air raid.'

'How convenient. Lock the door, would you, please.'

Brandt hesitated and went to say something before obeying.

'Who was he?' Koch said to Hofer. 'The dead man in the Odeonsplatz? The truth, please, or I shall lose my temper.'

'One of my men,' Hofer said, hoping the lie would not show on his face.

'And the orpos he killed?'

'I don't know. There are difficulties. Perhaps they weren't simply orpos.'

'I don't suppose you have more men out there, tracking him – Rotach?'

Hofer shook his head.

'Somehow I don't believe you, Herr Major, but it would appear to me that the best way to deal with this situation is to find Rotach – your Valkyrie.'

'Are you really that naïve?' Hofer asked.

'I am trying to approach this situation with something like a clear head. I have considered the possibilities. I have considered getting into a motor car I keep parked around the corner and heading for Switzerland, but that would not be a smart option. And I do not have the requisite papers.'

'I am telling you the truth,' Hofer said.

'A truth, perhaps. Nebe seemed confident you would accept his name. Why?'

'I know him. What are you going to do?'

'I should obey my orders; trust in my superiors . . . but he killed her. And I will follow him to the ends of the earth for that. Nebe was right. It is personal. And very clear.'

'How long have we got?' Hofer asked.

Koch shrugged. 'Nebe suggested midnight tonight for your release.'

'Into the fog.'

'Indeed. I have a vision of Prinz Albrechtstrasse . . . something Max Weg said.'

'There is an elevator to the cells,' Hofer said.

'My vision is more pronounced.'

'Welcome to reality, Herr Kriminalkommissar.'

'The thing is, I suspect, Herr Major, you are a traitor; but to what I am not sure. You are also a murderer. I am not in the business of letting murderers go. I am a simple man. Or I thought I was.'

'I'm loyal, Koch, believe me. I'm loyal to Germany.'

'That would appear to be irrelevant at the moment. We are allies of convenience. But we need help.'

'From where?'

'Führer headquarters. Rattenhuber. He is an old colleague.'

'Himmler's his boss.'

'Technically, yes. But it's the only choice left to me. And the RSD are independent of the Reich Security Main Office and therefore somewhat beyond the machinations of the Prinz Albrechtstrasse set. At least, I hope so. I once tried to enter the RSD and was refused.'

'Terrific. What did you do? Hit the Führer?'

'I used to think it was because I had arrested him in 1923. Now I know it was something else . . . something I thought was routine. Routine work can often have bitter consequences.'

'And if Rattenhuber throws your case back in your face . . .?' Hofer asked.

'I am open to all suggestions, Herr Major. My options are extremely limited. I have a wife, whom admittedly I can't abide, and a son who is going into the army. And I am afraid now, Herr Major. Unlike you, I am merely a policeman. But I want Rotach. I want him more than I fear for myself.'

Koch stood up and walked over to where the spider was making its way up the damp undulating wall of the cell. There was a small web at the top of the wall. He examined it and saw that there was a fly caught in it.

The guard shouted Rosenheim for the third time and the Salzburg train began to slow. It had been on the tracks for over three hours now, behind an ammunition train and a passenger train bound for Innsbruck.

Ruth Wachs watched an old man get out of his seat and reach for a suitcase on the luggage rack overhead. He was a frail man, wearing a Nazi Party badge of honour in gold, signifying he was one of the first one hundred thousand members of the Party. He smiled at Wachs and she nodded a kind of salute and let her eyes drift to Kaestner, who was staring out of the window. He had his hand on the window sill, clenched into a white fist, and she could hear the breathing from his nostrils over the sound of the train and the muttering of the overcrowded mass of wool and flesh.

The first specks appeared in the sky about treetop height and two or three kilometres out, like a flock of sparrows or perhaps flecks on a photograph. Kaestner saw them first, though it was a soldier sitting beside him, reading a book, who sounded the warning. By then the air-raid siren had started in Rosenheim and the sparrows had become hawks.

On the stalled Innsbruck train ahead SS Paratroop Sergeant Michael Thann was drinking *sljivovica* when he saw the aircraft. 'Oh, shit!' he shouted. He rubbed his mouth, swigged another mouthful of plum brandy and watched the RAF De Havilland Mosquitoes approach in formation. 'I hope you have insurance, Herr Sturmbannführer,' he said to Haas.

Haas saw the first flashes of the cannon fire from the British aircraft; then a rocket hit the stalled munitions train in front of them.

13

RUTH WACHS PITCHED forward as the train braked and tried to prevent herself crashing into the man sitting opposite. It was a vain attempt, as the train approaching the Rosenheim rail junction could not possibly decelerate at anything like an acceptable rate in the time given before it impacted on the back of the stalled Innsbruck train ahead. The sirens were already blaring and the ammunition train that had held up the line for an hour was trying to get moving again as more RAF Mosquitoes peeled off from treetop level and angled up for the attack.

The second rocket hit the engine of the burning ammunition train while desperate troops were trying to get out of the packed goods wagons in full kit, some of them firing at the incoming British bombers. But even the two flak wagons at the back of the ammunition train were of little use against the rockets and twenty-millimetre cannon of the low-flying aircraft. One of the flak guns was destroyed at the same time as the engine exploded.

On the Innsbruck train, there were equal amounts of panic and chaos because the Salzburg train had rammed into the back of it at the same time as the Mosquitoes had begun firing, many of the civilians thought the train had been hit by a rocket. Erich Haas found himself sprawled out on the corridor staring at the jump boots of the paratroop sergeant, Thann. Other SS paratroopers on the Innsbruck train were trying to pick themselves up and deal with the confusion as it developed. Then two rockets hit the train's engine and a third and fourth hit the carriages either side of the one Haas was in, and the people who had not panicked when the Salzburg train hit them from behind did so now.

*   *   *

Ruth Wachs had hit the jaw of the man opposite her, broken it and almost knocked herself out.

The Salzburg train was an open-plan local, packed with women and children heading to the various towns and small villages between Munich and Salzburg to get away from the war, and immediately after the crash there were a few minutes of screaming. The sound of the first rocket impacting ended the screaming as people scrambled to get off the train. Wachs crawled over two bodies. Paul Kaestner was flat on his back in the aisle, trembling. 'My ribs are broken,' he said. 'Get me out. Please. I can't stand it. Please.'

A Mosquito passed right over the the train and let go two bombs which fell either side of the last carriage. One of the explosions took one of the carriage walls out. Then two more Mosquitoes opened fire with cannon and machine-guns, before releasing their rockets. The rockets tore into the front of the Salzburg train where it had rammed the back of the Innsbruck train. And Wachs was thrown off Kaestner.

Civilians and soldiers were on the tracks, running in all directions, while the remainder of the Mosquitoes sped in low over the junction and delivered their loads. A family was killed by a single machine-gun burst, and ten soldiers died running down the tracks, trying to get away.

When Erich Haas pulled himself to his feet, the SS paratroop sergeant, Thann, was trying to get two of his men out of a compartment that had been peppered with cannon and machine-gun rounds. Two more of his men were lying dead by the window, and the overhead racks and luggage had fallen down and blocked the exit.

'Give me a fucking hand,' he yelled at Haas. 'We're on fire.'

Haas looked around him: part of the carriage had been ripped away at the centre and there were two women lying in the hole as if they were holding one another. On the other side of the hole was the fire. And the screaming.

Haas could feel blood on his forehead; he was experiencing dizziness. He began to take deep breaths but the smoke and cordite made him cough. He crawled over and helped the paratroop sergeant.

'Four and a half years of war and we get it sitting in a railway station in Bavaria,' Thann said. 'Come on, get the door, pull it now . . . Jesus, my fucking shoulder.'

Haas shoved his boot in and the two men pulled the door between them and removed a luggage rack which seemed soldered to the metalwork. The sergeant reached in and pulled one of his men out, but the man was dead.

Ruth Wachs dragged Kaestner along the floor of the carriage and helped him to the tracks. Police and soldiers were carrying the wounded from the trains, and an officer was yelling at his men to get the ammunition in one box-car out before a fire in the next car spread to it. But his men were not keen.

Wachs sat down by the side of the Salzburg train and examined Kaestner.

'I panicked,' he said. 'I'm sorry. Claustrophobia. Jesus, I feel terrible.'

'What can you feel?'

'I think I'm bleeding inside. Check if there's blood in my mouth.' He opened it.

'You're bleeding a little. But you've bitten your tongue.'

'But what colour is it?'

'Red. Look, stop whining, you're all right.'

Wachs examined herself. Part of her coat was torn and there was a gash on the lower half of her left leg and her hip felt like someone had struck it with a hammer. She rubbed her face and surveyed the devastation.

'Are you all right, madam?' a polite voice asked.

Wachs looked up. The first thing she saw was a column of smoke; then the squat features of a fireman interposed themselves between the smoke column and her eyes.

'Yes, yes, I think so,' Wachs replied.

'And your friend?'

'My ribs are broken,' Kaestner said. 'I need a doctor. I may be bleeding.'

'He's fine,' Wachs said, shaking her head.

'Oh, my heaven, it's awful,' the fireman said. 'Awful. There are children dead everywhere. Schoolchildren, coming from school. They hit the carriage with the children. Oh, my God, I've never see anything like it. You're not a nurse, madam?'

'No, I'm not, no,' Wachs said.

'I thought you might be a nurse. You hear about that, about people being nurses and doctors. We need help.'

Then the fireman left them and wandered down the tracks as if he were in a daze.

'This is going to hurt you more than me.' Wachs lifted Kaestner up, put his arm around her shoulder and struggled with him to the station platform, tripping along the railway lines as they went, bumping into people who were trying to get away from the burning trains. Occasionally, there was an explosion, but no one seemed to pay attention any more. The officer who had been trying to persuade his men to go into the ammunition car on the first train had given up and was now telling everyone to get back. His men were way ahead of him, running towards the safety of the station building.

'It's going to blow, it's going to blow,' the officer screamed, and when Wachs was pulling herself on to the platform it did blow and knocked her back on to the tracks. Kaestner sat down against a wall, held his chest and moaned. 'I have to see a doctor,' he said.

'Stay here. You're all right.'

He stood up, using the wall for support. 'I'm going to get a doctor.'

'I told you to stay.'

'What are you going to do? Kill me?' he asked.

It did cross her mind. Kaestner held his chest with one hand and waved her off with the other. 'It's over,' he said. 'Over.'

Erich Haas was sitting beside the Innsbruck train, smoking with the paratroop sergeant, Thann, when the ammunition wagon exploded.

'I bet it wasn't as bad as this at Prokhorovka,' Thann said.

'No ...'

'Look, you're not such a bad bastard for an officer, Herr Sturmbannführer.'

'I'm going to have you on that charge, Oberscharführer.'

'You see him?' Thann said, nodding at the body of one of the SS paratroops who had been killed. 'We joined up together. Went everywhere together. Committed every offence in the book together. Now I'm the last one left from my class. You know what I mean?'

'Last one left puts out the lights, Oberscharführer,' Haas said.

In his cell in Ettstrasse, Max Weg stood up and bowed.

'Frau Gern ... I did not expect ...'

'Nor did I. They said I could see you. You still have many friends, it seems.'

'I cannot say how sorry I am about Ilse.'

'You didn't do it, Herr Weg. No more to be said. He tricked us all. I'm sure this misunderstanding will be sorted out. Look, for you . . . cakes.'

She held up the wicker basket she carried as if to show him, sat at the table and placed the basket on top. Max Weg searched her sounds and smells for signs. 'I want to explain,' he said.

'There's no need,' she said. 'I have lost much in this war and the last. My husband died in the last, right at the end. And now Ilse. You know I hoped you and I could . . . well, a woman does, you know.'

'I would have liked that, had the circumstances been right. But I'm not exactly in a position to . . .'

Gerda Gern nodded. 'Please. I just wanted to see you.' She touched his hands.

'Frau Gern, the situation, you must not say these things. Distance yourself from me.'

'They say you're a Red.'

'Worse. A Jew.'

'Oh, my heaven, oh, my heaven.'

'Well, half Jewish. So we would have been committing an offence. See, I saved you from that. I didn't know he'd kill Ilse.'

Gerda Gern shook her head and began to cry and Weg took her hands now and held them.

'They're only holding you on suspicion. I'm trying to get you free,' she said. 'I've been asking people. They say there's a chance . . . you did nothing wrong. How were you to know about Rotach? I don't want to hate for the rest of my life.'

'No. Thank you for the cakes.' He reached out and touched her hand.

The cell door opened and a guard entered. 'Time's up, madam.'

Neither of them argued.

When she was going, Frau Gern slipped the guard several hundred Reichmarks. Max Weg broke one of the small cakes and put a piece in his mouth. It had a bitter almond smell.

Ruth Wachs watched a medic clean the dried blood from her leg and then tear a bandage in two and tie it tight so that the skin and muscle seemed to buckle. A thin red line appeared on the stained reused material, and some of the hairs on her leg, close to a vein and a tendon, suddenly stood up, as if in shock.

'It's either this or stitch it, love,' the medic said, 'and I haven't got time to stitch it. You're way down the treatable list. I'm only doing this because I hope you'll grant me sexual favours later in the bar over there.'

Wachs did not answer; she was scanning the clumps of humanity that seemed to be wandering around the area of the Mittertor in Rosenheim as if they were all lost. And it had begun to rain.

A line of soldiers sat outside a church and shouted at a group of girls sitting around an arcade of shops, most of which were shut because there was nothing to sell or the owners were in the army or dead.

When the medic had finished with her leg, she reached down and touched it. 'How many are dead?' she asked.

He shrugged. 'There's a hall full of them over there, and there's a whole heap of the worst down at the police station, and then there's another lot still in the railway station. Have you seen the kids? They were on the last train.'

'I was on it. I didn't see them.'

'I have cigarettes.'

'I'm married. And I have to find my husband. Where are the doctors?'

'Down that way. Near the Mittertor. You don't need a doctor. You need me.'

She stood up and, without replying, started to walk towards the centre of the town.

When enough rain had gathered on her face, she started to clean her skin. Once, she reached into her pocket and touched the Mauser. A policeman nodded to her and checked the papers of three Danes, who said they were going to Berchtesgaden to work for Hitler. The policeman did not believe them.

Erich Haas sat in the doorway of a small shop that had closed a year before because the owner had been drafted into the army. The door was boarded up and there was a notice saying one of his sons had been killed and another saying that he had been awarded the Iron Cross. It did not say which class. There was a message to his customers, something about looking forward to seeing them again. Twenty metres away was a fountain. The sun was dipping its head below the mountains and greedily taking the spring warmth with it; a light from one of the windows showed the thin lines of rain falling on the silver of the fountain.

Haas picked himself up and began walking. He had no particular plan; he just felt better walking than sitting there and opportunity favoured the mover. As he walked, he checked his uniform, straightened his coat and put on his cap. And as he did this he saw that people made way for him.

Paul Kaestner slid down the wall, holding his ribs. He touched his tongue and studied the colour of the blood again.

'You all right?'

A man in German army uniform, wearing steel-rimmed glasses, a dog-collar and a chaplain's armband, leaned over him.

'I think I'm bleeding inside, Pastor.'

'I'm Catholic, actually.'

'I'm looking for my wife. We got separated. She's up that way, I think. I'm finding it hard to breathe. There's a queue for the doctors.'

The chaplain put his hand to Kaestner's ribs. 'They're broken,' he said. 'You should see a medic if you can't see a doctor.'

'I did. He said what you said. He had nothing to strap them with. They're out of everything. Is my tongue bleeding?'

'No.'

Kaestner swore and then apologised.

The car was parked outside a small house with flowers on the walls. Haas approached it slowly, looked it over and then reached into his pocket for a set of skeleton keys Ben Kramer had sworn would open the gates of heaven.

'Hey, where are you going, Herr Sturmbannführer?'

The SS paratroop sergeant, Michael Thann, was just behind him, holding two black bottles and smoking a cigarette.

'I have a girl waiting for me in Innsbruck, Oberscharführer. I'm on one week's leave and I expect to spend tonight with her. I'm taking a car so I can get there. And I've decided to drop the Court Martial.'

'Kind of you. Listen, you should wait here. There's Military police everywhere. Take that and you'll only be joining us in Yugoslavia. Hey, I didn't say thanks for the help . . . but thanks. Look, want to come and join us? You probably need that head seen to. Come on, you can get the first train tomorrow morning. Guaranteed not to be shot up. It never happens twice. How about that? Anyway, I want to buy you a drink. Or steal you one.'

Haas touched his forehead. The blood was running down his neck along a hardened channel. 'I have a girl . . .'

'You have balls, I'll say that, sir, but you should at least see a medic, I think. Come on.'

He touched Haas's arm and Haas smiled and rubbed his forehead and looked at the blood on his hand. 'Yes, I suppose so. It was a mad idea, wasn't it?'

'I won't mention it.'

Haas reached over and took one of the bottles from the sergeant and pulled the cork and drank from it. 'Jesus, it's that firewater from Yugoslavia,' he said.

'We're over there, in a café a couple of streets back. We've taken it over as a temporary headquarters, so we're helping ourselves to what's on offer. There're some women from the trains. Couple of the hotter little bitches will do anything for a cigarette and a sausage. Got any money?'

Haas laughed. 'Some,' he said.

Kaestner saw Haas in profile first. Again, it took a minute or more to make a positive identification. And then he was gone again. He reappeared from behind a stone arch and then there were soldiers marching in formation and he disappeared again.

'It's him,' Kaestner said.

'Sorry?' the chaplain said.

Kaestner shook his head slowly and pulled himself up. The chaplain reached out but Kaestner brushed him aside. He shoved his hand into his coat pocket and turned on the Joan-Eleanor.

The death's-head cap reappeared.

For a few seconds, Kaestner walked towards Haas very slowly, convinced the assassin would just disappear or change when he got close. And the people coming at him bumped into him with the frequency of the raindrops now spitting from the mountains to the south.

Then he lost him again.

He stopped and glanced around at the heads. Caps, caps. He kept looking for officers' caps; he jumped and it nearly tore his lungs in two. Blood trickled from his mouth. He began to move faster.

Some children ran across the street in front of him and he almost tripped over one of them as a horse slipped on a broken cobble and the cart behind it jack-knifed. There was a fight between the driver and a group of mountain infantry who were playing skat under an arcade: the cart had upset the rhythm of their game.

Ruth Wachs stopped at a junction and turned a full circle and jumped above the heads.

'Excuse me, but your leg is bleeding.'

The chaplain with the steel-rimmed glasses smiled and then pointed at the spreading red stain on the dirty bandage.

'Is there an SS unit around here?' Wachs asked him.

'I saw some SS paratroopers earlier. At least I think they were. I used to be with a tank regiment. I think they're in a bar down there.'

He pointed down a curving street, where families sheltered in doorways from the rain and boiler-suited civil defence workers handed out bread.

'I'm looking for my husband,' Wachs said. 'We got separated.'

'He's SS?'

'No.'

'I'm glad. They're a penal battalion. I've seen the penal battalions and they are difficult men.'

'My husband's a sweetie.'

She began moving down the small cobbled street, looking in the windows she passed. The chaplain stood for a few moments and watched her limp and thought about going after her but someone came over to him and asked him to attend to a dying woman.

Wachs reached the end of one street and then moved on to the next. Down the windows, sometimes going right up to them.

An SS officer turned the corner in front of her and crossed the street, his back still to her. Wachs kept her eyes on his collar patch runes and began to draw her weapon. Then he turned and it was not Haas. She let the Mauser slip back into her pocket and swore to herself.

Paul Kaestner spun on his heel, looked left and right and then started back. Then he stopped. For about a minute, he just listened. To the sounds of the overcrowded town, to the background noises, to the distant shouting of men, to the backfire of a vehicle, to the gathering force of the wind. And somewhere in all that, to the faintest whine of a harmonica and the hum of singing voices.

It took him another five minutes to trace it to a specific street. He pushed past people, gripping his pistol, tapping on his Joan-Eleanor.

Blood was running out of his mouth. One or two people commented, but he ignored them.

Ruth Wachs stopped at a corner and searched the street signs. The rain was heavier now, a translucent screen which forced her to squint. And it took the blood from her leg in dirty fan-lines which spread out around the hairs until the water diluted them into oblivion. She moved to the rhythm of the cascade around her, rubbing her face.

Wilhelm Koch bent over Max Weg and listened for breath. The skin was tight and the muscles rigid.

'Cyanide,' Theo Brandt said.

'How did he get it?'

'He must have had a phial or something,' the guard said.

Koch ran his finger through the crumbs on the table. He lifted some of them and touched his tongue.

'Who was in with him?'

The guard stiffened, turned a paler shade of his usual colour and spontaneously opened the pores of his forehead. Pinpricks of liquid appeared.

'The autopsy'll tell us,' Theo Brandt shouted at the guard. 'Then you're going east.'

'A woman. I was told to facilitate her. She was only with him ten minutes. I didn't realise . . . she gave him cakes, two small cakes.'

'Frau Gern . . .' Koch said. 'Who told you to let her in?'

'I didn't know . . .'

'So who gave the order?'

'The Higher SS and Police Führer's office, the Kriminaldirektor said, sir. I was just following orders, sir.'

'Shit,' Koch said.

'Will I order the arrest of Frau Gern, Herr Kriminalkommissar?' Brandt asked.

'No,' Koch said, 'no point; but you'd better speed up your SS membership. You may need it sooner than you think.'

Koch touched Weg's eyes.

It was a small bar, with broken windows and plain wooden benches inside. The counter was made of fresh pine and you could smell the cut still over the smoke and the beer. It was packed with SS paratroops in their camouflaged *fliegerbluses*.

And each of the tables with soldiers had four or five girls, bartering.

Kaestner stood at the door while the harmonica and singing died, and then moved over to a table to his right while the soldiers who had glanced over at him began singing again. There were three civilian men and two women at the long table where he sat. A pretty blonde waitress approached the table, dodging the advances of the soldiers.

Kaestner ordered a glass of white wine. One of the women at the table asked him if he was all right. He nodded but kept his eyes on Erich Haas.

Haas was sitting in the corner with his back to Kaestner, talking to a sergeant and two other soldiers, both of them officers.

The waitress was coming back through the tables with the wine when Michael Thann got up from where he was sitting and went over to the bar. He leaned over it, grabbed one of the barmaids by the top of her blouse, pulled her to him and kissed her. She pretended to be offended before kissing him back. Then the sergeant, urged on by his friends, pulled her on to the bar and kissed her again, to the cheers of the soldiers.

Kaestner took one sip from his glass and stood up. The cheering and singing meant that no one noticed him. One of the women at his table said something about doing the same because she thought he was going to leave. But Kaestner walked straight across the floor, pushing through shoulders and kicking legs out of the way. Some of the paratroopers made comments, one or two shouted abuse when he kicked their shins, but Thann was still kissing his barmaid, and the singing and music and shouting were raucous now.

Kaestner pulled his Mauser out about ten metres away from Haas, just as Haas turned his head.

Two paratroopers at another table saw it and reached for their weapons. One of them raised his Schmeisser machine-pistol. Kaestner shot him through the neck. The second man dropped to the floor and yelled a warning. And an officer beside Haas drew his pistol just as Ruth Wachs came through the door.

Wachs shot the paratroop officer in the head. Haas dived left and flicked the sleeve-gun down, but he was too late. Kaestner had his Mauser lined up on the side of the assassin's head.

The first shot hit Kaestner in the shoulder and he spun to the right and fired a wild round that hit a mirror behind the bar. Michael Thann's second shot missed Kaestner and hit a girl by the far wall.

His third shot hit Kaestner in the chest and knocked him back across one of the tables.

Wachs swung her Mauser at Thann, who pulled the barmaid he had been kissing between them. The barmaid took three of Wachs's rounds in her back. Thann rolled back over the counter.

Haas fired at Wachs and hit her in the shoulder, then pulled a table over. Wachs staggered back against the door and fired off two rounds at the table before falling back. Kaestner tried to train his Mauser on Haas, pulling himself up on a chair. Two SS paratroopers shot him in the back and pitched him over the chair.

Ruth Wachs turned her weapon on the two paratroopers, hitting one of them in the head, the other in the chest. The second man fired off most of his Schmeisser clip while falling back, hitting flesh and plaster and wood and forcing Thann back behind the bar counter again. And Erich Haas rolled through a back door to a small kitchen.

Wachs fired just as Haas was going through the door, and Thann fired just as she did, catching her in the side and spinning her across the floor. Kaestner stood up and fired the remainder of his clip at Thann, then smashed into the small kitchen after Haas. Wachs reloaded, fired four shots and followed.

She found Kaestner holding himself up against a stone wall in the alley behind the bar.

'I've lost him again,' he said.

She pulled him over her shoulder, dragged him along the alley, then kicked a wooden door open and pulled him into a hallway.

'I think I'm hit,' he said.

'Stop moaning.'

'Just a scratch?'

'Yeah.'

She pulled his shirt open. 'I can't leave you here, Paul. I can't,' she said.

'Oh, for Jesus' sake, Ruth, just get me to a doctor. No one'll know. I'm German, my papers are German.'

She leaned in close. 'You want to fall into their hands?'

'Oh, Christ! We should have left it. I told you. You fucking bitch, I told you.'

She put her hand over his mouth. 'Shut up. Just shut up.'

He tried to pull himself up. 'Jesus, I'm freezing. Get me a coat.'

'I want to, Paul, I want to. I want to call a doctor. I want to. I just can't.'

'You're a serious case, you know. I hope Adolf knows what I did for him. You think they'll give me an Iron Cross?'

'I can't leave you here,' she whispered to him.

'You expect me to take my pill? Fuck you.'

She kissed him on the forehead. 'I'm sorry . . .'

'You're not Italian? That's very Italian. Jesus, I'm dying, aren't I? It's so bloody cold. Must mean I'm not going to hell. I mean, hell is so . . .'

He shuddered a fraction when she fired.

There was only the sound of evening birdsong now. Erich Haas walked towards the centre of the old town and then began to swing wide towards the outskirts. Once, a police truck went by and one of the orpos inside stared at him for a moment, but Haas affected a look only Waffen-SS officers had and the policeman turned his head while the colour of his skin turned the colour of the mountain peaks. *Ostheeritis*, they called it, and it always struck young men doing home duty when they saw veterans from the fighting in the east. One or two were known to faint at the sight of a gold or silver wound badge, and an infantry assault badge could get you off any offence bar treason if you were decorated, too.

Michael Thann kicked Kaestner and then leaned down to check what he already knew.

'Who the hell is he?' an officer asked.

'I thought he was going to kill the Herr Sturmbannführer,' Thann said. Then he looked around and saw that Haas was not there.

'No, he killed Stroop,' a paratroop officer said. 'He was going for Stroop.'

'And the bitch?' Thann asked

The officer shrugged.

Thann leaned down and rifled through Kaestner's pockets. Down the alley, the bar owner was shouting at the paratroopers to get out, they would give his bar a bad name, and someone else was calling for the military police.

Wilhem Koch did up the buttons of his trousers very slowly, checking that the toilet was clear around him. Brandt was washing his hands in a basin, looking into a mirror. He could see Koch.

'Look, Theo, I think you might do well to take some sick leave today. I'll authorise it. Anything you've done has been on my orders.'

Brandt held his hands under the taps and watched his boss. 'I think I'll stay on the case, sir, if you don't mind.'

'I don't think I made myself clear, Theo . . .'

'You have, sir. I'm not a complete careerist, you know. I'm not sure what's happening here but I'm one of the ones it's happening to, if you understand. And praised be that which hardens, as the Reichsführer says.'

'You know, you're all right, Theo.'

'You, too, Wilhelm.'

'I'm going to have to make a decision in the next few hours.'

'Whatever you decide, sir . . .'

The first car Haas saw was parked in a narrow alley beside a house with geraniums around the windows. The geraniums were red-flowered and they hung from the wooden balconies of the houses in baskets that swung in the evening breeze. The rain had stopped. Haas pulled out the skeleton keys.

'I told you Innsbruck could wait, Herr Sturmbannführer.'

Haas did not turn round.

'You're in a hell of a hurry, Herr Sturmbannführer.'

'As I told you, Oberscharführer, I have a girl.'

'Yeah, I heard you. You left the bar very quickly.'

'I don't remember it saying in army regulations that a *sturmbannführer* has to explain himself to an *oberscharführer*.'

'It's in the small print. Only penal battalions ever read the small print. It says, and let me get this right, it says that where an *oberscharführer* is holding a Schmeisser machine-pistol to some smartarse *sturmbannführer's* back then the *oberscharführer* shall indeed be listened to and the *sturmbannführer* had better show some respect or the *oberscharführer* might remember that he is in a penal unit and open fire. I'm sure the military police wouldn't ask too much about it all, being as I'm trying to arrest you.'

'Why?'

'Well, they were going for you, weren't they, Herr Sturmbannführer? That stiff and the ugly bitch back at the bar. Oh, I know old Stroop got in first and probably saved you but the Mausers were gunning for a certain *sturmbannführer*.'

'You're just sore I nearly took your arm off, Oberscharführer. Now when they're dangling you by your balls after a general court martial, I'll make sure they break everything.'

'That piss may work with virgins and green infantry but I'm neither of them. Now what are you about, Herr Sturmbannführer? Who were they, why were they gunning for you and what are you running from?'

Haas turned his head slightly.

'Keep your head turned and put your hands on your head if you don't mind. What kind of trouble are you in?'

'I suppose I should thank you for saving my life.' Haas slowly raised his hands to his head.

'Let's just say you owe me one. Now what's it about?'

'It's about money, Oberscharführer. It's about a million American dollars in a Lisbon bank account.'

'Go on, I'm listening.'

'I'm going to pick it up.'

'And the lady?'

'She wanted to stop me. It's a long story. If you fire, the money dies with me.'

The sergeant laughed to himself. 'How do I know this is true?'

'You don't. But then you saved my life, so I figure if you let me out of this one I'll owe you something. Do you want to go back to Yugoslavia?'

'I take it there's no girl in Innsbruck?'

'Not in the traditional sense.'

'You are a wanker, Herr Sturmbannführer.'

Haas slowly turned around. 'There's a certain trust involved,' he said. 'I've deserted, Oberscharführer. I figure my regiment has done enough done enough for this Reich of ours, and all to what avail? So I'm heading for Switzerland, and then . . . well, wherever sounds very nice.'

Thann lowered the machine-pistol. 'I like you, you know, Herr Sturmbannführer,' he said. He rammed the barrel of the Schmeisser into the front passenger window of the car. 'All right, let's go. Half and half . . .'

Haas grinned and, very slowly, lowered his hands.

The sergeant got into the passenger seat. Haas sat in the driver's seat. Thann put the Schmeisser between his knees. Haas put his hands under the steering wheel.

'So who were they?' Thann asked.

'Who knows?' Haas said. He found the wires he was looking for and then folded his arms.

'What's the matter?' Thann asked. 'Getting greedy? I'll use this.' He picked up the machine-pistol.

'Shouldn't have put it down, Oberscharführer.'

Haas fired the sleeve-gun. Thann's head cracked off the window rim and he slumped over the broken glass in the passenger window.

Haas leaned over, Searched the sergeant's pockets, opened the passenger door and kicked his body on to the ground. Then he pulled a bullet from his own pocket and began to reload the sleeve-gun. The two paratroopers who came round the corner took about two seconds to realise what had happened.

They fired into the car just as Haas was checking the reloaded sleeve-gun and reaching for Thann's machine-pistol. The paratroopers hit the open passenger door and a piece of metal clipped Haas's arm. He fell back into the driver's seat, loosed off a volley of machine-pistol fire through the windscreen and pressed the accelerator. As the car jerked forward rounds smashed into the bodywork.

He drove at the paratroopers, who fired another volley at point-blank range.

Haas felt something strike his head and fell sideways, almost out of the open passenger door, but he kept his foot on the pedal.

He hit the first paratrooper and sent him into the air in a somersault; the second man dived out of the way and fired a burst into the back of the car, hitting the hand Haas had on the steering wheel and sending the car into a skid. It hit one wall and bounced off. Haas tried to regain control but the car rebounded off a tree and into a second wall.

Haas pulled himself to the edge of the passenger seat and grabbed the Schmeisser from the floor. The second paratrooper was walking slowly up to the car, machine-pistol extended. Haas slid on to the street on his blind side, and when the paratrooper fired at point-blank range into the car, he rolled over and fired a burst that killed the man before he hit the ground.

A small crowd gathered at the end of the street; they saw Haas drive off.

When Arthur Nebe skipped up the steps of *Prinz Albrechtstrasse* that evening, out of uniform, he had the strain of a man sitting on a razor blade etched into his oversized face.

'I'm afraid the meeting's cancelled, Arthur. A developing situation.'

Heinrich Müller was sitting in the central hall, right at the top of the stairs, on a bench that resembled a church pew, between two busts, one of Hitler, one of Göring.

Nebe stopped and waited for two of his officials to catch up. 'My business is private, Heinrich.'

'Not when it concerns treason. This is Gestapo headquarters, so it would be common courtesy, Arthur.'

Nebe glanced in the direction of the elevator that led to the cells, then at his two officials, who were now flanking him.

'Sit down, Arthur,' Müller said. He nodded at several of his men, who had gathered between the staircase and the doors leading to the back stairs, to back off and provide a space. Nebe held his cool, licked his lips and told his men to wait downstairs.

Müller looked as if someone had grafted his uniform on, and Nebe felt that if you tried to remove it you would not be able to, so much was the uniform the man and the man the uniform now.

'Don't worry, Arthur. Consider yourself a guest, not a client.'

'You have a thug's face, Heinrich, Now I know you're an intelligent man, but you have a thug's face. And thuggery does have its place. To frighten old women and children, things like that. But not me, Heinrich.

'You know what they say the difference is between the Kriminalpolizei and the Gestapo, Heinrich? Gestapo are heavies trying to be policemen and Kripo are policemen who have been forced to be heavies.'

Müller shoved his hands in his pockets and stretched out his legs. 'Your friend, Hofer: it's sorted out?'

'Of course.'

'I look forward to meeting him.'

'Out of my hands now.'

'Who knows, we may be seeing more of one another, Arthur!' Müller grinned.

Nebe came to attention and gave the *Deutscher Gruss*. Then he walked very slowly over to the stairs, paused until his aides caught up and then walked out of the building.

Müller nodded to two of his men, who followed Nebe and his party. Then he stood up and straightened a Nazi flag hanging from the wall before going back to his office.

*   *   *

Theo Brandt came into Koch's office, short of breath. 'There's been an incident, in Rosenheim,' he said. 'Shooting. One of the men involved dropped a sleeve-gun. It's just come in.'

Koch, who had been rereading Hofer's statement, looked up. 'Rotach – Valkyrie?'

'Brief description could be him. In SS uniform.'

'Who else knows?'

'I took the report.'

'Right. Get Hofer up here, Theo. We're going to move. You're sure you're with me, Theo? There's still time to save your career.'

'You let me worry about my career, sir.'

When Hofer was brought up, Koch locked the office with just the three of them in it. 'All right,' he said, 'you two are going to Rosenheim. I want you to find Rotach. Whatever it takes. Whatever it costs. You're going to earn your SS spurs now, Theo.'

'And you, sir?' Brandt asked.

'I'm going to do what I said. The only thing left to me. Go to Obersalzberg with the file. To Rattenhuber.'

'You're a damn fool,' Hofer said.

'And you're a traitor. If he makes a false move, Theo, kill him.'

'Herr Kriminalkommissar. How are we going to get out of here unseen, if you don't mind me asking? I suspect our SD watchers will not be pleased.'

'I'm not without moves, Theo. And if we move before dark we'll have a head start before we're noticed. There's a tunnel under this building leading to the Frauenkirche. Very few people know about it. It was built years ago, after the communist uprising here, so the police would have a way out in difficult times.'

'You're a smarter man than I thought,' Hofer said.

'I'm protecting myself. And I want this man, Herr Major, I want Rotach. If he is who you say, Hofer, then he's going in one direction. If he is not, it won't matter.'

'Rattenhuber'll do what the Reichsführer says,' Hofer said. 'You'll come back in a box.'

'That's a possibility. But Brigadeführer Rattenhuber is a policeman' Koch said. 'If he puts a toe wrong, Theo, kill him.'

'You may depend on me, Herr Kriminalkommissar.'

'I'm hoping I can, Theo.'

Koch put his arm on the sergeant's shoulder.

14

ERICH HAAS OPENED one eye and rolled it. The room seemed bare and he shivered. He closed his eye and then opened the other one.

'Awake?' the pustular man standing over him said. 'Good! I was beginning to believe you wouldn't.'

It was a small room with very hard wooden furniture and a flagstone floor and the man's high boots slapped hard on the floor. He was middle-aged, with a pocked hairy face and calloused hands, and he wore jackboots and corduroys and a collarless shirt and braces; and underneath his shirt was a vest.

His chest hair came over the top of his vest and it was the same shade of grey as his head hair. Below his hair his face was a ruddy mix, browned by something more than the sun, maybe a liver complaint, Haas thought, and his hands had a slight tremor. His nose was large and spread out across his face and his face had a kind of facetious know-all grin. The kind you often see on teenagers.

'You are feeling better?' the man asked.

Haas nodded. 'As well as someone knocked out by Max Schmelling might feel. Where is this?'

'This is Oberdorf.'

'And where is that?'

'Well, Innsbruck is that way and Munich is that way and Salzburg is that way. That's where Oberdorf is. Actually, this is my farm and Oberdorf's about a kilometre that way. But you may refer to this as Oberdorf for geographical reasons. Population one hundred and fifty, evenly split, main industry agriculture – and tourism before the current difficulties. The population has been somewhat diminished by the war. There's a memorial to all the dead that way. A rather grandiose thing.

233

Better if I explain that all the young men who graduated in 1939 are dead. As are all the young men of 1940 and 1941; 1942 and 1943 had no young men leaving school. This year there are five but they are already in the army. Some of their fathers are in the army, too. The army isn't fussy who it takes any more. And we have been told to prepare to supplement our population with refugees from Munich and Stuttgart. There are Poles or Russians or Czechs being sent to help with the farms. I'm expecting a couple. So, that's where you are. Now who are you?'

'Sturmbannführer . . . it's there, written in my *soldbuch*, my Party *ausweis*, my *urlaubschein*, my personal *ausweis*. Take your pick . . . Ulrich Beck.' Haas put out his hand. 'Where is my coat?'

The farmer nodded his head. 'Over there, Herr Sturmbannführer . . . I'm not the type who rifles coats. Not while people are unconscious anyway. There's a gun in it, I can tell that. My, you were in a hell of a mess. I cleaned your wounds. You looked like you might have been shot.'

'I was; there was a train and we were attacked . . . Mosquitoes. I was wandering, I think.'

'Rosenheim . . . yes, I heard. My God, you wandered a long way.'

'Waffen-SS . . . I passed out a few times. I might have hitched a lift. What time is it?'

'Oh, about three, I think. I don't carry a watch. Here, get this into you.'

Haas looked at the wooden bowl.

'Soup. The best I can provide. I have put meat in it.'

'How long have I been here?' Haas asked.

'A few hours. I found you in my shed. I have cows in labour. One delivered earlier, another's due. And I have to do my duty. Wars may come and wars may go but cows have to be delivered. I think you've lost a bit of blood. Where were you going?'

'I'm not sure. Innsbruck, I suspect. That's where the train was going. There's a girl.'

'There's always a girl. I'm afraid I have no pretty daughters for you, Herr Sturmbannführer.'

'I'm not in any shape . . .'

'Ah, yes, shooting up things all over the countryside, they are now. They really are terror flyers. You'd think they'd concentrate their efforts on the battlefront instead of killing innocents here.'

'Do you have a vehicle? I need to get to Innsbruck.'

'Not tonight. I have a truck but no fuel. I'll ask in the village later and see if there's anything going that way and we can have them pick you up.' The farmer touched Haas's Ritterkreuz. 'Knight's Cross? Nice. And a gold wound badge. I was in the last one, you know. Got wounded so many times I lost count. Reached sergeant. I should have been an officer but they were snobbish about that in the last war. That's changed now. You don't have to be from the right family any more to get a commission. You just have to be smart and brave. Like you. Das Reich Division? Where are you based?'

'Can't tell you that.'

Haas pulled himself up and rubbed his neck and checked his wounds. The farmer had put small bandages on each of them.

'Don't rub them. You'll open them. You might have bled to death, you know. Or at least frozen. You were lucky. I've seen men frozen to death in these mountains. Even in a shed. I've seen men bleed to death, too. One lad in France during Verdun took four days to bleed to death. Sitting with him in a shell hole, listening to him crying, passing in and out of consciousness, turning that brighter shade of pale, you know. He was a good kid, plenty of fun when he was okay, but a pain in the neck when he was dying. That's how I remember people, how they died. If they died quickly I liked them; if they made a meal of it I didn't. Some guys just weren't there any more. You weren't there, were you? You look too young but just seeing you there made me think.'

'No, I wasn't there. Russia.'

'Oh, right. Well, then you know. And here am I like a big fool telling you about bleeding to death and you already know. Listen, eat this soup. It's good soup with real vegetables, not stalks.' He handed Haas the bowl and some dark bread. 'The bread's shit but it's all we have now. But as shit goes it's the better kind. I bet you're a city man. I can tell.'

'You talk a lot.'

'Of course. I'm alone here. Wife's dead. Just making small-talk. I'm the only one here most of the time – there were two lads here but they were sent east last year and I haven't heard from them since. So here I am. That's the way it is here, a few women and some kids left and old men in farms who wonder where it's all going. And now they want us to take in refugees. They'll bleed us dry, refugees, and they'll all be city types, with stupid accents and bad smells. We don't like foreigners here.'

'My apologies.'

'You're my guest. Look, it's getting near time and I have work to do. I'm even supposed to enforce the blackout around here, and some kind of curfew. I mean, I ask you, a curfew here. Oh, I don't know. My back's aching and I'm having trouble with my teeth again. You have trouble with your teeth?'

Haas shook his head.

'It's the war,' the farmer said. 'The diet. You can sleep some more when you're finished.'

'Exactly where am I? Do you have a map?'

The farmer went over to a wooden table, pulled open a drawer and took out a map. 'Here, look at this. Kufstein is here. And we're just off the road to Bad Reichenhall. St Johann in Tirol and Erpfendorf are that way. Don't worry, when you eat and rest some more, it will all appear much clearer. It's difficult to appreciate where you are in these mountains. It all looks the same, especially in the snow, and if you're not sure you run the risk of going round in circles. But you were lucky. And maybe the cold kept you bleeding to death. There's a thought. How long have you been with the SS?'

'Too long.'

'I thought about joining the army again, you know, something in admin, but I didn't fancy being in a city or somewhere like that. I'm more suited to this, being a farmer. We need food. And I like the freedom it gives me. But don't let it fool you, there's nothing happens here I don't know about: escaped prisoners, black marketeers, draft dodgers, I can spot them a mile off. We're getting a lot of draft dodgers around here these days, trying to lie low. Some of them near freeze themselves. But I help bring them in when we find them. I figured you for a draft dodger at first but you're too old. You're lucky to be alive. I've lost count of the people we've seen die in these mountains. Usually city people. Hikers and suchlike. No idea what the mountains are about.'

Haas finished his soup and put the bowl down on the floor.

'Like some schnapps?' the farmer asked. 'I have some schnapps but no coffee. I'm trying to get hold of some coffee from a supplier in Innsbruck who has a brother in Zurich. But getting it here is difficult. I suppose I should not be telling you this.'

'I didn't hear.'

'Good. Schnapps?'

'Why not?'

The farmer took out a bottle and poured two glasses. 'So, when will the invasion will be?'

Haas shook his head. 'I don't know. You say that like you are interrogating me.'

'I'm sorry, I'm a nosey old devil.'

'What's your name?'

'Hermann . . . Hermann Luft. Sky's the limit. It's a little joke of mine.'

Haas smiled. 'Hello, Hermann.'

'I'll do my cows,' Luft said. 'You rest. We'll talk some more later.'

'If there's time.'

'There'll be time.'

After cleaning them, Claude Dansey replaced his glasses and also replaced the white sheet over Teddy Giles's face. Kim Philby's aftershave fought with the formaldehyde in the small morgue.

'It was a sneak raider,' Philby said. 'Probably a Junkers 88. The bomb hit a gas mains. There's a whole family dead up the street.' He stood back against the yellow-stained tiles.

'What the bloody hell was he doing there?' Dansey asked.

'We were meeting for a drink,' Philby said.

'So why aren't you lying there with him?'

'I was late, sir. Vee Vee asked me to stay back. I still have Ryder Street business.'

'Aren't you the lucky one, young Philby?' Dansey said.

'He was my . . . friend . . . sir.'

'We don't have friends, Philby,' Dansey said. 'Allies, some; enemies, many; friends, none. Bloody nuisance, this. Look, you'll have to fill in for Teddy. I don't want anyone else in on this Valkyrie thing. I'll clear it with Vee Vee. No more Ryder Street work for the time being.'

'Won't he be curious?'

'He's not a very curious man, is he? Anyway, this is a priority affair. Be in my office in an hour. I'll brief you.'

Dansey pulled the sheet back one more time and allowed his personal grief five minutes before ushering it out for ever.

It was the purple time just before dawn, as the colours are splashing at the edge of day, when Brigadeführer Johann Rattenhuber came strolling down the winding road that leads from Hitler's Berghof to Berchtesgaden.

He had been up all night and his tiredness had given way to an elation of sorts. He walked through the cold with his hands behind his back and his dimpled double chin balanced precariously on the knot of his tie.

The guard post, manned by detectives of Dienstelle 1 of the RSD, was a wooden building on a stone foundation, with the roof topped with small rocks in the Bavarian tradition, in order to prevent large amounts of snow gathering on the structure.

The three detectives at the outer perimeter of the Führer area on Salzbergstrasse were all wearing field-grey greatcoats and rubbing their hands. The temperatures at that time of the day made men on guard duty swear a lot. Rattenhuber, a big nebulous lard of a man in the semi-darkness, stood for a moment while his men saluted, and then stepped inside the guardhouse.

'Herr Kriminalkommissar, I should be smart and say I've been expecting you, but I am genuinely surprised. If you think you can give yourself up to the Führer personally and rely on some kind of birthday leniency, I think you've come a long way for nothing, Wilhelm.'

Wilhelm Koch looked up from where he sat, his face paler than the snow-capped tops of Watzmann or Hochkalter mountains to the west, holding his side. 'I must talk to you, Herr Brigadeführer . . . there is an assassin . . .'

'Yes, and it would appear – from the nature of the warrant I have read – that you have aided and abetted him, Wilhelm. I have to say I'm disappointed.'

'No, Herr Brigadeführer, not I. If this were the case, would I come here and surrender myself? Would I?'

'There's more than one way to skin a rabbit. I personally think you should invest in a good lawyer.'

'I was ordered to release Hofer. By Gruppenführer Nebe.'

Rattenhuber thought for a moment. 'And you can prove this, I suppose?' he asked.

Koch shook his head slowly. 'Look, there is an assassin,' he said. 'I've met him. He is working for the British, and he will kill the Führer, Herr Brigadeführer. And then you will be out of a job.'

'You were always opinionated, Wilhelm. You've created a hell of a fuss. You must have really had the hots for that lady in Munich.'

238

'I have a file.' Koch glanced across the guard hut. 'Read it.'

'It's late – or should I say, early – and I've had a hard day. You should have got Nebe's order in writing, Wilhelm.'

'Please,' Koch said. 'Hear me out. His code name is Valkyrie, but I know him as Karl Rotach. He's a German, working for the British. Part of a unit run by Hofer. Tod, they call it. A department of Abwehr Two. Hofer was trying to stop him. Hofer told Ohlendrof and Schellenberg. That night he was arrested. SD Inland were going to kill him. Read it all. I've tried to get a personality check on Rotach from Berlin. Nothing came. Look, he killed three paratroopers in Rosenheim yesterday.'

'The Reichsführer's office say it was a shoot-out between soldiers – SS penal troopers with too much booze and nothing to do.'

'And the Gestapo?'

'It's a military matter. They have no jurisdiction.'

'Just read my file, Herr Brigadeführer. Read it and and judge it as a police officer and protect me.'

Rattenhuber was silent for a while, then he spoke very deliberately. 'You're in a lot of trouble, Wilhelm. You could help yourself by telling me where Hofer is.'

'I don't know. Somewhere between here and Rosenheim, I suppose. Looking for Valkyrie. Herr Brigadeführer, there are people who want this assassin to succeed. Look at the details in the file, sir, show it to the Führer. He is blond. His eyes are somewhere between blue and green. He has posed as a book-binder. Hofer even sketched a likeness of him. There are written testimonies. There is evidence. The report is thorough. Hans, I'm asking you as a police officer to consider all of this. As an old friend.'

'You're a cool one, Wilhelm, I'll give you that. Or a terrible fool. Are you so arrogant that you cannot see you might have been used? You must realise that stories like this are Hofer's stock-in-trade. And his boss, Von Freytag-Loringhoven, he says he knows nothing about any of this.'

'But I've met Rotach – Valkyrie.'

'So, let me get this straight,' Rattenhuber said. 'Gruppenführer Schellenberg, Gruppenführer Ohlendorf and Reichsführer Himmler are wittingly or unwittingly covering the fact of a British assassin and, instead, are pinning the whole thing on an Abwehr major who just happened upon the information in the course of his otherwise flawless intelligence career. Of course, the fact that this Abwehr officer has cocktails with known enemies of the state, has murdered two of the state's security officers, is a past master of sabotage and subversion and is probably up to his arse in conspiracies with foreign agents – this has no bearing on events.'

'I am a serving police officer. I have gathered evidence. I have seen this man. He killed a woman in Munich and very probably the paratroopers in Rosenheim. And others. Look at my evidence. I don't know about the Reichsführer or Gruppenführers Ohlendorf and Schellenberg, but I know Valkyrie and I know Gruppenführer Nebe told me to let Hofer go.'

'You are persistent,' Rattenhuber said. 'What's his name again? This assassin of yours?'

'He will kill the Führer.'

'Over my dead body.'

'Very probably.'

Koch pulled his eyes directly in line with Rattenhuber's and the RSD commander saw something which his police experience and his years of guarding Adolf Hitler told him to take notice of. He called his men back into the guard hut. 'Right, get him up to the Turken, get a doctor for those bruises; and nothing about this until I say so, hear?'

His men nodded.

'You have the sanctimony of a perennial loser, Wilhelm. And if it is a hoax? If, while we're searching for this shadow, your friend Hofer makes a move, will you explain to the Führer why this happened?'

'I accept that as a possibility. I ask you to use your police skills, Herr Brigadeführer. This man is no shadow.'

'You know, all things considered, I think the Führer made the right decision about you, Koch. You'd never have fitted in here. You consider that while I decide what to do with you, Herr Kriminalkommissar.'

He opened the door of the guardhouse and looked out at the breaking dawn.

Dawn on 19 April 1944 broke in lower Bavaria and that part of the eastern Tyrol, north of the Kitzbuhler Alpen, with a series of short rain showers no one but the mountain farmers and the early morning shifts in the factories noticed.

The rain twisted the light around the silver peaks and broke the white into colours, and a secret mist hung on in folds like protective netting above the mountains. Martin Hofer rubbed his eyes, shifted his body in the seat, then nudged Theo Brandt. Brandt woke with a start. Then both men straightened their clothing.

'It's like looking for a speck of rust on a needle in a haystack,' Brandt said.

'He had to hold up for the night,' Hofer said. 'That buys us time. This road is still our perimeter.'

'And there're a dozen scattered villages and a hundred isolated farm and outhouses up here. And us. I'm probably on a wanted poster now. Christ, what a career move!'

He pulled Haas's sleeve-gun from his inside pocket. 'I stole it in Rosenheim. When that orpo lieutenant was looking at you. Nasty little device. They'll be all over us soon, you know.'

'If we bring them to Valkyrie then it'll be worth it,' Hofer said.

'Jesus! What kind of a fighter pilot were you, Herr Major?' Brandt asked.

'The kind that liked flying but didn't care for the rest of it. There were two distinct breeds in the air war, the killers and the flyers. The killers weren't as good flyers as the flyers and the flyers weren't anything like as good killers as the killers. I'd say we complemented one another, though in my estimation the killers had a greater life expectancy. The flyers ran out of steam most of the time and gave up. You can only kill so many people when it is not your nature. Are you an SS man by nature, Brandt?'

'God, no. I'm joining the SS now because I see young guys with down on their chins getting promoted while I'm still a sergeant and I says to myself, look, Theo, you have nothing except this career and you had better either play the game of your career or get out. So I play the game.'

'Until now.'

'I have more integrity than I thought. Unforgivable, really. I suppose I expect to be rewarded when we find Rotach – this Valkyrie. Or not. All right, I'm rash.'

'I don't think so.'

'I never served, you know. Maybe that's why I'm doing this. My brother was killed in January.'

Brandt started the car and they rolled along the mountain road for about two or three kilometres. Three men trundling along the road in boiler suits, their shoulders bent, smoking a tired cigarette, which sagged as they passed it around in the wet, disappeared around

241

a corner. Hofer nudged Brandt and rubbed the car window to get a better look. Brandt eased the car around the corner.

'What was the make of that car they said he stole?' Hofer asked.

Brandt stopped the car and ran his hand through his hair. 'Stoewer Arkona.'

'Three point six litre?'

'Yeah. Black, like that.'

The car was up an embankment, embedded in a wire fence. Two of the men in boiler suits were looking inside; the third was telling them to leave it, he wanted to get home.

'There might be something useful,' the youngest one said.

'I'll get you two years or a posting to the eastern front if you're not out of there before I blink my eyes.'

Brandt showed his Kripo ID and pushed one of the men aside. 'Anyone see the man driving this?'

'Wearing SS uniform, mid to late thirties. Black hair,' Hofer said.

All three men shook their heads.

'We thought . . .'

'I know what you thought,' Brandt said. 'There's blood in here, Herr Major. What's nearby, lads?'

The man who had wanted to go home and was now picking his nose, pointed in the direction of the forests. 'Couple of farms. You'll break your axle.'

Brandt looked at Hofer.

'That's where he's headed,' Hofer said.

Brandt pulled out a Mauser pistol and cocked it. 'This man does not play games, does he, Herr Major?' He reached under his coat and extracted a second weapon. 'You had better have this.'

Hofer took the pistol and checked it.

'What are you waiting for?' Brandt yelled at the three men, who were now looking at the automatics with a mixture of fear and fascination. They backed off and began to move quickly down the road towards Oberdorf.

'Shall we dance?' Hofer said.

Brandt grinned.

'You lead, Herr Major. He's your man.'

The clouds had cleared over the Obersalzberg when Adolf Hitler pulled his greatcoat collar up and threw the stick as far as his shaking arm would let him; the Alsatian bitch barked and chased the stick and the Reichsführer-SS grinned slyly when the animal brought the stick back to the Führer. '*Gruss Gott*, my Führer,' Himmler said.

'Still the Bavarian bourgeois, Heinrich,' Hitler said. 'I don't believe in that God. Christianity is a social depressant. It's Christianity which has us facing the kind of people who would plot against their Führer and country in its hour of greatest need. You have him, then? Our Abwehr traitor who can slip through fingers like melted butter? And his Kripo accomplices?'

Himmler hesitated and looked around at the RSD guards, standing off. 'Nothing yet, my Führer.'

'It would appear that not just the Abwehr will have to be watched in future, Herr Reichsführer,' Hitler said. 'I didn't sleep last night. That's why I'm here so early. On my own.' He stared at Himmler. 'I don't fear him.'

'Of course not, my Führer.'

Hitler let his eyes drift across the valley to the Untersberg mountain and then left over the pine trees to the Hochkalter and then behind that the Watzmann and the Hoher Goll. 'I could stay here for ever,' he said. Then he rubbed his eyes. 'But I shall have to go in, the light's too strong for me.'

Himmler was left standing. He gave the *Deutscher Gruss* to Hitler's back. Above them, standing on the wooden balcony of the Hotel Turken, next to the Berghof, Brigadeführer Johann Rattenhuber watched the day take shape in the valley below. He stayed watching it until the Reichsführer-SS sat in his car and was driven off in the direction of Salzburg.

When Wilhelm Koch looked up from where he was sitting at the bear-like silhouette in the shadow of the doorway, Johann Rattenhuber did as much as he could to feign a smile and then stepped into the cold concrete room.

'Rotach's a complete fake,' he said. 'Gestapo confirmed it five minutes ago.'

Koch attempted to stand up but the light had disoriented him and he sat down again.

'It seems you may indeed be on to something, Wilhelm,' Rattenhuber said then. 'But what, I'm not sure. However, Gruppenführer Müller is anxious to interview you. Gruppenführer Müller and Gruppenführer Nebe are not soulmates, which is perhaps to your advantage. My primary concern is for the safety of the Führer.'

'And my evidence?'

'The jury's out, so to speak. You should have informed me immediately, you know. RSD has mechanisms. As secret military police we have access to everything.'

'I was under orders. Reich Security Main Office orders.'

'That is what we are here to establish. Your case is very circumstantial. And you're still the man who will have to answer most of the questions. The peculiar thing is, no one's looking for Rotach, even for the Gern murder. It's hard to order a hunt for a ghost. They are hard to find.'

'He's very real.'

Rattenhuber sat his bulky frame down on the small table. 'Know where you are?' he asked.

'Führer headquarters. Obersalzberg.'

'No. You're under the mountain. We have many tunnels here. They go all over the place. But it's quiet and we like to use it for things like this. You could easily disappear here. You see, what I see is a fading police officer and a man beaten in love, who could easily be a dupe for an elaborate coup. You're opinionated enough and not quite clever enough. Perhaps you should have just obeyed your orders.'

'I did.'

Haas found a drawer full of old photographs. There were snaps of the farmer, Luft, and his children taken years earlier, and ones of Luft and his grandchildren. One of his grandchildren was in the Hitler Youth. Haas found himself flicking through the photographs while he rechecked Luft's body for any signs of life. Then he put the photographs down on the table and continued searching the kitchen.

'I hope you had reason to kill him.'

Haas paused before he turned to the voice behind him. He thought about reaching for the Navy Luger laid out in front of him. But had no magazine in it.

'Hello . . . Valkyrie,' Martin Hofer said. 'You don't mind if I call you that? Code numbers are very disappassionate.'

Haas studied the face as if he were having problems and as if the man who was speaking his name might be making a mistake.

'Your hands where they are, please. I'm not him.' Hofer gestured to the dead farmer. 'I know the trade. By the way, the man covering you from the left is Kriminalmeister Brandt of the Munich Kripo and he wants to talk to you about murder – and other things.'

Brandt showed some of his body at another door.

'You have me at a disadvantage, gentlemen,' Haas said.

'Put your hands on your head,' Brandt ordered.

'You're a hard man to track down,' Hofer continued. 'Almost makes me proud.'

'Look, I don't know what he's told you, Herr Kriminalmeister, but I'm Hauptstrumführer Ernst Voss, Gestapo. This man, Hans Luft, was running a smuggling and black market racket with the Abwehr.'

Brandt glanced over at Hofer.

'Come on, you can do better than that,' Hofer said to Haas. He walked over to the farmer, lying on the floor and touched his body.

'No. it's true, Kriminalmeister,' Haas said. 'Check my papers. My warrant disc. The Abwehr have been running a currency and contraband racket through here for years. Check with Berlin. Check with your own office, for heaven's sake. It's an on-going investigation. We've already hauled in a number of Abwehr people from Munich. You must know this.'

'You will walk over to the wall and face it,' Brandt ordered.

'Just check my identification and ring Berlin.'

'Be careful,' Hofer said. 'Be very careful, Brandt. Everything he says is a lie. And keep your distance. Don't go near him. If he moves, kill him.'

'He's going to kill me anyway,' Haas said. 'And you, too. He's the damn ringleader. His name is Hofer, Major Martin Hofer, he runs Abwehr Two's Tod programme. Among other things. How would I know that? I don't know what he's told you but whatever it is you've been had, man.'

'Shut up,' Hofer said. 'I'm going to frisk him. Cover me, Brandt.'

Hofer came up to him and put his pistol to Haas's head. Very slowly, he began to frisk him.

'Long time no see. Your handiwork has a remarkable consistency. Now, Kriminalmeister Brandt wants to bring you back to Munich. We have a car. I will insist you travel in some discomfort, if only for my own security. I do not relish the thought of having my neck broken.'

'What has he told you?' Haas said to Brandt. 'I'm not going to make it to Munich, you know. He'll kill me; he'll kill you, too. My God, man, can you not see what he's up to? What has he told you? Tell me, please.'

'You are here to kill the Führer,' Brandt said.

Haas laughed. 'Jesus Christ, not that one. And you believe him? A specialist in sabotage and subversion? Think about it. How did you know where to find me?'

'Good detective work,' Brandt said. 'We saw your handiwork in Rosenheim. You left a trail, Herr . . . Rotach, or whatever your name is. I'm a good detective.'

Haas laughed again.

'Rosenheim? Have you checked out those guys? SS paratroopers, from a penal unit. I was following them. They work the currency scam out of Yugsolavia and Italy. Through Turkey. The Abwehrstelle in Istanbul. I've been set up. Do you understand?'

'Come on, let's get him out of here,' Hofer said.

'You won't make it, Brandt,' Haas said. 'You'll die, too.'

'Cuff him,' Hofer said to Brandt. 'I'll cover you.'

Haas went to move from the wall.

'I told you to stay put,' Hofer said. 'The cuffs, Brandt.' He pushed his boot into the back of Haas's knee and punched him in the back and Haas went to the floor on his knees.

Brandt cuffed him and stood back. Then Hofer brought his pistol across Haas's head. He slumped to the floor.

'Right, get the car,' Hofer said. Brandt hesitated. 'I said, get the car.'

'I want to see him alive when I get back, Herr Major,' Brandt said.

'I'm not a murderer, no matter what you may believe,' Hofer said. 'Anyway, I need him alive to clear myself.'

'You'll have to kill me, Herr Major, you know that,' Haas said. 'Gestapo get me and work on me with whatever, who knows what I'll say.'

'Get the car!' Hofer shouted at Brandt. 'Do it! We don't have much time.'

Brandt nodded and left, leaving the back door open.

Immediately, Hofer started to kick over the furniture and smash the crockery.

'You are going to kill me,' Haas said.

'It's politics,' Hofer said. 'I don't think you'd understand. You always did have a juvenile attitude to the whole thing. And now you're just a hired assassin.'

'I've always been a hired assassin. I just make more money this way. They sold me out. Gestapo and SD. Someone gave me to them.'

'So Richter was careless. Welcome to the real world. They want to hang me.'

'Let me go.'

'I can't.'

'You think Churchill and Roosevelt will protect you from Stalin?'

'We have no choice.'

'God, who's juvenile now. You people are living in Cloud-cuckooland. I've heard of building castles in the clouds, but you people want to move in.'

'I am protecting my Führer's life,' Hofer said.

'I think you and I are being had.'

'All the time', Hofer said, 'all the time. I do not expect to live much longer. I am wanted for treason.'

'I have a million American dollars coming to me . . . let me go, let me kill him,' Haas said.

'If it was up to me, then I would.'

'Bullshit. You're like all your class. You throw responsibility for your actions anywhere and everywhere, just to keep yourselves clean. You all took an oath to him and when he was victorious you cheered him. You're spineless people and I hope to God he kills all of you. I have a job to complete. I will complete it.'

'You know, I almost believe you,' Hofer said. 'Stand over there, please,' Hofer picked Haas up and shoved him across the kitchen. 'You know, my father was a gambler. Always approached each day like it would be his last. He killed himself one morning when he woke to find he could not care less if it was his last or not. I watched him try to avoid that day.'

'There's a point to this?' Haas asked.

'I've had this same feeling for some time now.'

'I've always had it,' Haas said.

'They'll deal with us when they land,' Hofer said. The British, the Americans.'

'My arse. They'll use you. They'll deal with the Russians.'

The air was heavy. Hofer was sitting at the wooden table having poured himself some schnapps. Haas stood at the far end of the table with his hands cuffed behind his back.

'His death now would do no one any good.'

'There're some Jews who think otherwise.'

'It'd just bring Himmler to power. He's waiting for the chance. He wants you to do it, you know.'

'You'd say anything now, Herr Major. To justify yourself.'

'Why do you think you've got this far? The British told us about you and I told Schellenberg. So where is the manhunt?'

'The British tried to stop me. They failed.'

'I saw one of their corpses in Rosenheim. I will not fail.'

'Why, you're sweating, Herr Major. Having second thoughts? Thinking about asking me to give my word? That's not the Tod way, is it? Kill me quickly and get it over. Then you'll die. Futile, isn't it? Himmler'll string you and your friends from every tree from here to Berlin.

'I'm doing my duty.'

'Of course you are . . .'

Haas moved to the left and Hofer swung his pistol and fired; but Haas rolled and the shot hit the floor beside him. Hofer aimed again but he knew he was too late: Haas brought his right boot up and kicked the pistol up towards the ceiling, where the next round went, and slammed his head into Hofer's stomach. Hofer roared and buckled and Haas came up and caught him with another kick to the chest and Hofer seemed to explode and fall back across the table. Haas followed him and slammed his knee into Hofer's face and his foot into his neck and Hofer collapsed on to the floor.

Haas sat down on the floor and began pulling his cuffed hands around the back of his legs, watching Hofer writhing across the floor, gasping for breath, his colour shifting to a deep purple. Haas got his hands to the backs of his knees.

'I'm going to have to kill you, Herr Major,' he said. 'I don't want to, but I'm going to have to.'

Hofer looked at him and seemed on the verge of passing out.

Haas smiled. 'Out of practice,' he said. He had his hands down at his ankles.

Hofer then suddenly threw himself across the floor at Haas, caught him with a kick to the face that sent the assassin reeling on to the concrete flagstones, cracking his head and reopening one of the wounds there. Haas got one leg free of the cuffs but Hofer was up now and he caught him under the shin with his boot, and when he stamped the sole of his other foot into the small of the assassin's back, Haas collapsed on the floor.

'Not quite,' Hofer said. He walked back across the kitchen and picked up the Mauser pistol and cocked it and came back to Haas. 'Still the best, teacher,' he said, smiling. 'Still the best.'

Haas spat blood from his mouth. 'Get it over with,' he said.

Hofer stood over him and levelled the pistol. 'I wish there was another way.'

The silenced round sent Hofer spinning across the room. He sank to the ground, tried to pick himself up, but his spine was shattered, then he swung his weapon but could not control it and fell across the stone floor. Theo Brandt looked at the sleeve-gun and then placed it in his pocket. Haas scrambled across the floor, trying to get out of the cuffs again. Brandt swung his service pistol at him. 'Don't move . . . please!'

He walked across the floor, turned Haas over and undid the cuffs. 'Let's just say I work for a serious institution anxious for a positive outcome to your mission,' he said.

Haas was rubbing the blood on his mouth. 'Himmler?'

'No. More serious than that.' He reached into his pocket and pulled out the sleeve-gun and handed it to Haas. 'You'll need this, I suspect.'

'And him?' Haas asked.

'A murderer and a traitor. Now get out of here. There're a couple of police coming along a mountain track on bicycles.'

Haas walked around the kitchen, collecting the things he needed. He assembled his papers and weapons.

'There's a car parked down a track about a kilometre that way,' Brandt said. 'Take the track and then head east. It'll bring you to the main road to Salzburg via Bishofshofen. Then you're on your own.'

He went over to Hofer's body and checked it for papers. 'I liked him.'

Haas reloaded his sleeve-gun and then pointed it at Brandt. 'I can't leave you alive,' he said.

Brandt did not get time to reply.

15

CLAUDE DANSEY SAT down on the iron bed and rubbed his hands.
It was dank in the cell and the smell was sharp. The frosted breath of
the two mouths seemed to touch and rebound and then mix.

'Treating you well?' he asked.

Ben Kramer tried to lift his wooden leg but was unable to. 'I'd
like a view, sir.'

'I'll see what I can arrange. How are you feeling?'

'Not terrific, sir. Wretched stuff is gathering strength and I'm
losing it. I get tired.' He pulled the grey blanket beside him over
his shoulders. 'I get cold, too. When do I face court martial?'

'There'll be none. You're here under 18B. You'll stay that way for
the duration or . . .'

'Until I croak it. Convenient. How's Sussex going?'

'Good. We're beginning to place the teams. You did fine work
there, Ben.'

'It's just a pity I became unsound.'

Dansey closed his coat and tied his scarf.

'Kim Philby's probably going to get the Soviet Desk.'

Kramer turned his head to Dansey and very slowly began
to grin.

'Perhaps it's for the best. He's the nearest thing to a real Chekist
I've ever talked to. So maybe he'll do well.'

'I wanted you, Ben,' Dansey said . . .

He stood up.

'Would you look in on Maurice Hallan's widow, sir?' Kramer
asked. 'As a favour.'

'I'll do something there, don't worry. You know, I admire you,

251

Ben. I see something of myself when I was younger in you. We may need to talk about the situation in Palestine again.'

'You know where to reach me,' Kramer said. 'What day is today? I get confused.'

'Thursday, 20 April. About three minutes past midnight.'

'Hitler's birthday. You haven't stopped him – my man – have you?'

'I'll see if I can get you that view.'

The face appeared slowly from the shadows on Konigseerstrasse in Berchtesgaden.

'Gestapo. A4,' the man said. He flashed his silver warrant disc at the three Liebstandarte SS soldiers. The moonlight caught it and made the metal seem molten for a second.

Corporal Peter Neumann, who was on his second all-night sentry duty in three days, glanced at the warrant disc twice and then nodded at the Gestapo agent, who adjusted his glasses in the spitting rain. The Gestapo man seemed bulkier than his face would warrant, but it could have been the overcoat. 'Is there an RSD officer here?' he asked.

'No, they're all in bed, or at Klessheim with the Führer. We get this shitty work.'

'And I suppose you can give me the Führer's itinerary, too, Unterscharführer,' the Gestapo agent said to Neumann. The SS corporal stiffened, aware that he had made an error.

'Check my papers, please,' the Gestapo agent said.

Neumann examined the man's papers. '*Heil Hitler*, Herr Hauptsturmführer . . . Voss,' he said, reading the Gestapo agent's identification. The man had a *sonderausweis* for the Führer area on the Obersalzberg, complete with RSD stamp for the month of April, 1944. And a letter signed by Heinrich Himmler.

'Special attachment,' the Gestapo agent said. 'Look, I know it's dirty weather, Unterscharführer. But do your duty.'

Peter Neumann and his men came to attention. Erich Haas walked on. A fourth soldier coming down from the direction of the railway station watched him stroll up towards a bus-stop and acknowledged him, but concentrated his mind on what was coming from the sky.

Haas vanished into the darkness and the soldiers rubbed their hands and swore.

*   *   *

Wilhelm Koch struggled now with the lack of light as the two RSD detectives escorted him through the tunnels under the Obersalzberg.

He was taken up a flight of stairs, past an unmanned underground machine-gun emplacement and up another flight of stairs into the Hotel Turken, the headquarters of the RSD in the Führer area. The room was old and decorated with pinewood and had a large log fire burning. Koch watched the various hues of the fire before focusing his eyes on Johann Rattenhuber.

'Herr Kriminalkommissar, we bring you back from the underworld, so to speak.'

Koch shook his head and straightened himself. He was shivering; the stone of the tunnels had sapped the last joule of heat energy from his body and he was beginning to slip into that euphoria which signalled that he would not last the length of the speech the fat man was making.

'Come closer to the fire. Warm yourself up, Wilhelm,' Rattenhuber said. 'There have been developments, and you may be somewhat absolved, as they say, but not released from custody. Play this right and you may escape with your pension rights intact.' He leaned against the door and shoved his hands into the pockets of his uniform. 'It appears we have found Major Hofer. Unfortunately, it also appears he is dead. In a farmhouse near Oberdorf, west of here. Two other bodies also. We're awaiting official identification but one of them may well be a sergeant of yours, Theo Brandt.'

'Rotach?' Koch asked without emotion.

Rattenhuber shook his head.

'I am beginning to believe that what Hofer said about him was true: he is a ghost,' Koch said.

'Nonsense. For a police detective you are displaying a remarkably unprofessional approach to this investigation, Koch.'

Heinrich Müller's entry into the room made Rattenhuber swing round and stiffen to attention.

'No formalities, gentlemen, there's too much to do. I hope you slept a bit while in Rattenhuber's custody, Koch, because I'm going to need you today. Have you eaten?'

Koch shook his head.

'Get him some food, Hans.'

Rattenhuber signalled to one of his men. The man left the room. 'We have copious supplies of vegetarian gruel, fruit, dry biscuits and mineral water,' Rattenhuber said. 'The Chief insists.'

253

'Why do you think Nebe ordered you to release Hofer?' Müller demanded.

'I don't know, sir,' Koch answered.

'Of course you don't. And Nebe's indisposed, would you believe. Taken ill. I'd expect that. It's a redundant argument now, anyway, who told whom what in relation to Hofer. It only becomes important again if we capture your bookbinder alive. Then the Gestapo and the RSD can start to make some sense of all this. And for that, your safety is imperative. No automobile accidents, no tripping up in the bathroom or swallowing poisonous foods, or anything like that. If you understand me.'

'I'm beginning to understand more than I ever wanted to,' Koch said.

'You do your duty, Wilhelm,' Rattenhuber said.

A waiter in a white tunic came into the room, carrying a silver tray. He placed it on the table, saluted and left.

'Meat!' Müller said. 'You've been given the royal treatment, Koch.'

'I'm honoured.'

'You may well be a traitor, Herr Kriminalkommissar,' Müller said then. 'But I need you, so I treat you well. You help me and I will help you. Understand?'

'I understand, Herr Gruppenführer. I want this man as much as you do.'

'If he indeed exists. Now fill me in on what you know and none of this rubbish about ghosts. I'm not going to the Führer to tell him he's being stalked by a demon. The Reichsführer will have me relieved if I do.'

'If he is a ghost, he's a very deadly ghost.'

Erich Haas cut through the outer perimeter fence of the Führer area in under a minute, and rolled under. Then he moved snow to cover up the breach, brushed over the snow with a tree branch, looked around and moved into the pine trees ahead, making sure not to step in the patches of snow that still lay on the mountains at that altitude. He glanced up at the moon and then at the Kelsteinhaus, perched on a crag high above the Obersalzberg. No one would be there now.

In the trees, Haas found a crater made by a fallen tree and took off the civilian clothes he had been wearing over his mountain infantry camouflage. He rolled the civilian clothes up in a belt, untied two mountain boots he'd had suspended from his neck and put them on. Then he adjusted his equipment and made sure the white camouflage was sitting right before setting off.

It took him two hours of hard climbing, sometimes almost straight up, to reach the top, through snow that often came up to his waist. The moonlight reflected off the clouds in the valley below and whatever heat the ground had collected during the day had already released itself into the silvered darkness.

Haas was soaked through when he reached the Kehlsteinhaus; the moonlight spread fingers across the whole of Berchtesgadener Land and the rain fell in thin sheets from the fingers of light.

He lay on his back and felt the heat he had generated himself in the climb dissipate through the cold limestone. He began to shiver. If he did not get inside he would freeze to death before he could act.

He hauled himself up with the same will that had brought him out of Moscow in 1941 through fifty kilometres of Russian patrols and a counter-offensive; with the same will that had brought him through the Quattara Depression in late 1942, and a dozen other assignments he had undertaken.

He pulled out the Navy Luger, loaded an armour-piercing round, screwed on the silencer, knelt down on one knee, rested the barrel of the weapon on his left arm and aimed at the lock on the small door in front of him.

The door opened with the second kick.

The Great Hall in the teahouse was furnished with chintz-covered easy chairs which seemed to jar with the tapestries and candelabra on the stone walls, with the wooden beams overhead and the great marble fireplace which was the focus of the room. Haas cringed at the lack of taste when he peered into the other rooms and saw the pinewood panelling and hunting-lodge rugs. He expected to see an animal head until he remembered what he had read about Hitler's distaste for hunting.

He went through to the balcony and took out a pair of binoculars and trained them on the crude outlines of the Hoheitsgebeit on the Obersalzberg a thousand metres below him.

In Schloss Klessheim, twelve kilometres away, Adolf Hitler was carefully studying a painting of his mother, hung between two of the windows in his bedroom. The painting came from his study in the Berghof and he would take it with him when he returned later that day. He checked something in the portrait, using his glasses, and then picked up a magnifying glass to study it more closely. 'How long will it take to confirm?' he asked

Heinrich Himmler went to move from the position he had assumed near a desk. He was almost at attention but ill at ease. 'The bodies will be officially identified this morning.'

'But Hofer is dead?'

'That is the indication.'

'Last year you gave me the Warsaw Ghetto; this year an Abwehr traitor planning my death. What will next year bring? I ask myself.'

'Victory, my Führer,' Himmler said.

'It was betrayal, you know . . .' Hitler looked directly at his Reichsführer-SS for the first time in the conversation.

Himmler was confused. 'What, my Führer?' he said, gasping for saliva.

'My mother. She died on me. Left me. Perhaps it was a test of my will, my strength. I did not come home. I could discard her: she had served her purpose.'

'Your strength is Germany's, my Führer,' Himmler said.

'Yes. I wish people would remember that.'

Claude Dansey stared at the blackout curtains on the window and imagined things. His breathing was tight and his chest felt as if someone had placed a great weight on it. He could hear intermittent footsteps on the street below. 'I think you had better get inoculated, Philby,' he said.

Kim Philby remained impassive. Something that annoyed Dansey even more than the information he had just received. 'It's a joke, Philby,' he said. 'I used to threaten Teddy Giles with Africa.'

'I see, sir.'

'Do you, Philby? Some of those African diseases make your insides turn to mush. Can we get confirmation of Kaestner's death through Switzerland?'

'Being sought. Things are confused.'

'Ever so. Ever will be. You know, I imagine us landing in Normandy only to find two men with vodka waiting for us. Christ. We could be facing a situation, Kim. You have to hand it to Ben Kramer . . .'

'And the Germans . . .?'

Dansey shrugged. 'I don't know everything, Philby. I wish I did. I wish I knew where Wachs was.'

Ruth Wachs pulled herself over the last crag before the Kehlsteinhaus and slumped to the ground. Then she pulled out her Mauser, checked the clip, cocked it, took another look at her wounds and stood up.

The door was ajar. She touched it with her foot, pushed and swung her weapon inside. Occasionally blood oozed from under her parka and ran down to the floor. She held her breath and slid along a marble wall. Somewhere ahead of her a tap dripped.

The suit of clothes was hanging over the first chair. Wachs stopped. She held her breath, put her foot out into the centre of the corridor, then slammed herself against the far wall with the Mauser raised. She scanned the Great Hall, then slipped her weapon round the corner and stepped inside. Then she swore.

A glass of water, some American biscuits and a bar of chocolate were all that remained of Haas. And the suit of clothes neatly draped over the back of the chair. Wachs slumped into a chair.

Erich Haas knocked on the door of a small house above the hamlet of Oberau, east of Berchtesgaden.

'Yes?' the old man rubbing his eyes said.

'Geheimestaatspolizei,' Haas said. 'Checking the district. Routine. May I come in?'

He flashed his silver warrant disc and the old man looked at it. Then he looked at Haas's white mountain uniform and mountain infantry cap with its edelweiss badge.

'It's cold,' Haas said. 'They gave me this uniform for the cold.'

'It's very early,' the old man complained. 'And usually we have RSD for this kind of thing. I give them schnapps.'

Haas closed the door behind him. 'Well, you can give me schnapps. Sicherheitspolizei drink, too.'

The man smiled. 'I'll get some. The Führer's birthday, yes?'

'Yes,' Haas said. 'Special precautions.'

The old man went into his kitchen and opened a small press and took out a bottle. 'I make it myself,' he said. 'Don't ask how. The Luftwaffe are interested in the recipe. They have made an offer.'

He laughed and took out two small glasses and poured a measure of alcohol into each one.

'Seen anything or anyone suspicious in the last couple of days?' Haas asked.

'No, nothing. And up here I'd notice if a new bird landed in one of the trees. I can see everything from my window.'

Haas nodded. 'It's beautiful.'

'I think so.'

Haas noticed a shotgun in the corner of the room. 'That yours?' he asked.

'I hunt sometimes. The Führer doesn't like hunting. Göring does. I've been on the mountain with him. With the Reichsmarshall.'

'Good stuff,' Haas said.

'It can make you go mad.'

'I am warm. When does the snow clear finally?'

'Should be soon. Next month it'll be nearly all gone. You in from Munich?'

'I should see the rest of the house, please. We'll begin at the top. After, maybe we'll have another drink.'

Haas followed the old man down a passage and up three flights of old stairs and into a small heavily timbered room with beams so low he had to stoop.

'It's an uneven room. We're on a hill and I think there's subsidence,' the old man said.

'Good view,' Haas remarked.

'The best.'

'And the woods back there, where do they lead?'

'It's pretty wild out there now. You're not thinking of checking it all yourself? It's dangerous.'

'No, I'll get the soldiers to do that. All right, let's start down, then.'

Haas looked out of the gap in the wooden shutters to the road, the onion dome church across the small valley and the T-junction, the small river and the bridge in between. He felt the kind of excitement he only felt this close to a kill, and it made him stop for a moment and move his eyes left to a ski run that wasn't functioning any more. 'There's a clear shot from this window,' he said. 'For an assassin.'

The old man came over and looked out. 'Maybe five seconds, maybe seven. I was a sniper in the last war. You would have to be set up. You're not going to make me seal the window?'

'Not up to me.'

'No. Forgive me.'

Haas swung the piano wire around the old man's neck and lifted him off the ground. He slammed his knee into the old man's back, snapped his spine and held him until he was dead.

Three hours later, on the outskirts of Salzburg, Gruppenführer Heinrich Müller came to attention and handed Reichsführer Heinrich Himmler a buff folder. A gentle flurry of snow twisted in the breeze outside and the train, Heinrich, shifted slightly. Outside, feet crunched on gravel and voices shouted through the crisp mountain air while shadows played with the jaundiced light escaping through the various shades and curtains on the train.

'Summation?' Himmler said, turning the pages.

'From the evidence and testimony, it is certain there was another man in the farmhouse. We are still gathering statements. You'll see we already have a statement from two people who saw this fourth man, an SS officer.'

'And when was Brandt's car found?'

'Fifteen minutes ago. Near the river. About two kilometres that way. The photograph is how he looked then.'

Heinrich Himmler drew breath through his pained attentiveness. 'Conclusions?' he said then, looking at Müller first, then Ohlendorf and Schellenberg.

'The assassin, Valkyrie, exists,' Müller said. 'He murdered a woman in Munich and some paratroopers in Rosenheim. And he may or may not have been sent here by the British. But all that is irrelevant until we find him.'

'Three dead bodies tell you all this?' Himmler asked. His upper lip was beginning to sweat.

Müller opened his briefcase and pulled out another file. 'This is the report of Kriminalkommissar Wilhelm Koch of the Munich Kriminalpolizei. It documents the evidence.' He almost dropped it on Himmler's desk. 'The Gestapo apprehended Koch last night. And with what happened in Oberdorf and Rosenheim, I feel there is definite cause to believe there is a killer out there. I have taken the precaution of calling out all available troops and establishing checkpoints.'

You could have heard a pin drop in the carriage.

'A ring of steel?' Himmler asked then, trying to read Koch's file and compose himself at the same time. 'Yes, a sensible precaution. But why wasn't I informed of this development? Of Koch's arrest?'

His chicken face began to assume the proportions of a bird about to be ringed.

'I rang earlier this morning, but you were indisposed, Herr Reichsführer.' Himmler had called on his mistress, who lived near Berchtesgaden, after visiting Hitler at Klessheim. 'I think I left a message.'

'And where is Koch now?' Himmler asked.

'In the custody of Brigadeführer Rattenhuber at Obersalzberg, Herr Reichsführer. He is a valuable asset. Kriminalkommissar Koch is the only one who can identify Valkyrie with any degree of sureness.'

Himmler continued to read, as if he did not know what was in Koch's file. But he was using the time to compose himself. 'You believe this?' he asked Müller.

'It seems that much of what Kriminalkommissar Koch reported is turning out to be less than inaccurate,' Müller said in reply.

'Seems is the appropriate word,' Himmler commented.

'Yes. This could be just an elaborate ruse by the Anglo-Americans to divert our resources in a time of urgency,' Otto Ohlendorf said.

'Would you like to put that to the Führer with your latest morale report, Otto?' Müller asked.

'Any reports to the Führer will be mine,' Himmler said. 'We just have to be sure what it is we are reporting.'

'The Kriminalkommissar may be an innocent dupe, or a key figure in something bigger,' Watter Schellenberg said then.

'Koch claims to have been ordered to release Major Hofer by Gruppenführer Nebe,' Miller said.

Again there was the kind of silence you only experience in morgues.

'You have asked Nebe about this?' Himmler said.

'Alas, Arthur is unavailable for comment at this moment. He's sick, I'm told. Gone to recuperate at a lakeside lodge in Bohemia. I've sent someone for a comment. He'll deny it, naturally.'

'Naturally,' Himmler said. 'I should like to talk to Koch, if that's all right with the Gestapo and the RSD?'

'Of course, Herr Reichsführer,' Müller said. 'As you order. He'll be here in half an hour.'

'Unfortunately, I have to attend the Führer's birthday celebrations at Klessheim soon,' Himmler said. 'Perhaps after lunch.'

There was a long pause and each of the men at the table studied the others' faces.

'Gentlemen,' Himmler said then, 'it is my belief that there is a strong possibility of a second assassin. This train will be the nerve centre for the security operation.'

'The Führer is vulnerable at Klessheim,' Müller said. 'He has to move back to Obersalzberg.'

'I will advise him thus. But you will protect him, Herr Gruppenführer, no matter where he is.'

'Yes, Herr Reichsführer,' Müller said, pushing back from the table. 'And Walter, I believe we have been duped. The question is by whom?'

The previously suspicious faces now set like granite, with the shade of a snow cap. Himmler regained himself in the face of the onslaught by his Gestapo chief. 'There are forces in this state who would seek to bring down the structures which keep it together,' he said. 'We must be constantly vigilant.'

Arthur Nebe paced from the door to the window and from the window to the fireplace. He picked up a log and threw it into the fire and waited for it to catch light. Sap poured from the centre of the log and a grey steam obscured it. Nebe scratched his face and went back to the door. He held the door handle. 'I was obeying orders. That is all I have ever done. Obey orders.'

'I wouldn't make that the cornerstone of my defence when Gruppenführer Müller's men are pushing broom handles into your anus.'

Nebe's nostrils flared and his large nose seemed to cover his face. 'I will not be talked to like that, Herr Von Trott, not by some Foreign Ministry dilettante.' He let go of the door handle for a moment and began to wring his hands.

'You'll have to vanish.' Claus Von Stauffenberg stepped out of the shadow where he had been standing, to the left of the fireplace. He came to attention. 'To be quite honest, Herr Gruppenführer, there is nothing I would like more right now than to see you in the welcoming arms of Gruppenführer Müller at Prinz Albrechtsrasse 8. But I have more pressing problems and my own preferences must take a back seat. You have, in your inimitable way, jeopardised us to a point where our whole movement is in the gravest peril. You have snaked your way between us and the Reichsführer, playing one off against the other, to the extent that I seriously considered killing you when I walked in that door. What have you been telling him?'

Nebe's eyes darted around the room. He touched the door handle again. 'Nothing.'

'Don't worry, Arthur,' Von Trott said. 'My dilettante sensibilities have convinced Claus that you are still more useful alive than dead.'

'It is the word of a *kriminalkommissar* against the word of a general,' Nebe said.

'I wouldn't argue that either,' Von Trott said. 'You do see our problem, Arthur. Koch appears to be the focus of the hunt for Valkyrie, and yet he is the one who could deliver you to Müller and all of us to very sticky endings.'

'The Reichsführer may bump you off anyway, just to avoid the difficulties.'

'You have to vanish, Herr Gruppenführer,' Von Stauffenberg added.

'And we have to pray – if you understand the meaning of the word, Herr Gruppenführer – that the man who can sink you will lead Müller and his men to our assassin. Stay here for a while, think it over. I'd say you still have a few hours before some of Müller's people come calling. We must get back to Berlin. I have a meeting with Allen Dulles this evening.'

'And Arthur,' Von Stauffenberg said, 'don't go anywhere near the Reichsführer. He will kill you if he has to.'

Erich Haas took out the Navy Luger, laid the parts on a table and began screwing them together. The old man's body was dumped in the corner. Haas had the bottle of schnapps on the table and he took a drink when he had assembled the Luger and was adjusting the sight and the metal shoulder butt. He then took out about a dozen bullets. They were simple lead projectiles, hollowed out at the top, and with the low muzzle velocity of the silenced Navy Luger they would do maximum damage to the tissue they struck.

Ruth Wachs stuffed the smaller piece of torn tablecloth into the ragged tissues of the wound in her shoulder and then tied it off with the longer piece. Twice she had to pause. Once she passed out. Perhaps for a minute. When she was ready, she stepped into the Kehlsteinhaus elevator and dropped 124 metres to a tunnel, which ran through the rock and two sets of doors with ruptured locks to a car park and the snow. A single set of footprints in the snow led into the trees.

Wachs touched the prints and stared at the valleys below. Then she began to descend through the snow, following the footprints, breath caught on the edge of her lips, while the morning sunlight wrestled with the mist and cloud cover that shrouded the mountains in the morning. Below her, the church bell in Oberau rang. It was followed by others in the valleys, a solemn cacophony in the stillness.

In Salzburg, a church bell was ringing when Wilhelm Koch examined Theo Brandt's Citroën, parked near the river. He picked up the SS officer's uniform folded on the seat, and examined the papers of Sturmbannführer Ulrich Beck.

'Why would he leave us a photograph of himself?' he asked. 'And why dump the car here? Look at where we are. It's bound to be found.'

'It's a diversion.' Johann Rattenhuber said.

'Obviously. The point is, for what?'

'Or for where?' Rattenhuber added.

At Schloss Klessheim, while Adolf Hitler stood watching a Panther tank going through its paces, Heinrich Himmler walked towards him at a controlled pace.

'An accomplice?' Hitler asked, when Himmler had finished whispering in his ear.

Heinrich Himmler felt his stomach twist a little more. 'There is developing evidence, my Führer; Rattenhuber thinks you should return to Obersalzberg. For security reasons.'

'Just like that?' Hitler asked. 'I should run on the basis of shadows now? My security cannot protect me from such dangers? Heinrich, I have just witnessed the best German engineering can produce, a tank that if manufactured in sufficient numbers, if backed by our new jets and rockets, will turn the tide of this war in our favour, and you wish for me to run from a possibility.'

'I am only thinking of your security, my Führer.'

Hitler grinned. 'You know my doctor is sick. Professor Morell sleeps worse than I do. My own doctor and his health is getting worse than mine. That's a metaphor, you know. I used to have parades in Berlin for my birthday, whole armies lined up for me. Now I have a couple of tanks, a few ageing field marshals and a security service which runs scared from possibilities. Just tear Salzburg apart. Arrest everyone if you have to. House to house.'

'It's being done, my Führer, but it takes time.'

'Yes. Time, time, always time. I do not have enough time for all I want to do. All right, we'll go as soon as we're ready; you've ruined any enjoyment I had here. I think I'm getting a headache.'

Corporal Peter Neumann had a headache. He had been on duty now for twenty-four hours without sleep and the woman ahead of him, in the brown corduroys, was not even pretty. He looked at his three men, strung out along the road to Oberau, greatcoat collars turned up, rifles over their shoulders, hands rubbing one another in a robotic fashion, and made a face.

'For the Führer!' the woman said. 'Birthday present.' Her right shoulder seemed to dip. Then she produced some daffodils and forest flowers from behind her back.

'Very nice,' Neumann said. 'But you can't go any further.'

'I would like to give them to him myself.'

'He's not here,' one of Neumann's soldiers said. He was small and wearing glasses and did not seem to fit her notion of what a Liebstandarte soldier should look like. He wore the ribbon of an Iron Cross second class and a silver wound badge.

'Where is he?' she asked.

'You look terrible, love,' Neumann said to her. 'Are you sick?'

'Dying, I think.'

He stepped back from her. 'Look, go home,' he said. 'I'll give him the flowers when I see him.'

She pulled the flowers back. 'No. Where is he?'

'I should arrest you for that,' Neumann said. Then he smiled, which seemed to relieve his headache. 'All right, all right, suit yourself. But you can't go any further here. You know that. Look, he'll be coming from Salzburg soon. We've just had word. Throw them into his car when he passes. All the women do that. There'll be a crowd of them down at Oberau; there usually is.'

'Oberau?'

'Yeah. And see a doctor, for God's sake.'

She smiled and turned and started walking towards Oberau.

'Hey!'

Only when Neumann had shouted three times did Ruth Wachs turn. He was only ten metres from her; his men were ten metres behind him, in a group. He reached out with his hand. 'I have to

264

check you out. Papers, that kind of thing. Otherwise the Gestapo get cranky. Christ, you're bleeding!'

Wachs shot him in the head. The other three men were still trying to unsling their rifles when she shot them. She threw the flowers away and started to run.

The SS lieutenant approached Johann Rattenhuber and Wilhelm Koch with something approaching fear. Very deliberately, he came to attention and gave the *Deutscher Gruss*. 'There has been a body discovered in Berchtesgaden, Herr Brigadeführer,' he said. 'The police just reported it.'

'Who?' Koch asked.

The lieutenant paused to check Rattenhuber's countenance before answering. 'A Herr Keller. A Herr Helmut Keller.'

'How?' Rattenhuber asked.

The young lieutenant paused again, as if to consider the question.

'How did he die?' Koch said.

'He was found at the bottom of his staircase. Neck broken, I believe.'

'Keller's an old Party man,' Rattenhuber said. 'Lived there for years. Used to be a university lecturer. Mathematics. He has a collection of old fifteenth-century mathematics books . . .'

'He's there,' Koch said. 'Valkyrie, he's there.'

'Get on to Klessheim, tell the Führer to stay put,' Rattenhuber barked at the SS lieutenant.

'How long ago?' Heinrich Müller almost spat his coffee out. He swung round with the phone and slammed his cup into the table. 'Get a bloody platoon together,' he said into the phone. 'Whoever's available. Someone's going east for this.'

As his convoy snaked along the mountain road from Salzburg to Obersalzberg, Adolf Hitler was thinking.

Theo Morell's concoctions and any morning elation had completely worn off, and the shadows from the afternoon sun had begun to haunt him. All the time he touched the small Mauser in his pocket.

The Mercedes splashed along the wet road at a steady fifty kilometres an hour, Führer speed, as it was known, and Hitler sometimes tapped his SS driver, Sturmbannführer Erik Kempka, on the shoulder if the officer exceeded his stipulation.

The mountains around him sported the darkness of spring growth and thin veils of the wispish cloud that gave Berchtesgadener Land its special feel, that of another world, apart from reality.

Erich Haas pushed the hollow-nosed bullets into the clip, one by one, and then snapped the clip into the Navy Luger. He checked the time and then watched a small group of people come together near the bridge at Oberau. To his right, the first Mercedes had entered Oberau. He opened a window and felt the sharp touch of the air.

Wilhelm Koch passed a Schmeisser machine-pistol over the car seat. Johann Rattenhuber took it, checked the breech and then let it rest in his lap. He handed Koch a piece of paper. 'There's a Belgian worker unaccounted for on the Obersalzberg,' he said. 'He came in last night but never checked in with the construction company he was hired by.'

The car threw mud and slush around the mountain road and Koch watched Rattenhuber and the speedometer with equal fascination.

Hitler's convoy had entered Oberau when the Führer tapped Kempka on the shoulder to tell him to slow down on the steep hill that led through the main part of the village.

The cavalcade of Mercedes cars, with RSD outriders on the running-boards, began to slow as it came down the Oberau road to the T-junction at the onion-domed church.

It passed a small *gasthof* and an altar with a giant crucifix and martyred Christ. A group of schoolchildren in Hitler Youth dress gave the *Deutscher Gruss* and several single men in *lederhosen* stood to attention where they were. More people came out of their houses.

In the passenger seat of the first car, Adolf Hitler saw the small strings of people gathering, and held his head up. He was, as usual, propped up higher than the window in the passenger seat; to his right, strung between two trees, a small banner wished him a happy birthday . . .

The RSD detectives around him, and in the other cars, watched the surroundings and each other.

Kempka began to slow rapidly as he approached the T-junction at the church. The ice on the roads made him feel as if he might continue on down to Unterau and the main road between Salzburg and Berchtesgaden or roll off the road altogether.

Adolf Hitler took a moment to look at the wall of silver mountains ahead of him and to his left, shrouded in a very thin afternoon mist. High over the Obersalzberg, on Kehlstein, he could see the teahouse he hoped he would not be asked to visit for his birthday celebrations. The mist had parted either side of it, making it appear as if it were floating in the clouds.

Up on the third floor of the house above the T-junction, Erich Haas had the Navy Luger tucked into his shoulder.

Ruth Wachs scanned the houses as she ran, glanced down again at Hitler's convoy coming towards her, gauged distances, trying to pick up speed, sucking air in, close to collapse, elated beyond feeling, blood streaming from her wounds.

Adolf Hitler saw the small girl with the flowers standing beside the bridge on the other side of the small river, and smiled. Her apricot frock shivered in the mountain breeze and the sunlight danced on the colour and made the Führer squint.

Haas followed the convoy of cars with his telescopic sight. In their usual protective formation, the cars began to turn left at the T-junction, between 100 and 150 metres away. He levelled the Navy Luger at the Führer's car, then took aim on Hitler's neck.

And Ruth Wachs saw him. She fired at Haas, out of effective range, but the fifth round clipped the window sill beneath him. Haas swung the Navy Luger and shot Wachs in the chest. He swung back to Hitler.

At that moment, Erik Kempka lost control on the ice, and Hitler's Mercedes slid across the road, which made Kempka turn into the skid and neglect to slow down as much as he might. The car slid out of Haas's sight. Kempka regained control of the car just before the bridge. Two women gave a *Deutscher Gruss*, which their Führer nodded a reply to.

Haas refocused.

The car crossed the bridge. Adolf Hitler smiled again as the little girl in the apricot frock on the far side of the bridge was picked up by her mother, less than half a metre away from the car. The little girl had a bunch of spring flowers in her hand. Two RSD detectives behind Hitler tried to stop the woman holding the little girl, but she pushed her daughter over the car window, and the little girl dropped the flowers into the Führer's lap.

Ruth Wachs hauled herself up on her knee, unscrewed her silencer, levelled her Mauser and fired the rest of her magazine at Hitler's car. Three of the rounds hit the Mercedes, near the radiator.

Erich Haas fired at the same time as Kempka braked and swerved.

The little girl in the apricot frock cried out. The mother felt something heavy push her off the running-board of the Führer's Mercedes. She thought it was one of the RSD detectives in the rear of the car. She fell back and staggered and rolled in the snowy grass by the side of the road. Her child rolled away from her. The mother was about to yell at the Führer's car, when Erich Haas's second shot hit the front windscreen; then the woman looked at her daughter, lying in the snow, and at the blood streaming from her apricot frock.

Hitler automatically fell forward and shouted at his driver to accelerate. The RSD detectives in the car with him, and the men around him, swung their machine-pistols at Ruth Wachs, who could not raise herself from her knee any more. She was already dead when their bullets hit.

Kempka struggled desperately for grip and the car sped right by the dead body of Wachs, into the cover of the winding mountain road and the trees that flanked it, Kempka hugging the left-hand side of the road to offer more protection to Hitler. Two RSD detectives were lying across the Führer in the passenger side of the car, telling him to keep down.

Three people across the road, huddled together behind a low wall and shouted at the RSD detectives in the other cars that someone else had fired.

Above them, Erich Haas was swearing to himself.

RSD detectives were already out of two of the support cars, backed up by a squad of SS troops, shouting directions at each other and asking the civilians for information.

Haas took aim again and shot one of the SS soldiers between the eyes; then he shot an RSD detective.

Soldiers and detectives rolled into the snow and began firing volleys at the farmhouse above them.

Haas killed another soldier and wounded two more, then slipped out of the back of the house and into the woods behind and went down on one knee and shot a civilian.

It had the desired effect. The sight of the hollow rounds in the bodies of an SS soldier and another RSD detective made the rest of his pursuers hold back for a few minutes more.

Haas scrambled up the steep wooded incline, rolling and crawling, jumping small gullies where he had to, the Navy Luger strapped to his back. Behind him his pursuers were regaining their courage, pulling themselves through the snow-covered fields, yelling at their comrades to move wide of the target house and try to cut off any possibility of escape. Haas was clear of the trap before it could be closed.

When he reached the top of a hill, he could see two trucks coming from the Obersalzberg, full of SS troops. He could not see Hitler's car any more.

The pursuers approached the house with caution; one or two called out for whoever was inside to come out. A young Liebstandarte lieutenant had an argument with an RSD captain about who should go in first. Then everyone opened up.

As the house exploded, a small group of people gathered round the body of Ruth Wachs. No one but her mother bothered about the small girl in the apricot frock, Doris Schieff.

16

ADOLF HITLER PULLED off his greatcoat and walked around the conference hall of the Berghof in diminishing circles, watched by various aides, staff officers and RSD detectives. It was a scene of half-panic, half-anger.

Julius Schaub, his senior ADC, scrunched up his rodentine face and slapped his leg with his own gloves. 'You're alive, my Führer, alive,' he said.

'I am aware of my biological status, Julius,' Hitler barked. 'Get me Bormann! Where on earth is Bormann? Screwing one of the secretaries, I'll warrant. Rattenhuber!'

Johann Rattenhuber stood on the steps of the conference hall, hands behind his back, a frown on his fat Bavarian face. 'You're alive, my Führer, thank God,' was all he could come up with. He knew it was as stupid as Schaub's sentiment, and because Hitler expected more of him, he waited for the riposte on the balls of his feet.

'God had nothing to do with it, Brigadeführer, nothing. It was providence, and Kempka's bloody awful driving. And if one more person tells me I'm alive I'll have him shot. Well, don't just stand there, Hans, don't just stare at me like I'm some modernist sculpture, hacked out by a dirty little Jew pervert, tell me you have who did it.'

'We have the woman.'

'She's dead. I mean the other one. The one with the bullets that put holes the size of grapefruit in you.'

'All efforts are being made. A fire is still raging.'

'Well, call the fire brigade . . .' Hitler's blood-streaked eyes almost jumped out of their sockets. 'This woman. I don't suppose you can tell me who she is?'

'We're investigating it,' Rattenhuber said. 'There is some difficulty there. We were not aware of a woman.'

'The man you want is a British-hired assassin called Valkyrie, my Führer, though I know him as Rotach, Karl Rotach, and he has had other names.'

'And who the hell are you?' Hitler asked.

Wilhelm Koch stood to attention. 'Kriminalkommissar Wilhelm Koch, my Führer, Munich Kriminalpolizei.'

Hitler looked Koch over, then stared at the now screened picture window in the conference hall, which before the installation of camouflage netting could be lowered by motor to provide a panoramic view of the mountains. He looked Koch over again and then glanced at Rattenhuber. 'Yes . . . yes . . . they told me you were wanted . . . Hans?'

'A misunderstanding, my Führer,' Rattenhuber said. 'Kriminalkommisar Koch is the one who warned us about Valkyrie.'

Hitler shook his head violently. 'Well, I want him, I want him alive, and all those responsible for this. The British . . .?' He looked at Koch again. 'They've tried before. That bloody watchmaker in Dachau, the one who tried to blow me up in '39, he was their man. And Himmler wants me to consider a dialogue with such people. If this man escapes, I'll have heads.'

'My Führer,' Koch said, 'I don't think escape is on his mind. This man is a professional assassin, trained to operate in the most extreme conditions, trained to survive against all odds.'

Hitler's face went pale. 'Are you telling me I should cower? From one man? In here? I want him found, gentlemen. What am I not being told? Come on, spit it out.'

'He's Abwehr-trained, my Führer,' Rattenhuber said. 'Part of their Tod programme, and they did their job well.'

'Abwehr-trained? This man is German?'

Martin Bormann came into the conference hall at that moment, flanked by four RSD detectives. His appearance distracted Hitler.

'The Führer area is secure; a speck of dust will not fly by without being checked.'

Hitler sat on the long marble table by the picture window and reached across for the globe beside it. 'I shall check your word with a white glove, Herr Reichsleiter,' he said, 'and if I find a speck of dust I shall be very angry. This man is a German? My God.' He shook his head, then picked up his riding crop, lying on the table.

'That little girl, the one who was shot, I want her family taken care of, Martin, taken care of, you hear? I want her buried with honours. Family provided for. It's providential. Providential. How many times have they tried, Martin, how many times have they tried? They cannot kill me. Where's Himmler? Where's Himmler when I need him? Get him, Martin, find him. If he's with his mistress, drag him away.'

'Cancel all appointments!' Bormann barked at Schaub. 'Nothing is to disturb the Führer.'

Schaub's displeasure was lost in Hitler's reaction.

'No,' Hitler said. 'I will not allow this to interrupt me for one minute longer. Proceed as normal. I will meet whomever I must meet, talk with whomever I must talk, smile when I must smile. Reichsleiter Bormann, Brigadeführer Rattenhuber, you will root this cancer out wherever it is. Perfidious Albion. Isn't that what those Irish republicans always say? I will show them, I will show them. When the V-weapons begin to wreak their havoc they will change their tunes. They will beg for peace terms. And I will cry unconditional surrender.'

Bormann began to clear the room, slowly and around the Führer's outbursts, which were getting more and more manic; at one point, Koch went to follow a group of RSD detectives but was held back by Rattenhuber. At the end of these manouevrings, Bormann, Rattenhuber and Julius Schaub were left in the conference hall, with Wilhelm Koch standing beside the RSD detectives at the door.

Hitler was now sitting on the large marble steps in front of the fireplace, rubbing his hands together. 'What are you boys doing at the Turken, Hans?' he said to Rattenhuber. 'Why didn't you prevent this?'

Heinrich Müller pushed past two RSD detectives and into the conference hall. 'Because there has been a concerted effort to deceive,' he said.

'Deceive?' Hitler said to himself. 'By whom?'

'Unclear, my Führer.'

'Well, make it clear.'

He jumped up and stamped around the room clicking his fingers. He was beginning to feel a terrible pain in his head. 'And get me Professor Morell, Martin, get me the professor, please. I'm going upstairs to lie down. Müller, you're with me, and you . . .'

'Koch, my Führer.'

'You tell me about this assassin, everything you know, Herr Kriminalkommissar. And, by the way, my niece did kill herself . . .'

Koch responded automatically.

Erich Haas had cut into the woods high above the Berghof, where the snow was thick and the weather was closing in around him. He crept low along a small stream bed and then up a treeline and down the other side of a hill, making sure to walk where there was no snow. Every so often, he doubled back on his trail and then headed in a different direction. And when he had done that he climbed. He climbed higher and higher until the snow was all there was.

Below him, he could see trucks and cars moving along the Konigseerstrasse and along the line of a small tributary called the Hollgraben towards Scharitzkehlstrasse, the main mountain road leading from the Jenner in Austria to the Führer area on Obersalzberg.

He had cut through the outer fence beneath the snow, where no one would notice, and continued on up Kehlstein from the Austrian side, once or twice within earshot of voices. And now, in the distance, there was the barking of dogs.

To his right, between the trees, he could see the silver of Mount Watzmann, and he thought of the old legend that said all the mountains surrounding Berchtesgadener Land were the family of an evil ruler turned to stone. They might still be watching the proceedings and laughing. The smell of aspiring spring was everywhere, the evening was bringing a new mist from the south, and when he reached the Kehlsteinhaus, he fell down and watched the sky change colour.

Across the valley, the mist was closing in rapidly.

Heinrich Himmler stood to attention for nearly a minute in front of Hitler's desk; the Führer was writing and finished the letter before taking off his glasses and acknowledging his Reichsführer-SS. 'You're late,' he said.

'I have been co-ordinating . . .'

'Müller says Nebe is dirty,' Hitler interrupted.

'Upon what evidence?' Himmler asked.

'The *Kriminalkommissar* from Munich . . . Koch, the one who . . . well, he claims to have been ordered to release Hofer by Gruppenführer Nebe. On your train.'

'I allow my officers to use Heinrich where necessary. There may have been a misunderstanding.'

'We seem to be knee-deep in then. When will Nebe be here?'

'Tomorrow morning.'

'We will sort it out then. Müller would like to settle it in Berlin. He wants your job, Heinrich.'

'I am aware of his ambitions, my Führer.'

'And what will you do about it?'

'He's a first-rate officer.'

Hitler stood up and replaced his glasses and walked past Himmler. 'Keep your friends close and your enemies closer?' he said forcing a smile. 'I will get to the bottom of this.'

'I have ordered an immediate investigation into the whole affair, my Führer. When we have this assassin, alive, we will be in a better position to establish credibility.'

Hitler put his hand on Himmler's shoulder. 'You know I trust you, Heinrich. I trust you above all of them. We'll have to make a move, before the year is out . . .'

'My Führer?'

'Against those who could betray me. Root and branch.'

'You have my unconditional loyalty, my Führer,' Himmler said.

'I'm inspired, Heinrich. Now let's go downstairs and celebrate the remains of my birthday.'

Darkness had fallen when Johann Rattenhuber picked up a coffee cup and shook his head. He stared out of the window of the Hotel Turken and caught the lines of the camouflage netting around the Berghof.

'We've lost him,' he said. 'The weather's closing in, too.'

'Do you want to call off the search?' Heinrich Müller asked. 'We need this man. We need him alive.'

'You can't see beyond your nose out there,' Rattenhuber said. 'We'll pick him up. Tomorrow.'

'If he planned a way in, then he planned a way out,' Müller pointed out. 'And we'll lose him.'

'If he's gone.'

Both men turned to Wilhelm Koch, standing by the fireplace.

'Continue the search,' Müller said. 'Round the clock.'

17

ERICH HAAS SAT in the snow and watched the torch beams pass. Two dogs barked and three SS soldiers had an argument about a third dog, which had gone missing. Haas waited an hour and the third dog's corpse got colder.

He entered the Hoheitsgebeit near the Platterhof Hotel, between two foot patrols, slipped across the road between the Platterhof and the work camp for the legion of labourers on the mountain, and cut through the inner fence.

After a short rest to draw breath, he moved quickly between the SS barracks and the staff quarters of the Platterhof, then stopped in scrubby undergrowth, waited for a few minutes more, before crossing a small path into the trees behind the Berghof.

The moon was hidden by cloud and the silver of the Untersberg and the Watzmann were the only sources of reflected light.

Haas looked at his watch, sat down and waited.

Adolf Hitler shook hands with the last of his birthday guests and left the conference hall. He paused briefly at the bottom of the stairs to listen to the singing that had started up in the conference hall after his departure, pouted and shook his head. 'Tell them to keep the noise down, Julius,' he said to his chief adjutant, Schaub. 'There are people trying to sleep.'

Then he turned and plodded up the stairs. Halfway up, he swung round. 'Julius, keep me informed,' he said. 'Of everything.'

Schaub came to attention. As did the RSD detectives on guard at the top of the stairs. Hitler acknowledged them.

*   *   *

Erich Haas looked at his watch and then crawled, very carefully, to the left of the Berghof. The ventilation shaft was exactly where Ben Kramer's plans said it would be.

He used a small bottle of concentrated acid and a hacksaw to break into the shaft, then crawled his way to the the first machine-gun posts in the tunnel complex. They were unmanned.

After the machine-gun posts, he was able to stand up. He waited for a while and then swung left before the underground guest rooms and stopped again at the foot of a staircase leading up to the Berghof. Then he checked the Navy Luger, now shortened to a silenced handgun, and looked at his watch again.

'The Kehlsteinhaus,' Wilhelm Koch said.

Johann Rattenhuber looked up from where he was reading. Koch put the telephone down. 'They've found the locks broken on the doors,' he said. 'There're civilian clothes there. And food.'

Rattenhuber stood up and grabbed his cap. Heinrich Müller pulled his pistol from its holster, checked it, then took a small pistol from a pine dresser and threw it to Koch. 'For the duration,' he said. 'And don't get any ideas.'

'I don't think you realise how much I want this man,' Koch said.

'I want him just as much,' Müller said.

Erich Haas dragged the dead RSD detective into a small room beside the staircase leading from the Berghof to the tunnels, and put the man's tunic on. He could hear laughing from the conference hall and snatches of song and people telling one another to be quiet. Then there was shouting outside on the veranda and the sound of running jackboots.

He slipped through the hall, past two bathrooms, to the main staircase. The RSD detective on guard at the bottom had no time to think of an answer to Haas's question.

'They've found a dead dog near the Platterhof!' Heinrich Müller yelled from the Berghof terrace.

Koch and Rattenhuber were at the bottom of the stone steps leading to the Berghof. The camouflage netting overhead was flapping in the breeze.

'And there's a hole in the fence!' Müller added.

He was already moving.

*   *   *

The RSD detective at the top of the main staircase in the Berghof saw the uniform first and then the RSD *sonderausweis* being flashed. He never really saw the Navy Luger. One shot sent him back against the wall; his colleague, who had been in the bathroom and heard the noise of the body falling, came out with his pistol drawn. But Haas shot him back into the doorway.

Wilhelm Koch was at the bottom of the stairs, the lumbering bulk of Johann Rattenhuber covering him while Heinrich Müller shouted for support over the sound of singing from the conference hall.

Erich Haas entered Hitler's study from the Führer's bedroom. For a moment he stood perfectly still, as if he were having one last thought.

Adolf Hitler looked up from where he was sitting at his desk, writing.

'My Führer,' Haas said then. 'Your hands where I can see them.'

He raised the Navy Luger. Hitler remained impassive. 'You cannot kill me,' he said.

'I must,' Haas replied. And he aimed and fired at Hitler's heart.

Hitler fell back.

'Valkyrie!'

Wilhelm Koch burst into the study from the landing and fired at Haas, who was trying to turn. The first bullet caught him in the chest and threw him across the corner of Hitler's desk, the second hit him in the neck, the third in the abdomen. Haas swung the Navy Luger back at Koch and loosed off two shots. One hit the picture of Hitler's mother, the other the heater. Koch threw himself across the carpet. Haas was trying to aim again when Johann Rattenhuber fired from Hitler's bedroom and hit him in the shoulder. The assassin fired off a last shot and then fell to the ground beside Hitler.

'My Führer!'

'Don't say it, don't say it, Rattenhuber. Yes, I'm alive.' Hitler pulled open his jacket to reveal the bullet-proof vest he had on. 'I think my chest has been crushed. Get my doctor.'

He pulled himself up and stood back from the dead body of Erich Haas. Rattenhuber's attention had drifted across the room. Wilhelm Koch had been hit through the forehead. He lay dead under the picture of Adolf Hitler's mother.

The study began to fill with men, all armed – RSD detectives, staff officers, adjutants. Heinrich Müller was barking orders and enquiring about Hitler's health. Hitler sat on his desk, looking at the body of Erich Haas.

'I am the only one who can kill me,' he said.

THE DEPORTATION OF Hungary's Jews began on 28 April 1944. In late May, the SS made an offer to exchange Hungarian Jews for Allied trucks. The Allies rejected it. Over half of Hungary's Jews were exterminated.

Ben Kramer died of cancer in July 1944.

Jake Coll and his aircraft were found in the Swiss Alps in 1957; he was buried quietly as a righteous gentile in Tel Aviv; his wife and child were at the funeral.

Arthur Nebe was executed for treason in 1945.

Claude Dansey died in 1947.

Otto Ohlendorf was hanged in 1951 for war crimes.

Walter Schellenberg died in 1952, having escaped the gallows.

Heinrich Müller vanished in 1945; one report had him in Moscow in 1948. Before he died, Walter Schellenberg maintained that Müller had been a Russian agent all along.

In April 1994, German federal investigators, charged with making a report on the whole incident, dug up the grave of the assassin known as Erich Haas or Valkyrie. There was no body in it.